RAVEN UNVEILED

GRACE DRAVEN

ACE

NEW YORK

ACE
Published by Berkley
An imprint of Penguin Random House LLC
penguinrandomhouse.com

Library of Congress Cataloging-in-Publication Data

Names: Draven, Grace, author.
Title: Raven unveiled / Grace Draven.
Description: First Edition. | New York: Ace, 2022. |
Series: The fallen empire
Identifiers: LCCN 2022010970 (print) | LCCN 2022010971 (ebook) |
ISBN 9780451489791 (trade paperback) | ISBN 9780451489807 (ebook)
Subjects: LCGFT: Novels.
Classification: LCC PS3604.R385 R39 2022 (print) |
LCC PS3604.R385 (ebook) | DDC 813/.6—dc23
LC record available at https://lccn.loc.gov/2022010970
LC ebook record available at https://lccn.loc.gov/2022010971

First Edition: November 2022

Printed in the United States of America
1st Printing

Book design by Elke Sigal

To Anne Sowards, who embodies the virtue known as patience.
Thank you, Anne.

RAVEN UNVEILED

CHAPTER ONE

After two months of relentless tracking, the once feared empress's cat's-paw had finally run his prey to ground outside the haunted ruin of Midrigar. If Siora thought to hide from him here in the hopes the stories of the trapped and restless dead might scare him away, she knew him not at all.

He'd once been the lackey of a demon dressed in a beautiful woman's body and survived the employment. Nothing so insipid as a ghost would stop him from hunting down his treacherous servant.

She probably thought he meant to kill her. He'd been an assassin after all, and his fury over her betrayal had nearly consumed him once. The anger still simmered inside him, but he hunted her not to kill her but to make her apologize—on her knees if necessary—to a small child. That, more than vengeance meted out through death, was what drove him across the Empire.

The moon played coy behind tattered clouds and spilled argent light over the shattered city, casting the broken bones of its towers in stark relief against a star-salted sky. An unquiet tomb under an indifferent heaven.

Gharek growled, the sound making his horse's ears swivel back. He patted her neck, wishing he was comfortably ensconced in one of the better inns' finer rooms, with a sweet-smelling whore to keep him company. Or better yet, out of Kraelian territory altogether, safe with his daughter and the people he'd paid a fortune to see to her care while he roamed a collapsing empire in search of the beggar bitch who'd turned on him and ruined his and his daughter's lives.

Instead of a posh room shared with an accommodating woman, he rode through a woodland devoid of sound, its silence absolute, as if it dared not flutter a leaf or creak a branch for fear of attracting the attention of what might lay behind Midrigar's tumbled walls. Despite the strangeness that sent a crawling feeling over his skin, Gharek didn't waver in his tracking.

A trek through the forest was as good as any for avoiding Kraelian troops on patrol. Despite the raids from Nunari clans, the main trade route remained a busy one, serving Guild and free traders as well as battalions of Kraelian soldiers sent to fight the rebellious Nunari. He stayed off the road for those reasons and others, as much a fugitive as his quarry, as fiercely hunted by those he'd once wronged.

Gharek's search for Siora had finally proven fruitful in the last week. The right questions asked of the right people in the villages where he'd stopped had yielded reliable information. A woman, not much bigger than a child but with the knowing gaze of a crone, had offered to act as liaison between the grieving living and their beloved dead for the fee of a *belsha* or two. She'd managed to swindle coin out of their families before others drove her away. Shade speakers were barely tolerated even when many believed in their talent.

He'd set off for Wellspring Holt, a bustling trader's town that had so far managed to escape the worst of the raids. Siora would find it easier to hide there than in the smaller towns and villages. Hiring a tracker might prove a faster method for finding her, but Gharek preferred working alone, especially since he had his own secrets to keep. As the empress's cat's-paw, experience had taught him that his skills weren't suited for teamwork. The mad empress might be draga spittle splattered on Domora's battlements now, but it didn't change the way he hunted quarry—always alone.

While he'd altered his appearance with a new beard and shorter hair to avoid being recognized, he wasn't taking any chances by keeping company with anyone for any length of time. Bounties for the cat's-paw, alive or dead, were generous, and those hoping to claim such rewards numerous.

He'd crossed a sea of fields—some plowed and seeded, waiting for harvest, others left fallow—and came upon a stone circle in the middle of a pasture. No sheep or cattle grazed nearby, and Gharek's mare balked when he tried to steer her closer. He gave in to her protest and rode past the monument erected to some long-forgotten deity. These ancient places held on to their power long after their supplicants had turned to dust. Whatever lingered here, his mare wanted nothing to do with it.

If anything hid within the circle, he'd have seen it already, but nothing disturbed the wild flowers growing there, and he disregarded it, turning his attention toward a ramshackle barn nearby. The horse offered no resistance when they stopped in front of the structure. Gharek tied her to one of the few posts still standing from the remnants of a fence and went inside, his instincts practically making his veins hum with the certainty his target had stopped there or was still there.

Sunlight had cascaded through holes in the roof, illuminating a half dozen empty stalls. Mice fled in every direction on a chorus of tiny squeals when he entered, their feet leaving patterns in the powdery dust coating every surface.

But it wasn't their tracks that held his attention. He'd crouched to examine a set of much larger prints—human, those of a woman or child with flat feet who walked lightly. The shoe tread pattern was unique and Gharek instantly recognized Siora's distinctive footprints. Nothing else in the barn so far gave him a clue to her presence, and the prints might well belong to someone else, but his gut had yet to fail him. This was Siora's marker.

The prints tracked in two directions, and he'd followed the pair leading farther into the barn's depths to what was once a provender room. He paused in the doorway, letting his eyes adjust to the greater darkness there. Patterns on the floor's disturbed dirt told him she'd slept here, at least for a short time, likely taking what shelter she could find during the night away from other predators, besides himself, that hunted during the small hours.

He'd pivoted, noting the walls with their cracked plaster and bowed framing, the slope of the roof on the verge of collapse. A stiff wind would bring the place down in a rotting heap. Best not to linger and end up entombed beneath the wreckage.

The sight of one of the room's walls as he turned to leave had made him recoil.

As Dalvila's erstwhile cat's-paw, he'd witnessed levels of depravity and cruelty that defied description and decayed a part of his soul every time. The empress had more than earned her reputation as a mad and murderous ruler. Her subjects didn't know the half of it. Gharek remembered every person he'd dispatched on her orders, though unlike her, he meted out death in a manner efficient and quick. Time had made every memory sharper, made his spirit ever more numb to his actions, but even he sat up some nights and brought in the dawn with a flagon or two of wine, afraid to close his eyes and subject himself to the nightmares of remembrance and the empress's monstrous indulgences upon her victims.

He'd sometimes wondered if she was even human and had decided that in the end it didn't matter. She was vile, and he served her will, thus making him as vile as her. He was as beyond redemption as she was, holding on to his last scrap of humanity for his daughter's sake. Estred would never know the depths to which he had plunged in order to keep her safe and cared for. If she did, she'd hate him. Rightfully so.

People didn't turn the labor of their creativity toward provender rooms where the only witnesses to works of art were field mice and farmhands, and yet laid across one wall was a display of horror in shades of black and rust executed by a gleeful hand. Gharek had studied the repulsive mural. If Dalvila had seen it, she would have commissioned the artist to paint something similar on one of her bedchamber's walls or maybe the ceiling, a visual feast to look upon while she raped her latest plaything. The work half revealed in the room's shadow displayed pleasure in torture, a lust for another's fear. A multitude of faces crushed together, their mouths stretched wide in silent screams, their eyes bulging with terror as they stared at some horror he couldn't see. Why such an abomination was displayed on a derelict barn's wall was a mystery, one he had no desire to solve.

He hadn't gone closer for a better look, and the longer he had stared at the grotesque images, the more certain he became it wasn't paint that rendered them on the wall.

While he hadn't run from the room, his strides were long ones, and he'd released a grateful breath when he was outside once more under the sweltering blaze of a summer sun with the song of insects serenading him.

Had Siora seen the wall when she camped in the barn? A true shade speaker might not fear ghosts, but there was more to that hideous mural than a callous mockery of the dead. Surely even she would be horrified at the sight.

He'd ridden away, following more of Siora's tracks while doing his best to shrug off the feeling of being watched that skittered down his back on spider legs. No wonder the fields surrounding the barn were abandoned and the building left to decay.

Experience and weeks of fruitless searching had taught him that to rush toward Siora's latest hiding place did him no good and often worked against him. It was uncanny how she'd managed to outsmart and outmaneuver him without ever truly outrunning him.

Were she a wealthy noblewoman with numerous connections and friends, he'd assume she made use of a vast network of helpers who would render aid either in the service of friendship or for profit. But this was a beggar without a *belsha* to her name beyond what she might scrape together for a meal. She was also a shade speaker, a fact she'd failed to mention when he suffered a moment's weakness and offered her a place in his household as thanks for saving Estred from a stone-throwing mob. He'd paid a heavy price for that foolish kindness.

He'd tracked her through the day and into evening, not toward Wellspring Holt, but here to an eerie expanse of woodland whose perimeters stretched for leagues in a gentle curve that hugged the trade route and clung to the remains of Midrigar. The forest offered a possible hiding place for brigands and fugitives. And shade speakers on the run.

Moonlight lit the treetops but most of the woodland slumbered in full dark. It was slow going as his horse picked her way through the underbrush. Gharek held a small lamp aloft to illuminate the path ahead. He didn't worry that the fragile light might be seen in the distance and alert someone. His mount's hooves crushing sticks and brittle deadfall would accomplish the task long before the light did.

The music of insects and bird calls had been loud just before he crossed the tree line, a cacophony of whistles, rustles, and chirps. Those sounds died away the closer he rode to the ruins of the dead city until the silence itself held its breath and only the gloom shrouding the trees breathed. His amiable mare stopped suddenly then pranced backward, tossing her head and snorting. Gharek tapped his heels against her sides to coax her forward. She'd have none of it, fighting the bit in her mouth as she pivoted on her hooves to trot back the way they'd come.

Gharek reined her to a halt, considering whether it was wise to continue his scouting in another direction or make camp nearby and wait until morning to resume his hunt. He'd lose time with camping but trying to find anyone in this darkness while riding a spooked horse was an exercise in futility. Besides, he could make up the time in daylight. Siora was on foot, he on horseback. He'd cover far more ground in less time than she would, and the chance she'd outrun him if he spotted her was nonexistent.

He guided the mare to retrace her steps, and this time she readily obeyed the command, eager to put distance between them and the city that squatted like a pustule on the landscape. But she'd taken no more than a pair of steps when something wrapped icy fingers around Gharek's spine and wrenched him backward. He flew off the saddle as if lassoed from behind and landed on his back. The ground beneath him vibrated from the beat of his mare's hooves as she bolted past him into the labyrinth of trees.

He lay there for a moment, stunned and winded. The ice shard wedged against his backbone remained, though whatever had ripped him from horseback didn't press him into the dirt. A few more breaths and he lurched to his feet, unsettled by his unusual clumsiness, alarmed by the violence of an invisible force that had so thoroughly unhorsed him. There'd been no trip rope to clothesline him, nor had he been riding fast when he fell. The lamp he held had fallen when he did, lost somewhere in the underbrush when its flickering light had guttered. Darkness hung thick enough to scoop with a spoon.

His muttered curses sounded loud to his ears as he peered into the sepulchral black, hoping he might spot the mare standing nearby or at least find a partially cleared path that led back to open pasture. He took a step only to suffer a hard clamp on his backbone, as if the icicle there had suddenly transformed into a shackle locked around his middle. Invisible tethers seized his arms and legs and he was jerked to one side and then the other as if by a drunken puppeteer with their hands on the strings.

Gharek staggered, struggling to keep his feet, struggling to free himself from the bonds that held him in an unbreakable grip that both dragged and yanked him in the direction of Midrigar's walls. He careened through the dark, along a jagged path that propelled him into tree trunks before spinning him away to tear through the underbrush. He tried planting his feet in the dirt to no avail, his boots carving skid marks as he was pulled along like a cur on a leash. His palms left bloody smears on the bark of those trees he tried to grip for purchase and was wrenched away with little effort.

The iciness slithering down his spine spread in creeper tendrils throughout his body, wrapping around his lungs and heart, his liver, even his tongue so that his curses and snarls slowly ebbed away and his struggles waned. Speaking was an impossibility, breathing a challenge, and he was reduced to nothing more than a grunting, shambling mute driven inexorably toward an ancient city of the damned and a fate he could not know but feared with every part of his soul.

His sense of a thing waiting, hungering for him, grew stronger with every drunken step toward the black silhouettes of buildings. The image of a landscape where deserts were bloodred, seas obsidian, and skies the yellow of bile filled his mind's eye even as his vision sharpened with an inhuman accuracy.

He heard the rustle of movement and caught the flit of a shadow from the corner of his eye. Perspiration beaded his skin from the labor of turning his head even as his feet carried him relentlessly forward. The shadow rushed him, small, quick. Had he the ability to speak, Gharek might have bellowed his triumph at the brief glimpse of familiar delicate features and large eyes with their far-seeing, enigmatic gaze. Siora. Her name was a gurgle in the back of his throat. She raised her arms, gripping a stick like a club in both hands. Unable to dodge or deflect, he could only stare, helpless, as she swung the makeshift club. A bright flash of pain immolated the image of the strange landscape and snapped the puppeteer's strings. Darkness.

CHAPTER TWO

Siora stared at her nemesis lying motionless at her feet. He had once been her employer and unlikely savior, a notorious and dangerous man who'd given her shelter and food, first as thanks, then as wages. To a homeless beggar like her, he had been a dark blessing—fearsome, fascinating, coldly calculating. A roof and regular meals bought a great deal of forgiveness, and she'd not been put off by his notorious reputation as the empress's cat's-paw. More fool her.

Some might say she had a choice to make: club him to death while he lay helpless and steal the horse still lingering nearby or render aid. In her mind, the moment she'd whacked him with the stick, she'd chosen to help. Had she wanted him to die, she would have simply stood aside and watched as an invisible and powerful entity of malevolent purpose dragged him through one of Midrigar's broken gates, never to trouble her again. She knew deep in her bones that what waited on the other side of the city's walls offered neither a quick death nor a clean one.

Gharek of Cabast had pursued her across the fracturing Krael Empire, an untiring nemesis in his quest to exact revenge on her. A quest that had become the crusade of the devout. He'd held to the snarled promise he'd made months earlier that she'd find no sanctuary in the Empire, no place where he couldn't track her. For one cold-blooded moment, she'd been tempted to stand by and watch as he was reeled in like a hooked fish, a silent, terrified scream stamped on his features. If he died, she could reclaim her life once more, such as it was. Beggar still and scourge to some, but no longer hunted. Then the image of Estred's face had risen in her memory.

The young girl, intelligent, sweet, and loving, had inspired the violence of a rock-throwing mob simply for the crime of her appearance. Empire society was merciless to those considered lesser, broken, or strange. She needed a parent as ruthless as Gharek to keep her safe, to guard her. Siora might condemn him for his many heinous acts, but she remained undecided regarding his motivation for them. Parental devotion honed to a lethal edge cut multiple ways, and she'd often pondered whether or not she'd go to the same lengths as him to protect a beloved offspring, especially one as vulnerable as Estred. She'd once told a draga that nobility was the indulgence of those who only had themselves to consider. In that moment she'd embraced the idea as a way to justify her own betrayal of Gharek. The best of intentions sometimes had the sharpest teeth and spilled the most blood.

Gharek was heavier than his slim build led one to believe, and Siora muttered soft curses under her breath as she dragged his limp body through the brush and away from the shadows cast by the city. He'd wear a wealth of welts and scratches by the time she got him a distance she deemed far enough away from whatever foulness had bewitched him and attempted to drag him to an unseen lair.

The invisible tethers binding and pulling him across the

ground had snapped when she'd struck him senseless, a sound not heard by the ears but by the soul. It was followed by an enraged howl that nearly sent her fleeing pell-mell in terror in the opposite direction. She planted her feet instead, shivered like a sapling in a storm, and watched as a pulse of muddy yellow light burst from behind the city walls. Shades cast by the trees suddenly bent at strange angles. A low thrum, like the far-off beat of a war drum, vibrated the earth beneath her. The sickly luminescence pulsed to the slow pump of a poisoned heart and for a moment hulked over the battered battlements in twisted shapes carved from malice and ancient night. Even the moon seemed to draw farther away and the stars dimmed, as if repulsed by the sight.

By the time Siora paused from dragging Gharek across the forest floor, her clothes were wet with sweat and he looked as if he'd been mauled by a pair of angry wild cats. Midrigar was no longer visible, and the music of insects and frogs had replaced the funereal silence surrounding the city.

She laid him in a patch of clover. A pair of fireflies flashed bright as tiny lamps over his head, and a spider scuttled across his chest to disappear into the grass. Normal creatures in a normal part of the wood.

Siora leaned against one of the trees to catch her breath and wipe the perspiration from her face with her skirt hem before retrieving the abandoned lantern Gharek had dropped. An inquiring equine nicker sounded close by. His mare ambled toward them. Not a brave horse but a loyal one. She hadn't gone far when she bolted. With any luck, Siora could coax her close enough to grab the reins. A horse with supplies meant fast travel, something to eat, and maybe a *belsha* or two.

Her empty stomach rumbled its support of the idea, and Siora clicked her tongue against her teeth to coax the mare closer. Though the wait was excruciating, she stayed in place and let the horse come to her. She didn't dare leave Gharek unattended, at least not as he was—still unconscious but also unbound.

While the mare took her sweet time reaching her, Siora scanned the blackness that painted the forest and turned the trees into whispering obelisks. Gharek lay as the dead, though there were no ghosts roaming this woodland for now, not even Siora's father, for which she was profoundly grateful. Coincidences were rarely so in her experience. Gharek's struggles as he resisted the demand of his invisible captor had been much like the pitiful spirits discovered in the abandoned barn she'd entered two days earlier, the horror etched into his face just like theirs as he tried to grab on to anything for purchase and slow his unwilling journey toward Midrigar.

She had stopped at the farmstead in search of sanctuary and found the monument to a nightmare etched into a plaster wall. The overwhelming sense of something old and avaricious had made her back out of the provender room only to pause as an ethereal swarm of terrified ghosts descended on her. Siora had fled the barn, her own screams trapped in her throat. Hiding in the forest surrounding Midrigar had been a matter of choice driven by desperation. The thing that ate ghosts lingered in the damned city. She felt it in her bones the moment she stepped into the woods. But who was the greater threat? An unseen malice that hunted the dead or a vengeful cat's-paw who hunted the living? She'd chosen the woodland.

Gharek's own cries had been no more than feral grunts trapped in a frozen throat. The barn was a distance from Midrigar, but Siora was as certain as the sunrise that she'd witnessed the trapping of another unwary victim by the eater of ghosts. Why and how it had chosen a living man to attack was anyone's guess, as was her own resistance to its summons. Still, the idea of its power and its reach froze the blood in her veins.

A whuffle and snort sounded close. Gharek's mare emerged from the deeper darkness, at first a shade of indeterminate shape, then a graceful head, long neck, and slender legs as she picked her way toward her fallen master. Siora casually caught the reins in one hand and patted the mare's neck. "Hello, love. Kind of you to return."

The horse stood docile, lowering her head once to nudge Gharek with her nose. He gave a soft groan but didn't move. Siora spoke softly to the mare as she wound the reins around a low-hanging branch before pillaging the packs tied to the saddle. She found a length of rope as well as a knife, flint, and a lump of tinder fungus. She used the last three to relight the lamp so she could see to bind Gharek's hands and ankles.

She watched his face as she worked, treating the annoying flutters in her gut as simply fear at being this close to him once more. He looked different since she'd last seen him. Still handsome but more haggard, with a scruffy beard hiding the planes of his face and his hair clipped much shorter than she remembered. The beard still didn't hide the pinched tightness of his mouth, though his closed eyelids obscured the intensity of his gaze. His changed appearance didn't surprise her. Siora might be hunted by the cat's-paw, but the cat's-paw was hunted by everyone now. He'd need to disguise himself if he wanted to go among people anywhere in the Empire.

The knots would hold long enough for her to get away and far enough down the trade road before he'd have the means to track her again. She'd be long gone with his horse, his supplies, and his coin. She wasn't a thief, at least not by trade, but she'd be a fool if she left behind those things that made it easy for him to catch her. Some would say she was a fool for bothering to save him in the first place.

It would have been wiser to have been done with the bindings and put distance between them as soon as possible, but she set caution aside for a moment to slide her fingers along his nape and scalp. The lump left by her striking him promised a nasty headache when he woke and one more reason he could add to his list for taking revenge on her. His skin was warm under her fingertips, his hair like down feathers. Siora caught her breath and yanked her hand back, mortified at those brief observations. She lunged to her feet and wiped her hands on her skirt before returning to the mare.

Gharek's saddlebags contained enough rations to last her more than a week if she didn't indulge and supplemented them with begging and shade-speaking if necessary. The coin he carried she'd reserve for other purposes such as bribery. Blindness and denial were expensive services but necessary ones for those like her who were on the run.

The saddle strapped to the mare's back had a very low pommel, a cantle, and stirrups to aid the rider in keeping their seat. Siora was glad for the last. She was a small woman, and this was a tall mare. A stirrup would provide the leverage she needed to climb atop the horse's back, and Gharek had tied them low to accommodate the generous length of his legs. As long as the mare stayed still enough, Siora could climb onto the mare without much difficulty.

Surprisingly, the horse proved to be disagreeable to the idea. Every time Siora slipped her foot in and grabbed the saddle, her four-legged companion shuffled sideways with a protesting snort.

"What is the matter with you, horse?" she snarled under her breath.

"You're trying to mount from the wrong side. She isn't used to it."

Foot still trapped in the stirrup, Siora stumbled at the sound of Gharek's slurred voice and lost her balance. She hung off the side of the disapproving, snorting mare for a moment before falling to land on her backside. The horse eyed her with contempt.

Siora leapt to her feet, picking sticker burrs out of her palm and off her skirt. She peered at Gharek lying where she left him, careful not to get too close.

He'd turned on his side to face her, his body contorted from her binding him. His face was obscured by the night, but she felt the weight of his gaze on her, a wolf watching the activities of a clueless sheep and deciding when best to pounce. He was awake and no doubt working furiously at the knots she'd tied. Time to leave.

"Where am I?" He sounded a little less groggy.

"Woodland outside the cursed city," she replied, careful not to say Midrigar's name out loud. To do so invited the attention of things best left unaware of your existence.

"You hit me," he said.

She nodded, forgetting he probably couldn't see the movement. She circled the mare farther away from him and this time took up a spot on the proper side for mounting. "I did. Whatever held you let go when I did so."

He winced. "Gods protect me from saviors like you. You've made my life a misery with your brand of liberation." Angry sarcasm had seeped into the groggy confusion muddying his voice. He wiggled in his bindings. "And you've trussed me like a pig."

Wary, she widened the distance between them. "For my own protection. Were our circumstances reversed, what would you do?"

The thin, humorless smile he offered didn't reassure her, nor surprise her. "Do you really want me to answer that?"

Siora cringed inside. He'd probably watch with a smile as the ghost-eater dragged her into the city and wave a casual goodbye. She expected such from him, but it still stung. She reached inwardly for stoicism and said, "It crossed my mind not to be so merciful."

"What stopped you?"

One answer to that question she chose not to dwell on too closely. A second was much easier to espouse. "Estred."

He jerked in his bindings, hands busily searching for the knots she'd made so he could untie them. "You aren't worthy to say her name. You betrayed her when you betrayed me, and then you abandoned her. You cut your wounds deep, beggar woman."

A clutch of bitter tears hurtled into her throat before seizing it closed. For a moment Siora forgot caution, forgot the urgency to leave and the risk she took in staying any longer. Estred had grown very attached to Siora in the months that they'd been nursemaid and charge. And Siora had returned the affection. Had Estred's father been any man other than the cat's-paw, she would have stayed and braved his fury at her betrayal.

"You've hunted me for months now," she said, proud of the way her voice sounded calm, even emotionless, though inside she was a turmoil of emotions. Gharek wouldn't hesitate to turn any chink in her armor into a weapon. "For what? The vengeance you promised when I revealed the whereabouts of an old woman you abducted and used as bait in the hopes of carving up a draga disguised as a man?"

That fateful decision had altered the life courses of several people. She'd never wavered in her belief that it had been the right thing to do for all involved, but some nights, regret overwhelmed her and she wished fiercely that circumstances had been different. Gharek's accusation only made it that much worse. Still, she defended her actions. "Your present fate is as much your fault as it is mine. Your daughter would be shamed by the idea that you'd shed innocent blood for her, and whether or not you choose to believe me, if I hadn't told Malachus where Asil was, you'd be bones under dirt right now or a soot stain on the floor. And then where would Estred be? She may not have her nursemaid any longer, but she still has the most important person of all—her father."

Gharek's upper lip curled and his gaze in the thin lamplight nearly drowned her in its contempt. "Painting yourself the heroine? That's rich. And you can take your golden sanctimony and shove it straight up your arse."

Her fingers curled around the mare's reins in a fist. She was tempted to throw all caution aside, step in front of him, and land a solid kick on his bound body for his remark. A glint in his eyes told her he hoped she'd succumb to such an impulse. She'd be within reach then and, bound or not, he'd figure out a way to capture her. His words sliced sharp and no doubt sincere, but they were said with purpose. In the time she'd come to know the cat's-paw, he never did anything without purpose.

She didn't fall for his trap, turning instead to hoist herself into the saddle, this time from the correct side. The mare stood still as Siora adjusted her skirts. The stirrup lengths had worked well in helping her get into the saddle but were far too low to be of any use to her now that she was seated on the mare's back. She'd have to ride carefully to keep from falling off. Beggars were lucky to own a pair of shoes much less expensive horseflesh, and it had been a long time since Siora had ridden a horse.

She tossed Gharek's knife into a bramble bush not far from him. She hadn't saved him from a Midrigar demon only to leave him completely defenseless. He'd figure out a way to retrieve the knife, bound or not, but by then she'd be far enough away that it wouldn't matter.

"You're stealing my mare." Loathing melded with the anger in Gharek's voice. "Not only a traitor but a thief as well."

Siora tired of his insults. She'd been the unwitting accomplice to his imprisonment of an innocent woman. She'd known of his reputation but had willingly turned a blind eye to it. As a servant in his home, she'd learned more of the man than the henchman, had seen him as a loving parent, a fair employer, and even on occasion when he thought no one observed, a melancholy, vulnerable man. Those things had seduced her into the delusion that he was simply misunderstood or judged too harshly because he worked for the empress. Guilt still rode her hard at such willful delusion; not because she'd turned on him, but because she hadn't turned on him sooner.

She paused in guiding the mare toward the path leading out of the woodland to the trade road and Wellspring Holt in the distance. Her reasoning told her he was most likely using every tactic at his disposal to delay her long enough so he could free himself, recapture his horse, and kill her.

"Borrow," she snapped back. "You're welcome to her when I'm far enough away from you. And I'm no traitor. My loyalty was always to Estred, not you. Your fear for her has blinded you to compassion, to mercy, even to humanity. Estred needs her father, not the father you were becoming." The more she spoke, the angrier she grew, the more indignant. The more reckless. "You had no right to abduct Asil and hold her captive. As for this mare, consider her repayment for saving you."

"There's no debt," he snarled, making thrashing noises in the brush.

"So say all who feel neither guilt for a cruelty visited nor gratitude for a kindness offered." Siora touched the mare's sides with her heels to coax her into a steady walk away from Charek.

"You can ride across the entire Krael Empire and you'll never get far enough away, Siora!"

It was the first time she'd ever heard him call her by her name, and it sent both hot and cold shivers riding along her skin. She shrugged. "So has it been since we began this dance, you and I." The dark prevented her from pushing the mare into a pace faster than a cautious walk, even with the aid of the lantern's pallid light.

"I just need to stay far enough ahead until you give up this quest, remember you're no longer the empress's cat's-paw, and return home to the child who misses you," she said over her shoulder.

"Why do you think I'm here?" he shouted after her as she rode toward the wood's edge and away from him.

"To take your promised revenge," she replied in a soft voice he couldn't hear. "But not today."

His virulent curses followed her through the trees, finally fading until all she heard was the rhythm of the mare's steps and the sounds of woodland creatures. Compared to the barren silence surrounding Midrigar, the woods here were almost noisy, and Siora kept her ears open for the howl of wolves and her eyes wide as she guided the horse through the maze of sentinel trees.

She thanked any gods who might be listening when the wood thinned, and she spotted hints of the trade road, a silver ribbon under the moon's light. The crackling tread of hooves on underbrush gave way to a louder clop when the mare stepped onto the road's hard-packed dirt.

During the small hours, as the night waned but dawn was still beneath the horizon, the road was deserted, at least by the living. Siora's gladness at traveling the road alone and unaccosted changed to horror at the sight of several ghosts once more rushing toward her, wispy, tattered flags caught in a wind she didn't hear or feel. They twisted and clutched the air, silently screaming as they resisted the draw of a force that pulled them toward the wood, toward Midrigar in a relentless tide. They wore the same expressions as those pitiful faces on the barn wall and in the fields as she'd fled from Gharek.

They broke against her and the mare before spilling around

the pair like waves against a great rock. Their terrified expressions tore at her, and Siora reached for several, offering herself as an anchor. It was a futile gesture. Revenant hands passed through her clothing and hair, leaving cold trails on her skin as they clutched at her. She peered into every face, no matter how gruesome or decayed. Her heart thundered in her ears as she searched, frightened she'd find her father's ghost among these captive unfortunates. Relief at not seeing him combined with horror as the dead were sucked toward Midrigar while she stood in the road, helpless to stop it. She'd managed to save a living man from this evil. She couldn't save the dead.

Whatever scooped ghosts up as if they were fish in a net and bewitched Gharek until he was no more than a puppet pulled on harsh strings, Siora remained immune to its power. She'd felt the frigid abyss of its regard in the woodland near Midrigar, understood in the instinctive way of a rabbit being stalked that it would devour her if it could, but for reasons unknown, it held no sway over her.

Her imperviousness to its power had allowed her to help Gharek, an irony in itself considering what bound them together. There was no ethereal weapon she might wield to break the grip this thing had on spirits. She was a shade speaker, not a necromancer. She could speak to and hear the dead but possessed no death magic, knew no spells to beat back an entity that stalked the departed. She was merely a voice for the voiceless and could only watch as each ghost was snatched toward the black wood, where it disappeared into its depths.

The mare snuffled and shifted her weight, either unconcerned or unaware of the ethereal chaos swirling around her. Siora peered into the tree line a final time, listening for footsteps or sepulchral voices. The darkness, and its sister, silence, stared back. Her sympathy for the dead would get her killed if she returned to the wood, and she didn't believe the mercy she'd shown Gharek would be returned. She urged the mare into a trot, away from the wood, and cursed Midrigar, away from the dead empress's assassin.

Wellspring Holt offered temporary safety, a place where she might briefly catch her breath before fleeing once more in the hope Gharek wouldn't find her and, if the gods were kind, finally put aside his need for revenge.

The town was just waking when she reached its outskirts. A rising sun crested the horizon, riding a fiery line that burned away the night. Morning dew sat cool and damp on her shoulders and hair. Tired, hungry, and yawning from lack of sleep, Siora maneuvered her way through a growing crowd of vendors and customers filling the streets, the first to set up their stalls, the second risen early to buy the choice items for sale. She dodged beggars, who watched her pass with the same weary, desperate expressions she wore when she begged, and avoided the vile-smelling trenches that lined the cobblestone streets and alleys and carried the effluvia tossed from chamber pots.

Prolonged scrutiny from others as she made her way through Wellspring Holt made her shoulder blades itch and reminded her she needed to find a stable quickly. Gharek's mare had been an unexpected boon, and Siora wished she might keep her, but the horse was a fine mount, obvious to anyone with an inkling of knowledge about horses. Far too fine a possession for a beggar woman in rags to be riding unless she stole it.

The last thing Siora wanted was to draw attention to herself.

Even when she took the risk of offering her services as a shade speaker, most only remembered what she told them about their dead loved ones, not what she looked like. A gutter rat atop a fine mare attracted notice.

Her talent for communicating with spirits had sometimes bought her a night in a stable or barn among the cattle and horses or sometimes the dinner of a meat pie or bowl of potatoes. It also created problems. Charlatans claiming to have the same talent as she had turned it into a travesty to be mocked, disbelieved, and, on some occasions, punished. Still, the Empire considered shade-speaking a kind of second sight instead of magic, so it wasn't outlawed. Siora was happy most people thought her a trickster and her gift a sham, even as they gave her money to speak to the spirits that still lingered on the earthly plane.

She halted in front of a stall setting up to sell iron nails. The vendor gave her a suspicious look when she asked the whereabouts of the nearest public stable yard. His distrust didn't lessen when she told him she'd been charged to drop her mistress's horse off with a farrier. He pointed in the direction of a cluster of ramshackle buildings, then shooed her away with a wave of both hands.

His directions were easy to follow, and she soon discovered the stable yard, a bustling hive of activity with groomsmen and stable lads rushing to and fro, customers dropping off horses for grooming, vetting, or boarding, and the horses themselves, jostling each other for space at the feeding or water troughs. No one noticed Siora among the controlled mayhem, which suited her fine. She could leave the mare and simply walk away with none the wiser.

It was a shame she couldn't sell Gharek's mount, but attempting it guaranteed an unfriendly visit from the town's constabulary armed with questions, suspicions, and the strong possibility of a night spent in the gaol, caged and waiting for Gharek to stroll into town and find her.

She found an out-of-the-way spot in the stable yard to dismount and strip anything of value from the tack and saddlebags, tucking them out of sight in her bodice and the pockets she'd sewn into the folds of her skirt. She kept all of Gharek's coin, as well as a shirt, a tunic, a pair of trousers, a knife, and the half full pack of road rations he carried. She turned his tunic into a makeshift satchel, shoving all but the coin and the knife inside before tying it off. The saddlebags she left with the saddle. Of good quality and well-made, they were far too nice for the likes of her and would only draw notice.

She coaxed the mare to a cluster of other horses still tacked and saddled, whispered a "thank you" for her help, and left her at one of the hay racks before striding away from the stable yard. Soon enough someone would inquire about her owner. By then Siora intended to be on the other side of town, hiding in some niche where she could sleep a few hours and plan what she'd do next.

She hurried past shops catering to the town's wealthy citizens: perfumeries and tailors, confectioneries and specialty cobblers, silk merchants, a sword smith, and even a book purveyor. The last made her pause for a moment to stare longingly at the bound volumes displayed in cases, the lettering on their spines hinting at the treasures between the covers. Her mother had taught her to read when she was a child. The skill had served her as well as speaking with the dead, though she considered it a gift while the other was sometimes a burden.

"Get away from there, ya lice-ridden tar leather!"

A piece of fruit hurtled through the shop's open doorway. Siora sidestepped it and jogged away from the scowling shopkeeper who raised his arm to throw something else at her. She did stop long enough to pick up the fruit. An orange. She grinned as she sprinted down the street. The well-fed merchant might think nothing of wasting food in such a way, but Siora blessed such good fortune literally thrown at her. She had something to eat and didn't have to spend any of Gharek's pilfered money yet.

Her stomach grumbled, reminding her she hadn't eaten in a day and a half. The orange wasn't much but she could enjoy it, along with a little of the road rations she'd taken to keep the hunger pangs at bay. They'd been her constant companions for many years, with only a few short respites from their presence, including the time she'd lived in Gharek's household.

She wove a path deeper into the town, away from the main roads used for commerce and onto the narrower back streets and alleys, lined on either side by houses. Some boasted ornate doors studded with rows of expensive iron-nail caps. Others were carved or painted in lavish designs with family crests or murals depicting some familial event for which the occupants were most proud. All spoke of the wealthy living behind them and a message that rabble like her had no place here.

What this neighborhood lacked in welcome, it more than made up for in peacefulness and quiet. No one lurked in the doorways. Children didn't play in the streets nor did women stand on their stoops to sweep and exchange gossip with each other or share in the labor of laundry from communal washtubs. It was an odd kind of distancing, one Siora welcomed. A gathering of people familiar with each other and their day-to-day lives would be quick to note and remark on the appearance of a stranger in their midst, even one simply journeying through the town on the way to other business.

Relieved that this street lacked the bustle of others, Siora followed a winding alley dividing the back walls of several homes, searching for a hideaway where she could rest without being noticed. She found what she was looking for in a tiny lean-to, empty of whatever it had been built to shelter. Just large enough for her to crawl into and obscured by a pair of overgrown bushes and numerous lines of damp laundry hanging above it. The perfect place to sleep for a few hours, out of the sun and safe from prying eyes.

Tucked into the space, she ate the orange and a little of the road rations. The makeshift bag holding the food and clothes acted as a pillow, and she lay on the ground, thankful for its coolness in the lean-to's stifling stillness. The day's heat and a night of running from her pursuer made her lethargic. She closed her eyes, skating the edge of sleep, wondering at the vagaries of fate that had turned a man, who'd offered her his reluctant but significant trust into a vigilante who'd chased her across half the Empire to exact revenge against her.

The memory of his daughter, small, fragile Estred, crying as she huddled in on herself while a vicious mob bellowed their outrage and hurled rocks at her, made tears seep beneath Siora's closed lashes. The girl hadn't even been able to protect her head from the stones with her arms because she had no arms. Courage had engulfed Siora in a red tide of indignant fury at the sight. She'd flung people twice her size out of her way to reach the terrified child and used her own body as a shield to protect her against the hail of stones raining down on them.

The battering had lasted a lifetime, or so it seemed to her bruised body, until it gradually stopped, and the angry shouts turned to fearful cries, screams of pain, and running feet. Siora had found herself unceremoniously flung to the side, the crying child ripped from her arms. She'd rolled, only to gain her feet, ready to launch herself at this newest attacker. She'd halted at the sight of the little girl held tight in the embrace of a man who stroked her hair and whispered soothingly into her ear. He'd stood amidst a scatter of stones and a trio of lifeless bodies, their blood pooling beneath them or trickling in serpentine rivers across the cobblestone street. The mob had fled and left its dead behind.

Unnerved by the dichotomous sight of what must have been the child's father comforting his offspring while standing among those he'd killed to save her, Siora had begun edging away, wincing with each step from the bruises and cuts made by the stones that had struck her .

The man had lifted his head to stare at her. "Wait," he'd said, and Siora had obeyed, captured not just by the grim, commanding voice but by the expression in his eyes—sorrow laced with murderous fury, and a bleak desperation that made her heart clench at the sight.

She had done as he ordered and waited. And while that decision had brought her to this moment, she didn't regret it. It was a bittersweet draft that she drank, where the bitter was stronger than the sweet, but the sweet made it worthwhile.

That grim memory faded as she sank into sleep, only to be replaced with restless dreams of writhing phantoms and Gharek's merciless gaze promising retribution for her betrayal of him and his plans. Siora heard herself speaking, an insistent command to wake up. As she climbed her way back toward wakefulness, she discovered the demanding voice wasn't hers, but a deeper one. And familiar.

Her eyes snapped open to see her father Skavol's nebulous apparition crouched in front of her, afternoon sunlight piercing him with golden spears so that he flickered and sparkled in a haze of dust motes. "Hurry, Raven-girl," he said in the hollow tones of the dead. "Run!"

Siora didn't hesitate or question him. He'd been a constant presence in her life after he died but only when she was in danger, his warnings and help saving her numerous times throughout the years. He was how she'd evaded Gharek this long. She clutched her belongings and scuttled out from her hiding spot. The ominous smell of smoke teased her nostrils and, in the distance, shouting and the thunder of hooves echoed through the streets.

Scavol's misty shape hovered at her side, one translucent hand resting on her arm to urge her to a faster pace. "Run, daughter! Horsemen!"

His enigmatic order didn't reveal much but the smoke did, as did the increasing volume and proximity of shouts and frightened cries.

The labyrinth of hanging laundry that had offered welcome obscurity now hid her view of anything beyond the last bedsheet. She ducked around the fluttering shields, thrusting them aside, no longer caring if anyone saw her. Even those who did spare her a quick glance forgot about her instantly as people left their houses to spill into previously empty streets and gape at the roiling columns of black smoke pluming skyward from the opposite side of the town.

Uneasy calm shattered when a stripling lad suddenly rounded a corner and raced toward them, waving his arms wildly above his head, his features stricken and pale as any ghost. "Nunari!" he yelled as he dashed down the street. "Nunari attacking Wellspring!"

His frantic warning instantly turned the milling crowd into a panicked stampede. People fled in every direction, either back into their houses or through various streets, some toward the columns of smoke to join the fight, others away from them to flee the danger.

Caught in the mayhem of a frightened human tide, Siora shoved and elbowed her way toward one of the side streets leading away from the city's center. She struggled to stay upright amid the mob that twisted and convulsed like some great, dying beast. If she fell, she'd die, trampled underfoot.

Once free of the press of bodies, she zigzagged a path through the town, taking every street with the fewest number of people clogging the way, her heart pounding as the sounds of fighting and the acrid smell of burning wood filled her ears and nose. She skidded around a corner and plunged straight into a nightmare.

Ghosts newly freed from their fleshly cages swarmed one of the town's smaller squares, phantasmic hornets emitting an ethereal cacophony of wails and keening sorrow. They swirled around a mob of fighters slashing and stabbing at each other with swords, axes, knives, and spears. Bodies—human and horse alike—littered the ground around them in dark puddles of gore. Those battling one another were a mixed lot of civilian townsmen, Kraelian army, and invading Nunari who fought both on foot and from horseback. People fell before the blade like wheat stalks under a scythe;

men shouted and cursed while blood sprayed the walls of nearby shops and houses and turned the streets into a slippery mire.

Siora froze for a moment at the horror of it, the brutality of the fighting. It was one moment too long. A Nunari fighter spotted her. Painted in the ghastly shade of blood crimson, he flashed her a murderous grin, hefted his sword, and lunged toward her.

She spun and fled, the scream trapped in her throat as she bolted for another street, no longer sure of her direction, only certain that her pursuer was close behind and getting closer. She fancied she could feel his breath on her back and prayed for her father's presence, his guidance for a way to turn, a means to lose the man chasing her through the burning town, but no familiar specter appeared to aid her; only those newly made and still in shock over their own savage endings flitted past her.

"Keep running, little bitch," a voice snarled practically in her ear. "You still can't get away."

His words and her terror gave Siora's feet wings. Her lungs burned, but she ignored the splinters in her chest every time she inhaled. She darted toward a busy street, crowded with people—those who fled or those who fought or both. It didn't matter. Anything that offered an obstacle for the Nunari chasing her and an opportunity to outrun him.

Once more the thunder of battle boomed around her as she raced through the center square where only a few hours earlier Wellspring Holt had hummed with business and townspeople going about their day, unaware of the madness about to descend on them. Now the square was a raging mayhem of burning buildings, flame and smoke, screaming people and runaway horses, bloody skirmishes between Nunari invaders and desperate citizens defending their families and themselves.

She plunged into the thick of it without looking back. Her own cry drowned in the chaos as a stinging pain burst across her scalp and neck. Her head snapped back and she was wrenched off her feet. She hit the dirt hard, the impact flattening her lungs. The leering face of her Nunari pursuer loomed above her, and from the corner of her eye she saw her braid, her one small concession to vanity that had become the means of her capture, wrapped in his hand. He raised the bloodied sword he held in his other hand, and Siora stared at death with tear-filled eyes.

Months of running, hiding, and surviving by her wits, her luck, the help of her dead father, and the arbitrary mercy of the gods, and now she'd die not by Gharek's hand but by some nameless steppe nomad looking to loot, plunder, and kill.

The thought was briefer than the breath she couldn't take, chased away by the sight of the sword blade flashing in the sun as its wielder brought it down to cleave her in two.

Death came fast and savage, but not hers. Another blade met the first with a dull ring, blocking the lethal blow, and Siora managed to snatch a thin inhalation as the second blade slid free to slice through her attacker's neck. Gouts of blood fountained in every direction, splashing her in a hot wave. She rolled away just before the Nunari's headless body collapsed onto the spot where she'd lain, his sword clattering harmlessly beside him. His head bounced a short distance before stopping with his face turned to the sky. His wide eyes blinked slowly as if mystified by how he'd ended up in his current position.

Terrified of facing a rescuer who was just as likely to kill her as the dead Nunari, Siora scuttled backward on her haunches and elbows, half blinded by blood not her own dripping down her forehead and into her eyelashes. A hand grabbed her arm, the grip as unyielding as the one that had held her braid. She twisted to see who imprisoned her.

Fear fought with relief at the sight of her captor. Gharek's implacable features were soot-stained and as bloody as hers. He hauled her to her feet, giving her a slight shake to emphasize his displeasure. "Stupid girl, stop fighting and keep up," he snarled.

He didn't give her a chance to reply or resist. His fingers wrapped around her wrist, shackling her to him, and he pulled her deeper into the havoc around them. There was no time to puzzle out why he'd chosen to save her instead of letting the Nunari cut her down. She stayed close behind him, using his body as both shield and battering ram as he clove a path through the square.

Buildings consumed by flames collapsed into fiery heaps of red-hot timbers and glowing showers of sparks. Heavy smoke made it hard to see and breathe. Riderless horses, terror-struck by the fire, galloped through the crowds, trampling anyone too slow to get out the way. A man enrobed in flame and blazing brighter than any pitch-soaked torch staggered along a hastily cleared path, screaming in a voice no longer human. A woman, face resolute and smeared with soot, tossed a baby from the second story window of a burning house into the arms of an older girl waiting in the street. She closed her eyes in obvious relief just as the roof collapsed on her with a dull roar and an explosion of sparks.

The hazy shapes of ghosts mingled with the serpentine swirl of smoke in Wellspring Holt, both so thick in some places a person could carve their name in the miasma and have it linger. The chance for Siora to escape Gharek came when he let her go to capture a runaway horse by its trailing reins. She didn't take it. The man who'd chased her across Empire lands was, for the moment, her ally and her best chance at survival.

The animal skidded in the dirt and reared before settling down. Its wide eyes rolled and its nostrils sprayed snot with every frightened, bellowing breath. Gharek grabbed Siora, flinging her onto its back so hard she nearly flew off the opposite side. He mounted behind her, using the reins as a lash. The horse jumped to a full gallop, and Siora clutched the saddle pommel to hold on.

We're going to die. We're going to die.

The chant played over and over in her head as they raced through Wellspring Holt. Gharek plowed the horse through a small knot of fighters, using his sword to cut down a pair of Nunari who tried to halt their escape. Siora spotted one of the town's two gates so close, though it might have been in another kingdom for any chance they'd have of reaching it alive. Gharek lashed the horse to greater speed. The gods only knew what threat lay on the other side—no doubt more Nunari invaders riding on a second wave of attack to finish what the first wave had started.

They didn't slow, and the horse raced through the breached gate at a dead run. Siora flinched and closed her eyes for a moment, expecting a hail of arrows to descend on them, death from above, painful but hopefully quick. She opened her eyes again at Gharek's bellowed "Oh fuck!" and yelped when their mount reared once more, pivoting hard on its back hooves before crashing down again. Siora narrowly avoided biting her tongue as her teeth snapped together from the jarring landing. She caught a quick glimpse of what looked like an ocean of uniforms, a landscape of shields, and a forest of spears stretched as far as her eye could see. Instead of Nunari horsemen waiting outside Wellspring Holt, an entire battalion of Kraelian soldiers stood at the ready.

A voice rose above the din behind them, sounding both surprised and triumphant. "Holy gods, it's the cat's-paw! Catch that fucker!"

Panic engulfed her when Gharek turned the horse back toward the gate, toward the burning town, and the fighting within. She struggled for space in the saddle, enough to fling herself sideways and off the fleeing animal. She sent up a brief prayer that she wouldn't break anything. She never got the chance.

Two loud cracks split the air, followed by agony so sharp she thought she'd retch. Like the vicious edge of a mirror shard, the pain cut across her upper arm, tore along her collarbone, and bit deep into her other arm before she was wrenched from the saddle. The world turned a somersault in her vision an instant before another breath-stealing fall to the ground rattled every bone in her body. A last tiny huff of air burst past her lips in a whisper when Gharek landed on top of her with a hard grunt.

CHAPTER THREE

Gharek sat, bound and bloody on the saddle of a trotting horse, and swallowed back the foul-tasting bile that hung in his throat. The view in front of him offered little in either interest or comfort—a solid wall of mounted, armored Kraelian soldiers. They rode toward some unknown destination, absolute in their intent that Gharek go with them. He scraped his tongue gingerly over his split lip, wincing at the sting there. He didn't complain. They could have broken his jaw and made him spit teeth, and that was before they might have entertained the idea to crack his spine like a broomstick or gouge out his eyes. Kraelian soldiers weren't known for their civility or their mercy. He would know. He'd been one before taking up the far more lucrative and dangerous role of Dalvila's cat's-paw.

The blessing of no life-threatening injuries didn't stop him from cursing inwardly, not only over his rotten luck but also his own foolish mercy toward Siora. Had he not tried to play the role of hero, he wouldn't be in this sorry predicament right now, a prisoner of some faction of the fracturing army with plans for him that no doubt included a slow, agonizing death at the hands of one or more of the countless enemies he'd made in the Empire. The only question was who among that considerable number would have the pleasure of weaving his entrails through their garden gate or displaying his severed head on a pole outside their front entry.

He'd realized the second his horse had cleared Wellspring Holt's gate that he'd ridden into an equally grim situation. A full Kraelian garrison's worth of soldiers had gathered outside, weapons drawn, as they waited for the command to charge inside the city and battle the Nunari ransacking, pillaging, and looting. Any hope that he might simply ride past them had died when one voice rang out, urgent and demanding.

"Catch that fucker!"

A trio of soldiers had leapt at the command, using whips to wrap around both him and Siora. Gharek didn't even get a chance to turn his mount in a different direction before the whips tore into his clothes and cut his flesh as thoroughly as any knife. When they fell, he'd fallen on Siora, certain he'd crushed her to death with the impact. A pack of soldiers pounced on him with the speed and ferocity of starving wolves, punching and kicking him while he did his best to protect himself and the small woman still trapped beneath him.

In no time he was bound, gagged, and tossed atop the horse he was yanked from, a soldier riding beside him, holding the reins. Siora, also bound but free of a gag, shared a saddle with another soldier. Gharek only caught glimpses of her stiff shoulders and back as she rode ahead of him, doing her best not to touch her companion.

That she hadn't been raped by their captors still astounded him. The Kraelian army was no better than the Nunari tearing apart Wellspring Holt behind them, its townspeople in as much danger from their saviors as they were from their invaders. But the man commanding this party had threatened to geld anyone who even twitched in Siora's direction for a better look at her ankles.

"Probably nothing more than a whore," the leader said and spat at Siora's feet, even while his flat gaze traveled over his underlings with unmistakable warning. "But you shitheads don't get to find out. Only the general does. So until we deliver these two to him and he decides what to do, it's hands off or I'll cut your balls off and force-feed them to you." After that grotesque threat, the soldier riding with Siora was no more eager to touch her than she was to touch him.

They were a party of sixteen, carved out of the large battalion gathered at the gate outside of Wellspring Holt. They rode away with the Kraelian battle cry ringing in Gharek's ears. If there was anything left of the town by the time the day was done, he'd be amazed.

The bodies of Nunari nomads and some of their horses littered the roadside as they passed, signs the Empire's troops hadn't arrived here without some resistance. Their much greater numbers allowed them to overwhelm the lesser force of Nunari, either caught unawares or unable to flee in time and warn their kinsmen already in the town that the enemy fast-approached.

The group Gharek and Siora rode with traveled hard along a narrow path that forked north of the main trade road to run perpendicular with the borders marking the Nunari hinterlands. Gharek might have assumed this was a renegade band turned slavers, who'd decided to sell their two captives to the enemy, if it weren't for overhearing their leader's remarks.

They rode toward a destination where a nameless Kraelian general waited, and Gharek's stomach twisted into a knot. Half of Domora's surviving elite were hunting him, and someone among these men had recognized him as Dalvila's cat's-paw. Gharek understood hatred and vengeance. Both dictated how he lived his life. He didn't delude himself into thinking he was unique in being driven by such forces. Another felt the same about him. Whatever punishment they wished to bring down on his head for any of the numerous crimes he'd committed while serving Dalvila, it would be prolonged and it would be brutal.

He pushed away the rising despair along with the image of Estred's innocent face, the one shining light in his dark thoughts. He'd not go down without a struggle. He'd failed at many things in his life, but he knew how to survive, to start over, and to prevail. He didn't have the luxury of dying just yet.

They rode for several hours, stopping once to water the horses. Siora used the time to answer nature's demands, hiding behind a cluster of horses for privacy. Gharek found it odd that only one soldier paid attention to her movements, and that was the guard assigned to her. Even he didn't leer but kept a respectful watch only in the sideways glances he sent her way.

Kraelian army men were a vulgar lot, more feral than a pack of pit dogs most of the time, with little knowledge or concern for property, or so it had been Gharek's experience when he was a soldier. These men were unique among the ranks, and he wondered who commanded them in such a way that they acted with such restraint.

A soldier pulled down Gharek's gag long enough to tip a flask of water to his mouth. He downed several gulps before he was gagged once more and shoved toward the waiting horse. Siora's gaze followed him, though she remained silent as her guard lifted her onto the saddle and mounted behind her.

They were off again, their path a steady ride along the boundaries of Nunari territories. A pair of scouts rode farther ahead before circling back to cover ground the party had already tread, reporting to the leader any movement or activity. Tension ran high in the group, everyone braced for a Nunari raiding party to suddenly crest one of the adjacent hillocks and bear down on them with spears and a hail of arrow fire.

The Nunari had revolted against their imperial overlords and allied with their Savatar neighbors to attack and lay siege to the once-great capital of Kraelag. With both the emperor and the empress now dead and the powerful Kraelian families slaughtering each other in their bid to seize the contested throne, the Empire fractured even more, and the Nunari steadily clawed back bits and pieces of Empire territory into their grasp. They'd set their sights on Wellspring Holt, and in Gharek's opinion they'd take a lot more in a short period of time if the army didn't crush the invading forces soon and without quarter.

Twilight had cast a gossamer veil across the sky by the time the commander called a second halt and ordered his men to set up camp. Gharek knew this territory. As the erstwhile cat's-paw, he'd traveled all over the Empire to do Dalvila's often bloodthirsty work. He didn't need a map or a guide to tell him they were headed toward the burned out remains of Kraelag; a city so destroyed by god-fire it had taken months to stop glowing red from the heat. Its fiery light had been seen from as far off as Sokoti Island, where the locals there had crafted charms and wards against the spirits of thousands who'd burned in the conflagration. If Siora was indeed a true shade speaker, she was about to greet an entire city of the restless dead in the next few days.

The camp was a spartan affair with only bedrolls laid out to provide a barrier between the sleeper and damp ground. A frail breeze provided the only relief from the lingering summer heat, and the vault of sky above them sported only a few clouds, none promising rain. Neither Gharek nor Siora got a bed, only a stake rammed into the ground to which each was tethered. He took a long, grateful breath when one of the soldiers removed the gag. His relief didn't last long, and he stiffened as the group's leader approached.

The man squatted in front of Gharek and inclined his head toward Siora before returning his attention to the cat's-paw. "Here's how this works. I have two guards to keep an eye on you, so you'll have a hard time trying to wiggle out of your bonds without some-one noticing. I don't know if the whore means anything to you, and I don't care, but if either of you try to escape, I'll break one of your legs. Then I'll break one of hers." His mouth turned up briefly at Siora's gasp, though his gaze remained steadfast on Gharek, who scowled.

"You won't allow your men to rape her, but you'll break her bones if I try to run?"

The other man's smile widened even more. "They're a careless bunch of fucks who'd end up killing her while they took their plea-sure, and swiving a whore serves no purpose. Making sure neither of you decides to run off does serve General Zaredis's interest. I won't be showing up in his camp without you, even if I have to cut your feet off to keep you docile."

Zaredis. Gharek recognized the name though he'd never met the man or seen him at court. One of Dalvila's most capable generals. Capable enough and ambitious enough to be a threat, but one too valuable to have assassinated. She'd exiled him instead, to quell and control the rebellious southern territories with their barbarian tribes who fought even harder against the Empire's yoke. Why Zaredis wanted the cat's-paw, Gharek could only guess.

He glanced past the captain to Siora behind him. In the shadows cavorting around her, she looked paler than the moon, her mouth thinned to a grim line. "Don't run," he warned her.

She shook her head, and her eyes narrowed. "You either, cat's-paw."

The Kraelian captain flashed a full grin before standing. "Wise decision. Let's see which of you keeps to it as the night wears on." He rose and strolled away to join the others around a communal campfire.

Gharek's stomach rumbled at the idea his captors would soon cook their supper over that fire. He hadn't eaten since before Siora walloped him with the branch to break Midrigar's bewitchment and then stole both his horse and his supplies. Nor was there any guarantee he'd eat anytime soon. He glared at Siora, who divided her attention between him and the guards set to watch them. Her gaze finally settled on him and stayed, as steady and far-seeing as he remembered when she still served in his household.

"Why did you save me?" She tilted her head to one side. "When I left you in the forest, you warned me there was no debt."

Were he driven simply by the revenge he'd promised, he wouldn't have done so. His fury over her treachery still threatened to swallow him whole, even after all these months. Fury and a nameless hurt that demanded recognition he struggled not to acknowledge. But it was Estred's grief that had sent him after Siora, not his revenge. Her grief and his promise to her that he'd bring back the wayward nursemaid and make her beg his daughter's forgiveness for abandoning her had sent him on his search. If he had to drag Siora back in chains to the home of those who took care of Estred while he traveled, then so be it.

Siora believed he'd chased her for the opportunity to kill her, and he'd entertained the idea more than once, especially during those first hard weeks when he'd taken Estred and fled Domora, terrified they'd be caught—he executed for his crimes and Estred executed for the offense of being his offspring. That or for offending the delicate sensibilities of those who believed only the undamaged and unblemished had the right to live. He'd spent many a sleepless night rubbing his daughter's back while she cried in her sleep and muttered Siora's name. It was during those times he sank into the black depths of silent rage and wished the nursemaid dead.

"Why did you save me?" she repeated.

"Because you're more valuable to me alive than dead, and you owe Estred," he snarled. "And for the moment the why doesn't matter. We're both someone else's captives now. If you pray and believe in the compassion of gods, now's the time to act the supplicant and beg for their help."

A puzzled frown creased a line in her brow. She didn't flinch away at his waspish reply. "Do you know this Zaredis?"

His shoulders were killing him, and he shrugged in his bonds to try to ease the ache in his joints. "Only by name. If he's anything like the mistress we both once served, you and I are already walking corpses." And they'd beg to die by the time it was over. He pushed the thought away. For the moment there was nothing he could do, no plan he could make until he could judge who pulled the puppet strings in this scenario.

He focused his attention back to Siora. "I would ask you the same question. Why did you save me?

She didn't hesitate. "I already told you. For Estred, who needs her father." The frown line between her eyebrows smoothed out, and her expression and voice softened. The regret in her eyes shone like guttering lamplight. "How is she?

He twisted the knife. "She grieves and she fears." Her eyes turned glossy at his answer, and he offered her the barest hint of a cold smile. "You make little sense. You betray me and her to help the draga—supposedly for Estred's sake—then risk your life to save me from whatever thing sleeps in Midrigar, knowing that I've hunted you all this time and thinking I mean to kill you. Again for Estred's sake, but thanks to your actions, I lost everything I'd built for her in Domora."

His daughter was safe—as safe she could be—with a relative of his steward in a town some distance from Domora. They'd agreed to watch over Estred for a handsome sum that bought not only their care but also their silence regarding her fugitive father. No doubt it also helped that his steward let his relatives know that with the generous payment came the surety that if they failed in their task, they'd pay with their lives. The cat's-paw didn't hesitate to dispatch those who crossed him, especially where his daughter was concerned.

A snide voice laughed at him inwardly. *And yet Estred's nurse still lives.*

Melancholy had joined regret in Siora's gaze. "My father died in the Pit during one of the melees for the Rites of Spring years ago. I was Estred's age at the time. He was a good man. Strong, protective. He loved my mother and me, and when he died, we were broken." The light from nearby torches caught the telltale sheen of tears in her eyes. "I can't help every fatherless child, but I can try to help one, and Estred shines with you as her parent."

If he wasn't bound like a trussed pigeon, Gharek would wrap his hands around her neck and squeeze from pure frustration. "Then why did you turn against us when I had the draga in my trap? His blood might have helped my daughter, given to her what she was robbed of at birth." If the draga had been honest—and Gharek believed him, despite his innate suspicions—his assumption about the blood was despairingly incorrect.

Siora sighed. "You know that isn't true. If it were, Malachus would have offered you his blood willingly. You can't even say it aloud, can you? She was born without arms, lord. A burden yes. A struggle through life, but she's undeterred and has risen above that limitation, yet you've been so blinded by what you see as her lack that you almost got yourself killed facing a man who was something other than human and far more dangerous." Her distant gaze now did its best to peel away every one of his defenses and see beyond. Gharek didn't look away. She'd find nothing. Just hollowness.

"Why," she continued, "must you hold an old woman with the mind of a child hostage and put your own life at risk fighting a draga in order to change Estred?

His cackle held an edge that would do any sword proud. "First, your belief in a draga's generosity is ridiculous. And second, be-

46

cause we live in a world where a girl who eats with her feet is hardly seen as human, much less accomplished. Have you forgotten how you ended up in my service in the first place?" The reminder of that moment, when he'd raced through the streets of Domora hunting for his errant daughter, half mad with terror, made his heart seize in his chest. He'd never forget hurtling into an alley, drawn there by a shouting crowd, knowing what he'd find, and made sick to his soul.

Estred was there all right, cowering and frightened and sobbing as the good citizens of Domora threw stones at her. She'd come away from the ordeal with only a single cut to her cheek thanks to the incautious bravery of a beggar woman hardly bigger than Estred herself who'd used her own body as a shield. Bloody, bruised, and smelling worse than a public piss pot, Siora had entered his household for a bath, food, and physicking and ended up staying as Estred's unlikely nursemaid. She stayed long enough to gain his daughter's love and Gharek's reluctant trust. Then cheerfully set fire to both before running away.

"I'm through talking," he declared, and closed his eyes against the sight of her.

She was relentless. "What purpose will capturing me serve? What is so important that you've put your vengeance aside yet still hunt me across the Empire?"

Gharek kept his eyes closed. "You will come back with me, willingly or not. You're going to face Estred and apologize for leaving her. You will get down on your knees, assure her it wasn't her fault that you left, and beg her for her forgiveness. And if she bestows that forgiveness on you, you will leave us and never show your face again." He opened his eyes and turned his head to stare at her. "If you do, I will hunt you once more, and this time *it will* be for vengeance."

All the blood had drained from her features, leaving her as pale as the dead. A hollow bleakness filled her eyes, and the muscles in her throat tightened convulsively with the effort to speak. When she finally managed to push the words past her lips, her voice was barely a whisper, washed out and unsteady. "Estred thinks it's her fault?" She didn't wait for his answer. Her eyes closed and her jaw tightened even as tears cascaded in rivers down her cheeks. "I never wanted that," she said in the same whisper, shaking her head. "I didn't know . . ."

He was merciless. "And obviously didn't care."

"That isn't true!" She darted a glance at the soldiers set to guard them. Both scowled at her.

Gharek didn't reply and she didn't continue. The silence between them was an ocean neither chose to cross, at least until one of the Kraelian soldiers approached them. Gharek watched warily as the man drew closer with two bowls from which tendrils of steam meandered to fade into the night air. His mouth watered at the enticing smell coming from those bowls, and his belly sent up a series of growls that could be heard across the encampment.

The soldier thrust both bowls and their spoons at Siora. She grabbed them with her bound hands before the man could drop their supper carelessly into her lap. He pointed to Gharek. "The captain says you both stay tied. You're to feed him his share."

His words killed Gharek's appetite. Before he could protest, the soldier walked away to return to his comrades drinking ale around the fire. Siora had set down one of the bowls and knee-walked closer to him with the second bowl. She'd wiped away her tears, though her gaze remained sad. Gharek bared his teeth at her in warning. "I'm not hungry."

She rolled her eyes and pointed at his rumbling midriff with the spoon. "That's a lie. Put aside your pride, lord."

Had she admonished him in the tone of a tutor to an errant student, he would have snapped his tethers to reach her. But she'd spoken in a tired, defeated manner, and some part of him, a part he wished might die a quick and convenient death, suffered a pang of guilt. "Pride has nothing to do with it," he grumbled.

The stew smelled better than the finest plate of delicacies served at the royal palace, made even more tempting by the sight of it mounded on the spoon Siora held up to tempt him. "Then put aside your suspicions," she said. "Trust me." She pursed her lips to blow on the spoon and cool its contents. She possessed a full mouth, one he'd noted smiled readily and often when she'd taken care of Estred, and on occasion had even curved upward for him, startling him. He looked away, cursing inwardly at the errant observation. He'd never been one to think with his prick, and now wasn't the time to start.

He surrendered to the scent of hot food and the demands of his stomach and accepted the bite she offered him. It was probably a good thing he was tied and dependent on her to feed him, or he would have wolfed down the bowl's contents in two bites. She fed him the rest slowly, waiting until he finished each bite instead of shoving it between his teeth and trying to choke him.

During one pause he asked her, "Why do you wait to eat? You

could enjoy yours in front of me and make me watch as you savored each spoonful."

"Because if it's poisoned, you'll be the first to die."

Gharek gaped at her, the sour burn of bile-tainted stew surging up from his stomach to his throat. Gods, she was right! He lurched back from her as if she offered him a diseased rat instead of the ladened spoon, only to stop at the hints of amusement dancing in her eyes and playing around the faint lines that bracketed either side of her mouth. "You bitch," he breathed, feeling the hot blush of embarrassment crawl up his neck, into his cheeks, and set fire to his ears.

Her tut of disapproval only fueled his outrage. "You deserved it for throwing my good intention back in my face. I fed you first because it's a small kindness most of us will do."

"Sorry," he snapped. "I'm fresh out of medals today." When had this strange, quiet woman developed claws and the willingness to use them? Against him? Several times now.

Another sigh, and she shook her head. "And almost out of your share of the stew. Do you want more?"

"No."

This time she shrugged. "More for me then," she said, and proceeded to eat the rest of his dinner and hers as well, completely unconcerned at the idea of the food being poisoned. "I told you to trust me," she said as she put the now empty bowls aside.

He should have left her to her fate in Wellspring Holt. "I did that once and look where we are now." His shoulders were on fire and his hands had gone numb. Gharek clenched his jaw, unwilling to show any hint of his discomfort, especially in front of this beggar maid who'd just done a damn fine job of making a fool of him.

"I accept the blame for Estred's sorrow but not for the failure of your foolish plan. It was already ruined before you even returned to the house to face the draga." She wiped her hands on her tattered skirts. "I hope they give us water or ale. The stew was filling, but I'm parched."

As if her remarks summoned him, the same soldier who'd brought them food returned with two cups of tepid water.

"No ale?" Gharek asked, unable to keep the sarcasm out of his voice.

Siora made a distressed sound, and the soldier's eyes narrowed before he said, "I can piss in it for you. You'll have a nice warm cup of ale in no time."

Siora plucked the cups out of the man's hands. "We like water. Our thanks for bringing it."

The soldier's gaze moved from her to Gharek and back again. "Most of the time, I'd say a man can do better than a used-up whore, but in this case I'll say you can do a lot better than him." He nodded once to a grim-faced Siora and planted a solid kick against Gharek's outer thigh before sauntering away.

A pained grunt escaped Gharek's tightly closed mouth despite his best efforts to hold it in. Siora gave a sympathetic cluck, which set his teeth on edge. "You know you invite your own misery," she said.

"Obviously," he replied. "I brought you into my house, didn't I?"

That sympathy evaporated in an instant, and her mouth thinned into a harsh line. Her hands tightened on the cups she held. He fully expected her to douse him in the face with the contents from one of them. Instead, she set one cup down next to her and carefully tilted the other one to his lips. Her patience only infuriated him even more, though he stayed silent and drank the cup dry. He had plenty of other opportunities to slash at her without going thirsty for it.

When he was done, she knee-walked back from him and drained her own cup before setting it aside and stretching out on the damp grass. The air hung hot and humid around them, and in both torch and moonlight, he saw the silvery sheen of perspiration on her forehead as she stared up at the stars.

He envied her the ability to stargaze. With his arms wrenched up behind his back and tied, lying supine in the grass didn't appeal, nor was it possible unless he wanted to be in agony instead of just pain. He bent his legs and curved his back so he could rest his torso against his knees and take the pressure off his spine. Siora glanced at him before returning to her study of the night sky.

"Are there ghosts around us?" he asked. Gharek never had use for idle conversation. If it didn't serve the purpose of gleaning information or entrapping someone, he preferred to remain silent. However, sparring with her earlier had taken his mind off his discomfort.

She turned her head to regard him, light and shadow carving her features into strange angles. "You know I'm a shade speaker?"

He tried to shrug and regretted it. "The villagers where you plied your trade were happy to give me that information." It might explain the strangeness of her scrutiny at times. Did she see ghosts always hovering around the living?

"And you believe me to be an authentic shade speaker?"

"Whether or not I believe it doesn't matter. Most who claim themselves necromancers are charlatans."

She bolted into a sitting position, all scowls and thin-lipped annoyance. "I'm not a necromancer. There's a difference."

He'd hit a nerve. Delighted by the discovery, he tucked away that small weapon for future use and arched an eyebrow. "Indeed. An important distinction if you want to survive in the Empire. One is true magic and the other mere bullshit. It's the only reason your kind aren't outlawed like others who possess magic; no one really believes you."

A soft breeze rose suddenly to tumble the stifling air and provide welcome relief to the oppressive heat. It stirred tendrils of hair that escaped Siora's braid and coiled around her slender neck. She plucked them away to rest behind her ears. Her scowl didn't lessen. "If no one believed us, they wouldn't pay for our services. More believe than you think. They're just afraid to say so because of ridicule or pity from others. And no, there are no ghosts lingering among us at the moment."

"Was that thing pulling me toward Midrigar a ghost?" He shuddered inwardly at the memory of whatever foul bewitchment had managed to sink its claws into him and drag him toward the cursed city's tumbled walls and the dark silhouettes of its ruined towers. He was used to being a puppet to a power greater and far more vicious than he, but Dalvila had been human—or at least wore the façade of a human—while whatever dragged him through the forest had been something so otherworldly, his very spirit shied away from dwelling on it for too long.

Siora's gaze bore deep holes into him before she finally answered in a flat voice, "No."

He'd half expected just that answer, but it still took him by surprise. And scared him. Wandering spirits didn't scare him. Confused ghosts who didn't know they'd worn out their welcome were harmless. Whatever the entity was that captured him in its grip wasn't harmless. "Are you sure?"

She nodded. "Quite. Whatever it is—was—it devours spirits. Swallowing whole crowds of the dead like a leviathan of the deep might swallow a ship." The idea of this unseen, ravenous adversary obviously frightened her. She didn't bother to hide her shudder as Gharek did.

He pondered her words, recalling his sojourn across empty, moonlit pastures; the wild, silent wood that ran along one side; a dark, mysterious wall. "When you were running from me, did you stay in an abandoned barn near a circle of stone?"

Her round eyes rounded even more. "Yes. Did you go in there?" She scooted a little closer to him at his nod.

"I thought you might have taken shelter under its roof," he said. "One wall of the barn had a mural. A grotesque painting." Beyond grotesque. Nightmarish, and Gharek had seen many things in his time as the empress's cat's-paw to understand the true meaning of both words.

Siora nodded. "Many faces. All screaming." The breeze brought another cooling exhalation. She shivered.

"Yes. At the time I wondered who would paint such a thing," he said.

"It isn't a painting." Her voice, already soft, had taken on a more hushed quality, as if she feared that what they spoke of was listening and might come calling to join the conversation.

Her words revealed some things but puzzled him even more concerning others. He might be dead inside, but he was still a living, breathing man. "If it only eats spirits, how was it able to bewitch me? And me but not you?" He'd wondered about the second while he worked free of the knots she'd made in the rope she'd used to bind him so she could steal his horse. Gharek decided he was thoroughly sick of being tied up by one person or another.

Siora offered a shrug, making him wince at the reminder of his aching shoulders. "I don't know. It's as much a mystery to me as it is to you. I only first encountered it in the barn when I saw ghosts struggling and fighting against whatever captured them. I felt none of what they did, or you, for that matter. No compulsion to turn toward the cursed city." She hugged herself as if the gentle breeze was a winter gale that cut through clothing and stripped warmth from her very bones. "Everyone knows that city is more than a mass grave, that those who risk going in for treasure or artifacts don't always come out. If any place should have been destroyed by god-fire, it was that place, and I say that as a woman who was set to burn in the Pit as a Flower of Spring."

Gharek started. Of the revelations she'd treated him to since he found her in Wellspring Holt, this surprised him most. In the months she'd served in his household as Estred's nurse, she'd never once mentioned it, and he couldn't imagine how she'd survived to tell of the ordeal. Flowers of Spring were burned alive in Kraelag's arena as sacrificial tithes to the gods for good luck and a bountiful harvest, and the Empire brooked no disobedience from those towns and villages forced to give over a woman for the great burning. A long-dead emperor had made a lasting example of Midrigar for showing such resistance. Punishment had been swift, monstrously cruel, and eternal.

"How did you . . ." he began, only to be interrupted by the arrival of a different soldier this time.

"Finish up," that one said, his leer intensifying as he ran his gaze over Siora from head to foot. "You're through chatting."

Gharek watched, fascinated as her features changed, adopting an expression that made him slide back a little and made the soldier retreat a step even as his leer faded.

"Your sister Fan asks that you remember her tears." She looked directly at the man, though her gaze saw through him to something—or someone—else only she could see.

Even in the torch-lit gloom, Gharek saw the soldier blanch before his face took on an ugly look that made Gharek's hackles instinctively rise. "I have to piss," Gharek said in a loud voice, and either his tone or his volume distracted the other man from making a lunge at Siora, who still looked beyond him, seemingly uncaring that she'd just narrowly avoided an attack.

The soldier remained dead-man pale, and he shivered before looking over his shoulder at those of his comrades still seated around the fire. "Keep an eye on her," he called to them. "I'll be back." A few sour mutters and nods were his reward, and he hauled Gharek to his feet, ignoring his captive's pained hiss.

Siora rested her hand briefly on Gharek's leg just before the soldier dragged him a short distance. The pleading in her gaze had replaced that far-horizon stare. "Don't run. Please."

He would have taunted her if his guard hadn't nearly yanked his arm out of its socket pulling him in the direction of a cluster of shrubs at the camp's perimeter. A few humiliating moments later and he was hauled unceremoniously back to his spot next to Siora, where the soldier shoved him down and walked away with the command to shut up and go to sleep or end up gagged.

His companion lay on her side, bound hands folded together under her chin like bruised wings. Gharek lay down next to her, facing her, trying his best to balance on his side and not roll to his back. Grass blades partially obscured Siora's features as she watched him struggle to get comfortable.

"Thank you for not running," she whispered.

He glanced at the cluster of soldiers nearby. None of them turned their way. "Did you see a ghost when you spoke of that man's sister?"

She nodded. "His younger sister, defiled by a neighbor's son. She died the following year of a fever."

The matter-of-fact tone in her voice lent truth to her statement. She'd answered his odd question without embellishment, as if chatting up the dead was a thing she did all the time. "How do you know this?"

Siora shrugged. "Her spirit told me. The dead are willing to talk if one is willing to listen."

The curve of her cheekbone cast a shadow across the hollow beneath it. There were more hollows at her throat and in the dip of her collarbones, and the trough of her waist between rib cage and hip was deep. She was a slight woman who'd noticeably missed more than a few meals since she fled the sanctuary of his house. She watched him with a steady expression, as if fully expecting his mockery. Had he not personally experienced an evil that tried to reel him in like a caught fish, he might have expressed his disbelief. There were indeed charlatan shade speakers. Siora, he was fast coming to believe, wasn't one of them.

Instead, he gave a disdainful huff and closed his eyes against the image of her next to him, more shadow than flesh and anchored to earth by the thinnest of threads. "Then the dead suffer the same weakness as the living. All are willing to talk. Few are willing to listen."

He cracked an eyelid open at her soft chuckle. "That, lord, is very true."

She said no more, and exhaustion swept over him, conquering the pain in his back and shoulders enough that he fell asleep, though not for long. It seemed only a series of breaths had passed before someone rudely woke him with a kick to the backside and a harsh voice belting out orders to his abused ear.

"Wake up, cat's-paw. We're headed out, and I'm eager to turn you over to the general so I can get back to important things like fighting the Nunari instead of playing nanny to you and the whore."

Gharek struggled to a sitting position, staring blearily at the group's captain. His shoulders had gone completely numb, and his fingers tingled in warning that they would soon do the same.

Unlike him, Siora stood and gave the captain the same disapproving look she'd leveled on Gharek numerous times so far. "I'm not a whore."

The man raked her with a cutting glance. "You have a cunt. You're a whore," he said flatly, and walked away.

Siora glared after him. "If there's any fairness in this world, that man's mother is dead and he has no sister, no wife, and no children to suffer his presence."

It was Gharek's turn to scoff. "I think you're the most patheti-cally hopeful person I've ever met."

Unlike the captain's comment, Gharek's mockery bounced off her without any noticeable mark. She shrugged. "Of course I am. After all, I didn't let you stumble into Midrigar."

They traveled through the day and beyond sundown, riding over ground both Gharek and Siora had just traveled going the oppo-site direction two days earlier. Pastures and fields rolled out on either side of the road, lush carpets of green under the hot sum-mer sun. Deceptively peaceful despite the turmoil that was tear-ing apart the Empire at every seam.

They stopped not far from the southern perimeter of the same forest that hid Midrigar from view to take a piss break and water the horses at a seasonal stream. Gharek fancied he smelled the smoke that plumed occasionally from Kraelag's ruins, still smol-dering so many months after its destruction. The men consumed their meals from horseback—travel rations of hard bread and dried fruit. They offered none to Gharek or Siora.

Full night had chased away the last of the gloaming when they finally reached a sprawling camp teeming with Kraclian soldiers and lit by hundreds of torches. Banners displaying a crest for the noble House of Varan fluttered from the peaks of several tents, with the biggest one flapping above the largest tent.

Gharek knew every house banner of the Kraelian nobility, and though he'd never seen or met Zaredis, he recognized the stylized design of the black wolf and bear locked in eternal combat on a field of green and bronze.

A crowd of soldiers hailed the new arrivals and several curious stares followed their prisoners as they were led toward the camp's largest tent. Gharek was shoved to one spot not far from the entrance and ordered to sit. A soldier did the same to Siora but put her too far away for them to exchange conversation. No doubt a purposeful move from a commander used to dealing with spies. He'd played spy now and again.

He settled down to wait, thoughts racing as he scrutinized what he could see of the camp from the limited scope of his vision. Horses were penned in a corral near the edge of the camp but not so far that predators would risk the light and the smell of humanity to attack one. Others grazed idly just outside of tents, some still saddled, others wearing bridles and horse blankets. A makeshift forge had been erected, open to the air except for a short awning pulled over the cold iron waiting to be hammered into weaponry or horseshoes. An impressive rack of spears and other pole arms bristled next to a wall of shields.

The camp hummed with activity, a hive of hundreds if not thousands of soldiers and camp followers brought across the Maemor Channel's turbulent waters on ships left docked on the Karadoc shores. Everyone knew the southern territories turned green soldiers into hardened fighting men. If it didn't, it was only because those lads didn't survive the experience. A general like Zaredis, de facto monarch himself over a realm of savages who, given half a chance, would eat his raw entrails straight out of his gutted belly while he was still alive, was even tougher than the soldiers he commanded. Gharek wasn't at all surprised that he'd returned to the heart of the Empire, most likely intent on wresting the throne from the latest usurper and crowning himself emperor. Gharek couldn't care less who sat on the blood-painted chair. His worry sprang from the fact that a man with such grand ambitions had put out the order to hunt him. There was no scenario he could imagine here in which his head didn't end up mounted on a pike.

He had expected to wait much longer—hoped he could wait much longer—before being summoned to the general's tent, but no more than an hour passed before the captain of the escort came for him and yanked him to a standing position by his tunic front.

"Hard to believe looking at you that you were once the most feared bastard in the Empire," he said, eyes a little glassy from drink and dark with contempt.

"That's what every fool thought before I killed them," Gharek replied, smiling the smile he always used on those he'd been sent to murder. And just like them, Zaredis's man lost his mocking bravado. He shoved Gharek away with a growl, made uneasy by a threat he sensed more than heard.

Gharek stayed upright, dropping his stance in anticipation of dodging a blow. He was crippled by his bonds but not completely defenseless as long as his legs were free. He'd knocked out a few teeth and broken bones on more than one occasion with a well-placed kick. He might die and his remains fed to the camp dogs before the night was over, but this rejected whelp of a poxy tar leather wasn't going to use him as a boot scraper.

Heartbeat thundering in his ears, he waited for a punch that didn't come. The captain eyed him, then the large tent where his commander waited to have his audience with his captive. "The general wants to see you. And the whore too." He crooked his fingers in an impatient gesture and two soldiers soon took a place on either side of Gharek. Another brought Siora to join them. She fell into step beside Gharek as they were marched to the tent and pushed inside.

As tents went, this one bore more similarities to a rich man's abode than the humble shelters that kept most of the elements out. Supported by lattice walls, ropes, and a center pole whose girth equaled that of a draft horse's middle, the general's tent offered comfort afforded to the most spoiled and entitled Kraelian aristocrat. Carpets covered the ground, providing a soft foundation for the feet and backside. Several braziers were scattered in spots through the tent, though only one was lit to boil water in a trio of kettles. Oil lamps hung from hooks attached to the roof supports. They swayed gently on chains in the breeze that swooped in from the roof's open peak and blew into the lattice exposed by the wall coverings that had been rolled up and tied to let cool air in and warm air escape.

No fewer than four armor stands, clad in a mishmash of armor styles reflecting Kraelian and Galagus influences, acted as the backdrop to a simple stool placed on a modest carpet-draped dais. Behind that, a great banner with the Varan coat of arms hung in green and bronze majesty.

Gharek took it all in with a single glance before setting his focus on the man seated on the stool watching him. Every instinct he possessed, already fine-tuned to danger, strummed a vibration through his body. This general, who had yet to say anything, swallowed the air in the tent with just his presence. Worse, Gharek recognized him. Recognized him when he'd never met him before or seen his picture. Recognized him because he'd delivered a man with the same face to meet a brutal end at the hands of the empress.

Zaredis stood. A man of average height and build, made muscular by the demands of his position and made scarred by the battles he'd fought, he seemed a giant in a tent no longer spacious. He strolled casually toward his wary guests, and his dark eyes burned bright with a light Gharek immediately recognized every time he saw his own visage in a reflective surface. Vengeance.

That burning gaze rested briefly on Siora with little interest before returning to Gharek with an intensity to make a dead man sweat, and Gharek had no doubt he'd soon be a dead man.

"Do you know who I am?" the general asked in a gruff but quiet voice.

Gharek nodded once, swallowing to unlock the muscles in his throat. "General Zaredis of House Varan, supreme commander of the legions occupying the Galagus Gate lands and consul of the four prefectures there." He offered an honest observation, certain such a man as this would instantly recognize—and punish—empty praise. "Of the generals who served under Herself, you were the one she feared most."

Beyond the flaring of the fierce light in his eyes, Zaredis's expression remained controlled, his voice even quieter. Every hair on Gharek's nape rose. Zaredis tilted his head to the side as if considering the puzzle known as the cat's-paw. "Yet it didn't stop her from torturing and killing my brother Kalun when he tried to help her." Those dark eyes narrowed. "You played a principal role in his death."

Gharek's instincts for survival didn't fail him now, and he stayed quiet as well while Zaredis slowly circled him and Siora before returning to stand in front of them.

"You aren't quite what I imagined," he finally proclaimed after a silence. "Dalvila's cat's-paw had a reputation throughout all the Empire. He was feared. He was hated and, in some quarters, admired. I expected someone . . . I don't know." Zaredis waved his hand as if to capture the right word. "Bigger, maybe. Child of an ogre woman with daggers for teeth and the snout of a boar." Gharek's eyebrows climbed at the description. "Someone who turned every head when they walked into a room and made women and men faint with terror." Zaredis's burgeoning smile lacked any humor. "But that would make you memorable, wouldn't it? And a good assassin never wishes to be memorable."

Had he not served as the dagger in the dark for the most lethal, unpredictable woman in the world, Gharek might have floundered with how to respond, but years spent running the gauntlet of verbal traps that defined conversations with Dalvila had left him well-prepared for how to respond to Zaredis. "Your captain recognized me."

Zaredis's grim smile turned even grimmer. "Enough people with clear memory and a wish for your death were happy to describe your appearance to an artist with a flair for drawing faces, including those with or without beards. I honestly never expected to find you, though I've a bounty on your head to make a man and two generations after him wealthy. That Captain Horta crossed your path in the town and recognized you was luck or the beneficence of the gods."

The gods and their beneficence could kindly go fuck themselves, Gharek thought sourly, uncaring that some outraged deity might hear his private blasphemy and strike him down with a perfectly aimed lightning bolt. He held his tongue and waited for Zaredis to confirm what Gharek already knew. His stomach dropped through the floor when Zaredis finally ended the waiting.

His smile that was more a grimace disappeared, and his nostrils flared. Gharek stiffened even more when Zaredis's hand dropped to the hilt of one of the daggers sheathed at his belt. "My brother," he said, biting off each word with his teeth, "was one of three physicians summoned to the royal palace to try and save the empress from dying of a poisoned wound."

A hum started in Gharek's ears, high-pitched and panicked. Blood froze in his veins and images of his sweet Estred at every year since he'd found her spooled across his vision, blocking out Zaredis's cold visage.

Three physicians. The best the Empire had to offer brought to the summer palace with orders to save Herself. They'd succeeded, but not in the way Dalvila had hoped, and she'd punished them in a manner that left every witness to their deaths vomiting or fainting in the corridors once they were allowed to flee the throne room. Gharek, who'd thought himself numb to the sight of the worst sort of violence, had retched so hard he saw black spots dance in front of his eyes. He'd gone home and drank himself into a stupor, revisited, after a long absence, by a guilt that warped and wefted his insides into a tapestry of misery. He'd been the one sent to fetch Zaredis's brother to the palace.

"Kalun was a good man, a skilled physician." Zaredis continued to bite through every word. "He didn't deserve to die, nor did he deserve the death Dalvila meted out to him. He's beyond my reach now, just like the bloodthirsty bitch who ruled us all." He closed the distance between them until no more than a cloth's thickness separated him and Gharek. The fires of pure hatred had turned his eyes into hot coals. "But you aren't."

Time and silence froze on a sword point as Gharek stared at Zaredis and saw the promise of his own slow death there. Both were shattered when the woman he'd forgotten beside him spoke in a gentle voice.

"You're wrong, general," Siora said. "Your brother stands right beside you."

CHAPTER FOUR

I f silence could be woven like thread, then the silence that descended in the tent after Siora's statement would have made a blanket thick enough to insulate against the cold of a blizzard. Her heart thumped hard against her ribs as every eye turned toward her. Even the ghost standing next to the general had leveled a stunned gaze at her. It seemed it was as easy to surprise the dead as it was the living. If the mirror image of the living general was a true indicator, this ghost was Kalun, Zaredis's unfortunate brother.

The spirit vanished only to abruptly appear in front of her. Were she not used to this behavior in ghosts, she might have jumped, startled. But ghosts had appeared before her since childhood, been playmates to her and companions on occasion. They'd sought her out to tell their story, relay a message, or simply to stand there and weep over some tragedy that might have happened long before Siora was even born. A few were hostile, and these Siora still feared. Most though deserved her pity, not her fear, including this one.

She offered him a small smile, knowing how odd, not to mention rude, it looked to everyone else in the room, who only saw her ignore the general and stare off into space, wearing a mysterious smile.

You can see me, Kalun said, his ethereal voice as surprised as his expression.

I can, she replied with the same thought conversation she always used to converse with the dead, and which had earned her more than a few puzzled or disapproving looks from others over the years when she'd seemed to drift into a dazed state. People weren't particularly tolerant of those they thought of as odd.

Zaredis, nearly incandescent with fury, flung a hand at her and said in a guttural voice, "Get her out of here!"

A trio of soldiers lunged for her, their grip on her arms rough and bruising as they dragged her toward the tent's opening. Gharek took a step in her direction only to be shoved back. His eyes were dark mirrors reflecting back the same shock the other occupants in the tent displayed.

Siora struggled in her captors' hold. "Wait, please! The cold. Have you not noticed it?" The space encompassing her, the general, and Gharek had grown bone-chilling, so much so that their breath was visible as if they stood outside on a midwinter morning instead of inside a sweltering tent during the height of summer. "It's because he's here. He could be mistaken for you except for a mark along his jaw, paler than the rest of his skin."

At her words, Kalun reached up to touch the sickle moon shape of a thickened scar that curved along his jaw to end just below his cheek. *A gift from my brother during a brawl over a girl*, he said, his face wreathed in a wide smile.

The guards paused in dragging her, unsure what to do. They let her go at another gesture from Zaredis, who'd forgotten Gharek and turned all of his wrathful attention on her. "How do you know Kalun?"

"I don't. I've never met him before now. His spirit lingers here, drawn to you." She glanced at Kalun, who nodded.

"For gods' sake, Siora. Shut up if you want to live." Gharek's voice rasped harsh in the pulsing quiet.

The command earned him a sharp blow from Zaredis, and he stumbled. When he straightened, blood ran in a bright ribbon from the corner of his mouth and his cheek beneath the beard was red. He glared at both Siora and Zaredis but this time kept his tongue behind his teeth.

Zaredis ignored him after that, as if he were no more than a pesky fly he'd swatted out of the way. Siora backed into one of her guards when Zaredis approached her. "A shade speaker," he said, not bothering to hide his contempt. "Why am I not surprised that Dalvila's cat's-paw keeps company with such worms?"

His opinion only mattered to her in the context that he believed her to be authentic. If she could convince him of that, she might find a way to help Gharek, or at least buy him time to find a way to save himself. And this time it wouldn't be a betrayal. She held out a hand to Kalun. *Go ahead*, she said. *Take my hand.*

Siora rarely offered such a gesture to spirits and never in front of witnesses. The one time she had, it hadn't ended well. The ghost's living relatives were so terrified of the vision before them, Siora had to flee a mob of villagers armed with scythes and shovels. It was a huge risk to do it again. The tent was crowded with people more than willing to carve out her heart if the general commanded it, and Zaredis himself looked ready to give such an order or do it himself.

Once more for Estred, she thought. And for Gharek too.

Sneers and snide insults from their audience at seeing her hold her hand out to empty air changed to gasps and startled shouts when Kalun wrapped his icy fingers around hers and shimmered into visibility.

Siora's grin matched his. *I see you, and now they do too.*

Zaredis gawked at her and then at Kalun, his mouth moving in soundless exclamation, his eyes nearly bulging from their sockets as he stared at his dead brother, who shook with silent laughter at his sibling's amazement.

Siora risked a glance at Gharek. He looked as startled as the rest but only for a moment. A calculating glitter brightened his eyes, and he gave a small nod. Whether it was approval or simply an acknowledgment of the truth of her claim, she didn't know, but she returned the nod with a brief one of her own before returning her attention to the two brothers.

Her fingers were numb from the cold of Kalun's grasp, but she held on as Zaredis stretched out a tentative hand to touch his sibling. A shadow of despair passed over his features when his fingers passed through Kalun like water, leaving only ripples behind it. Kalun's grin slipped away at the reminder of his ethereal state.

"What sorcery is this?" Zaredis said, voice thickened by grief.

Siora shook her head. "Not sorcery, only truth. I understand your disbelief. The pretenders are many. I'm not one of them."

Kalun stared at his brother as intently as Zaredis stared at him. Their likeness was remarkable. Twins were uncommon, but she would wager hard-earned coin that these two men had shared their mother's womb at the same time. The thought saddened her. Two parts of a whole. Had the general sensed when his brother died? Death of a loved one was difficult for any of the living, but this would have been a cleaving of a more profound kind, and some sorrows were harder to bear than others.

Can you hear me? Kalun asked. Zaredis only peered more intensely at his twin as if trying to make out words in the movement of Kalun's lips.

Siora spoke for him so all could hear. "I can hear you but they can't. If you have a message for your brother, I'll tell him for you."

Before Kalun could say anything more, Zaredis spoke, words stuttered and slowly released as if held down so deep, he labored to dredge them up and past his throat. "Forgive me for failing you. I wasn't there when you needed me most."

From the corner of her eye, Siora glimpsed Gharek start, and his bloodied lips nearly disappeared against his teeth as his face tightened.

The softness that had crept into Zaredis's expression disappeared. "But I can avenge your death." Hatred turned the fire in his eyes black when his gaze settled on Gharek.

Siora swallowed a gasp, cold fingers clamping down more tightly on Kalun's hand at Zaredis's words. "I beg your mercy for the cat's-paw," she said. "Surely when the empress sent him to fetch your brother, he didn't know what she would do." She went to her knees before Zaredis without letting go of Kalun. It was a weak argument at best. It would be a miracle of untold generosity from the gods if Estred didn't end up an orphan when this was over.

Kalun's voice held the memory of agony and the outrage of injustice. *He was her cat's-paw. He knew her well enough to guess what horror she might have in store for us if we couldn't save her arm. We should have let her die.*

"She is dead. I don't ask mercy for him but for his daughter, whose safety is the reason for all of his deeds." Siora didn't expect absolution for Gharek from either brother, but she had to try. Gharek loved Estred with all his being, and Estred needed him. Killing him wouldn't bring Kalun back to the living.

Kalun didn't budge. *It doesn't excuse him or absolve him.*

"No, it doesn't. It's why I ask for mercy instead of forgiveness."

"What is he saying?" Zaredis snapped.

Kalun gestured for her to rise. *You can crawl on your belly and it won't matter. So you might as well stand.* She gained her feet and was about to answer Zaredis when Kalun continued. *Tell my brother he didn't fail. He's a great general, an even better man, but he isn't a god to change fate or know what things will come to pass. Tell him I blame him for nothing, that I linger in the world to help him take the throne if I can. The Empire might survive under his rule.*

She did as he instructed, making certain to repeat every word exactly as spoken. During that time, Zaredis said nothing, only watched his brother with a yearning as if he'd trade a kingdom just to hear him speak one more time in his own voice. Siora had seen that look on many of the faces of those who paid her to speak with their beloved dead. In those instances—and this one—she was reminded why her mother had always called her macabre ability a gift.

Everyone in the tent jumped when Zaredis finally addressed her. "You can speak with him. Can you bring him back?"

The inevitable question, one she hated as her inevitable answer drained hope and made a mockery of wonder. Even if she could resurrect the dead, she'd lie and deny it. The Spider of Empire might be dead and the Empire itself fast plummeting into lawlessness and chaos, but the latest usurper on the throne had made no attempt to repeal the laws regarding sorcery. Admitting to it, practicing it, were crimes punishable by death, and while shade-speaking wasn't considered magic, necromancy definitely was.

She shook her head. "I cannot. I'm a shade speaker, not a necromancer. My ability isn't born of magic."

Keep speaking for me. Tell him I'm content not to return, Kalun said. *Tell him I don't suffer, and this shadow existence isn't a trial.* His fingers flexed against hers. Strong for a spirit. Icy. She repeated his words to Zaredis.

A cunning glint, not unlike the one still flickering in Gharek's eyes, lit Zaredis's gaze. "Kalun was in the summer palace, in the inner sanctum. Does he remember how to get there?"

Kalun shook his head. *No. We were hurried down corridors, through locked doors, and up staircases. It's a maze in that place.* Siora conveyed his answer.

Zaredis uttered a salty curse. "Can you go there and come back to tell me?"

Behind Zaredis, Gharek's eyes narrowed. Siora fancied she could almost hear a plan take shape in his mind. She met Zaredis's eyes and answered for Kalun. "They who linger don't possess that kind of power."

"I know the summer palace as if it were my own home." Gharek's voice was even raspier than before and held an enticing note of knowledge, the kind that might buy him a stay of execution, at least for tonight. Siora promised herself that if they made it out of this scenario alive and with all body parts intact, she'd remind him to thank her for her help.

The cold in her fingers had gone from numbing to burning,

and her nail beds were turning blue. She raised her and Kalun's clasped hands. *I have to let go for a short time.* He nodded his understanding and released her hand.

Zaredis's panicked bellow nearly made her jump out of her skin. "Bring him back! Kalun!" He leapt at Siora, dagger drawn and blade to her throat before she could draw another breath. "Bring him back," he repeated, baring his teeth as if he'd forget the knife and clamp his jaws on her jugular to rip and tear.

The sounds of a nearby scuffle teased her ears, but she concentrated on taking the shallowest breaths. Even those didn't ease the press of the blade, or the tiny stings that sent ticklish ribbons of warmth down her neck. Terror made it hard to speak. "Your brother is still here, lord," she whispered. "He just let go. I was growing too cold."

A chilly brush of air on the back of her hand, and Kalun flickered into view for a brief moment. Zaredis's exhalation steamed out of his nostrils like fog and disappeared with Kalun. He lowered the dagger and released her. "Now you know what will happen if you lie to me, shade speaker."

Siora swayed for a moment and blinked back tears of relief at finding herself still alive and breathing, her jugular intact. She resisted the urge to touch her neck where a warm wetness tickled her skin. Her knees trembled so hard she feared she might fall.

He's always been the more hot-tempered of the two of us, and the most protective, though I'm the oldest. Kalun wore an apologetic look.

How much older?

A few moments only. The midwife told our mother when I came out that Zaredis had his hand wrapped around my foot, unwilling to let go.

Siora latched on to that small bit of information and passed it on to Zaredis as further reassurance of his brother's continued presence. She'd guessed rightly. They were twins.

Once more the barest hint of softness settled briefly on Zaredis's face before it turned grim again. He'd blocked her view of Gharek and when he moved, Siora gasped at seeing the cat's-paw no longer standing but on his belly, the side of his face pressed into the carpet while a soldier knelt on his back and wrenched his arms even higher behind him. A groan of pain burst from his mouth.

"Stand him up," Zaredis ordered. He glared as Gharek was hauled to his feet. "How you came to be with a shade speaker is a question for pondering later, cat's-paw. She seems honest enough, but my reasons for distrusting her are based on the fact she's keeping company with you." He was almost standing on Gharek's toes and lightly brushed his dagger's edge along Gharek's neck this time. Gharek didn't cower or shrink away. "Why," said the general, "should I believe what you say about the palace? Why shouldn't I kill you right now?"

Siora admired Gharek's calm. She was sure she hadn't looked so serene with that same knife at her throat.

"I wouldn't believe me either," he said. "But in this I'm telling the truth. As for why you should believe me, again, I am—was— the empress's cat's-paw. It was my duty to know every corner and stair tread of the summer palace, every secret door, every spy hole, and hidden room. Not only to know where they all were but how to navigate such a maze without being seen."

A murmur rose among those in the tent observing the exchange. Even Zaredis's eyebrows had risen, and he'd lost a small bit of the fiery anger that so obviously tempted him to disembowel

Gharek on the spot. He tilted his head to one side, considering his prisoner. "And why would you give up such valuable information?"

"I'm not giving up anything. I'm negotiating," Gharek said.

There it is, Siora thought. *The bait to dangle.*

"You want inside the palace. Conquest from within is always easier and less bloody than from without. I want to live."

Siora noticed the nods and thoughtful looks exchanged between Zaredis's men. Gharek's proposed exchange had merit. It also had value. Information for a life.

Zaredis didn't look at all impressed. "I have no guarantee you won't slip away and disappear the moment your guard looks away. You'll probably even betray me to the current usurper for a price— coin or measure of power in the new court."

"You have my word."

Siora's own disbelieving snort matched Zaredis's louder one. "The word of Herself's cat's-paw is worth less than a pile of dog shit." He gestured with a lift of his chin to one of the guards at the doorway. "Tell Rurian I want to see him." The man bowed and slipped out of the tent. Much to Siora's relief, Zaredis finally sheathed his knife and stepped away from both her and Gharek. "You'll meet my sorcerer," he said, and he bent that same derisive smile from before on Siora. "Not a lowly shade speaker," he said.

Siora held her tongue though her thoughts whirled. A sorcerer, and Zaredis had admitted his presence in front of many, completely unconcerned that someone might report back to those currently controlling Domora. He was very sure of his power and place, this fierce general, flaunting the abilities of a man Dalvila herself would have set her dogs on had she even a whiff of his presence inside her borders.

My brother has always been a confident man, Kalun bragged beside her. *A man worthy of it, ever since he was a boy.*

Imagine that. He wasn't telling her anything she hadn't observed or concluded so far. Even now Zaredis and Gharek held a silent contest to see who could outstare the other, both wearing stoic expressions and no doubt thinking how much they'd enjoy killing each other.

The staring battle continued in the tent's awkward stillness. It lasted until another chill, not made by Kalun, surged down Siora's arm. She glanced at him, belly clenching at the new terror in his face. She'd seen its like recently. *What's wrong?* she asked, though she already knew.

Darkness. He spoke the words with all the horror of one who'd looked upon the nightmare hiding in writhing shadow and prayed with an acolyte's fervency for deliverance. He reached for her, wrapping both hands around her arm as if to find purchase, an anchor to hold him in place.

As terrified as he, Siora stretched out her other arm to the perplexed Zaredis, acting on a desperate hunch. "Hold on to me! Now!"

A quick glance at the now visible Kalun's face and Zaredis didn't hesitate, grasping her forearm and hand with both of his—just as Kalun did—with a strength that slowed the blood flow to her fingers.

She stared at Gharek, who had turned a shade paler, his eyes wide. Siora didn't invite him to grab on to her. Even if the thing he and Kalun sensed rushing toward them now tried to bewitch him, it would have to fight a crowd of soldiers just to force him out of the tent. Held fast in the grip of three, all with sword points aimed at his torso, he didn't move. His face looked as it did when she found him lurching toward Midrigar, fighting every step of the way. He wasn't lurching now, but his knees were bent and his back hunched as if braced against the relentless pull of an unseen leash.

"It comes," he said in the eerily hollow voice that reminded her of how the dead spoke in her mind.

Kalun replied, as if reciting the stanzas of a dark invocation. *A thing foul and starving.*

"Hold tight to me," she commanded the brothers just as a shrieking wind blasted through the tent, carrying with it the rot of the grave and a touch so alien and strange, her flesh walked across her bones in recoil. The strength of the maelstrom tore part of the tent away from its lattice frame. The center supports creaked in protest but held in place even as the felt covering peeled back like the hide off a butchered animal. The shadows of panicked horses raced past the tent, chased by men surprised by a sudden freakish storm.

Never before had Siora felt something so abjectly vile, so abyssal and malevolent, as if the black of nightmares had formed a mouth and stretched wide around the tent, ready to tear it apart with merciless teeth and devour the pieces.

Soldiers yelled and cursed, chaos erupting as the howling gust blew over the lit brazier, sending a shower of embers to land on the one remaining swath of tent wall not yet torn away. The hiss and whoosh of felt catching fire sent more men scurrying in every direction, bellowing for water or knocking over the contorted lattice so they could stamp out the flames licking the fabric. Lamps swung wildly on chains still hanging from the slender spoke-wheel joists, the oil inside their high-sided bowls sloshing threateningly close to the bowls' rims.

A chorus of voices shouted for Zaredis to get out of the tent. He ignored them, his attention solely on Kalun while he nearly broke Siora's arm in an ever-tightening grip. "Brother," he yelled above the wind howl, and his shout was no more than a whisper. Kalun's fading apparition solidified, became less transparent, strengthened by the power of his name uttered by his twin.

A new voice cracked across the mayhem in the tent, slicing through the roar of noise like a blade. One word in a language Siora didn't know, followed by a flare of blinding green light. The fetid wind instantly died as if cut off mid-rush with the slam of a door. Siora gasped, her own thoughts echoing the many voices raised in relief and confusion.

"What the fuck was that?" chorused through what was left of the general's tent as soldiers stared around them and at each other. More tried to right the furniture tossed about like twigs and gather up the armor flung off their stands as if it were leaves in a whirl-wind. Siora's left hand and right arm were numb thanks to the twins' touch, living and dead. Kalun still stood before her, unde-voured and visible to his relieved brother.

Gharek no longer held the braced stance. Instead he slumped, swaying on his feet as if exhausted. Rivulets of sweat painted silvery lines from his temple to his jaw.

"Are you well, lord?" she asked him. Something glittered in his weary gaze, but he only nodded in reply.

A figure entered her field of vision, circling around Gharek with only a slight pause before halting in front of Zaredis. Like the general, this man would turn heads in a crowd, but for very differ-ent reasons. He carried himself proudly, even in the homespun sleeveless tunic and trousers he wore. That wasn't what held Sio-ra's attention. Many men of every station walked proudly.

This new person sported tattoos the same way wealthy women wore their jewelry; generously, flamboyantly, and for all to see. He was a living mural of symbols and scenery, inked into his skin in rainbows of color, some vivid, others faded. They decorated his arms from wrist to shoulder. In some places she caught a glimpse of telltale shimmers and glows along those designs that looked suspiciously like sigils or wards. More of them encircled his throat and climbed up his neck to his chin while others peeked out from the neckline of his tunic, edging his collarbones. One followed the line of his jaw to partially cover one cheek, where it stopped at the corner of his eye.

His elaborate markings were emphasized by his strange coloration or lack of it. Pale hair, bleached eyebrows, and skin the color of milk. He was striking and unhandsome at the same time, and if the shimmer of those tattooed sigils hadn't given it away, she'd guess he was either a priest or a sorcerer or both.

Zaredis practically shouted his name. He still didn't let go of Siora's arm. "Rurian! Thank the gods for your magic. You chased off whatever demon paid us a visit." He frowned at the havoc around him.

"I think I took it by surprise," Rurian replied. He had a pleasant voice, calm and accented in a way that the words were broad and flowed into one another, unlike the clipped patterns of a Kraelian's speech.

"What was it?"

Rurian shrugged, his pale eyes flitting back and forth between Zaredis, Siora, and Kalun. "I don't know. A demon as you said maybe, but it seeks the dead." He turned his head to stare at Gharek for a moment. "And even a few of the living." He continued staring at Gharek, who stared back as Rurian addressed Zaredis. "This is the one you were hunting?"

"Yes." Zaredis leveled a threatening scowl on Gharek. "Were you responsible for what happened here?"

Gharek arched an eyebrow. "Had I such power, I wouldn't be here, bound before you."

Siora tried to shake free of Zaredis's death grip. He finally let her go with the warning not to do the same with Kalun. She shook her arm, grateful for the return of feeling, certain she'd have a chain of bruises mottling her skin before the evening was done.

Rurian continued to watch Gharek. "I believe he's telling the truth, general. Whatever passed through here did so of its own free will. A hunter ancient and powerful."

Siora wrapped both her hands around Kalun's when his voice echoed low and despairing in her mind. *I cannot fight such a creature. Even with your and my brother's aid, I barely held on.*

Zaredis paced, ignoring the bustling activity around him as people continued to restore the tent, erecting the lattice walls, re-covering them with the felt that had been torn away and tossed in the grass. "What does it want with my brother?"

Siora answered this time. She, more than this sorcerer, had seen firsthand what this thing was doing. "It wants all the dead, not just Kalun. I've seen what it wrought in other places nearby." She shivered at the memory of the screaming faces melded into the wall of the abandoned barn's provender room. "I think it dwells in Mi . . . the cursed city." It seemed especially unwise now to say Midrigar's name out loud.

"That's a day's ride from here."

She had a feeling, given enough time and nothing to stop the thing from expanding its hunting grounds, an ocean wouldn't protect the dead, much less a day's ride on horseback. "I don't think distance matters to it. If it grows stronger from eating the dead, then its reach grows longer as well." The combined weight of both Zaredis's and Rurian's regard rested heavy on her shoulders, not to mention Gharek's, which she was used to but which was no less weighty.

"You found a witch," the sorcerer said.

Siora stiffened, her hand tightening on Kalun's. "I'm a shade speaker, not a witch. I can see and talk to the dead. Nothing more." Judging by Rurian's expression, the difference was indistinguishable.

"They aren't sorcerers," Zaredis explained. "Not as the Empire would define them. Most are charlatans. The few that aren't, work more like soothsayers. They don't possess magic." Her heartbeat accelerated when he stepped closer to her, and she observed, alarmed, the way he caressed the hilt of the dagger he still held. Surely he wouldn't harm her. If not for her, he would lose the connection with his brother. Such practical reason did nothing to slow her heartbeat. "You, however, just did much more than chat with my brother. You stopped our visitor from taking him. How?"

Kalun echoed him. *Yes, how?*

Should she lie and present her guess as fact? Built on some knowledge she held from past experience? The thought came and went. Every instinct she possessed warned that neither Zaredis nor his mage would believe her.

"I don't know how," she said. She held up her and Kalun's clasped hands. "I don't think I'm what anchors him here. You are," she told Zaredis. His eyes widened. "Siblings who share the womb at the same time forge connections beyond that of ones born months or years apart. You're brothers but more than brothers. Two sides of one coin. Two bodies of a split soul. I'm merely the means by which you can see and speak with him. You're the tether and the shield that protects him."

Zaredis watched her without speaking before exchanging a glance with Kalun. "Why are you with the cat's-paw?"

Her answers were numerous, convoluted, and scarcely sensible to herself, wrapped up in emotion instead of logic, fed by affection not only for a small child but also—unwillingly, unbelievably—for that child's father. In the end, she chose the simplest explanation. "He saved me from a Nunari who chased me through the streets of Wellspring Holt intent on killing me."

Zaredis wasn't so easily satisfied. "Why would the infamous cat's-paw rescue a prostitute?"

Simple answers, she reminded herself. Complicated ones became traps. "Maybe for the same reason I saved your brother." She glanced at Gharek, who listened silently to their exchange. "I needed the help."

"Hard to resist a beautiful woman." The mockery in Gharek's voice made her blush. There were things about him she admired, things she feared, and things she detested. His occasional biting sarcasm firmly occupied a space in the last, though somewhere in that serrated comment was a startling echo of sincerity.

Kalun's accusatory tone distracted her from her embarrassment. *You're lying. You plead for his life for a daughter's sake. This man is no stranger to you.*

Thank the gods only she could hear him. *I'm not lying. Your brother asked his questions. I answered truthfully.*

And wove the truth to your benefit.

She jerked her hand out of his grip. He faded from view a second time. "Still here," she assured Zaredis. "I need to warm my hand." And she wasn't interested in hearing disapproval from a ghost after the ridicule of an assassin and the abuse of a Kraelian general who'd threatened to slit her throat. She could lay the blame for the lack of kindness on their gender, except the Empire had once been ruled by Dalvila, and these men were merely playful puppies compared to the lethal malevolence of the Spider of Empire.

Despite Kalun's accusation, and her selective truth, her actions must have earned a fragile trust with the general. He accepted her word about Kalun with a single nod and turned that steely gaze back to Gharek. "Strip him," he ordered the men surrounding him.

Gharek's curses fell on deaf ears, and his struggles were futile as half a dozen soldiers untied him and yanked his clothing off. They then kicked his legs out from under him. He fell with an *oomph* and was once more bound with his hands behind his back. Only now he was naked, except for a simple cord with a charm tied to it that he wore around his neck.

One soldier handed Zaredis his clothes. The general searched the garb, checking any pockets or hems for contents, even shaking them to see if anything fell out. He even shook out Gharek's boots. When they were first captured, Captain Horta had made certain neither Gharek nor Siora kept anything sharp on them. He'd also relieved them of all money as well as weaponry. She doubted there was anything of value to be found in Gharek's garb.

Zaredis tossed the clothing aside in disgust. "Nothing," he told Rurian.

The sorcerer stepped closer to Gharek, pale eyes like ice chips in his bloodless face. "Oh, I don't know about that." He lashed out with one hand. Just as fast, Gharek jerked back, but not fast enough. Rurian snagged the leather cord and yanked. The cord snapped and Gharek bellowed as Rurian held the humble charm aloft.

Gharek lunged toward the mage only to be shoved back. "Give it back, dog mage. That's mine."

"And obviously of great value to you." Elegant fingers slid over the charm, nothing more than a small braid of hair decorated with a tiny bead and a dirty scrap of ribbon. A distressed squeak escaped Siora. She recognized the hair color as well as the bead. She'd woven a bracelet with such beads for Estred as a gift and tamed Estred's wavy tresses into a neat plait with such ribbon. At some point either Gharek had made a charm of his daughter's hair and a bead from the bracelet or Estred had done so and gifted it to him. Rurian was right. They might have discovered a king's treasure house worth of gold sewn into his clothes, and none of it would have equaled the value of that charm. At least not for Gharek.

"Can you take anything from it?" Zaredis asked the mage.

Rurian continued stroking the charm, his eyes half closed as if he listened to some secret the trinket was imparting to him. "I need a map," he finally replied.

In short order a map of the Empire was rolled out across a nearby table. Gharek fought his bonds and cursed their names until one soldier punched him sideways and he was gagged and tossed against the tent wall. It didn't stop the hatred burning in his gaze or the venomous promise of revenge there. He'd worn that same look when Siora told Malachus she'd take him to where Gharek had hidden the old woman Asil.

Zaredis and Rurian bent over the map, speaking in low voices as the sorcerer held the charm above it as if warming it over a fire. "Here," he finally said, loud enough for her to hear, and pointed to an unseen coordinate on the map. "The cat's-paw's child is here." His head tilted to one side as if he'd discovered something unusual. "A child without arms."

Zaredis straightened, a cunning triumph in his expression that made Gharek's face wash nearly as pale as Rurian's. He motioned for Captain Horta to join him, pointed to the same spot Rurian had, and told him, "Find a small child with no arms. Ask around. Someone will spill any secret for the right price. When you find her, bring her here."

Desperate sounds, nearly inhuman in their panic, escaped past Gharek's gag. He writhed against his bonds, the muscles in his arms, shoulders, and chest flexed and bulged as he struggled to break free. Siora tried to reach Zaredis. A soldier's hard grip kept her in her place. "Please," she pleaded to the general. "I beg you. The cat's-paw and I will do anything you wish if you will show mercy to his child and not hurt her."

His eyes narrowed. "So not just a random prostitute in need of saving after all. I thought as much." He signaled to Gharek's guards again. "Get him dressed. Remove his gag but tie him again when you're done."

Siora flinched when they did as commanded, for they weren't gentle in their enthusiasm to obey. Soon, however, Gharek stood next to her, garbed and bound but no longer gagged. Zaredis came to stand in front of them. Rurian joined him. The gloating smile he wore made Gharek growl. "So the notorious cat's-paw has one notable weakness."

Gharek's growl rose in volume, and Zaredis's smile widened.

Next to Siora, Kalun voiced more of his disapproval, only this time it wasn't for her. *This is wrong and not like my brother.*

The general swung the charm on his fingertip. Gharek's eyes followed its motion. "Now we negotiate," he said. "I've sent trackers throughout the Empire looking for you, Gharek of Domora. The gods have a sense of humor because after all this time and having no luck in finding you, I discover you've ridden into the middle of one of my battalions." The gloating smile fell away and the murderous expression he wore mimicked Gharek's. "You're responsible for my brother's death, and you'll die for the crime, but not before you help me."

Gharek's derisive snort sounded loud in the quiet tent. "Why would I help you if you plan to kill me anyway?"

He knew why, Siora thought. He knew and still he goaded Zaredis, reckless in his fury over his predicament.

"I think we both know why." The general raised the charm a little higher, swung it a little harder.

"Leave her alone!"

Unfazed by Gharek's shout, Zaredis shrugged. "No. She's now as valuable to me as she is to you, just for different reasons."

"If you hurt her, even your soul won't be safe from me. Even death won't stop me from destroying you and everything you love."

For the first time since they'd been shoved into this tent, Siora saw a waver in Zaredis's confidence, a fraction of a breath in which doubt seized him, and maybe even a little fear in the face of Gharek's promise. It was gone so fast, she might have imagined it, but she was sure of what she saw, and if she interpreted Rurian's expression correctly, he'd seen it too.

"I've no intention of harming her. Yet. In fact, she'll be well taken care of while you return to Domora, gain access to the palace, and discover a way to retrieve the item Herself called the Windcry. An artifact of great power. You'll bring it back to me and provide me with a map of all accesses to the palace and any changes you discovered while you're there."

Several gasps greeted his statement, and Gharek's features went slack for a moment before he stared at Zaredis as if he spoke gibberish. "You must be joking."

"I'm not one to waste time on useless humor," Zaredis said.

Siora dared to venture a question. "What does the Windcry do?"

She expected the general to answer or order her to be silent, but it was Gharek who replied.

"It's a weapon of magic. Before the old emperor outlawed all sorcery and had his mages slaughtered, he had them craft a weapon that could circumvent the defenses of a walled city. The Windcry could turn a fortification to a pile of rubble in an instant. The old histories tell of it being used against the cursed city."

No wonder others in the tent had made noises of surprise. She hadn't known such a thing existed. Then again, she wasn't like Gharek or the general, who mingled with the aristocracy of the Krael Empire and were privy to secrets no one else knew.

"You want to use the Windcry on Domora's walls," Gharek said.

Zaredis nodded. "If I have to. I'd rather take the city from inside. If you're telling the truth, you're one of the few with the knowledge I need to navigate the palace's labyrinth of traps to reach its inner sanctums." He quoted Gharek, "'I know the palace like my own home.'"

Gharek's mouth curved down into an even deeper frown.

"And you'll hold my daughter as a hostage to gain and keep my cooperation."

The general remained unapologetic. "I demand your success as well. You'll still die, but I will make your death swift instead of slow and tell your child you died a hero."

Siora looked not at Gharek or at Zaredis but at her feet. This scenario played out yet again, with one of the players a repeat performer, only this time it wasn't Gharek who wielded a vulnerable hostage as a bargaining tool against someone else. This time he occupied Malachus's place, a man with something of value forced to exchange it for the life of a loved one. The awful irony of it made her eyes blur with tears, and she felt Gharek's gaze settle on her. She refused to look at him, wondering if he somehow blamed her for this fateful circle or if he believed as she did; that fate had a way of balancing scales, often in the worst way. Ruthless plans made under the impetus of loving intention had terrible consequences.

Gharek was obviously less than impressed with the general's bargain. "A dead hero is useless to my daughter, so spare me the bait as you wield the whip. What reassurances do I have from you that you won't harm her while I play your dog and fetch this stick?"

"I'm not Herself."

A succinct reply but spoken with a sincerity that challenged anyone's disbelief in Zaredis's words. And its impact was profound on Gharek, whose bristling defiance bled out of him. Siora prayed that the general stood behind what he said. Of course, claiming a less cruel nature than Dalvila and making it true wasn't difficult to do. The twisted empress had stood solitary upon that pinnacle.

She frowned when a small voice—not Kalun's, but her own

inner one—whispered to her, and its message was harsh. *You stand here and beg mercy for Estred. What would you offer to help assure it? How truly great was your own sacrifice when you betrayed Gharek's secret to Malachus?*

At the time it felt enormous. She'd willingly walked—no, ran—away from regular meals, a warm bed, a dry roof, relative safety, and the company of a bright, loving child and her broken father. She still didn't regret it, but maybe she'd worn that decision as a martyr's cloak. If so, it was time to shed it and leave it behind.

"I'd like to go with him," she told the general.

He and Gharek gaped at her, and both said in unison, "Why?"

Another question whose best answer was a complicated one, so she did as before and kept it simple. "Because I wish to help."

"Gods save us all from your kind of help," Gharek snapped.

Her cheeks burned at his cutting remark but she continued, undeterred. "The dead sometimes share secrets, give information or warnings if they're so inclined at the time. My father has done so for me all my life. He died fighting in the Pit years ago. He was the one who told me I was in danger in Wellspring Holt."

"That doesn't explain why you offer to help the cat's-paw." Zaredis gestured to Kalun. "I want you here. Where you can defend my brother in case that thing comes back and so I can speak with him."

Hand on the heel, Kalun said, and there was amusement in his voice. *Zaredis hasn't changed much as he's aged.*

Siora didn't repeat what Kalun said, but she noticed he didn't back his brother's insistence that she stay. "My lord, for the dead to walk on living ground, it takes strength, power—and it isn't limitless. It's like if you or I ran a long distance. We have to stop and rest at times. So it is with the ghosts among us." She turned to Kalun. *You already fade even as we touch.*

He nodded. *Will I return?* His shade darkened for a moment, and his features adopted a more cadaverous look, all hollows and angles and deeply sunken eyes.

She wished she could tell him yes for certain. *I hope so.*

"I can't defend Kalun against an enemy I can't see and don't understand," she admitted to Zaredis. "I'm of no use to you here in that capacity. I said before I think it's you who's the one anchoring him here, but maybe I can be of use to you both if I go to Domora with the cat's-paw. If something in the palace has changed and Charek's knowledge is no longer accurate, I can coax a spirit to help." The idea sounded far-fetched to her own ears, and she feared Zaredis would think so as well.

Support for her suggestion came from an unexpected source. "I can ward this camp against whatever this thing is." Rurian swept a hand to encompass the tent and all the camp in his gesture. "I banished it before. If it comes back, I'll be ready."

Zaredis tapped his chin, swooping black eyebrows pitched toward each other as he frowned. "Nothing is free. What price for helping my brother, shade speaker?"

Triumph made the blood sing in her veins though she kept her excitement behind a stoic mask. "Protection for the child Estred while she's under your care. You've told Charek she'd come to no harm while she was here, but a bargain struck is better than assurance given, no matter the trustworthiness of the person giving it." She offered the last to him, praying she didn't give insult for not accepting his declaration as an unalterable truth.

GRACE DRAVEN

His gaze flickered back and forth between her and Gharek. "Why such concern for the cat's-paw's get?"

"I was once her nurse."

This time his eyebrows winged upward. "You failed to mention that earlier."

He sounded very much like his milder-mannered twin at that moment. "You didn't ask."

"Why isn't she Estred's nurse anymore?" He aimed the question at Gharek, who gazed at Siora as if trying to comprehend what she was doing and why.

"She betrayed me."

Such a wealth of dark emotion in those words. Worst of all, it wasn't the anger that made her guts knot, but the disappointment, not so much in her but in himself. Had he truly trusted her? Let down the wall of suspicion thicker than the curtain walls surrounding Domora and placed some small measure of faith in her? She tried to swallow around the lump in her throat. No wonder his fury ran so deep. It encompassed himself as well as her.

Zaredis snorted. "Discovered your true character, did she?"

"I've always known it," she said softly. *Though not nearly as well as I assumed.* She kept that only in her thoughts. Gharek was a study in conflict, a man of shifting character, gaping wounds, and a frayed soul. He possessed one defining, consistent trait—absolute, unwavering devotion to his daughter, even at the cost of anyone else, including himself.

The general tucked the charm of Estred's hair into a hidden space inside his tunic, ignoring Gharek's feverish regard. "I'll give you my answer tonight." He waved a hand toward her and Gharek. "Take them outside and feed them. Loosen his bindings but change

92

leather for iron." He answered the cat's-paw's unspoken question. "You won't run. I don't possess a shackle stronger than the one you made for yourself, but I'll not leave you completely free."

Before the soldiers escorted them out, Zaredis brought them to a halt. "Will my brother return, shade speaker?" The hope in his inquiry reminded Siora that while he acted as warden, extortionist, and possible executioner, he was also a man grieving for a murdered brother.

"I believe he will, lord, though I can't say for certain. He was at your side when I arrived. You're why he's drawn here, not me. I'm merely the means by which you can speak with him. Remember, when you grow cold in the heat, he's nearby." Zaredis nodded and waved them away.

Once outside, they were marched to a spot near the middle of the camp, out of the way of traffic but still in a space visible to all from every direction. There were no structures to hide behind or use as cover, even if they could get free of their bonds. Gharek's leather shackles were exchanged for iron ones, though now he wore them with his hands clasped in front of him. The leg irons they clasped around his ankles were connected by a short length of chain with another one hooked to it and staked to the ground by a peg hammered deep into a tree stump. Siora was tethered as well but by rope and only at one ankle. Zaredis was far less concerned about her escaping than his primary quarry. She just happened to be in the wrong place with the wrong person and managed to make herself useful to him.

Gharek squatted on his haunches, bowing his shoulders forward and wincing as the muscles there unstitched slowly from their strained position of earlier. He regarded Siora in the aging evening's lengthening shadows. "Your offer to help me changes nothing. You're still treacherous, and you'll still kneel before Estred and beg her forgiveness."

"Take it anyway. Even bearded, you're recognizable by some. If we travel to Domora, there are places in the city I can go that you can't. Only you hunt me. Many hunt you." He scowled but didn't argue her points. She gave a deep sigh. "I wish I'd known you hunted me for a reason other than to kill me. I wouldn't have run." His disdainful snort told her he didn't believe a word of it. The effort to convince him otherwise would fall on deaf ears.

She changed the subject. "Did you feel the entity's pull on you when it entered the tent?" Why he fell to its bewitchment in the first place puzzled her. She'd first thought her own resistance to such darkness was because she was a shade speaker, but none in the tent, except dead Kalun, suffered any effects.

Gharek gave a contemptuous sniff. "Proximity," he replied. "We're far enough away now. I felt nothing when it entered the general's tent."

"That's a lie," she told him, disregarding the hostile sparks in his narrowed eyes. "I saw your face. You felt the draw of its power just like Kalun did. Maybe not as much, but you felt it."

Before Gharek could snap back with an answer, a guard brought them food and water. Arguments and accusations fell by the wayside in favor of eating, and Siora devoured her bowl of cooked fish and scorched flatbread with relish. Gharek did the same, frowning into his bowl as he did so, as if the food revealed some displeasing foretelling of future events.

They'd barely finished their meal when they were escorted back to the tent. Zaredis once more sat on the stool placed on the small dais near the tent's center. All had been put to rights, and except for the burn patterns and tattered holes on one side of the tent's covering, there was no visible reminder of the ghost-eater's visit. A few of his counselors hovered nearby, and directly behind him, the pale, tattooed Rurian regarded them with a hooded gaze.

Zaredis addressed her first. "I agree to your terms, shade speaker. You leave before dawn. Two horses with supplies. You don't have limitless time." He then spoke to Gharek. "I expect you both back here in a fortnight at most with every detail of the palace's hidden accesses as well as something that will deliver the Windcry into my possession. I'd prefer that you brought the Windcry itself, but that isn't realistic. If you haven't returned by then, you better be dead because if you aren't . . ." He left the threat hanging unspoken and didn't he wait for a verbal agreement from either of them before dismissing them from his presence. Once more they were tethered to the tree stump and each given two blankets to use for bedding.

Siora might have crowed at their improved circumstances except they weren't truly improved, just changed. Zaredis still intended to kill Gharek, and soon he'd have Estred in his custody. There was also an abomination out there, its darkness long and becoming longer as it stretched questing claws into new territory searching for prey. But she and Gharek were still alive, still able to affect or change the course of their fate in some small way, to pray to the gods for mercy or intervention or both. Gharek's task was a difficult one to fulfill, fraught with numerous perils. She hoped she could truly help instead of hinder him.

As if he heard her thoughts, he lay down on one of the blankets given to him and balled the other one up to act as a pillow. He reclined on his side, facing her. Endless long legs, wide shoulders, high cheekbones bruised and thin mouth still swollen from Zaredis's earlier strike. His eyes were dark as ink in the camp's dull torchlight. "If you betray me again and endanger Estred, I'll show you no mercy, Siora," he said in the sultry tones of a lover.

All the hairs on her nape rose. She swallowed, her mouth devoid of saliva and her throat tight. "I won't betray you, Gharek. I swear it."

He studied her for several moments without speaking, and Siora refused to break their stare. Finally he rolled onto his back, hands relaxed and palms flattened to his chest, and closed his eyes. She stayed in her reclining position a little longer, unabashedly admiring his profile with its prominent nose and hard jawline. An unforgiving face for an unforgiving man.

Her eyelids grew heavy, drifting further down with each blink until she slid into sleep. She dreamed of her father and the Nunari who chased her through Wellspring Holt, of Estred holding up her favorite comb with her toes to ask Siora if she would plait her hair, of Gharek, who in one stunning moment that made Siora forget to breathe, laughed at something Estred said. A booming guffaw of unrestrained amusement that altered his entire demeanor and gave her a glimpse of the man he could have or might once have been.

"Ah, Estred," he said in the dream, still wearing the grin that was more than just a baring of teeth. "You do make me laugh, love."

He repeated her name and then again and again until Siora clawed her way up from the fog of dreams and memory and found Gharek still beside her, his own sleep troubled. He twitched, hands closing and opening on the empty space where his precious charm would have rested had Rurian not taken it to give to Zaredis.

"Estred," he muttered as a frown carved a trio of lines into his forehead. "Estred."

Siora didn't dare touch him, afraid of an inadvertent blow if she startled him awake. Instead she whispered to him, hoping he heard and would settle once more into a peaceful slumber. "Safe, Gharek. Estred is safe." She prayed to the mercurial gods she wasn't lying.

CHAPTER FIVE

They set out just before dawn, wakened by a rough voice ordering them to get their lazy arses up and on the road. Gharek
had already been awake for a good hour, staring up at the fading
stars while he crafted and just as quickly discarded plan after plan
for escaping, for beating Zaredis's man to Estred's caretakers and
fleeing with her into the Empire's hinterlands, even stowing aboard
a ship to the lands across the Sevelon seas.

He wanted to blacken his own eyes for not doing that in the
first place. He'd always told himself that Estred came first. She was
the impetus for his every action. He'd lied to himself. Vengeance
had become the thing that drove him most, sent him down a foolish path because of pride, rage, and an odd hurt he refused to dwell
on for any length of time. Thanks to that recklessness and a chain
of events that defied the idea of random coincidence, he'd ended
up here, once more a puppet to a master, his daughter the weapon
used to yoke him.

He glanced at Siora next to him, half asleep in the saddle as
they rode toward Domora to fulfill impossible demands for a general who'd thank Gharek's efforts by killing him fast instead of
slow. She was a sorry sight. Bedraggled and dirty, her hair finger-
combed and only half tamed into a plait, she looked much like she

did when he rescued her and Estred from a stone-throwing mob in a Domoran back alley. She didn't smell much better either. Then again, neither did he.

The memory of that awful night was engraved on his mind's eye. It had taken only a moment to spot the mob's ringleaders, and as he cleaved his way through the crowd, he knifed two of the three, sinking the blade fast, deep, and lethally. He killed the third man the next day as he was taking a piss against the back wall of a tavern house. The crowd itself scattered in short order once a few within it recognized him.

He'd pulled a sobbing Estred into his arms to soothe her and ascertain there were no more threats. He then addressed the bleeding beggar who'd shown compassion and a foolhardy courage. She paused in backing away from him when he told her to wait. "Follow me if you wish repayment for your bravery." She'd followed wordlessly, a ragged scrap of a woman possessed of more kindness than any he'd known. Until she betrayed him and sank a dagger between his shoulder blades.

She must have felt him staring at her now for she lifted her head from a half doze and gave him a faint, sleepy smile that startled him. No one except Estred truly smiled at him, and the sight of Siora doing so sent a familiar frisson through his body. She might be an unkempt mess now, but he'd seen beyond the dirt and fatigue and remembered how she looked when she served in his household a lifetime ago. He'd been surprised by what a bath, food, and clothes that weren't rags did for a person. Small, too thin, and with an odd gaze that made the hair on his nape rise on occasion, she was pretty, with big eyes, wide cheekbones, a pointed chin, and a bottom lip that begged to be suckled.

Gharek blinked and shook his head to clear the cobwebs of memory and focus on his companion's words. She gestured with her chin to the two soldiers Zaredis had sent with them. They rode close enough to discourage a sudden race for freedom but still far enough away that they only caught scraps of conversation from her and the cat's-paw. "I thought it would just be us traveling to Domora."

He'd assumed differently and had been right. "Zaredis is a man with a lot at stake and who's not particularly trusting. Even with Estred as his hostage he wouldn't trust me enough to send us to the capital without a guard or two. Rightfully so."

Siora sat straighter in the saddle as she came more awake. "If holding Estred couldn't stop you from betraying the general to the usurper, how could a couple of his soldiers? They wouldn't make it out of Domora alive to warn Zaredis of any treachery."

That was true. They wouldn't make it alive to Domora if they were the only ones he'd have to contend with. "They're not here to keep me in line. They're just an escort until we reach the capital. I'd wager Zaredis has a number of spies in the city already. Once we get there one of these men will meet with one of the spies who'll then take over in monitoring the two of us and relaying information to another who'll feed that information back to the camp. If I dared say anything to the current emperor of the day, the general would know it in a matter of hours. If his sorcerer can work various magics, he'll know it instantly."

Zaredis's mage Rurian was a force he hadn't expected to contend with. The general was a near insurmountable obstacle himself. He'd have to adhere to their plans and complete his task, at least until Estred was safe. But he did not have any intention of meekly submitting to his own execution.

Siora interrupted his musings. "Have you ever seen the Windcry?"

He nodded. "Herself kept it under heavy guard with both soldiers and outlawed sorcery and brought it out for the court and visiting dignitaries to admire on certain feast days. A reminder of the Empire's strength. The Windcry isn't much to look at on first glance, but once you get close enough you can feel the power radiating from it."

He'd seen it more than once, a humble apparatus lacking any ornamentation except for the inscription of symbols he couldn't translate. They were engraved along the side of some type of lever attached to a disk that looked as if it would rock up and down, picking up speed thanks to the lever. He knew nothing else about it beyond the stories of its usage. And he had no idea what, if any, spell could break the powerful wards placed on it to deter thieves.

Siora was still speaking, keeping her voice low so as not to annoy their escort, who looked as if they'd take any excuse to use their cudgels on Gharek. "I remember listening to a free trader entertain a crowd in a village square with a story of some great magical item and how Emperor Attahulin used it to conquer the old Soquay kingdom by shattering its cities. If it's still under guard, how will you reach it?"

Another question whose answer was still nebulous. "I have a connection at the royal library who may be willing to help me. To a point."

They lapsed into silence that held through a brief stop at a farmer's well, where the man offered to water their horses. Though the farmer didn't invite them into his house, he offered a place for them to rest as well as a basket containing a pair of plucked chickens, two loaves of bread, and a few vegetables for a small price.

"You're welcome to this, but you'll have to cook your own. We're not an inn for travelers."

One of the soldiers tossed him a small bag of coins with a grunt of thanks while the other started a small fire in the shade of a tree whose trunk spiraled in a tight pattern before spreading a canopy of green leaves that whispered in the hint of a breeze.

The soldier who'd taken the basket rifled through it before giving both Gharek and Siora a gimlet look. "You want any of this, you have to cook it."

Siora shrugged and held out her hands for the basket. "I'll do it. I don't mind."

In no time, she had the poultry spitted over the fire and vegetables roasting in the coals. The guard who'd started the fire followed her as she foraged nearby for wild herbs she could use to season their supper. While both guards gave her a nod of thanks, neither showed an inclination to share their company and they sat away from their charges, close enough to keep an eye on them but far enough to discourage any attempts at conversation or eavesdropping. Gharek was perfectly fine with such an arrangement.

He slowly ate his share of the food, savoring each bite though the vegetables blistered his fingers and he had to wipe grease smears on the grass next to him from the roasted poultry. "This is good," he told Siora, gazing wistfully at the bare leg bone he held and wishing for more. "I'd forgotten your talent with a cook pot." Not only had she been a good nursemaid for Estred, she'd shown a deft hand in the kitchen when she could sneak past the cook. Her pleased expression lit an unexpected spot of warmth inside him.

"You had a well-stocked larder," she said. "It was a joy to work in the kitchen, at least when your cook wasn't glaring daggers at me for invading her territory."

He tossed the leg bone toward the fire. "She probably feared for her position, and rightly so. Had not Estred kept you busy as her nurse, I'd have tossed Cook out on her backside and installed you in her place. Maybe if I'd done that, neither of us would be in our current straits now." He couldn't resist throwing a barb. His anger ran deep, and the short history between him and this woman had made a significant impact on his present. She'd told him why she'd betrayed him, but he still couldn't find the sense in it. Betray him to save him. He worried at it like an abscess.

Her face fell, the flash of disappointment hiding behind a bland look, but not before he'd seen it. "I'm not your enemy, lord." The deference in her address to him had changed. No longer in his employ but still of lower social status, she called him *lord* instead of *master* now. It didn't matter to him either way, though a small voice far in the back of his thoughts wondered what his name might sound like on her lips. She went back to finishing her meal, her gaze no longer on him.

"I'm not a nobleman," he said flatly. "And while you may not consider us enemies, I don't consider us friends." He'd take her offer of help and use it in whatever way benefited him and Estred and leave her to whatever fate the world held for her. No debt on his part, he thought. She owed him.

She shrugged. "Somehow I doubt either of us have had much experience with such an attachment."

With their meal finished and the farmer watching from his doorway in an obvious hint for them to move on, they mounted their horses and set off to complete their journey to Domora. Siora held her tongue this time, and it was he who finally broke the silence.

"I will never understand your decision or your reasoning. You say you wanted to help Estred and save me? I didn't need your help or ask for it. You intruded where you had no business."

Before when he'd thrown darts at her she'd merely let them bounce off, or worse, stared at him with a pity that made his stomach curdle and his spirit rage. This time her delicate face lost its softness, sharpening into angles and a tight mouth. She still refused to look at him, but her eyes were narrowed to slits as she bore holes into the back of their point guard with her gaze. "You made it my business when you wanted me to coax information out of the old woman, when you bid me watch for observers as you took her from the house and hid her in that filthy abandoned forge, guarded by a man I wouldn't leave to watch a stray dog for me."

To his disgust, Gharek felt the red fever of an unexpected shame paint his neck and face. Rarely did he feel such regrets, and when he did, he crushed them under the justification of surviving the empress and her brutal desires or doing whatever was necessary to insure Estred had the best life he could offer. Siora's rebuttal reminded him sharply that sometimes a justification was merely an excuse.

"I love Estred," she said in a milder tone. "I think of her all the time." Once more that hideous pity he so loathed rose in her eyes. "You were so desperate, so certain you'd found a way to make her like other children that you were blinded. You didn't see Malachus's face, the look in his eyes. He didn't want to kill you, but you were forcing him into making that choice by refusing to give up the old woman. You refused to tell him where she was, so I did."

Nothing slaughtered guilt faster than being pitied as pathetic. "And you destroyed our lives," he all but snarled at her. "For all we know, the draga was lying. He used Estred against me, and you helped him do it."

Their rising voices made the point guard turn and glare a warning. Siora called out an apology while Gharek wrestled down the urge to send the man a rude gesture to let him know what he thought of his demand for quiet.

"He wasn't lying." Siora picked up where she'd left off, albeit in a near whisper now. "You simply refused to believe your plan hinged on flawed information and failed because of it. I'm sorry draga blood wasn't what you hoped it would be, but Estred without arms is still beautiful, clever Estred. Estred without her father would be forever changed, and not for the better. Telling Malachus what he wanted to know saved you to live another day for her. I can't be sorry for that."

Her preaching to him about Estred's strengths and his lack of appreciation for them made him want to grind his teeth. "Do you have children?"

"No." She eyed him warily, waiting for whatever weapon he was about to use to make an appearance.

"I didn't think so. Gods save us from the ignorant who seek to enlighten the experienced with their sanctimony."

This time it was she who went rosy from her collarbones to her scalp. "That's unfair."

"Spare me the hurt feelings. Estred could give you lessons on the meaning of unfair."

The quiet this time was a frozen thing between them, and Siora slowed her mount enough so that instead of riding beside

Gharek she rode just behind him. It frustrated him to no end that they had the two Kraelian soldiers with them like fleas on a dog. He was spoiling for a fight, desperate to lance the poison building inside him since the day the draga came to his house and destroyed his careful, if risky, plans with the help of his daughter's nursemaid. He wanted to fight it out with her, bellow in her face, and if he was honest, have her shout right back at him. Most of all he wanted her to apologize, to regret what she'd done—not to Estred, but to him. She hadn't, and she wouldn't, even if he threatened to end her life here and now. It wasn't a matter of pride for her in refusing to admit she'd wronged him and Estred. She truly believed she hadn't.

Submerged under all that fury, a question rose in his mind to make his heart's rhythmic beat stutter for an instant. *Why do you even care?*

He buried the thought and worked to cool his fury by turning inward to his recollection of the palace and its many corridors, hidden chambers, and false doors. At the moment, the patriarch of the Goroza family sat on the Kraelian throne, crowned emperor but merely a puppet to the real power behind the throne, General Tovan. Zaredis had a challenge on his hands if he hoped to wrest control of the Empire from Tovan. The two commanded armies of similar strength and number but Tovan had the advantage of already occupying the capital city, protected by its formidable walls as well as the two major rivers that brought in trade from the inland territories.

Gharek had never met Zaredis until now, but he'd crossed paths with Tovan several times. As wily and smart as Zaredis and just as power hungry. Knowing the man, Gharek suspected he'd already supplanted the old guard with his own, placing them in every strategic part of the city, on the lookout for anything or anyone who might be a threat to his control of the throne. That also meant a palace swarming with new soldiers unfamiliar with Gharek. That was both a good and a bad thing. His chances of being recognized were reduced, but so were his chances of bribing a few of them into turning a blind eye at the right moment. If, however, he could use one of Siora's ghosts to help him sneak into the chamber housing the Windcry, he wouldn't have to worry about who to bribe.

He slowed his horse to let Siora's catch up. She brought her mount almost to a stop, unwilling to narrow the space between them. Gharek sighed. "No more questions over a past event neither of us can change. At least not now. I have other questions for you, about your abilities."

Her expression went from frozen to curious and she gave in to that curiosity, allowing her horse to amble up next to his. "What do you want to know?"

"You said your father's spirit has guided you many times, and we all saw how your touch made Zaredis's brother visible to everyone. How long have you had the talent to speak with the dead?"

"For as long as I can remember." The echo of memory flitted across her face. "I would tell my mother of my friends that others couldn't see. She had the talent as well when she was young, but it faded away when she became pregnant with me. Maybe that's how the gift works. It shifts from one generation to the next." A tiny frown marred her smooth forehead. "Making Kalun visible to others is part of true shade-speaking and possible if the ghost is willing. He and Zaredis are twins. Kalun's spirit is more firmly anchored here than others I think because of that bond. It wasn't me holding him that saved him from the ghost-eater. It was the general."

This woman was more than a shade speaker whether she knew it or not, but he kept that to himself.

"Did you see your father die in the Pit?" he asked.

The shadow of melancholy darkened her eyes. "No, thank the gods. I almost died there too a year ago when I was a Flower of Spring. My father's ghost saved me and others. It helped that the Savatar were laying siege to Kraelag at the same time. I saw the Savatar fire goddess burn the city to ashes."

His eyebrows rose. She'd revealed that tidbit of information before as if it were as ordinary as saying she participated in the seasonal haying at one of the farmers' fields. The old capital of Kraelag always hosted the gruesome Rites of Spring with its carnage of slaughtered men, butchered animals, and burned women. Gharek had witnessed it once when he was much younger and well before Estred was born. One of the horrors that kept him up at night, at least until Kraelag had burned to the ground, was the idea of Estred being picked as one of the unfortunate Flowers of Spring. He'd reconsidered his abandonment of faith when word reached Domora that a vengeful Savatar goddess hadn't just burned the city, she'd reduced it to nothing more than a scorch mark of black glass on the earth. Yet somehow, some way, Siora had survived the rites and the city's immolation.

"How in the gods' names did you walk out of either of those events unscathed?"

Her smile this time was for a memory he couldn't see. "As I

said, with my father's help, along with the words of a prostitute's ghost, and the powers of a fire witch." She shrugged. "It all sounds ridiculous, I know, but makes for an interesting story."

He didn't doubt it. This small woman continued to surprise him as much as she angered him. His gratitude for saving Estred had altered during the months she was Estred's nurse, becoming a reluctant interest he did his best to ignore. He hadn't known she was a shade speaker then, just someone with the gift of making his daughter laugh and see the small pleasures in life. Just a beggar woman with an odd gaze, and yet so much more.

"I was in Domora when Kraelag fell," he said. "Preparing an account for the empress of all the activities her summer court had engaged in while she ruled from the old capital during winter and spring. Her torturers and executioners were already sharpening their knives and axes in preparation for dealing with Herself's latest crop of enemies." Dalvila's suspicions weren't unfounded. She was loathed almost as much as she was feared, and she knew that the moment one emotion superseded the other, she breathed on borrowed time. He doubted even she could have imagined the manner of her death.

"Did you know she would kill the physicians who saved her when you fetched Kalun to the palace?" Siora asked the question in a way that told him she dreaded his answer.

Kalun hadn't died by his hand, but his death was one Gharek felt responsible for and regretted. He'd carried out his task and retrieved the physician to help two others in saving Dalvila's life after the arrow wound she'd sustained from a Savatar archer had poisoned her. They'd succeeded but at the cost of the empress's arm. Instead of thanking them for saving her life, she'd punished them for maiming her, and their deaths had been the stuff of nightmares. Gharek had no wish to die and no plans to succumb willingly to that fate, but he understood Zaredis's fury and his desire to see anyone associated with his brother's death pay for the crime.

Siora's expression of dread had only increased with his delayed reply. "No. I knew she would if they didn't heal her. But her version of healing was different from mine, her expectations unreasonable. Crossing her path always carried great risk. Evil is often stupid as well as cruel, without thought or reason. Most of the time it's impossible to make sense of it. Dalvila embodied such malice. The draga did the world a favor by getting rid of that particular abomination."

The dread in her face had vanished and fortunately pity didn't replace it, only a general sorrow not for him but for Kalun. He didn't miss the glitter of a savage satisfaction in her eyes. It seemed she too applauded Malachus for doing away with the empress. "I wonder if she ever imagined she'd be eaten."

"I doubt she ever imagined dying at all. I'm sure she tasted vile."

Siora sputtered, hiding her laughter behind her hand. He liked the sound of it, remembered the pleasure of hearing it in his house as she entertained Estred. "Did you see it happen?"

He'd turn over a wagonload of *belshas* for the opportunity to roll back time to just that moment so he might witness the draga bite down on the evilest bitch to ever draw breath. "No. The instant I came to and the steward let me out of the buttery, I packed up Estred and what valuables I could transport and left Domora. You?"

She shook her head. "I saw the draga in the distance. I too had left Domora."

Fleeing from him, no doubt.

He changed the subject. "Why didn't the entity bewitch you? You were as close to Midrigar's walls as I was. And why me? I'm not dead. If it's an eater of ghosts, it should have no interest in me."

While her gaze rested on the back of the guard riding ahead of them, her sight had turned inward, lending that unnerving far-horizon look to her expression. "I don't have an answer for either question. Its reach goes beyond the city, as we saw in the abandoned barn and again in the general's camp. Every spirit is at risk but not every living person." She blinked and returned to the world around her. She studied him as if he'd suddenly grown horns. "Have you ever been inside the cursed city's walls?"

"Fortunately, the empress never assigned me a task that required it." If she had, Gharek would have found another way to achieve what he needed without going anywhere near Midrigar. He didn't like visiting the Maesor with its sour sky and unnatural light and the sense of detached otherness. If the scavengers who robbed Midrigar of its artifacts and managed to make it out alive told the truth of what they saw or faced there, it was more than a mass grave. A haven for demons and nightmares, and now for this thing without substance whose hunger threatened to overwhelm Gharek and bend his will to its commands, not once but twice. His skin began to crawl, and he shook off the sensation hard enough to make his horse whuffle a protest.

"Who knows what the emperor's sorcerers wrought when they punished the city, or how long it might have slept there and is now awake and starved," he said.

She didn't allay their fears. "And it can reach beyond the bewitchments they laid down to keep the darkness behind the walls."

What if it came back a third time? Siora had rightly accused him of lying when he said he didn't feel its call in the general's tent. Not as strong but just as demanding. An abyssal voice not only in his mind but in his soul, broadened by a chorus of the lamenting dead screaming their despair. Had she not knocked him out with the branch and broken the spell binding him to the ghost-eater, he'd be one of those. Had she hit him a little harder, he'd still be a meal for the thing. "Why didn't you kill me when you stole my horse? And don't feed me that tired refrain of doing it for Estred."

"I'm not a murderer."

He snorted. "I am."

"You could have killed me too," she said. "I'm more than willing to apologize to Estred, to make it right between us. But it would be just as easy to kill me and tell her you couldn't find me. She's young. She'd grieve, but soon I would fade in her memory, along with the hurt I've caused her. So why have you shown me mercy now that you've found me?"

The voice within him once more spoke to annoy him. *Because she's more than her betrayal, isn't she? Something more than Estred's beggar nurse.*

His expression must have looked sinister, for Siora's eyes widened and she guided her horse away from his. "Because Estred has suffered enough in her short life. She doesn't need the burden of guilt in thinking she's the reason you ran away. That, and you're useful to me at the moment," he said. "Zaredis was willing to bargain with you, and I'll work with anyone who'll help my daughter. Plus, a woman who can hear and speak to ghosts could learn many secrets."

The front guard's signal to pick up the pace ended any more opportunity to talk. They urged their horses into a canter, watching as the pale silhouettes in the distance darkened and sharpened to become a series of walls girdling the Empire's capital. Her graceful towers, built of white stone, gleamed in the sun, protected by a series of fortifications three moats deep and stretching for as far as the eye could see from their vantage point.

Domora had been Kraelag's fairer, younger, more elegant sister city, its palace the summer home of the emperor and empress when they wished to flee the heat and the stench of Kraelag and its harbor. Domora was the only capital now, and a new emperor sat on the throne. Gharek couldn't recall which number they were on. Third? Fourth? The Goroza patriarch might last more than the scarce months—and in one case, the few days—his predecessors did before someone assassinated him, especially with the support of General Tovan.

As familiar as he was with her seedy underbelly, Gharek was blind to Domora's surface splendors. Nothing more than a poxy whore wearing an expensive gown. He'd hoped never to see this place again, but at least he had the benefit of knowing its many secrets. Trying to suss out the weaknesses of an unfamiliar palace in an unfamiliar city might have been a challenge he couldn't conquer in the time Zaredis had given him.

The main road joined three others leading toward the city's first set of gates, growing more and more crowded the closer they got. The high walls towering over them were manned by soldiers wearing General Tovan's coat of arms instead of the one belonging to the Goroza family, the battlements rising and falling with the topography like a giant serpent sunning on a rock.

Once something he generally ignored, Gharek now surveyed the walls with an eye for their destruction. "Zaredis is ambitious. I'm not sure even the Windcry can bring down these walls," he told Siora in a low voice. Travelers heading for the city hadn't yet hemmed them in, but the crowds grew ever denser and closer.

She raised her head to peer at the guards and the colossal gates with their heavy barricades built and reinforced to withstand battering rams and stones lobbed by catapults. "A draga did," she said.

He harrumphed. "A few broken battlements. He was nothing more than a siege engine with wings whose sole purpose was to rescue one woman. Zaredis means to take all of Domora as his. Whoever controls this city controls the wealth of the Krael Empire, or whatever remains after the noble families destroy each other in civil war. One can only hope."

"Will you not be recognized once we enter?" Her doubtful gaze took in his appearance, nearly as grubby as hers.

"Maybe. Maybe not." He no longer looked the part of a wealthy Domoran. During their journey, he'd stripped off the sash snugging his tunic to his waist and wrapped it around his head. Many men wore similarly styled hats or caps, so his impromptu headgear wouldn't be out of the ordinary and noted. Most of all, he'd have to remember to change his stance, the way he moved, and other telltale markers of his body's language that might alert someone familiar with him, and who'd no doubt waste little time in notifying whichever Domoran family had issued a bounty for his capture. With any luck he'd be in and out of the city with what he needed before he was discovered.

They merged with the river of people flowing into the city.

Their two guards narrowed the gap between them until they were single file, and Gharek's horse practically nosed the haunches of the front guard while the rear guard's mount did the same to Siora's horse. Gharek slouched in the saddle, adopting the posture of a smaller, more sickly man. He squinted one eye as if partially blinded from some long-ago injury. No one paid attention to him or his companions from what he could tell, but he held his breath, tense with the expectation of some outraged voice shouting his name and pointing, or worse, hearing nothing except the deadly rush of air through an arrow fletching before a broadhead embedded itself in his chest or back.

Once inside Domora, the lead guard guided them out of the milling throng to a spot not so crowded. The noise around the gates was near deafening with the shouts of soldiers ordering people to not dawdle and vendors touting their goods to travelers willing to spend their *belshas*. Zaredis's man had to bellow for Gharek to hear him.

"To use while you're here," he said, tossing a bag of coins. Gharek snatched it neatly out of the air, cursing the man under his breath. Half the city's pickpockets had likely seen the exchange and were just waiting for their new mark to slip in his vigilance. The soldier looked not at all apologetic over the annoyance he'd just caused him. "Remember, you have two weeks." The second soldier thrust Gharek's confiscated satchel at him while the other continued issuing instructions. "Dismount and take your supplies. The horses go with us."

"How are we supposed to get back in a timely manner?" Siora grabbed her own tattered bag and swung down from her horse's back. She clutched the bag to her chest, sparing only a brief glance at their escort before scanning the people around them and the many eyes now on their movements thanks to the money purse toss.

The man shrugged. "Someone will bring you replacements when you're finished and ready to return." He snagged the reins of both horses and turned his mount back toward the gate to join the second river of people leaving the city.

On foot and left to their own devices, Gharek motioned Siora to follow him to where a fruit vendor hawked a pallet of melons to passersby. His stomach rumbled at the sweet scent of ripe fruit, but he ignored the pangs and rifled through his satchel as Siora watched, pretending to drop his coin purse in there. To his surprise, he spotted both of his knives. There was something to be said for a military man who understood that an already difficult task would be made even more so if he was unarmed. A sleight of hand hid the money purse inside his tunic where cutpurses would have to strip him of his clothes to reach it, and he slid the two knives in the sheaths still attached to his belt. This was a reconnoitering mission, but one never knew when something sharp might be needed to dissuade an adversary or do away with one. His satchel was now empty except for a few road rations. If a street thief managed to snatch the bag, they'd be disappointed in its remaining contents.

He pointed to the bag Siora held. "Was everything returned to you?" She'd taken some of his supplies when she stole his horse. In her reduced circumstances, he doubted Zaredis's men would want to keep what few things she called her own.

She pulled part of what looked like a thin shift from her bag and a pathetic-looking eating knife wrapped in a strip of leather to cover its edge and tip. A sad little blade, but Gharek never underestimated the resourcefulness of someone defending themselves. That little knife could do significant damage in the right hands, and he had no doubt Siora had used it once or twice in defense of herself. "This is all," she said in a voice reflecting neither surprise nor disappointment.

The soldier hadn't tossed two bags of coins, so Gharek assumed the one was supposed to see to him and Siora through several days while they were in Domora. He'd have to count the purse's contents later, in a more private spot where they weren't being watched by the city's human scavengers.

Siora shrugged on her satchel, clutching the strap with both hands as if expecting to fight someone for it. "What now?"

She was right to be concerned, and standing here much longer only invited such a someone to come sniffing about. Gharek didn't doubt his own abilities in a fight, but brawls drew attention, and it was the last thing he wanted. "We find a place to sleep for the night where the patrons and the bedbugs won't eat us. It's near dark, and I'm not inclined to wander the streets once the sun goes down. Domora is changed and I suspect more dangerous than it was before the empress died."

"It reminds me more of Kraelag now." Siora watched as soldiers marched past them through streets Gharek didn't remember as being so filthy or so crowded, even at the gates, which received a daily influx of visitors who gathered to gain their bearings before dispersing into the city's inner neighborhoods.

He reached for her hand, startling her when he entwined his fingers with hers. A small hand with delicate fingers. Her wide-eyed expression almost tempted a chuckle out of him. "I don't want to spend hours searching for you should we get separated in this mob." He drew her closer to him, noting her odd lack of resistance. "To any who ask, I'm Saborak, you're my wife, and we're from Beroe. Whoever might be looking for me won't expect to find me with a companion." He didn't keep a mistress or bind himself to any woman for more than a few hours. Nor did he have friends. All who knew Gharek of Cabast knew him as a loner. Having Siora with him strengthened his disguise, and he reluctantly admitted to himself she was becoming more useful to him on this trip than he had anticipated.

"Do you want me to change my name too?"

"Are you being hunted by someone in Domora?" As soon he asked the question, Gharek winced.

Siora smiled. "Just you."

"Then I think it unnecessary."

They set off for the city center. None of the finer inns in the posher districts surrounding the palace would allow him and Siora near their thresholds, much less rent them a room for a night, not looking as poor and ragged as they did. His funds were limited as well. The money purse sat weighty under his tunic against his chest, but the price for a night in one of the city's finer establishments would drain away the majority. Instead, he led Siora through a labyrinth of streets toward a lower rung of neighborhoods halfway between the gates and the palace district.

Here the streets were only marginally wider and no cleaner than those where the poor of the city lived. This was a borough of merchants who did their business from temporary stalls made of worn awnings and scavenged tree limbs, shops built of stone and mortar and everything in between. A marginally safer area of the city where the less well-to-do were ignored instead of shunned or chased off by their more successful neighbors.

They took several more turns before stopping in front of a three-story building painted a garish blue. Balconies with railings painted red graced the facades of the top two floors, and the entire structure blazed with light inside and out from numerous lamps. Its luminescence in the gathering gloom, along with the sound of laughter spilling from the door and open windows, invited passersby to stop and enter.

"You want to stay in the Blue Rat brothel for the night?" Siora's puzzled expression as she split her gaze between him and the building held a wealth of doubt.

He returned a similar look. "How did you know this was the Blue Rat?" While it would be easy enough to discern the nature of this business with one quick glance, there was no sign outside the door advertising the name.

She pointed to a spot not far from where they stood. "That's a good place to beg if the brothel's door minders don't catch you and the men haven't spent all their coin before they leave."

Gharek stared at her. He'd learned more about his daughter's nurse in the last few days than he had when she lived in his house for a season. He'd let her stay for Estred's sake.

May she stay, Papa? I like her. She's brave, and she likes me too.

Estred had rarely asked him for anything despite knowing he'd rearrange the stars to her liking if she asked it of him. Allowing some unknown beggar to become part of his household went against every instinct. He'd agreed first to letting her eat and tend the minor wounds she'd sustained from a well-aimed stone or two. Dinner had become a night spent by the lingering warmth of the kitchen hearth, then a sponge bath and cast-off but clean clothes to replace the rags she wore. Soon a day turned to two days and those to a week and longer. Much to the disgust of the rest of Gharek's staff, Siora had gained a place in his household as his daughter's nurse.

He'd kept a close eye on her at first, as did his steward, the cook, and most of the maids, certain she'd steal something and run. But she'd stayed honest and pleasant, and under her care Estred had blossomed. His household had never accepted the new nursemaid, who showed little concern for the ostracism. Her focus had been on Estred, and in brief, memorable instances, on him.

She'd once warned him to be careful and stay safe when he intended to travel Domora's streets in the late hours when the more feral members of the city's population roamed about. Her worry had puzzled him greatly. No one, except Estred, worried about him. He'd chalked it up to Siora's desire to keep a roof over her head and food in her belly.

Enslaved by Dalvila and hollowed out by the tasks she set to him as her cat's-paw, Gharek hadn't bothered to delve deep into the new nursemaid's history. It was enough that his daughter was happy and safe under Siora's wing, or so he'd assumed. He'd assumed wrong.

"You marked out a dangerous place to beg," he told her. "Those who purchase a prostitute's time are often just as willing to get it for free from a lone woman without a defender, even if she isn't willing herself."

She nodded. "I know. I've had a few close scrapes here."

Forgetting his disguise also depended on a wilting slouch, his back snapped straight at her revelation as a sudden wave of protective anger crashed over him. As brothels went, this was a safe one and accommodated not only men who paid for a few hours with a whore but also those couples who wished to be discreet about their affairs. Men who brought wives not their own to the Blue Rat were assured of secrecy by the owner and her women and clients. He'd chosen it for the safety and anonymity. If, however, any man in there dared lay a hand on his "wife," they'd learn soon enough they dealt with the cat's-paw.

"No scrapes tonight," he assured her. "We'll rent a room, buy a meal to share, and be gone by morning." He waited to see if she'd protest at having to share a bedchamber with him, but she only nodded and slipped her arm through his as if it were the most natural thing. "Shall we?" she said.

They were still in the middle of the street when one of a pair of door guards at the brothel's entrance met and stopped them. Had Gharek been standing straight, he would have been the taller of the two, but the door guard easily outweighed him, with hulking shoulders and arms and a brutish face that had seen one too many street fights and tavern brawls. He loomed over Gharek and Siora, a threatening shadow smelling of ale, grease, and pickled fish. His gaze stayed longest on Siora before his upper lip curled up with a sneer. "Friend," he told Gharek. "If you can't afford a better whore than her, you can't afford to rent a room at the Rat to fuck her."

Siora's fingers dug into Gharek's arm though she remained quiet and kept her eyes downcast. Gharek had expected such a confrontation as well as the casually cruel words. He brandished a single *belsha* in front of the door guard. "I can pay. One night and two meals." He snatched the coin back when the other man reached for it. "I pay the owner or the knock-shop madam, not you."

The door guard scowled when Gharek disappeared the *belsha* with a quick twist and turn of his hand. "Come on then," he finally said, motioning for them to follow him not to the front door but to the side of the building. "You'll wait in the scullery."

Gharek didn't ask him to explain. The front entrance was for clientele better dressed, better fed, and better smelling than he and Siora were at the moment. He had no doubt that even if they could get a room, it would be one on the ground floor not far from the midden and with the bare minimum of comforts. As long as there was a sturdy bar to set across the door and a decent-sized window to crawl out of, he'd be pleased.

The scullery was a busy place even at this hour, with several hollow-eyed women and boys toiling at slop sinks and washer tubs to clean dishes and wash bedding. The open door that led to the narrow alley Gharek and Siora had taken to reach this part of the brothel allowed in a teasing hint of a breeze, but nothing great enough to lessen the room's stifling heat. Those working in there barely glanced at the visitors and ignored the big door guard as he strode through the scullery for the main part of the brothel.

They didn't have to wait long before he returned, accompanied by a tall, elegant woman wearing garb fine enough to gain the envy of any lady in the Kraelian court. Her red hair shimmered in the lamplight, the effect enhanced by tiny jewel-encrusted pins placed in her tresses. Her sharp-eyed regard took in every detail in a single glance, and like the door guard, her gaze rested longest on Siora, but with curiosity instead of contempt.

"You're the owner or the house madam?" he asked her.

She stared at Siora as she answered. "The second. I'm Madam Cadinn. The door guard said you're looking for a room." Her gaze swept them both. "He says he doesn't believe you have the funds to pay."

Gharek flashed a trio of *belshas* at her. "I have the funds. For room, bath, and food." He pulled his hand back when the madam reached for the coins. "I think not. I've been here before. I know the house rules. Half after we see the room, half when we leave tomorrow."

Her drawn eyebrows rose in elegant arches, a glitter of respect in her eyes. "Those are indeed the house rules." Her lip curled a little as she inspected their garb. "For another *belsha*, I can get you both some decent clothing. Plain things but clean and not reduced to rags." She said the last with more emphasis as she stared at Siora. "Unless you want to barter your woman here in trade. A night on her back and she can pay for everything with a little left over."

Before Siora could protest, Gharek replied. "Not interested," he said shortly.

Madam Cadinn shrugged. "As you wish. One *belsha* for the room, one for the food and bath paid now. Another *belsha* in the morning, and don't try to bed-jump without paying tomorrow. Those who try it always regret it." The hard look she bestowed on him and Siora warned that she didn't bluff.

She signaled for a maid who, to his surprise, escorted them to a room on the brothel's second floor. Once Gharek nodded his acceptance, she held out her palm for the first part of payment, promising food and a bath would be delivered shortly.

The chamber was small but well-appointed and illuminated by softly glowing oil lamps.

Siora stood next to Gharek, frowning. "I think this is far too nice for us." She plucked at her grimy skirts. "I'm afraid I'll ruin one of the chairs if I sit."

"Nonsense." Gharek circled the room, inspecting it with a raptor's eye. The large bed with its bounty of linens and pillows beckoned with the promise of either sensual pleasure or restful sleep or both. A table and two chairs occupied one corner, and at the opposite corner, two chests took up space. Gharek knew from previous forays to the Blue Rat that they contained any number of interesting items to enhance bed play of all preferences. A pair of large windows offering a view of rooftops and the distant silhouette of the palace spanned half of the longest wall. He unhooked their latches and opened them, allowing the night's cooling breeze to swirl in and chase away the heat. "It should cool off soon enough."

Their dinner arrived before their baths. The servants worked quietly and efficiently, setting plates and covered dishes whose delectable scents filled the room. When they left, Gharek peeked under each covering and breathed deep. "Far better than road rations," he said. He glanced to where Siora hovered nearby, staring at the table as if she could hardly believe the bounty before her. He suspected it had been a long time since she'd seen this much food in one place at one time. "Come on then," he said, gesturing for her to sit at the table.

She grabbed a drying cloth from the stack the maids brought ahead of the bathwater and laid it across the chair's seat before perching on its edge. She eyed her skirts with disgust. "If this weren't my only frock, I'd burn it."

Her garb was in poor condition, its thread held together by dirt and prayer. Gharek mentally counted the money Zaredis had given him to use for necessary items during this trip. He hadn't been specific as to what constituted "need." Something to wear not caked in dirt, splattered in blood, and not coming apart at the seams was, in his opinion, very much a need.

Siora's clothes might have been filthy and her skin smudged from days on the road and nights lying on the ground, but she didn't touch their food until she'd meticulously cleaned her hands with cloth and the citrus-scented water the maids had left in small bowls alongside their plates. A memory surfaced in his mind of observing her doing the same thing when she shared a meal with Estred in Estred's room. She might be covered in layers of grime now, but the small shade speaker was fastidious when given the opportunity.

She stared helplessly at each dish as Gharek uncovered them, her incredulity making him chuckle inside. "I don't know where to start," she said. "I've not seen so much food in one place in months."

While he was the empress's cat's-paw, he'd partaken of meals far more lavish than this one, but with his stomach gnawing its way toward his backbone at the moment, this particular meal seemed superior to the culinary marvels prepared for Dalvila's and her courtiers' pleasure.

"Soup is always a good place to start," he said, lifting the lid off a tureen to take an appreciative sniff of the steaming contents. He motioned for her to hand him her bowl and ladled a golden broth into it. She took it and set it down on her plate but didn't immediately delve into it. "Eat," he said.

"I'm waiting for you to serve yourself."

Fastidious and polite. And kind. He'd seen that himself many times while she lived in his house. No wonder her treachery had taken him by surprise. Like the earlier voice, he banished the thought. What's done was done, he thought. He'd dwelt on it long enough and there was no changing the past. To keep dwelling on it promised to eat him alive. He'd saved her instead of killed her, and she had done the same for him. For now they were awkward allies, though he still remained astounded at her offer to accompany him to Domora to help.

Except for a few compliments to the brothel's cooks, they ate without conversation, pausing at one point for Gharek to rise and let in another crowd of serving staff who wrestled in a hip bath and several buckets of steaming and tepid water. Soon the tub was full and one of the servants left a cake of soap, drying cloths, and a stack of clothing on the bed. Gharek rifled through those, holding up a woman's split-sided tunic and loose trousers that looked like a skirt when the wearer stood still. "Will these do?" he said. "A *belsha* will buy you simple garb that won't become rags after a wearing or two, but nothing else."

Siora abandoned her second helping of food to join him. She took the tunic, slender fingers running over the cloth's weave. She smiled. "It will do very well. Thank you."

Gharek watched her features, noted the pleasure with which she accepted the clothes. She'd worn the same look when she came to thank him for the clothing his steward had purchased for her when she'd started work as Estred's nursemaid. It had taken the man and the housekeeper two days to calm down after the hide-stripping he'd given both when he discovered they'd tried to pocket the allotment between them and dressed Siora in cast-offs. His staff knew better, and after that incident, none of them tried such a stunt again.

Whoever had purchased the new garb had bought it with practicality and durability in mind. Plain and utilitarian, it worked perfectly in helping them both blend unnoticed into Domora's crowds. Gharek was pleased.

He watched as Siora set the tunic carefully on the bed and returned to her seat to finish her dinner. Maybe not so unnoticed, he thought. At least not her. Clean and with her hair coiffed, she'd draw the attention of some. She was a pretty woman beneath the dirt. He'd seen that firsthand and had been startled by the fact when she first presented herself to him after a scrub in the kitchens of his fine house.

This bath was meant to be shared, either together or one right after the other, and as they'd posed as a couple, it made sense the brothel's staff assumed the first. Siora stared longingly at the full buckets waiting to be poured into the tub before stepping back. "You first," she said. "You aren't as dirty as me. The water won't be fit to put out a fire much less bathe in if I go first."

He rolled his eyes. He'd expected this, and she hadn't disappointed. "We'll compromise. You take half the buckets, I'll take the other half. You can't submerge, but you can get clean enough with the water available. When you're done, we'll empty the tub and I'll take my turn."

Delighted by the solution, she wasted no time in pouring her half of the water into the tub, except for one bucket. Gharek expected some argument about him having to leave the room to protect her modesty and so finished the rest of his supper before it grew cold and he had to leave. Instead, she began shedding her clothes with impressive speed, pausing only when he said, "Do you wish for me to leave?"

Bent, with the hem of her threadbare shift clutched in her hand, she gave him a questioning look. "Why do you need to leave?"

Her trust turned him speechless, though she was right in believing she was safe with him. He'd committed murder on command, but he'd never raped and never would.

He'd assumed she'd strip down to bare skin, but she proved him wrong, leaving the shift on while she used one of the buckets of cold water to wash her hair. By the time she was done, the shift was soaked through, outlining her small frame. She might not have been much bigger than a child with the fragile bones of a bird, but she possessed a woman's curves and a natural sensuality in the way she moved as she dried her hair and wound the tangled tresses into a knot at the top of her head.

Desire surged through him as he watched her from his place at their supper table. Desire, not anger. Gharek dropped his eating knife to his plate and stood abruptly. Siora froze, startled by his sudden movement.

"Don't loiter," he told her in tones harsher than he intended. "My share of the water will be cold enough by the time I get to it. I have to speak with the door guard."

He was across the threshold and in the corridor before she could respond, closing the door gently on the sight of her puzzled face and the tempting shadows of her body barely hidden by the damp shift. Gharek leaned against the wall adjacent to the door frame and exhaled a long breath.

Court gossip spared no one except the empress, and that was

because no one wanted to be publicly disemboweled should she chance to hear of anything other than praise and compliments said about her. Everyone else was fair game. Even Gharek, feared for his position but also despised for his low birth, had been the subject of blistering commentary and insults, often in his earshot. Conjectures over his parentage, whether or not he was a eunuch, if he desired women or men in his bed. Even children or beasts. He ignored it all, considering the gossip and those who gossiped ridiculous and tiresome.

Only once had such tripe made him react. A group of court-iers at one of Herself's many banquets were gathered around the dicing tables, betting on everything from who would bed Lord Whoever's latest favorite concubine to which horse would win a particular race. All of it shallow and deadly dull until one young nobleman wondered aloud if anyone knew that the cat's-paw had a daughter. "The younger the flesh, the sweeter," he said and pro-ceeded to detail what he'd do with the cat's-paw's whelp.

One of Gharek's many skills was to make himself invisible in a crowd. There was no magic to it, just the ability to capitalize on others' inattention and with this crowd, their innate snobbery. None of them had noticed his presence nearby. Close enough to hear everything said and report back to Dalvila should she want to know the way the breeze drifted through her court at any given time. In this instance Gharek had no intention of mentioning anything to the empress, but he listened to every word, noted every face participating in the conversation.

Crude jokes and vulgar speculation about his daughter pep-pered their conversation as they placed their bets and rolled their bones. A week later, the body of the nobleman with a taste for the very young was retrieved in one of the pleasure canals encircling the palace. Someone else found his head in a flowerpot in another aristo's garden. Gharek continued to overhear remarks about his street-rat origins and his masculinity or lack thereof, but nothing—not even a whisper—about Estred.

If any of those gossiping twits could see his physical state now, they'd know for certain he was not a eunuch and that he very much desired women, even women he considered adversaries.

Was Siora truly an adversary now? The question raked across his mind, an annoying whisper that had grown in volume as it revisited his thoughts over and over, fracturing his outrage even more with doubt when the inner voice that refused to be silent asked, *Was she ever the enemy?*

She was definitely a distraction, one he couldn't afford to indulge in, not with this difficult task before him and Estred's life at risk. He pushed away from the wall, eyed the closed door, and took himself away from temptation.

The brothel's second floor was an elegant place with carpets soft underfoot and decorative lamps that lit the space with enough light to see but not enough to highlight a prostitute's flaws to her customer. Tapestries filled the wall space between the doors, aiding in muffling the noises drifting from the rooms' interiors—a man's guttural cries while in the throes of orgasm, a prostitute's practiced reply refined to sound sincere to all but the most cynical ear. Gharek ignored them, concentrating on the placement of windows and staircases, which doors were barred from the outside and which weren't.

Had they been in a different establishment, he would have searched for peepholes in the room given to them, but the Blue

Rat had a reputation in Domora for discretion and secrecy. The walls in the room he and Siora occupied were bare of any decoration and pristine. No holes, no cracks, no murals painted in such a way that they hid ways for the occupants of adjacent rooms to spy. The proprietors were clever. They wouldn't share their wealthy clients' valuable secrets to which they were privy with some court fop wanting a peek at his best friend fucking his other best friend's wife. Extortion only worked when the secret was known only by a few.

By the time he returned to his and Siora's room, he'd mapped out two easy escape routes and one risky one, and those didn't include the windows in their chamber. The Blue Rat was indeed safe—as safe as any place in a city where his name was a curse on numerous lips and an engraving on the haft of many head pikes.

He knocked on the door and said, "It's Saborak," before easing it open. The last thing he wanted was to startle her and end up with a thrown knife sunk into his eye. He doubted she possessed such martial skill, and he was quick enough on his feet to dodge most things, but he rarely underestimated people and their capabilities. The rare times he did, he regretted it.

Siora had resumed her place at the table. She motioned to him, gesturing with one of the pastries loaded onto the plate. Her wet hair was combed and neatly plaited, and she wore the new shift and tunic he'd purchased. The tunic's gray fabric, cinched at her slender waist by a black sash, suited her and the bath had done wonders for her appearance. He was reminded again of the first time he'd seen her clean and better garbed.

She had appeared very different from the women of the court, dressed in their bright plumage with their hard eyes in which either calculation or desperation shone. The empress's own beauty far surpassed hers, as the sun compared to a candle flame, and yet in that moment when Gharek beheld her, he'd thought of a sunrise. So it was now, and he turned away from her to shut the door.

"I hurried as quickly as I could," she said. "And left you an extra bucket of water to add to your share. It isn't hot, but it's still pleasant enough for a bath." A hesitancy entered her voice. "Would you like for me to leave while you bathe?"

"That's your decision," he said, untying numerous laces and straps before peeling off his garb one piece at a time. He went slow, allowing her the chance to decide what to do before she got an eyeful of him in only his skin. He had no intention of flaunting his nudity, but he damn well planned to scrub the layers of grime and dried blood off himself. If she didn't like it, she could walk outside like he had or turn her chair to the wall. She did neither, and Gharek hid a smile when she showed more interest in the pastry she was buttering than in him.

He made short work of his bath, dried and dressed in the long shirt he'd bought, and made sure the lock on the door was secured. No doubt there was more than one copy of the room's key in existence, likely kept on a ring with several other keys the knock-shop madam carried. Gharek dragged one of the spare chairs across the room and wedged it under the door handle. It offered nothing in the way of defense, guaranteed to splinter under a solid kick to the door, but any who might want to enter would lose the advantage of surprise.

"Are you expecting intruders?" Siora watched him while she rolled leftover bread, pastries, and fruit into napkins and tucked them into her satchel. He had no doubt if the satchel could hold liquid, she would have poured the soup tureen's contents into it as well. He didn't judge her. When you didn't know where or when your next meal might appear, you didn't waste food.

"I expect difficulties and obstacles. Always." He snugged the chair harder against the door before deeming it good enough and gave his full attention to his companion. He tapped a finger to his ear, pointed to the door and the walls, then tapped the same finger to his lips. Difficulties included eavesdroppers. She nodded to indicate she understood his gestures.

"While you're browsing the market, I'll explore the city. I hear Domora has many things to see and the market is one of the finest. Pick something for yourself while you shop. We can meet later and visit the royal library. It is one of the wonders of the Empire, filled with knowledge on everything from the histories of lost cities to the artifacts collected by the old emperors."

If he'd chosen his words right, and she was as quick as he always knew her to be, she heard the true plans under the surface ones. He'd reconnoiter the palace while she roamed the marketplace and kept an ear out for any information he might find useful. He'd then come back for her so they could go to the royal library.

"Oh, I've always wanted to visit the library," she said in a girlishly excited voiced so at odds with her somber expression. "My father once told me ghosts haunt the library. Do you think we'll see one?"

Gharek offered her a short bow. She'd understood just fine. "Maybe." He pointed to the bed and then the floor. "Come to bed then, my beauty." Like her, he'd affected a misleading tone to his voice. Siora froze for a moment before a bright blush swept her features. He even managed to startle himself with how sincere he sounded.

He approached her where she still sat at the table and bent low to whisper in her ear. "That should convince anyone with an ear to the wall or door. Now choose your sleeping spot. Floor or bed, and if it's the bed, we'll share, because I'm not giving up a comfortable bed over some misplaced sense of modesty."

She didn't hesitate. "Bed," she said before rising with an agile grace to skirt around him and claim her place on the mattress closest to the wall. She wiggled out of her tunic but kept on her shift and slid under the covers, leaving Gharek to gutter the lamps. He dragged the half full hip bath to a spot under the open windows—another warning system in place but still allowed him and Siora to take advantage of the breeze blowing into the room and cooling it down.

Siora scooted closer to the wall, whether to give him more space or to avoid touching him, he couldn't say. She'd been the one to make the choice. If she didn't like his proximity, she was welcome to stretch out on the floor.

They lay together in the peaceful room, she on her side facing him, he on his back as he gazed into the darkness and listened to the sounds of a city slowly falling asleep. Male voices murmured in the background, their deeper notes mingling with higher, feminine voices punctuated with sultry laughter and the occasional moan of pleasure from one of the other rooms nearby.

"The royal library will have every ward ever created recorded in some scroll or book," he said in a whisper. "Including the one that protects the Windcry from thievery. Our challenge will be to find the counter one we need to break it." Her soft breathing drafted gently across his shoulder. "It probably has what's needed to get rid of a ghost-eater, though I doubt we'll have time to search for such a thing among so many records." He turned his head to look at her, face cast half in deep shadow, half in pale moonlight spilling through the nearby window. "Much has changed since Dalvila died and you and I left the city. At first glance it looks the same, but there's no possible way that's so, not with the throne contested by every aristo wanting to claim the seat for themselves. There'll be plenty of gossip."

"There's already something different." She spoke in the same hushed tones, but something else there—an unspoken dread—made him roll to his side and face her. "It isn't just the living who make noise. Ghosts do too, even when they choose not to reveal themselves to me. Every place possesses such a sound. It's like a memory of life. Even the earth joins in sometimes, I think. But not in Domora, at least not any longer." The bed shook gently with her shiver. "There's a silence underlying the sound of the living that doesn't belong. Isn't natural. There should be spirits in the city. There were before. There aren't now."

After what he'd witnessed in Zaredis's tent, Gharek took her at her word. "Spoken like a true shade speaker," he said. "Can you not sense your father?"

Another shiver, harder this time. "Even if I could, I dare not reach out to him, not with whatever is preying on the lingering dead."

"But we're much farther from the cursed city now." He hadn't expected her reluctance to reach out to her father's ghost, especially after she'd admitted his warnings had saved her more than once from a sure death.

"Not far enough for my liking." She edged a little closer to him. "Besides, as I said before, I can't just summon a spirit. They have to come of their own free will."

He rolled to his back again, smiling into the darkness. "You lied to the general about getting a ghost's help."

Her voice rose with her agitation. "I did not." At his warning "shhh," she lowered it to a whisper to match his. "I said I could possibly coax a spirit. Not a lie. There's a difference between coaxing and summoning."

Somehow during her protest, her hand had found a place to rest on his chest. For a moment, Gharek forgot to breathe. No more than the perching of a butterfly, that delicate touch burned a hole through his shirt, and yet he refused to shrug it off. There was a magic about this woman that had nothing to do with ghosts or necromancy and everything to do with softness. Softness of the soul, of the mind, a calming for tortured thoughts and dark fury, of regret and despair. He had at turns considered her a gift, then a curse. Who knew what she represented now? Forgiveness? Hope? He mentally shrugged off the ridiculous idea of the last. He'd lost an understanding of that emotion long ago. Whatever sorcery the woman sharing his bed at the moment practiced, it confounded him greatly. And if he was honest with himself, frightened him at times.

They lay quietly together, her weight pressing ever heavier into his side just as her hand settled harder above his heart. Gharek thought her asleep until she spoke in a drowsy voice. "I dream of the sea sometimes. It sings a lullaby."

"It sings a dirge." He had no love for the sea.

Her body's heat enveloped him, and Gharek prayed for a stronger zephyr to cool him off.

"Who were you once?" She avoided saying his true name aloud, but he fancied he heard it come to rest on her lips. "Before you became a man of splinters and bitterness?"

He didn't remember. Not really. Nor did it matter. "Go to sleep, Siora," he ordered before turning onto his other side and putting his back to her, doing his best to ignore the skin-prickle sensation of her hand as it now hovered just above his spine—not touching—before she dropped it with a sigh and grew still.

CHAPTER SIX

Siora reveled in the feel of clean, new clothes against her skin. Except for the clothes bought for her when she first came to work for Gharek, they were the finest things she'd ever owned, matched only by a pair of sturdy shoes snugged to her feet with straps and real buckles. The rags she'd worn a day earlier were gone, whisked away by one of the troop of maids who'd sailed in once Gharek opened the door. Siora suspected they'd been tossed into the closest fire and were now part of the hearth's ash pile. She wouldn't miss them.

She and Gharek had stood out of the way as the others removed the tub and buckets and cleared the table of the previous night's supper, replacing it with a tray of pastries well as a pitcher of milk and another of ale. Siora had worn her napkin like an apron to keep her new shift as clean as possible and piled her plate high with breakfast. Anything left over that could be transported without going off or making a mess she'd wrapped in the napkin when she was done and stuffed it into her already packed satchel. She doubted she'd ever eat this well again in her lifetime.

No one commented on the odd placement of the tub or the sight of a scone peeking out of her satchel. These servants were likely used to seeing many strange things in the rooms they cleaned and prepared for their next clients and were warned not to speak of it. In fact they didn't speak to Siora or Gharek at all except for wanting to know if there was anything they were needing. When Gharek said no, they filed out in an orderly line without another word, marching down the corridor on quiet feet toward the stairwell.

"They remind me a little of your servants," she told him. Maybe not as quiet as these but very discreet and unobtrusive. They'd also never accepted her into their small group, so some of their silence around her was ostracism. Siora hadn't cared. She was warm, fed, and in the company of a cheerful, interesting child with extraordinary resilience. And every once in a while she'd caught glimpses of a man who was far more than the loathed henchman to a mad empress. A man who loved with a ferocious devotion. Life had been good in the cat's-paw's household.

"They're paid to serve, not socialize," he replied. "In my house and I expect in this one as well."

When she was dressed and ready to slip on her shoes, Gharek motioned for her to sit in one of the chairs. "Let me help you," he said, startling her with the offer until she recognized his ploy. She perched on the edge of a chair while he knelt in front of her, one of her shoes in his hand. He leaned in close enough so that only she could hear him when he whispered.

"Meet me near the Goldoka bridge when the pleasure boats on the palace canals set up for the evening crowd. If I don't arrive, it means I'm dead, and if I am, don't linger. You're resourceful. Find a way back to Zaredis's camp. Use what leverage you have to bargain with him. Estred's well-being for protection of his twin against the eater of ghosts." He slipped the boot onto her foot, his elegant hands those of a poet or scholar, not an assassin. Or so she'd like to fool herself into thinking. No doubt they were as capable of writing beautiful prose as they were of wringing a neck.

"Why wouldn't Zaredis send his sorcerer with us? Wouldn't it be easier for him to learn the lay of the palace and take the artifact instead of waiting for us to return to draw some map?"

Busy buckling the boot closed, Gharek paused and looked up, wearing a faint frown. "Have you forgotten what he looks like? There isn't a crowd large enough or a street deserted enough for him to go unnoticed. Besides, he's too valuable to the general to risk on such an endeavor. He'll need him when he launches his attack on Domora. This isn't Zaredis's only plan for taking the city; it's just the easiest one with fewer casualties for his army."

In short, they were expendable if things went wrong—and the sorcerer was not. "How do you know the general has more than one plan?"

He tightened the straps on her other shoe, taking his time buckling them. "Because it's military strategy and men like Zaredis, who've risen in the ranks to such powerful positions, always have more than one plan."

Golden bars of morning sun streamed through the open window, highlighting similarly colored strands amid the darker brown ones in Gharek's hair as he bent to fit her shoe. The angle of his head shielded part of his face from her. She saw just the tip of his nose and chin, and the jut of his lower lip. She'd always thought him handsome, if coldly grim, with an aristocratic nose and nostrils that flared wide when he was angry or displeased, which was often. High cheekbones made more hollow by the thickening of his beard and narrowed eyes lent his visage an even harder cast.

The few times she'd seen his face soften had been reserved for Estred, and those rare occasions she'd seen him truly smile and then laugh had taken her breath away. In those ephemeral moments she'd caught a glimpse of what he might once have been like before life, circumstance, and the role of henchman for the Spider of Empire had changed him.

"Done," he said, and rose in one lithe motion. "We can't linger. You've a market to explore," he said in a mildly bored voice as if he'd spend his time doing nothing more than harmless sightseeing.

Siora stood when he did, and the space between them was thin and hummed with tension. Her skin tingled from her feet to her scalp, a feeling not entirely unfamiliar when she was this close to him. It had suffused her entire body when they shared the bed last night. Sleep had been long in coming, finally weighting her eyelids shut while she counted the steady rise and fall of his chest as he breathed.

Fear? Attraction? The first made sense. The second, not at all. Not with what she knew about him, what she'd seen, and yet the two feelings entwined together. He had, since the first moment she'd met him, fascinated her. Her reason told her such a thing made for bad choices. Her emotions seemed not to care.

She'd bargained with Zaredis to help Kalun if he promised Estred's safety while she was Zaredis's hostage. The dead needed her as well, including her father. She didn't dare speak his name or even think it just in case it somehow summoned him and made him vulnerable to whatever was devouring ghosts. But she missed his nebulous guidance terribly. And she worried.

She might have stepped back to put more distance between her and Gharek, except the chair on which she'd sat blocked her.

It was Gharek who moved away, nostrils flared in the telltale sign of annoyance. He didn't say anything, only set to completing his own dressing. She was struck once more by the profound change in the way he looked simply by covering his head with the head wrap and hunching his shoulders in such a way that he looked older, weaker, and not at all like the formidable cat's-paw.

"I see why the empress relied on your skills," she whispered. "I'm only surprised one of Zaredis's men actually recognized you."

He shrugged. "I was careless."

They took the servants' narrow staircase to the kitchens instead of the grand one reserved for patrons. That led to the greeting rooms on the ground floor where the prostitutes who worked for the Blue Rat draped the furniture in languid enticement and gauzy fabrics to please their customers. Except for the servants going about their tasks and the new pair of door guards manning the front entry, the brothel was quiet. Gharek sent one of the scullery boys to fetch the madam.

She tutted as she approached. "You both look refreshed, something I don't usually see after a night in my establishment." She eyed Gharek with faint contempt and Siora with a touch of puzzlement as if she considered them an odd, rather pathetic-looking couple. There was no pity in her expression when she once again held out her hand for the balance of payment. Her "Enjoy your stay in Domora and at the market" confirmed every one of Gharek's suspicions that eavesdropping was alive and well at the Blue Rat.

Once outside in the street, among the bustle of other city dwellers, Siora hooked her arm with Gharek's. "You were right."

The sly half smile he gave her almost made her jaw drop. Had he ever smiled at her before? "Of course I was right," he said. "No brothel hoping to compete in Domora neglects its eavesdropping. It's practically a sport."

Even outside the brothel, they were careful not to speak too freely. Gharek guided her toward the sprawling marketplace in the city's center, its byways already crowded with shoppers and pickpockets. "Browse and listen," he instructed her. "You'll be amazed at what you'll glean simply by keeping your ears open to other conversations. You know where I'll be."

"And where I'm to meet you," she said.

He nodded. "My visit will take all of today. Tomorrow we go to the royal library."

"To see your friend?"

"And do some research. If we're lucky, my friend will give us some guidance without asking too many questions." He frowned for a moment. "We'll have to stay in rougher lodgings tonight if we want to make Zaredis's coin last."

Siora smiled. She'd spent more days of her life sleeping under open sky, in barns, and on quiet streets than she had inside such places as houses, inns, and brothels. "I don't mind."

The corner of his mouth lifted for a moment. "I didn't think so."

He pulled her into a loose embrace, startling her, but only for a moment. The unexpected gesture and his closeness sent her heartbeat thudding in her ears. Obviously for show among a crowd that likely didn't notice, Siora seized the opportunity and slid her hands over his wide shoulders in a return embrace. She tilted her face up to his. "I'll see you soon, husband," she said, her voice carrying just above the din.

Gharek's expression, guarded and a little startled as well, quickly adopted a false affection. He bent to brush his lips across her forehead in a brief kiss. "Don't shop all day," he said. They parted ways after that, Siora doing her best not to reach up and rub the spot on her forehead where the skin tingled with the memory of his touch.

Domora was much like it had been when Siora fled from it months earlier. The lives of the common folk altered little when the seat of power transitioned to someone else, at least after the fighting was over. Life continued amid and beyond the grieving, interrupted by the occasional plague, rebellion, or a draga eating an empress. To any who surveyed the city now, it seemed like none knew or cared that an army advanced toward them, that the Kraelian throne would once more become the prize for whichever armies would slaughter each other so that one person might rule and enjoy the benefits of power bought with blood.

The sun beat down on her head as she made her way through the market, moving slowly from stall to stall, pretending to browse and engaging in chitchat with the merchants. Most of their conversations consisted of the usual cajoling banter and tactics meant to manipulate a reluctant shopper into parting with their coin in exchange for that one thing they suddenly couldn't live without. Amid the bluster and empty praise, she winnowed out details about the city's feel overall, the tense waiting for something to happen, the beginnings of hoarding just in case there would really be a siege, the conjectures concerning what was happening in the illegal market known as the Maesor. It was an open secret everyone knew, but no one admitted to knowing if questioned by Kraelian soldiers or palace guards. A place where magic of every kind— from simple and beneficial to dark and complex—traded hands, and buyers and sellers risked life and limb to do business there.

Siora tucked each tidbit into her memory as the day waned, and she wondered if Gharek had success with sneaking into the palace to retrace the path to the Windcry's hiding place. She dare not think the worst. This was the cat's-paw. The empress might be dead and no longer in need of his skills, but that didn't mean he'd lost them. This was a man who knew how to survive.

She finally made her way toward the Goldoka bridge and the wealthy palace district with its man-made canals and pleasure boats for the Kraelian court to enjoy. Those of lesser status weren't allowed on the canals, but they could watch the spectacle of pleasure boats illuminated with decorative lanterns and crowded with Kraelian aristocrats as oarsmen rowed them through the water.

The boats lived up to their names as the wealthy who occupied them drank fine wine, ate expensive food, and sometimes swived each other for all of Domora to see. It was no wonder the Goldoka bridge was the most crowded and most popular place to be during the summer nights.

Already the bridge deck was filling with spectators claiming the prime viewing spots, and it was still late afternoon with at least another two hours before the sun coaxed the twilight in. By the time the first oarsman lit the first lamp to the cheers of those waiting on the bridge, it was a sweltering press of people and the perfect scenario for every cutpurse and pickpocket in the city.

Siora didn't have any money on her person, but she held tightly on to her satchel of hoarded food, prepared to brawl with anyone who'd try and snatch it from her hands.

She shoved her way through the mass of bodies until she reached the end of the bridge on the side leading away from the palace district. She would never spot Gharek, or he her, if she remained in the middle of that crush. Time passed on a crawl as she waited for him, peering into the mottled light cast by the lamps lighting the bridge deck. Full dark was upon them now as the boatmen slowly rowed their passengers under the bridge's archways.

Strong fingers suddenly wrapped around her arm and held tight. Siora jumped and just as quickly cocked her free arm back to strike whoever had hold of her. She squeaked out an odd noise of relief mixed with startlement at finding Gharek right beside her, scowling at the sight of her upraised palm ready to slam into his face and break his nose.

She lowered her arm. "It's you! Thank the gods! I feared you wouldn't come back. Did you see it?" The words tumbled past her lips like a river's fast current.

He snorted. "I can count on one hand the number of times someone has actually thanked anyone at all, much less the gods, for finding me at their side." He pulled her along with him farther away from the bridge. "Let's get out of here. I've already broken the fingers of two pickpockets who thought themselves faster than I was. The odds will only stack against me if I stay and wait for someone who is faster to rob me blind."

She didn't need to be coaxed, and they were soon far enough away from the teeming crowds and the shadowing light that did more to hide than to reveal and allowed the thieves to easily tag their marks.

Gharek answered her questions once they found a spot thinned of people. "I saw the Windcry. The ward is still in place and guards loyal to General Tovan now stand watch over the chamber in which it's housed. That's in our favor since the chances of one of them recognizing me is much smaller than if it were any of

Herself's guards on watch. What did you learn from the market gossip?"

Things he likely already knew about the city. Still, she repeated what she'd overheard from merchant talk. "Wagers exchanged in secret for how long this new emperor will hold the throne. Word is out that Zaredis has arrived on these shores with his army. Everyone knows he'll march this way soon and lay siege to the city. People don't seem concerned, as the river ports are still open, and Tovan's ships control Kraelag's harbor. Trade goods are still getting through from territories within the Empire and without. There are whispers of stranger things. No one trades in the Maesor anymore."

He tapped his bottom lip with a finger, a double row of frown lines creased into his brow. "Why not? The latest usurper is but a puppet more concerned with holding the throne than enforcing the sorcery laws and punishing offenders. The Maesor would thrive under such a ruler."

"Rumor has it those who once traded there have disappeared." She'd never visited the Maesor nor walked among Domora's elite to understand their thoughts and machinations. "There are whispers growing about those who enter the Maesor but never come back." Until today, Siora had been curious about the Maesor. No longer.

A queasy feeling settled in her stomach when Gharek said, "If we can't find what we need at the library, we may have to visit there ourselves. For a price, a vendor there with his thumb in every deal taking place in the Maesor can tell me who might sell a ward breaker as well as something to hold off whatever tried to consume Kalun and lure me into the cursed city." He gave her a measuring look as if he saw the growing dread she tried hard to conceal. "Or I'll go alone. I've been to the Maesor many times. I don't need a companion to hold my hand."

Siora returned his frown. She'd likely be in no more danger there with him than by herself in Domora waiting for him. If she repeated it to herself enough times, she might believe it.

"I'll go with you," she said. "When does the Maesor close?" If it was like the regular market, merchants would close their stalls as twilight rolled in.

One corner of his mouth lifted in the hint of a smirk. "This is the Maesor. There's no day, no night. Just an orange sky without a sun. People who trade in the forbidden market aren't ruled by the hours or the seasons. You can do business there at any time." His words didn't reassure her, but she didn't hesitate to grasp his fingers when he held out his hand once more to her. "Come, we can stay at an inn halfway between the library and an entrance to the Maesor."

They hadn't gone far when Gharek's demeanor gradually changed. Siora noted the way his features seemed to freeze, and he did something so surprising, she almost choked on a gasp.

He lifted her hand, bringing it to his mouth as if he meant to kiss it. Instead he whispered around her fingers. "We're being followed by two men," he said, the tight smile pinching his face a twisted parody of the real thing. "I've been recognized."

The news vaulted Siora's heart into her throat. She resisted the urge to spin around and see this pair. She knew exactly what he meant when he said he'd been recognized. Those who followed hadn't come to say hello. They'd come to kill.

"If you panic," he said, squeezing her hand hard, "we're both dead. Follow my lead and keep up. Understood?"

She nodded, and soon their leisure walk turned into a quick stride, then a jog and finally a dead run. Gharek led her through a labyrinth of gloomy streets that hugged the palace district like a crescent, his grip on her hand unyielding as she struggled to keep up with him. They raced past windows lit by candle and lamplight that gathered in pools of anemic luminescence on scattered cobblestone and hard-packed dirt. Those pools surrendered to shadow, and Siora struggled to find sure footing. Gharek suffered none of the partial blindness she did, his steps sure and quick. The cat's-paw must also have cat's eyes when it came to seeing in the dark.

They hugged the edges of Domora's seedier side where the buildings weren't quite hovels but were still ramshackle, and the streets weren't cleaned of horse manure like those in the wealthier districts. They tramped through ankle-deep muck whose smell was so strong it made her eyes water and her stomach curdle. Figures lingered in doorways, watching as they passed, or darted between narrow alleyways. More darkness and fewer lamps obscured the faces of those still roaming the streets.

Siora held on to Gharek's hand so as not to lose him and gripped her small knife at the ready with her other hand. She'd wandered into this area when she'd first come to Domora after Kraelag fell. While this was a far more genteel city than the old capital, it still had its underbelly, and she'd been quick to flee and do her begging and shade-speaking in a less dangerous place. Now she'd returned, running through its filthy streets and in the company of a man who was likely the most lethal denizen here now. Or so she hoped.

They finally halted before a building that reminded her of the Blue Rat, though it stood in disrepair, its front dark and uninviting. And abandoned. No lights shone from the windows, and the windows themselves were empty eye sockets that stared back at her and Gharek, the glass long broken. Tattered remnants of curtains fluttered through the openings like lashes in the night breeze. The front door hung askew, giving brief glimpses of shapes inside as it creaked and swayed on its hinges.

The glimmer of metal under moonlight caught her eye. Gharek held a slender knife, one much larger than hers with an elegant, slim blade and a double edge. An efficient weapon easily hidden in a sleeve and quite good at sliding between ribs. "What in the gods' names . . ." he said in a low, frustrated voice. "What happened here?" He didn't take his gaze off the entrance.

The night hung thicker than lamp oil and the corpse of the building in front of them seemed a far more sinister thing, especially with assassins behind them.

A shape suddenly hurtled out of the darkness at them, caught the edge of a light pool, and became a man wielding a dagger.

Siora had no time to scream before she was violently shoved to one side. She almost fell, managing at the last instant to right herself with a clawing grip on one of the building's decorative lintels. The precious contents spilled out of her satchel and into the street's muck. She hardly noticed, gaze frozen on the scene in front of her as she balanced on the balls of her feet, prepared to jump out of the way.

Gharek and his adversary faced off, each wielding their knives. The attacker feinted, then lunged, swiping at Gharek's torso. "I thought it was you I saw at the gate, cat's-paw. Your head will bring me a lot of *belshas*." He lunged again, and once more Gharek dodged the attack.

He didn't respond to the incitement. Siora marveled at the nimbleness with which he moved. Even a street made slick with wet horse manure didn't make him slow, and she could only imagine how quick he'd be without such a challenge. Her heartbeat pounded in her chest, and she glanced at their surroundings, peering into the obscuring shadows for the other would-be assassin to come flying out of the dark to join the fight.

The two men seemed equally matched, quick and deadly, their blades glimmering in the moonlight as they lunged and parried, attacked and retreated. It was a dance, a deadly one, with survival reliant on strategy and speed. And surprise. Gharek proved the second when he suddenly feinted toward his opponent's blade, taking a shallow slash on the arm as reward. But the unexpected move made the other man slip. His dexterity compromised, he lost his footing, and Gharek seized his chance. Another nimble twist of his body, and he was suddenly behind his would-be assassin. Siora flinched as his blade slid across the other man's throat and blood spurted down the front of his tunic. He was dead by the time Gharek let his body drop to the ground.

Her heart surged into her throat when he left the dead man where he lay and bolted toward her, bloodied knife gripped in his hand. He clutched her arm. "Hurry," he said as he pulled her toward the abandoned brothel's door. "That piece of shit will be joined soon enough by his partner." He kicked the partially open door all the way back and hauled Siora inside with him.

The building was an empty shell, a carcass hollowed out by scavengers, its remains left to decay under the ravages of time and the elements. With her eyes now adjusted to the dark, she could make out a few sticks of furniture too rickety for any use other than firewood. Cobwebs garlanded the ceiling and walls, and she caught glimmers of moonlight casting pallid spears through holes in the roof. Dust whispered under her feet and rose in choking clouds as Gharek strode toward a staircase tucked away at one end of the room.

"Pray we find better luck in here than we did out there," he said, and climbed the staircase.

"Where are we going?" She spat out the taste of dust swirling around them.

"This is—was—one of the entrances to the Maesor."

"I thought there was supposed to be a guardian who didn't let people pass without permission." She'd never been here herself, but she'd heard access to the Maesor wasn't given easily or lightly.

"Usually there is, but who knows now."

They reached the last stair and a landing that led to a long corridor. Gharek halted so abruptly that Siora nearly cannoned into his back. The corridor on the second floor reminded her of the layout in the Blue Rat. A long hall with doors on either side. But there the similarities ended. Instead of a wall and discreet servant's stairs at the hallway's other end, she stared at what looked like a hole or doorway punched into the back wall, its edges a rotating ripple of air and its center an open door or gate offering a glimpse of structures and a strangely citrine-colored sky.

"No guardian but still a gate," Gharek said.

A loud bang from the door downstairs made Siora whirl to stare back the way they came. She couldn't see anything, but every nerve in her body sizzled with warning. She glanced at Gharek, who hadn't startled like she had. He raised the hand still gripping the knife. Blood trickled down the blade to ribbon across his knuckles. He raised his index finger and pressed it to his lips to signal silence. She nodded when he pointed to the spinning gate. A faint scrape of a footstep sounded below them. The Maesor ahead of them, a new assassin below them. It wasn't a difficult choice.

Gharek's free hand slid from her arm to clasp her hand. "Run," he mouthed.

They raced down the hall and, without pausing, hurled themselves through the gate. Siora's stomach vaulted into her rib cage at the sudden disorientation, as if some great and invisible hand had flipped her upside down several times, then spun her around and around for good measure. Thank the gods for Gharek's steadying grip or she might have fallen to her knees when they emerged into the Maesor.

"All right?" he asked as she leaned against him for a moment to let her stomach settle.

"I will be."

"Even if you hadn't told me you'd never visited the Maesor, I'd have known it. The gate causes seasickness but only the first time you cross." She wanted to ask him why but didn't get the chance before he pulled her along with him down a long street lined on either side by stalls for as far as the eye could see. "Come. We need to make ourselves scarce in case our pursuer chooses to follow."

They darted into a side avenue. It too revealed more stalls packed with goods that encroached upon the traffic path and hung from tent poles for better visibility. All stood under a yellow sky blanketed in a murky orange haze that no sun shone through. The yellow itself wasn't the warm color of day she was used to but an acidic shade toned down only by the smoky film covering the sky. No sun, no clouds, and as Siora gazed around her at the sprawling Maesor with its black-market sorcerous goods, no people either.

They waited outside an empty stall, watching the gate, which from this side looked to Siora like the rippling surface of a mirror. Instead of showing the corridor of the abandoned brothel, it reflected back the Maesor and its yellow sky.

Gharek stood in front of her, tense, ready to face a second assassin coming through the gate. Several moments passed in funereal quiet but no one emerged from the other side, and the rippling mirror remained undisturbed. He glanced over his shoulder. "I don't think we'll be followed. Someone must have heard the same rumors in Domora's marketplace and chose not to risk a visit."

Siora shivered despite the ambient temperature. Neither hot nor cold here. No sun and no breeze. No people and no sounds except for her and Gharek's voices. Instinct warned her to keep her voice low. "Can you blame them? There's a wrongness here. Do you sense it?"

"Beyond the fact that it's completely empty of people? Yes."

She scanned the many stalls, all full of goods left as if frozen in a moment, nothing ransacked or looted. She'd never seen the like. Even graves weren't safe from thieves. "What happened to everyone?"

Gharek shrugged and stepped out of their hiding place, still keeping a wary eye on the gate. "That is an excellent question and one we can't answer if we linger here." He motioned for her to follow him. "I doubt he's here, but if anyone can tell us what happened, it's Koopman."

They returned to the market's main avenue. The stillness was eerie, a living thing that observed them from every shadowed stall and alley they passed. The hairs on Siora's nape rose and remained standing. She'd faced raging spirits, malevolent ones that made her grateful she'd never met them while they were still living people, battlefields swarming with ghosts, houses crowded with whole families of spirits not yet ready to leave this world—all of these she'd seen and experienced. This though was different, its strangeness making her feel as if something fundamental to her soul had shifted the tiniest bit, changed in a way she didn't understand but definitely didn't like.

They stopped in front of a large, lavish tent. There were no goods displayed at the entrance to entice a customer to step in and see what else the vendor sold, only a plain stool next to a forgotten walking stick.

"A blind guard who saw better than most and his dog always perched here," Gharek said. His mouth thinned to a grim line and Siora's alarm ratcheted even higher when he unsheathed a second knife. "Don't ride my heels. I need the space to fight if needs be," he told her. "But don't wander off."

Gharek slowly eased into the tent, announcing his presence in a casual voice. "Koopman, you've a customer. Your guard's gone missing from his station so I came in."

No one greeted his announcement from the tent's depths. Once Siora's eyes adjusted to the interior's dimness, she got a good look at its contents. This Koopman person was a textiles dealer judging by the number of carpets and tapestries piled on the floor or displayed on hanging racks. Such ordinary goods seemed out of place in a market known for selling demon bowls, curse scrolls, forbidden grimoires, and potions that actually worked.

"Don't touch anything in here," Gharek warned her as they moved cautiously through the shadowed tent.

"Why is a rug merchant selling in the Maesor?" she wondered aloud. As soon as she asked the question, she had her answer. They passed the ragged remains of a tapestry still stretched on a loom, its center exploded outward as if something had burst through it from the other side, snapping warp and weft in its escape.

Trap shadows. She recoiled from the tapestry, and her skin shrank tight against her bones in an effort not to brush against anything in the awful stall. Revolted by her discovery and frightened, Siora was tempted to disregard Gharek's warning and flee outside, leaving him behind to continue his search for a monster who trafficked in enslaved souls.

"I see you're familiar with trap shadows," he said, peering into various alcoves half hidden by beaded curtains or sheer drapery. "A lucrative business for Koopman along with extortion. Outlawing sorcery only made it exceptionally profitable." He stopped to stare at her. "Do you see any ghosts?"

The question brought her up short. She'd been so focused on the newness and strangeness of her surroundings, and the fact no other living person besides her and Gharek occupied the Maesor, she hadn't thought to note if the dead remained. "None, thank the gods," she said. At least she hoped their absence meant those who lingered chose not to do so here in a place scoured clean of anyone. She eyed the tapestry, wondering what happened to the imprisoned soul that managed to break free.

Finally satisfied that Koopman was truly absent instead of hiding from visitors, Gharek gestured for her to return outside. He didn't have to do it twice. Siora led the way, relieved to escape the tent and its vile contents. "Now what?" She hoped they wouldn't visit another stall like this one, though this was the Maesor. The gods only knew what else the merchants here sold, and she doubted demon bowls and potions were unique or that trap shadows represented the worst things traded.

"We check a few more stalls," Gharek said, disappointment etched into his features. "And then we leave. I'm not a scrounger or a mage to know what in these stalls might be of use to us without guidance from the seller. I'd have better luck at the royal library."

How she wished they'd gone there instead of here. She regretted her curiosity concerning the Maesor. No wonder whoever entered the brothel and stalked them chose not to go through the gate. "Do you think your friend Koopman disappeared with the others?"

Gharek snorted. "Koopman was no one's friend, just everyone's source. If that torn tapestry tells the story I think it does, Koopman is dead and his slave souls finally freed." He bent for a closer look at whatever floated in an apothecary's jar on a stand placed outside of a nearby stall. "It's why I asked if you saw any ghosts. The fact you haven't is a good thing."

No sooner had he uttered the words than an unearthly shrieking—horrific enough to freeze the blood in one's veins and one that nearly made Siora jump out of her own skin—shattered the market's stifling silence. A wind that wasn't a wind tore through the stall, snapping curtains aside and knocking over display cases. Invisible, violent, it hurled Siora hard enough against Gharek that he fell backward, taking her with him. Sharp pains tore across her back, as if something raked her with claws. She yelped, then yelped again when the shrieking entity yanked her hair hard enough to wrench her head back and bring tears to her eyes.

Gharek wasn't spared its aggression either. He clapped a hand to his cheek when a bloody line suddenly bloomed along his cheekbone, flesh parting under the same unseen talons that struck Siora.

As quick as the spirit attacked, it retreated with another blood-curdling screech and fled in a small whirlwind of dust. Siora caught a glimpse of it as it spun down one of the deserted alleys, a shifting, warping shape becoming vaguely human with the hint of a face twisted by absolute madness.

She and Gharek watched it until it disappeared and its shrieking died away, leaving only the suffocating silence. He turned to her, the nasty scratch marring his cheek dripping thin lines of blood like the teeth of a hair comb. He smeared the blood away with a swipe of his sleeve. "Are you wounded?"

Her back stung, though she didn't feel any warmth or telltale trickles on her skin. "I think it scratched me too, though not as deeply as you." She touched her scalp. "The hair-pulling hurt worse." She peered down the alleyway where the entity had disappeared. "Was that one of the trap shadows?"

"Most likely." He touched his cheek. "Vicious bastard, yet you can't help but pity them." He frowned at her raised eyebrows. "Anyone with a sense of their own existence would feel sorry for those creatures and pray such a fate would never become theirs."

Siora shook her head. "You always manage to surprise me, lord."

He regarded her for a moment, as if deciding whether or not her reply held some hidden condemnation. She chose not to enlighten him.

Fearing the trap shadow might return for another screeching round of scratching and hair-pulling, Gharek suggested they linger no longer and head back to the gate. "If we hadn't managed to avoid that second assassin, I'd call this a failed endeavor and a waste of our time," he grumbled. "I'd suggest raiding one of the stalls for something to sell, but the risk is too great. The Maesor holds many things that will literally eat you if you're not careful."

More than happy to depart, she hurried alongside him. She desperately wanted to leave but without anything in hand to break wards or help Zaredis's brother, Estred remained at risk and Gharek would surely be executed if the library too offered up nothing. "I hope the library has something," she said.

His features had grown grimmer with every step. "So do I. The records available to the public won't have anything we need, but one of the oldest librarians there was once my mother's lover. He may be able . . ."

Siora's heart knocked hard against her breastbone when Gharek abruptly went silent, clapped a hand over her mouth, and nearly tore her arm off yanking her into the stall behind them. In the semi-gloom, his eyes were wide as they stared into hers, pupils dilated like those of a terrified feline. He pursed his lips in a silent "shh" and, at her nod, eased his hand from her mouth. Body so tense he practically quivered against her, he pointed out furtive movement not far from the gate.

She stared at what he indicated, and her fear turned to horror, the kind that reduced one's knees to water and made your bladder forget to hold its contents. Like the trap shadow, this creature was human in shape but had a solidity to it the trap shadow lacked. The color of bleached bone with misshapen limbs far too long and lanky for its torso, the thing scuttled along the main avenue, pausing randomly to raise a bulbous head and sniff the air.

Only it had no nose. No eyes either, just a wide mouth with fleshy, crimson lips stretched partially over a cage of jagged teeth. The talons tipping its bony fingers looked as lethal as the teeth, with the same purpose of shredding whatever unfortunate victim it caught in its grasp. Those claws dragged across the dirt and cobblestones, making quick skittering noises as they spidered along the wooden supports holding up one of the stalls.

Every survival cue inside her screamed for her to run, yet also kept her frozen in place, barely breathing in case the abomination without ears heard her. Gharek, motionless beside her, had ceased breathing as well.

The thing drew nearer to where they hid, darting in and out of stalls, its movements quick and nimble. Here was the ultimate predator, a thing that made wolves seem like rabbits and lions like sheep, the Spider of Empire a sweet toddler who loved flowers. As it got closer, Siora's eyes blurred with tears and her throat seized closed on a scream. She knew what it was to be the hare under the serpent's stare.

She clenched her jaw to keep the scream in her throat trapped there when a misty shape suddenly took form in front of her. Relief made her knees buckle when she recognized the beloved, familiar wraith standing there.

Papa. If her thought had been voiced, it would have bellowed across the Maesor. Relief instantly changed to fear. *You shouldn't be here.* Whatever this new horror hunting the Maesor was, she suspected it was somehow tied to the eater of ghosts and the two were likely not far from each other.

Take my hand, daughter, so the cat's-paw can see me. Skavol held out his hand, and for the first time in her memory, Siora touched her father's ghost. Next to her, Gharek startled, his body twitching in surprise at the sudden appearance of an apparition in front of them.

Skavol's touch was as cold as Kalun's had been, but his beloved presence blunted the razor's edge of her panic for a moment.

You don't have much time before it reaches this stall. I can distract it. The moment you see your chance, don't hesitate. His phantasmic features hollowed with their own terror. *I won't have my daughter suffer the same fate the Maesor traders did at the hands of that thing.*

His revelation regarding the disappearance of so many, once more sharpened the edge of her panic, made it jagged, but she only nodded. *Thank you, Papa. Be careful.*

Gharek couldn't hear their conversation and Siora didn't dare speak and risk being heard, but he understood both her and Skavol's hand gestures, nodding once. When Skavol let go of her hand, he faded from Gharek's sight but not hers. She held Gharek's arm in preparation of giving the signal for when to run. Her father walked through the stall's fabric wall as if it wasn't there and for a moment the creature continued its inexorable approach to their hiding place.

It suddenly spun on its thin, skeletal legs, making a triumphant chittering sound so reminiscent of what she'd heard in the abandoned barn's provender room that every last hair on Siora's body stood straight up. She spotted her father's shade flitting quicksilver through the labyrinth of streets. The faceless predator spotted him too and bolted toward him in a ground-eating stride.

Gharek didn't wait for her signal. Instead, he shackled her wrist in a bone-cracking grip and nearly lifted her off her feet as he burst out of the stall at a dead run. The gate wasn't far but seemed a continent away. Terror gave her a deer's swiftness and she easily kept up with him as they fled for the gate; an enraged, inhuman cry behind them splitting the quiet.

Gharek's sudden epithet and his order that followed put wings on her heels. "Fuck! There's two of them! Run!"

The chittering screeches had changed to howls, one set directly behind them and another to their left. *Oh gods, oh gods.* The chant clanged in her head, a half-crafted prayer raised from despair, fueled by fear and the primal urge to survive.

She and Gharek leapt through the gate. The strange vertigo didn't plague her this time, but a new, even greater threat faced them. Entering a gate to the Maesor at one place didn't always mean you exited in the same spot. The street they hurtled onto bore no resemblance to one in Domora, nor did the blasted ruins around it.

Their sprint slowed to a jog, and the tightening of Gharek's already hard grip on her wrist told her he was as confused as she was, but only for a moment.

"Gods damn it," he said, not in fury but in despair, and the hopelessness in his voice sent her stomach plummeting to her feet. "We're in Midrigar."

As if saying the cursed city's name out loud conjured more of the repulsive, faceless hunters, a series of feral calls sounded all around them, some closer, some distant, a blood-hungry sound of anticipation as cold as the silvery moonlight plating the remains of the city's towers.

Gharek didn't need to tell her again to run, and this time they raced for another gate, one not created by sorcery but by human hands long dead and then destroyed by an army and its battle mages.

She stumbled when Gharek suddenly gasped and his pace slowed, though he strained to reach the gate. Siora recognized his expression. He'd worn it as Midrigar or whatever was imprisoned inside it cast a sorcerous net over him. She felt it as well, though not as strong, an insistent tugging on her spine and limbs as if some viperous vine tried to coil around her body.

She fought off the sensation, and now it was she who clamped an unyielding grip on Gharek and dragged him with her, fighting his weight and the bewitchment of a malice whose whisper in the mind coiled into her ears and slithered along her backbone.

"Come, meat. I hunger."

Triumphant howling bore down on them, and from the corner of her eye she spotted a pale, faceless hunter sprinting toward them.

Gharek tried to twist out of her grip. "Let go, you stupid girl, and run!" he ordered in a voice slurred as if the ability to speak took monumental effort.

"No!" She pulled even harder, and with a renewed burst of strength, hauled them both through the shattered gate to the other side of the walls.

She slammed hard into an immovable barrier, crushed between it and Gharek, who did the same. They both fell; Siora onto him before she rolled away onto her back. She didn't stay that way, levering herself up on her elbows and squinting as the glow of a raised lamp blinded her for a moment. The enraged screaming of the faceless hunters still cut the night but they remained trapped behind the walls and drew no closer. The eerie pull on her spine lingered, annoying, skin-crawling but no longer so insistent or with the strength of a command as it was for Gharek. Even now he tried to crawl back to the gate but was held down by someone's knee in his back and someone else's grip on his legs.

She blinked until her eyes adjusted to the greater light. Several silhouettes surrounded her and Gharek, their regard focused hard on them. A face came into clear view, lit by the lamp. A familiar face, a human one that hid so much more, and one she never thought she'd see again.

"Malachus?"

CHAPTER SEVEN

C*ome, meat. I summon you.*"

The command boomed inside Gharek's head, and his limbs convulsed with the compulsion to obey. To crawl, to lurch, to sprint back through the gates into the heart of Midrigar, where a dark god, served by pale demons, waited to feast upon him.

He and others had named this entity the eater of ghosts, yet the force of its enchantment on him, the idea of some drooling, ravenous monstrosity eager to snack on him body and soul, made the name a lie. This was an eater of the living as well.

He squirmed in the dirt, pressed down hard by a sharp knee in his back and heavy weights on his shoulders and legs. The far-off sound of voices speaking teased his ears, but deafened as he was by the sonorous command in his head, they were mere unintelligible murmurings.

His jaw locked as the pressure came off his back and he was jerked to his feet. He tried to speak, to beg for help from whoever held him. Tried to say Siora's name and confirm she was uninjured during their race to the gate. Only gibberish squeezed through his clenched teeth, and he twisted in a desperate bid to gain his freedom and race toward his own death.

His captors fought to hold him, and Siora's petite features, limned in lamplight, filled his vision. Her round eyes were wide, soft with a terrible sympathy. Horror too. She said something to him, but he couldn't hear it; his head throbbing from the bewitchment's order beating hard enough to crack his skull.

Some small part of him wondered if she might wield another stick and knock him senseless. He prayed she would. He'd beg her to do so if he could only speak.

The gods were a fickle lot who visited strife and blessings on humanity with unpredictable and puzzling choice. They chose to answer Gharek's prayer in that moment in an ironic manner with a dark-eyed enemy possessing the form and face of a man, but the spirit of a draga.

Malachus stared at him, and it was his voice, flat with dislike, that finally broke through the entity's cacophony. "We meet again, cat's-paw."

A thudding pain struck his chin, snapping his head back. A second punch stopped the entity's voice entirely, and Gharek welcomed the silence and the blackness rushing toward him.

He woke, still in darkness but in open space instead of under a canopy of trees. Above him the vault of a star-filled sky arched toward a limitless distance, vast and quiet.

It was quiet in his head too. No drumming dirge, no roar of demand to obey. His muscles were loose, his spine no longer a bowstring being relentlessly drawn by an unseen archer. His chin and jaw throbbed and his cheek stung. He soon discovered that while he was no longer shackled by sorcery to the eater of ghosts, he was tied to the spokes of a wagon wheel. He'd been given enough rope to move his arms and wiggle into a sitting position if he wished, but not enough to stand.

His life had never been one of ease, even when he lived in his luxurious house funded by his role as the empress's cat's-paw. He'd found himself in more than one bad scrape through the years, but these last several days had been a . . . challenge, and he was growing heartily sick of finding himself knocked unconscious and bound.

He took stock of his surroundings and cursed under his breath. Wagons parked in a semicircle, their brightly painted boards obscured by the night. Even if Gharek hadn't recognized Malachus's stoic visage just before the draga punched him, he'd know by the wagons that he was among free traders. Lucky him.

"You're awake."

Gharek turned his head to find Siora sitting next to him. She'd lost the petrified expression of someone staring into the jaws of a wolf, though she was still pale, even under the soft golden glow of a nearby lamp.

He managed to raise himself to a sitting position with her help. The throbbing in his head no longer came from the sorcerous voice, for which he was grateful. This was probably the first time he was happy to suffer from nothing more than an innocuous headache.

"Where are we?" he asked. His throat felt dryer than a desert. A nearby road ran into the distance, hard-packed earth rutted and pock-marked over time by the roll of cart wheels and the step of hooves.

Siora's fingers combed through his hair, a gentle soothing caress that made him want to lean into her touch. "Just off the trade road between the cursed city and Kraelag," she said. "The forest is on the other side of the wagons. The free traders brought you back to their camp. The ghost-eater's spell doesn't work at this distance."

He wanted to bellow his frustration and offer thanks at the same time. The first, because they were in a worse position and farther away from Domora than when they started out from Zaredis's encampment. His thanks he'd hold back for when he spoke to one of the free traders. They'd likely expect a generous helping of groveling as well. Considering his run of luck so far, it would probably be Malachus he'd have to thank and grovel to. Never before had he found himself in the conundrum of being grateful to someone for punching him in the face, but it had broken the spell that bound him to the eater of ghosts.

"There has to be a better way to break such enchantments than being struck in the head with a tree branch or smashed in the face with a fist," he said, his voice souring as another pain knifed from his face to his temple.

Memories of their flight out of Midrigar filled his mind—his command that Siora leave him behind and her flat refusal to do so. "You are incomprehensible. Why didn't you leave me in the cursed city? That thing with no face almost caught us thanks to the spell. Were you affected too?"

She nodded. "This time, yes, though not nearly as strongly as you. It was just a voice in my head and an itchy tug on my backbone." She stretched her tunic over her knees, hands smoothing out wrinkles. "As for why I saved you, my answer remains the same."

"Estred." The knowledge comforted and stung at the same time.

"And you." Her mouth quirked into a slight smile. "Believe it or not, cat's-paw, you're worth saving."

When she'd turned on him in Domora and helped the draga, Gharek had seen her actions as a betrayal not only of him but of Estred as well. Even when she gave her reasons for doing it, he didn't believe her, couldn't grasp what would move her to plant a knife in his back when he'd offered her home, hearth, and safety in his household. She'd risked his wrath and his vengeance and gave up creature comforts for the streets and possible starvation, then rescued him twice when it benefited her most to let him die. He hadn't wanted her help when she volunteered to accompany him to Domora, undaunted by his antipathy toward her.

All for Estred. A child not her own and whom she'd only met while trying to protect her from a vicious mob. Siora was not his daughter's mother, but for one bright moment of clarity, Gharek wished she was.

That inner revelation altered something inside him, blunted the fury he'd lived with since he reunited with Estred years earlier, broke the splinters and sweetened the bitterness a tiny amount. He was still a man hollowed out by his history and his deeds, but in the abyssal black of his spirit, a light flickered to life—one of guilt, of regret. He didn't try to snuff it out but embraced it where it danced along the edges of his soul and burned the edges of the numbness reigning there. *You're worth saving.*

How wrong Siora was.

"What are you thinking?" Her question held an odd, breathless note.

He didn't know how to answer her and lost his chance when a tall figure strode toward them, backlit by the communal campfire not far behind him. It made him featureless until he stepped into the circle of light spilling from Siora's lamp.

The draga.

Gharek tensed, preparing for another nasty hit to the face or even a more involved beating. He wouldn't take it passively this time. His hands were tied but his feet and legs weren't. He could still do significant damage to an opponent, even if he was outmatched in strength by a draga posing as a man. Malachus, he noted, stayed just out of range when he crouched in front of him.

"I'm not much of a believer in fate," he said, those dark eyes shifting briefly from Siora to pin Gharek once more. "And I've half a mind to think Siora is lying when she tells me she's here with you by choice, cat's-paw, especially considering what I heard you threaten when we last met. It seems, however, our paths were intended to cross again, this time as possible allies instead of adversaries."

"Why in the gods' names would you return to the Krael Empire, draga?" Gharek, along with everyone else who hadn't seen it firsthand, had heard the tale of the draga, a prize to be captured and butchered for the empress. The prize, however, had changed the game on Herself, destroyed battlements and killed Dalvila in a way every bard in the land earned their supper money recounting in taverns these days, then flown away not to be seen since. Or so most believed.

Malachus shrugged. "My family is here, so I'm here." As he made that statement, a woman joined him, and Gharek silently groaned when lamplight shone on her features as well.

Halani. The pretty free trader woman with the round face and melancholy eyes. He'd abducted her mother, Asil, as a hostage and turned Halani over to those who planned to deliver her to the empress as a gift from the cat's-paw. Those gray eyes, like rain clouds, weren't sorrowful now, but steely and utterly unforgiving. "Were it not for the fact I'm not a murderer like you, and that your woman risked everything to help Malachus save my mother, I'd toss you back into the cursed city and rejoice in your death," she said flatly.

"And I'd not blame you," he replied. Her eyes widened for a moment before narrowing with suspicion. "My reasons were misguided, though not based in cruelty for cruelty's sake, as it might have appeared." Her derisive snort and thinning lips told him her opinion of that statement. She thought he tried to cajole her, to justify what he'd done. "I regret few things, but I do regret taking your mother and delivering you up to the empress. I won't ask your forgiveness, as it isn't earned or deserved, but know you have my apology, sincere in every way."

Her obvious contempt didn't lessen, though for a moment a thoughtful gleam entered her eyes before fading away. She turned to Malachus, and Gharek understood why the draga had returned to a land where he was valued for his parts, not their sum. Halani was pregnant, her belly gravid, and the hand she rested lightly on Malachus's shoulder spoke of far more than platonic affection. A half draga child. How extraordinary.

"I won't physick him like I did Siora," she announced. "And I don't want Mama anywhere near him, but I can bring what's needed so that Siora may see to his scrapes."

Malachus's hand brushed across her knuckles, and he abandoned his scrutiny of Gharek to give Halani his full attention and a smile that verified everything Gharek assumed of this pair.

"Even if you offered, I'd convince you otherwise," Malachus told Halani. He gained his feet and motioned for Siora to join the two of them. "Come. You can bring back supplies to tend him." He nodded his chin toward the wagon wheel that kept Gharek tethered. "You run, cat's-paw, and we won't chase you. We'll herd you. Right into Midrigar."

Everyone except Malachus flinched at his casual utterance of the name. The draga rested his hand on the small of Halani's back and left to return to the camp.

Siora rose to follow. "I'll be back with food and something to take care of the cut from the trap shadow."

"It's just a scratch. What about you? The trap shadow targeted you first for its fury."

She smiled. "Halani saw to me. Scratches like yours but not so deep, only more of them. I didn't bleed like you did." Her expression turned somber. "They aren't ghosts. Souls, yes, but they linger as vessels of distilled madness. Nothing of who they once were remains." A shiver shook her small frame, and she retreated to trail after Malachus and Halani.

Gharek studied her back, admiring the grace of her walk and the curves of her body hinted at beneath her clothing. Admiring her kept his thoughts from staying too long on her words.

He'd always found such sorcerous items to be of the darkest sort of magic and repulsive beyond measure. They were the work of necromancers, and while Siora denied possessing that kind of power, he suspected she had within her the ability to wield it. She'd recoil if she heard his thoughts and vehemently argue with him. She was a compassionate woman motivated by a moral code he was just beginning to understand and would never fully embrace himself. She'd never do anything remotely as horrifying as enslaving a soul, especially as a trap shadow. *Unless she was made desperate enough*, the cynical part of him countered.

"Gods forbid she ever find herself in such straits," he said softly.

They lived in a world where life was hard, brutal, and often very short, and even death didn't guarantee peace or an escape. He wanted to believe that another person beyond his own daughter might retain the one element snuffed out in him and so many others: hope.

She returned alone, carrying a loaded tray, and set it down next to him. Gharek scowled. "No one offered to help you?"

Siora paused in unloading a covered plate, a small pot of ointment, and another flask of what he hoped this time might be wine or ale. She left the stack of neatly folded cloths, a second flask, and a basin in the tray. Her eyebrows climbed toward her hairline. "Of course they offered, though it wasn't necessary. I'm no delicate aristo woman. Asil was the first to offer help. I declined." She handed him a spoon and whipped away the cloth covering the plate to reveal a few pieces of cured meat, roasted squash, a hunk of bread, and a generous wedge of cheese. "I don't need someone to carry a supper tray for me." Her chin went up. "I'm stronger than I look, lord."

"No argument there," he said. "But stop calling me *lord*."

Darker shadows stained her cheekbones. "What shall I call you then? I've heard *bastard* and *arsewipe* used a number of times by those who've spoken of you." She winked at him and resumed her seat beside him. The odd look of cautious wonder he'd seen dance across her features at his disapproval that no one helped her with the tray reappeared before she hid it behind a studied mask of casual interest.

He gave in to a half smile at her teasing. The answer to her question might seem obvious to some, but he'd never allowed the use of his given name by those whom he employed or those with whom he did business. Most didn't even know his name. He was the cat's-paw. "Gharek," he said. "Just Gharek." He was no longer the cat's-paw, though the stain of that title would mar his soul throughout his life and beyond death. But he'd been something other than splinters and bitterness once, something better than a mad sovereign's henchman.

"Gharek then." Siora tucked her legs under her. "I've always thought it a good name."

"Just not for a good man."

"Your words, not mine. I don't believe a person is irredeemable."

He snorted. "You obviously never met the Spider of Empire."

They sat in companionable silence while he ate, and when he finished, she took his plate and returned it to the tray, trading out dish and spoon for cloths and washbasin. She handed him the smaller of the two flasks and kept the larger one for herself. "Yours has plum wine. Kursak swears it's the drink of the gods."

Gharek opened the flask and took a sniff of fruit and strong alcohol fumes. This was the kind of wine that kindled a fire in your gut with the first swallow. He'd have to be sparing and not drink too much. No doubt when Siora was done coddling him, Malachus or one of the other free traders would fetch him for a friendly interrogation. He refused to endure the ordeal cupshot. "Who's Kursak?" He took a drink from the flask and gasped.

Siora poured water from the larger flask into the basin and dipped a cloth in it. "One of the wagon masters for this free trader band." She wrung the cloth until it was just damp and pressed it to the scratch the trap shadow had inflicted. Gharek hissed at the sting. "I spoke with him and Malachus and the others while you were . . . sleeping." Once more a smile curved her mouth; her hands were gentle on his face as she tended what he guessed was an impressive new bruise decorating his cheekbone. "You're still handsome," she teased.

He stilled under her touch. There was about her an honesty that cut deep when she judged, and she judged him often since they'd become allies in this endeavor. Yet her simple compliment, so casually offered and without any coyness, cut deepest of all. He clasped her hand and stole the cloth. "I'll finish. Did they tell you why they were right outside the gates of the cursed city?"

If he didn't know better he might have believed hurt flickered in her eyes when he took the cloth. Trick of the lamplight no doubt. She didn't offer to apply the salve to the scratch and passed the jar to him in silence.

"They told me a little," she finally said. "They were retrieving Asil, who'd tried to follow her brother into Midrigar." Shadows flitted in her eyes. "She said it looked like someone was pulling him toward the gate with an invisible rope. Asil has a dog who barred her from following. Thanks to the dog, the free traders were able to save her. It was too late for the brother." She paled. "Like you, he was compelled by the eater of ghosts. But why?"

A sick feeling settled like a stone in the bottom of his stomach, and the rising nausea made him wish he hadn't eaten. Other living people enchanted and forced to answer a dark summons. Somehow the Maesor was connected to Midrigar. What if the living that were forced to answer the ghost-eater's summons were those who'd visited the Maesor? Did business there? Even lived there for months? Was this why it was an empty place now? Did those people try to resist and escape through the gate to the safety of Domora only to find themselves in Midrigar? Or had the faceless hunters descended on the market and ravaged its population without warning? Gharek didn't think the second scenario occurred. The market would have been made a shambles by fighting or even by the stampede of terrified people fleeing the creatures with their bloodred mouths and jagged teeth.

He took another swallow of the plum wine and passed it to Siora. "I don't know, but I have a suspicion."

She accepted and, like him, gasped after swallowing. "Obviously the gods enjoy strong nectar," she managed to wheeze, and wiped her watering eyes.

"Careful how much you drink," he said. His tolerance for strong spirits was high but already the fuzzy creep of languor threatened to dull his senses. "Once more you kept the wolves from my door. I don't much care for a long sojourn in the cursed city, even if the free traders plan to stretch my neck from the nearest tree."

"You aren't in good standing with them as you well know, but I don't think they plan to kill you. Yet."

"You're a woman of enduring hope, Siora." Gharek closed the flask and set it aside. "We'll need their help if we want to return to Domora in any decent time. We've lost at least a day and a night of the time Zaredis gave us. Time moves differently in the Maesor. We'll lose more if we can't get a horse." Panic bubbled inside him at the thought. They had nothing beyond his own confirmation of the Windcry's location and how to get to it through a series of hidden doors and corridors in the palace only he and Herself knew. At least for now. Whoever Zaredis sent to steal the artifact celebrated for its ability to shatter fortress walls, they'd find it easy enough with the cat's-paw's directions, but at the moment the

Windcry was going nowhere unless they found a way to break the wards protecting it.

A vision of Estred filled his mind. Dainty features with his wide cheekbones and her mother's long lashes and blue eyes. She'd started life in the grimmest way, born deformed, abandoned, then sold and used as an oddity to titillate and coax money out of curious crowds. Yet she'd taken none of her mother's despair or her father's ruthlessness as her own. She saw joy in everything, even a mob intent on killing her—because that close brush with death had brought Siora into their house.

Estred had been inconsolable when she'd discovered Siora had left suddenly and without a word. The child who smiled even during the grayest hours hadn't smiled for weeks. That more than anything had lit the fire of resolve, even greater than his personal vengeance, in Gharek. He still simmered with resentment, but that fire burned less hot as he came to know the shade speaker and parse out her motivations. She puzzled him mightily, but he no longer hated her. In fact, he'd . . .

He backed away from the path of his musings. He was involved in this tangle of problems with her for Estred's sake. They worked together for the common goal of getting his daughter back from Zaredis safe and sound. That was all. Nothing more. He simply had to stay alive long enough to accomplish the task—an unexpected challenge so far. Zaredis would still execute him and Estred would become an orphan yet again, but he was a man, not a god. He could only tackle one disaster at a time and do his best to prevail.

The weight of his money purse still rested solid against his chest where he'd tucked it securely in his tunic. "I can't believe I still have the *belshas* Zaredis gave us."

Siora sighed. "They're free traders, lor— Gharek, not thieves."

He scoffed. "Free traders are known to sidle off with things that don't belong to them, and they make no distinction in whom they steal from, living or dead. Those grave goods we've all seen at markets? Take a guess as to who's the biggest provider of such wares." She recoiled at his words. He was overly suspicious and she wasn't suspicious enough. "Don't tell me that as a beggar you never stole? Or as a shade speaker you didn't lie to a customer about their dead relative?" Her crimson blush told him what he wanted to know. "As I thought." He shrugged. "They've been kinder to me than I deserve and far more generous than I would have been were our places reversed. I don't judge them for their actions; my own are blacker by far. I just don't pretend they're virtuous."

"You have your own brand of honesty, I think," she said. "Though it bludgeons like a club."

"I've never boasted of possessing charm or even subtlety." He tapped his finger against his lip, thinking. "We'll probably have to sleep in the fields and on the streets, and go hungry for a day or two, but we need a horse more than we need lodgings, and free traders always have horses to sell and trade." If they didn't try to skive him too hard, he'd have just enough *belshas* to purchase a mare or gelding still on the right side of a knacker's cart.

"Let me ask them," Siora said, giving him a strange look, as if he'd grown a third eye when he suggested negotiating for a horse. "I'm not sure they'd sell your own head back to you."

She wasn't wrong, and he nodded his agreement. They slipped back once more into a comfortable silence, and Gharek tried to remember when another adult's company was this soothing. A thought occurred to him. "Was that your father's ghost who appeared to us in the Maesor and lured those things without faces away from us?"

Siora nodded, worry lines marring her forehead. "Yes. I hope the ghost-eater didn't sense him."

"Can you summon him to make certain?"

She shook her head. "Remember? Ghosts don't come at a shade speaker's command or even request. They reach out to us first. If my father's spirit thrives, I'll know sooner or later." She tried to disguise the doubt in her voice, but he heard it just the same.

He recognized the ploy to distract herself from worrying over her father when she said, "Tell me of your search through the palace. What does the fabled Windcry look like, and why do you think the royal library will have what we want when the Maesor doesn't?"

Gharek rested his bound hands on his knees, twisting his ropes gently in an attempt to loosen the knots. "The Windcry isn't much bigger than a child's toy and even less impressive in appearance. Its majesty comes from the sorcery embedded in it, and if stories of its power hold true, it will win Zaredis the throne if he can get his hands on it. Those who guard it now are soldiers loyal to General Tovan and have no familiarity with the palace's many hidden accesses. Getting past them to where the Windcry is will be easy. Breaking the wards keeping it safe from thieves is something else entirely."

"And you think the library has something that tells of how to break them?"

"I'm certain of it." But like the Windcry's wards, finding the tome containing a ward-breaking spell could prove daunting. "The royal library has thousands of scrolls and parchments, grimoires and maps, most forgotten by scholars and gathering dust. It would take a hundred lifetimes to find a single book if we attempted it ourselves without help, but there's a master librarian there whose memory is a vast storehouse and who can pull a scroll or book from the most forgotten corner and tell you its contents. He won't have the knowledge that Koopman did about how I can get my hands on a good grimoire, but he'd know how to choose several that, combined, might serve the same purpose."

"And he isn't one of the many trying to kill you?" That brief smile made an appearance once more before fading. Gharek almost asked her to smile again, then shuddered inwardly at the temptation.

"Surprisingly no," he said in his blandest voice. "Let's hope it stays that way for a long time."

Manaran had been one of his mother's many lovers, a scholar of note and reputation who'd given Gharek his first taste of the wonders inside the royal library. Gharek hadn't been much older than Estred was now and he possessed the same curiosity and love of books. Unfortunately, like others who shared his mother's bed and fleeting affections, Manaran hadn't endeared himself to her for long, and Gharek's visits to the library became few and far between. He'd still see the squinty-eyed scholar on occasion when he chose to leave the library and his role as master archivist there to engage with the everyday world. Gharek hadn't spoken to Manaran in three years. He hoped the old man remembered him and would be inclined to help.

Siora piled the tray with his plate and the healing supplies

Halani had sent, promising to return straight away. She didn't but Malachus did.

The draga bent and untied the ropes binding Gharek's hands. "Piss if you need to, then come with me. Siora's waiting by the communal fire and the rest of us want to talk to you."

Gharek stood and rubbed his wrists together. "You trust me not to run?"

Malachus made a scoffing sound, and Gharek swore he saw a tendril of smoke escape the other man's nostril. "I don't trust you at all, but if Siora is speaking true, and I don't have reason to doubt her, you need us more than we need you. You won't run."

Sound reasoning, and neither Gharek nor his bladder were eager to sprint off into the night with only the placement of stars to keep him in the general right direction. He took Malachus up on his offer of time to answer nature's summons and returned without a fuss.

The two men walked side by side to the camp's main fire, where a crowd of free traders sat waiting for them. Gharek wasn't sure if this was an audience or an impromptu tribunal. All eyes landed on him as he stood just outside the circle. Siora, sitting next to Halani, stood and claimed a spot on his other side—a wordless signal to all that she supported him of her own accord.

Malachus made the introductions. "This is the man who kidnapped Asil and held her hostage, and the one who sent Halani to the palace where she was imprisoned and used as bait by the empress to gain my cooperation." His voice was matter-of-fact in relaying the information, lacking any drama or embellishment. The crowd snarled in unison, like one great beast whose hackles just rose as it prepared to rend Gharek limb from limb. Beside him, Siora made an alarmed squeaking sound.

Malachus continued. "Siora has said they were adversaries and are now allies. She betrayed the cat's-paw to help me find Asil and bring her home."

Unlike the unified snarl Gharek received, a smattering of applause and cheers greeted that statement, and a childish voice rose above it all. "Thank you, ghost woman!"

Gharek followed the voice's direction and was startled to see not a child but the old woman Asil. In all the time she'd been in his clutches, he'd never heard her speak, and the young voice paired with the wizened face was startling. Even more startling was the dog lying next to her in a protective pose, head up, ears forward as it watched the crowd. Gharek recognized the cur. It had once helped a blind man who saw too much guard the entrance to Koopman's tent in the Maesor.

Siora smiled and bowed to Asil. She didn't reply but her gaze traveled to Malachus on Gharek's other side, half hopeful, half pleading.

Malachus continued. "They want to buy a horse from us and ride to Domora. They have money to pay."

"We don't necessarily have a horse to sell."

The rebuttal came from a man standing on the opposite side of the circle, a fearsome sort who probably did the job of camp guardian when the draga couldn't.

Siora leaned close to Gharek and whispered, "That's Kursak. The wagon master I mentioned earlier."

He sighed inwardly. Of the many free trader bands traveling

this road, why did it have to be this particular one he and Siora literally ran into outside of Midrigar?

Kursak cut across the circle's center, skirting the fire until he stopped a few steps from where Gharek and Siora stood with Malachus. "I'd hang you by your own entrails if it were solely up to me, cat's-paw, but it isn't. That being said, I won't sell you a dirty stocking until I hear how you ended up in the cursed city and why." He gestured to Siora. "She's told us some, but I want to hear your version of the tale."

And catch me in a lie, Gharek thought. He hid a smile. He was familiar with this game, played by one far more formidable than this wagon master. Dalvila always listened for the lie in any conversation she exchanged with her minions, courtiers, and any unlucky bastard who gained her attention. Her ear for a falsehood had been honed to an accuracy comparable to that of a hound with a scent. Gharek played the game and played it well. He was, after all, still alive to play it again.

He pointed to the dog beside Asil. The cur's lips peeled back in a silent snarl. "I know that dog. It once guarded the stall of a man named Koopman. Koopman sold tapestries and carpets in the Maesor. Trap shadows." Gasps and a visible recoil undulated through the crowd of listeners. "Koopman wasn't just a Maesor merchant. He was *the* Maesor merchant. No one did business there without his approval, and he was the person you went to first if you were hoping to broker deals with wealthy clients for rare magical artifacts or even to sell something as uninteresting as a love potion."

"Like a mother-bond," Malachus said in dry tones.

Gharek nodded. "Just so. We hoped Koopman could help us.

Something is roaming these lands, something that doesn't belong in this world at all, and its power is spreading ever farther out from its source in Midrigar. Some are calling it an eater of ghosts, but it hunts the living as well." If tension possessed true weight, it would be an anvil. He felt the crowd hold its collective breath as he spoke. "Siora told you of what she's witnessed so far? Of Kalun and what the ghost-eater did when it appeared in the woodland and later in the general's camp? Of what it left behind in a rotting barn?" At the many nods and wide-eyed stares, he continued. "Zaredis is holding my daughter as a hostage to make certain I give him information I possess about the palace. Accurate information, current information." He caught sight of Halani's expression, a strange dichotomy of sympathy for his daughter and of knowing triumph that fate had meted out an ironic kind of repayment. Gharek could almost hear Halani's thoughts. *Now you know how it feels, cat's-paw.*

He did know, and it was an awful thing. But it wasn't new to him. He'd lived with the consuming desperation and fear since Estred was a toddler. It threatened to overwhelm him every day, sometimes every hour. Toss in a generous helping of guilt, and it was a poisoned soup of despair and foolish decisions predicated by terror. He bowed briefly to Halani in acknowledgment of the hard hand that was poetic justice.

"Siora," he said, "bargained with Zaredis as well. Help for the ghost of his twin brother. She'd try to find a way to protect him from the ghost-eater in exchange for my child's continued safety."

He told them of his plan to either hire Koopman or scour the royal library to find a spell book that could block the eater of souls, a book of wards if possible. Anything that might prevent the entity from attacking again and making off with more of the helpless dead, including Kalun and Siora's father. He described the trap shadow and fleeing through the market for the gate with a scarlet-mouthed creature hard on their heels, of racing through that gate only to find themselves in Midrigar, leagues away from Domora. He mentioned nothing about the Windcry and prayed Siora hadn't either. If she had and anyone questioned why he excluded it from his narrative, he had an explanation prepared, a twist of these words, an assumption inadvertently made that wasn't inadvertent at all.

When he finished, silence descended among the group with only the background noise of livestock and the crackle of burning wood in the fire to emphasize it. The wagon master stared at Gharek for several moments before shifting attention to Malachus. "They match," he said.

Malachus nodded. "Agreed, though I'm curious." Gharek tensed when the draga turned to him. "Why do you think the Maesor was abandoned? And what do you think makes you or others more susceptible to this ghost-eater's bewitchment when many aren't affected at all? We had to hold you down to keep you from flying back into the city and certain death. We lost Asil's brother to the city and would have lost Asil as well if it wasn't for the dog." All eyes shifted to Halani's mother, who embraced the hound and kissed the top of its head.

Gharek had asked himself that question when the enchantment had seized him the first time. It made little sense that one living person was unable to resist it while another had no sense of the compulsion at all. Twice he'd been in the vicinity of Midrigar, netted like a fish each time by the sorcery waiting there. Siora, on the other hand, felt nothing the first time and only a hint the second.

One explanation had bounced around in his mind when they'd discovered the Maesor empty, and he'd grown more sure of its validity even if there were some holes in the reasoning that still needed puzzling out.

"The eater of ghosts compelled us. Of that I'm certain. Why me and Asil's brother and not someone else, I can only guess. I believe the Maesor is the key connecting us." He had the free traders' rapt attention now. "Somehow, the sorcery used to create the Maesor itself also created a corridor to the cursed city. I think it's the gates that did it. The Maesor is a wedge forced between the reality of two or more worlds, and the gates are how people cross from one to the other. We assumed the Maesor opened only onto this world, but what if we're wrong? What if there are gates we don't know about? Tears even, from which something beyond our knowledge or understanding has slithered through and now hunts?"

Saying the words aloud made them more real, so much so that the hairs at his nape rose. Siora shivered beside him.

"I've had business dealings in the past with Maesor vendors who acquire their illegal goods from those they call koops, who make a living at scavenging the cursed city for artifacts. It's dangerous work. The koops who make it out alive after such forays often say the city feels as if it only hovers in our world or floats like a boat without an anchor. There's always a sense of being watched, of feeling the breath of something on their back yet finding nothing behind them when they turn to see." He and Siora had run for their lives through Midrigar, so he hadn't lingered long enough to sense anything other than the entity's compulsion and his own terror.

Malachus added his opinion. "They're right. When you glimpse

Midrigar from the corner of your eye, it has a murk about it and a translucence to its edges, as if it were a rotting blanket and the weft is separating from the warp until it falls apart."

"The earth is poisoned there," Halani said. Others nodded in agreement.

"Maesor," Gharek said, "is an ancient word meaning *in between* and it has that same sensation of floating. All who've traded there know it to be a creation fashioned from the twisting and manipulation of sorcery. There's no life in the market beyond those who buy and sell within its confines. No trees or fields, no rain or breeze. No sun even or day and night. Only an orange and yellowish sky that never changes."

Siora had sidled ever closer to him, and he reached behind her to grasp her tunic and nudge her against him. He spared her a glance. Her eyes were wide and dark with the memory of her first and hopefully last trip to the sorcery market.

"Things hunt there now," he told the crowd. "Creatures that chased us through the Maesor and also in the cursed city. The two places are tied together, and I think the eater of ghosts reigns over both. The dead have no defense against it, nor do the living who've visited either or both places." He gestured to Asil's dog, who again responded with a silent snarl. "Except maybe the dog. I think its last master met his end." He addressed Malachus directly. "I know that Asil and her brother visited the Maesor when he tried to sell your mother-bond. I think that's why they fell under the entity's enchantment. It's the connection the thing uses to reel in its living victims if they get close enough to either place. I think that's why you found them outside Midrigar."

The free traders shuddered to a man. Gharek risked speaking

to Asil directly, ignoring Halani's glare. "Did you hear a voice speak to you inside your head, madam?"

Asil nodded, and the words she recited in that childish voice were bone-chilling. "'Come, meat. I hunger.'"

Horrified murmurs of "Gods save us" and other similar remarks echoed through the group. Halani wrapped one arm around her mother's shoulders and pulled her close. She stared across the circle at Malachus. Gharek could only guess at the wordless conversation between them, but he was sure it likely echoed Kursak's sharp orders.

The wagon master clapped his hands twice. "No sleeping," he barked. "We're out of here as soon as we have the fire quenched, the pots packed, and the animals harnessed. Get moving!" He'd barely finished issuing the order before people scattered, hurrying in every direction to obey, eddying around Gharek, Siora, and Malachus like a fast-moving stream.

The draga eyed him with a curious mix of suspicion and admiration. "Good thing you aren't welcome among us or Halani might find her place as the camp's storyteller usurped in no time."

Gharek found the comment odd but didn't get the chance to ask what Malachus meant. The free traders broke down their camp with impressive speed. A life on the road rarely guaranteed long-term safety, and free traders were only tolerated in most places and fiercely unwelcome in others. No doubt this camp and others like it were practiced at pulling up stakes and leaving in a hurry when things turned unfriendly.

He and Siora stayed out of the way until Kursak returned, leading a muscular gelding, saddled and bridled. Halani walked beside him, holding a bulging pack. She passed it to Siora. "To replace what you lost in the Maesor," she said, her smile lighting her gray eyes. "Enough supplies for two days. There are also two blankets tied to the saddle." She squeezed Siora's hands. "I've thanked you before but will do so every time I'm fortunate enough to cross your path. You helped my mother, who's most beloved and not just by me." Her features hardened when her gaze landed on Gharek. "My words for you are unkind, so I won't speak them except to say I'll pray for your daughter's safety. Too many of the innocent suffer for the sins of the corrupt."

Once more regret sat like a stone on his spirit. He bowed low to her. "I thank you for those prayers. And you're right." What more could he say beyond an echo of his apology, and he'd always known that no forgiveness would come from that quarter. He didn't resent her for its lack. In her place, he'd be far less sanguine.

Kursak held out his hand to Gharek, not in farewell but to demand payment for the horse. When he quoted the amount, Gharek grimaced but emptied out the required number of coins from his money purse into Kursak's palm. It left him just enough to fund a bribe and buy a loaf of bread. Thank the gods for Halani's generosity or he and Siora would have to cinch their belts a little tighter during the last part of their journey.

"Goodbye, ghost woman," Asil yelled as she skipped toward them.

Halani sighed and turned to head off her mother. "No need to shout, Mama. Go back and help pack the camp. I already told Siora goodbye for both of us."

Asil nimbly avoided Halani's grasp, the petulant jut of her lower lip warning her daughter she had no intention of obeying. "You might have told her, but I haven't." She grasped Siora's hand.

"Goodbye, ghost woman," she said before swiftly looping a woven cord over Siora's head. "A charm of good health and good earth." Her fingers pressed the tiny clutch of dried flowers and beads attached to the cord against her rescuer's breast. "A gift for you."

Siora folded her hand over Asil's and gave a squeeze. "Thank you, Asil. I will treasure it forever as well as the moment I finally heard you speak."

Asil stepped back, switching her regard to Gharek, who for the first time in his recollection found it difficult to meet someone's eye. The child-woman regarded him, unsmiling now, and there was about her scrutiny the judgment of one far older and wiser. "Do you love your child, cat's-paw?"

The sudden mature tone and the question itself startled not only him but Halani and Kursak as well.

"I do," he replied. "More than life itself. She's everything to me. The reason I still breathe." Even if he didn't still hope. Siora's hand rested on his arm, a reassuring touch, though he didn't take his eyes off Asil.

She maintained that same measuring regard, a different woman altogether in that moment. "Then do better. Make her as proud to be your daughter as you are to be her father."

Siora's fingers tightened on his arm. Gharek struggled for a reply that would do justice to such straightforward wisdom that allowed no excuses and took no prisoners. "You're wise, madam. I can't remake the past but know I'm truly sorry for what I did to you and Halani."

She sniffed. "Just don't do it again or to someone else," she said, and the youthful timbre had once more returned to her voice.

"I won't."

Halani didn't look nearly as convinced of Gharek's sincerity as her mother did. "You've said goodbye, Mama. Let them go. They have a long ride back to Domora." She coaxed Asil back toward the wagons and the hive of activity there.

Gharek helped Siora onto the horse's back first, then mounted behind her. Malachus had joined Kursak to see them off. He gave their gear a last check before stepping back. "You won't lose much time riding double. Suti here is a solid mount, and Siora isn't much bigger than that satchel Halani packed for you, so it won't stress the horse." He studied them for a moment without speaking. "I'm glad you didn't kill Siora when you found her."

He and Kursak both grinned when Gharek and Siora said in unison, "So am I."

Gharek reined the horse toward the road, Siora's slight frame hot against his chest. He didn't mind. In fact, he savored it. A thought occurred to him, and he nudged the horse back to where the two men stood watching. "Before I go, draga, tell me something."

A shuttered expression passed over Malachus's features and he visibly stiffened, as if he knew what Gharek was about to ask and braced for it. "What is that?"

"How did the Spider of Empire taste?"

Kursak guffawed loud enough to make others in the camp turn and stare. Malachus's sigh was long and pained. He pinched the bridge of his nose with finger and thumb and closed his eyes for a moment. "I hear this question in my dreams sometimes," he said in a resigned voice. He opened his eyes to settle a wry gaze on

Gharek. "I wouldn't know. I didn't eat the empress." He pointed to the road. "I suggest you don't delay before I change my mind about what I prefer for supper and put cat's-paw on my plate."

Siora shook against Gharek with silent laughter. He held back his own amusement, gave a nod of farewell, and turned the gelding onto the road leading back to Domora.

He kept the horse at a canter, with breaks into an easy trot so as not to fatigue the animal. The moon was bright enough for now to see any obstacles or pitfalls in the road, but the clouds thickened above them, dimming that brightness. They'd have to stop soon. He was disappointed but traveling in heavy darkness risked riding over dangerous ground and laming the horse he'd just bought with almost every *belsha* in his possession. He relayed the news to Siora.

Instead of a protest, she offered a suggestion. "There's a well-used drover path not far from here and a wet-weather stream just off the path with shelter in the trees and grazing for the horse. We'll need to leave at first light or keep company with herders and their livestock."

She continuously surprised him. "You've camped here before?"

Siora nodded. "Many times when I was younger. My mother and I moved from village to village to shade-speak. Often it was safer to camp than stay in a town and sleep on the streets. Sleeping in a tavern or its stable was too expensive most of the time anyway. The place I mention was one of our favorite spots."

He followed her direction, guiding the horse into a section of overgrown pasture dotted with clusters of trees tangled in underbrush but still passable enough for the horse to navigate without struggle. They found the stream Siora described and a place to camp under the lacy drape of a willow tree's branches.

Gharek took care of the horse, tethering him on a long lead rope to graze nearby and drink from the stream. He brought saddle and horse blanket with him to where Siora set up their camp for the evening. It wasn't the comforts he'd seen in the free trader encampment, but it was a huge improvement from the bare ground and knotted ropes that was the hospitality Zaredis had offered.

He laid the saddle blanket on the ground. His legs would hang off its edge, but it served to keep his back and flanks dry while he slept. He stepped aside to let Siora spread the blankets Halani had given them onto the saddle blanket. She smoothed the wrinkles with small hands and brushed her palms together, satisfied with her efforts. Her mouth turned down in a small frown. "Are you willing to share? It's wide enough for both of us." Her question carried a hint of challenge as if she waited for him to say no, in which case she'd most likely tell him he was more than welcome to enjoy his bed of grass then.

Gharek chuffed and allowed a smile to curve his mouth. "I don't know why you bothered asking. It isn't as if we haven't done this before."

He looked forward to it. Her presence was greater than her physical size and offered a comfort he hadn't known before. When they'd shared the bed in the brothel, he'd wakened to her pressed to his back, her arm draped over his torso so that her hand dangled just below his chest. Gharek had lain still for longer than he should have, savoring the press of her body against his, watching that delicate hand, browned by the sun and marred with scrapes and scratches. Two of her nails were broken, one nearly to the quick, and he'd struggled against the temptation to lift that hand and bring her injured finger to his lips.

She hadn't wakened when he eased out of the bed and quietly dressed. Nor had he commented on their closeness as they'd slept. He'd told her nothing then and said nothing now of those oddly sweet moments or his hope that he might experience them again in the brief hours they waited out the night under the willow tree.

They sat together on the blanket and shared a few of the food-stuffs Halani had packed in the satchel she'd given to Siora. Gharek had no doubt she would disapprove of Siora sharing with him, but he was grateful for the food.

He peeled an orange, handing half to Siora. "Still no visit from your father?"

Her eyes glossed with tears for a moment before she blinked them away. "No, though I truly believe I'd know or sense if he were in jeopardy. Whatever those creatures were roaming the Maesor, they aren't a danger to ghosts even if they serve a more dangerous master's will. The living though . . ." She shuddered.

Gharek understood the fear too well. His mind went back several times to the creature stalking the now empty Maesor, the weirdly extended limbs and featureless face except for the crimson stain of a mouth with its eel teeth. Worst of all was the sound it made; a whispering, chittering noise hovering just above a background gurgle, as if rats had chewed their way out of a bubbling fountain of blood. The sound was the fuel of any nightmare and sure to haunt his worst ones for many nights to come.

The last tendrils of silvery light that turned the nearby stream into a metal ribbon disappeared behind a swath of clouds. The night turned black enough to cut with a knife, and he no longer saw Siora beside him. The gelding snuffled nearby as it leisurely grazed on the lush grass growing around them. The willow sighed a lullaby. It was another world compared to the seething tension of a crowded Domora as it waited for an inevitable siege or the silent horror of the Maesor with its otherworldly wolves and only the memory of those who once traded there. For a moment, Gharek wished he might never leave the tree's shelter but stay enrobed in its green peacefulness with the stream's laughter to serenade him and a small woman of unshakable fortitude and steadfast honor to keep him company. There were nightmares like Midrigar but dreams like this as well.

He lay on his back and stretched out his legs, lacing his fingers behind his head, and stared into the tree's shifting shadows above him. The rustle and twitch of blankets next to him told him Siora was settling down as well. He couldn't see her, but even if she'd made no noise, he'd have known she was there. Her presence tickled the edges of his spirit as much as it thrummed along his skin.

Her voice was soft, close. "Why did you ask me if I had children?"

The question puzzled him until he recalled their previous conversation when she wondered why he'd go to such lengths to change Estred instead of accepting her as she was. It might have been no more than curiosity on her part, but a part of him had sniffed out its underlying criticism, its judgment. He'd bristled instantly and lashed out at her.

Hers was a hard question to answer because it forced him to reveal a part of his history, what he viewed as his failure as a husband and a father. He was a private man by nature, happier to cut out his own heart, or at least the heart of the nosy person who dared intrude on that privacy, before offering a sliver of information. Shame and the loss of hope burdened him, along with an icy rage that hollowed him out year by year, hour by hour. If not for Estred, he'd be more dead than the ghosts Siora spoke to and saw. *Tell her*, a small voice coaxed in his mind. *Tell someone.*

He blessed the obscuring darkness, afraid of what he might see once he told her what she wanted to know.

"If servant gossip didn't already inform you, Estred's mother left Estred in her sister's care, walked out of the house, and never returned. I was a soldier in the Kraelian army at the time, serving in General Ceder's battalions. We saw many battles in the Huzuran Archipelago. My wife, Tanarima, was pregnant when the general marched and then sailed us to conquer the islands. I didn't return home until a few years later, when Estred was three. I found our hovel occupied by someone else and no idea where my wife and daughter had gone or if they were even alive."

"The servants only spoke to me when necessary. How did you find Estred?" Her voice was a caress as seductive as her touch.

History was a merciless taskmaster, its memories more brutal than any Maesor wolf. "I found Tanarima's sister, Odigan, first. As poor as we were, she was in worse straits. She had six children of her own and had been made a widow shortly after Tanarima left Estred with her."

A soft gasp and then, "That's a huge burden placed on anyone's shoulders. Poor woman. Was Estred cared for?"

He smiled in the dark, even as recollections best left buried hammered into him. She offered sympathy to his wife's sister. It had taken years for his own hatred for both women to chill to indifference. "Estred wasn't there. I think Odigan almost followed her unfortunate husband into the deathlands from fright when she found me standing on her doorstep wanting answers as well as my daughter. I was a different man then. Were I then what I am now, I would have snapped her neck once I learned what she'd done."

"What did she do?"

The dark revealed a great deal in a voice, and he didn't mistake the underlying dread weaving through Siora's now. Old fury he thought snuffed out after so much time threatened to reignite within him. "She sold Estred to a grind show for a nice sum. It seems my daughter's lack of arms made her into what's known as an animal-girl. Exotic, not quite human. I don't think I slept more than an hour a night for six months as I searched the Empire for that show. I finally found it. They kept Estred in a cage. Either she learned on her own or someone had taught her to eat with her feet and play a few notes on a whistle with her toes."

"Oh, Estred." Siora's voice had thickened with tears. "I am so sorry." Neither of them said anything, and while Gharek didn't remember what it was like to shed tears, he listened to Siora's sniffles and sorrowed inside. "I've heard her," she finally said on a warble. "She played for me a time or two. I thought you taught her that skill."

"No. I only encouraged it. Something bright should come from such darkness." And the darkness nearly drowned him then. "The show master made up some crazed story of how Estred was the whelp of a sailor and a snake woman. They'd painted scales on her skin and taught her to wriggle on her belly like a serpent. The crowds loved her. I tried to buy her from the show master but he refused to sell her. I then offered myself in exchange. He used me for a night, then threw me out of the encampment without Estred." Her hand on his arm offered comfort, but he jerked away from her touch, horrified at the idea she might find him pathetic. "Save your pity," he snapped. "I'd fuck every Kraelian soldier from the piss bucket boys to the generals themselves if it meant keeping Estred safe. I think that might be why Herself never showed interest, though she sometimes complimented me. For her, sex was power and power was subjugation. As her cat's-paw, I was already subjugated to her."

"What challenge is there in a willing victim?" The revulsion in her words wasn't for him but for the empress and echoed his own at the idea of sharing a bed with the Spider of Empire. Her favorites hadn't been so lucky.

"Just so," he said.

"How did you manage to save Estred?"

"I slunk away, pretended I was defeated, and waited three days until the show master felt assured I was gone and no longer a nuisance. I returned in the middle of the night and cut his throat while he slept in his bed. I then strangled Estred's caretaker or guard, whatever you want to call him, and took the cage keys. After being treated like an animal, my daughter was almost feral. I lured her out of her cage with sweets, then bound and gagged her before wrapping her in a blanket. I then unlocked every other cage there and set the supply wagons on fire before I fled with Estred on one of their horses."

His heartbeat now mimicked its gallop of so long ago when he held a sobbing, squirming Estred in his arms and raced across a wheat field toward a waiting horse and cart, leaving behind him a conflagration of tents and wagons, panicked animals and shouting people. And a show master choked to death on his own blood.

"I won't tell you all the details of what it took for Estred to become the child you know her to be, but I will tell you this. I—more than you, more than anyone—know how clever she is, how beautiful she is, what strength she has. But that isn't what people see when they look at her. We live in a world where crowds feel justified in trying to stone her to death for the sin of being born different. And one day, when I die, she will be friendless and left to fend for herself. Our society will never accept her. That is why I abducted Asil and extorted the draga, why I sought to physically change Estred, and why I will always look for some magic or chance that might give her the blessing of arms. Not because she's lacking or because she failed me, but because this shit pit of a world has failed her, me most of all."

The catharsis of revealing to another that grim time in his and Estred's life was like lancing an infected wound, draining away a bucket full of pus from his spirit. He'd forever be tainted by his erstwhile profession, and the role of cat's-paw had made him hated by many, turning him into a target for vengeance. In his opinion, he'd still failed Estred in his misguided efforts to provide her with a better, sheltered life, and now she paid the price for his role as the empress's murderous henchman. He almost gasped for breath under the weight of guilt.

Siora's silence was deafening. Gharek didn't hear so much as an exhalation from her. This time when her hand brushed his arm, he didn't pull away. "I don't believe Estred feels that way, nor do I think she'd want you to use a vulnerable woman like Asil or even a powerful being like Malachus, whose only sin is also being born different, to help her. She already knows you love her."

He sighed. "Love is the concubine of both fear and desperation when you're a parent," he said flatly. "And ruthlessness has no measure. Just ask Tanarima's sister, who sold my child so she could feed hers."

There was nothing more to say. Siora stayed quiet after that, and Gharek rode the edge of sleep, pulled back briefly by her shifting positions and pressing her body against his—whether for warmth or comfort, he couldn't say.

"Estred will never be friendless, Gharek." It was the promise of a supplicant devoted to a cause. "Neither will you. I swear it." Her fingers dug into his arm. "On my father's spirit. I swear it."

They didn't speak of their conversation the following morning. Gharek was relieved. Talk like that was a flaying in its way, and one needed time to recover. Siora's behavior was no different than before his revelations, though she smiled more often than the previous day. Who knew what moved the emotions of this mysterious woman in whose arms he'd fallen asleep last night? Hard riding and few stops brought them back to Domora in short order. Gharek used the last of the remaining *belshas* to stable the gelding in one of the more scrupulous stable yards that guaranteed the animal and its tack would still be there when they returned.

Siora skipped alongside him as they hurried toward the royal library, a worry pinching her features. Crescent shadows of fatigue darkened the skin under her eyes. The spot they chose to camp overnight might have been a peaceful one, but neither of them had slept well. Gharek had dreamed of the night he'd rescued Estred, waking several times panting as if he'd run from Domora to Kraelag and back. When sleep reclaimed him, so did the nightmare. Whatever plagued Siora's slumber was no less unpleasant. She thrashed in her sleep, legs kicking out as she fought off some unseen assailant. Her mumblings were nonsensical except once when she called out for her father in a terrified voice.

That was memorable, for the air around them had turned cold as midwinter for several moments, and while Gharek couldn't see anything in the encompassing dark, he had the distinct sense they were no longer two under the willow but three. He'd been grateful to see the dawn.

He slowed his stride so she didn't have to constantly jog to keep up. The royal library wasn't far from the stable yard, but the way required navigation through narrow streets so packed with people and carts, it was easier to go on foot than by horseback.

Gharek scanned the crowd as he and Siora shouldered their way through spots where the humanity huddled thick and pungent. He'd swapped scarves with her, her brown one adorning his head as a wrap while she wore his around her neck and shoulders. It wasn't much in the way of disguises, and one would-be assassin had already recognized and tried to dispatch him, but there was no help for it. They didn't have the luxury of time. He needed Manaran's help now. Hiding out until the city shut its doors and went to bed for the night wasn't an option. Besides, there was a certain anonymity in streets teeming with other strangers.

The library was a grand affair, the legacy of the Empire's first emperor, who'd declared himself such when the title of king was no longer grand enough. Soaring columns supported a structure carved of white marble adorned in sculpted figures and reliefs of the Empire's rulers, gods, and other flourishes. It was the work of a thousand laborers, of skilled artisans and sculptors, and decades of time. What it housed inside was even more wondrous. Clusters of students from Domora's schools that educated the elite gathered on the library steps to debate one topic or another while harried scribes raced up and down the treads, arms full of scrolls, quills, and ink pots. Beggars lined the steps, hands out to coax or guilt passersby into surrendering a coin or two. One approached Gharek then thought better of it under his warning stare.

Siora still held his arm though they were no longer in the midst of crowded streets trying to stay together. She never hesitated to touch him, which he thought strange but had begun to appreciate and anticipate. He regretted the loss of that touch when she let him go at the top of the steps and pivoted to stare open-mouthed at the library's grand loggia as it came into view. He waited, enjoying her thunderstruck expression as she stared at the impressive architecture, gasping at each new discovery her gaze landed on as she continued to pivot and admire.

"You've never been here at all during the time you lived in Domora?"

She didn't spare him a glance, too enraptured by the library's dramatic design, only deigned to shrug. "There was never a reason to do so."

"Can you read?" It wouldn't be unusual if she couldn't, especially raised as she was.

Her chin went up in a prideful tilt. "I can, though not as well as some." She did glance at him then, from the corner of one eye. "They don't allow beggars into the library, and my time wasn't my own while I was Estred's nurse." She explained the last without resentment.

Finally freed of the library's spell, she turned fully to Gharek. "What if this librarian friend tells you that what you need to break the Windcry's wards can only be found in the Maesor?"

He snorted and waved a hand at the colossal doors in front of them that beckoned visitors to enter and behold. "Believe me, if the information isn't housed somewhere in there, it doesn't exist. The challenge for us will be convincing Manaran to let us search without telling him too many details, not to mention actually finding such a book or scroll in a vast storehouse of them."

"What's to stop him from running off to the new emperor to tell him someone is looking to steal the Windcry?"

It was a reasonable question from an honest person. "Deception isn't your strength, is it?"

Once more that proud chin went up. "I don't weep over the lack."

He reached for her hand again, tucked it into the crook of his elbow, and brought her closer to his side. To other eyes, they were a couple on an outing to visit one of Domora's landmarks. Her eyebrows lifted briefly, but she didn't resist. "Trust me," he whispered near her ear. "I'll know what to say. This kind of thing was part of my profession as the empress's henchman."

"Are you sure they'll allow us in?" Her clothing looked worse for wear after a chase through the Maesor and Midrigar and sleeping outside on a horse blanket under a willow tree. His garb was in even worse shape than hers.

He waved away her concerns. "Who says I intend to ask permission? We won't be going through the front doors anyway. I know another way to access these halls."

She gave him a doubtful look. "Do you know every secret entry and exit in Domora?"

"Yes."

He was as good as his word, bypassing the main entrance with its gauntlet of guards and territorial scholars, who exercised their own meager power by deciding who among the common folk they deemed worthy enough to cross the threshold into the hallowed interior. Instead he led Siora to the long portico stretching along one side of the library, where a forest of columns cast their diagonal shadows on more students, who ignored the passing of two grubby townspeople.

They reached the back of the building. The library's builders had wanted the world to marvel at their creation, at least the parts of it visible to most. The back of the building was another matter. Here there were no sculptures or ornamentation, no marble cladding. Only dirty stone, middens, and entrances to the library used by the lower rungs of workers tasked with maintaining it and by the staff who served the librarians and scribes who lived and worked there. Like the students on the elevated portico, the busy staff barely gave them a glance, and those were bored ones. Gharek confidently strode through one of the open doors with Siora in tow. Creeping about made people notice. Acting as if you owned the place did not.

While he'd chosen this route to avoid questions or confrontation, he found new difficulties in coaxing Siora along with him. She paused every few steps once they reached the library's main hall to stare at the wall nooks, like slots in a gigantic dovecote, that covered the surfaces from floor to soaring ceiling and were stuffed with scrolls. Others held books stacked one atop the other or displayed spine out for the browser to read the title.

Were they truly here for a visit, he might enjoy observing her awestruck reactions, but they were here for a specific purpose. Wonderment would have to wait. He tugged her along, avoiding the hall's center aisles to hug the wall. His destination was a stairwell tucked behind the meeting of two interior walls. Hidden away and unseen by visitors, the master librarians used it to descend from their lofty studies to briefly mingle, then flee once more up the same stairs for their musty sanctuaries.

No guards watched the stairs or stopped them from entering the stairwell. Those who knew of its existence ruled the library and didn't need permission to use it. Others were of the belief it was sacrosanct and reserved for the near mythical scholars who didn't just climb the stairs to their chambers but ascended them.

Gharek smiled inwardly at the memory of Manaran's humble and often self-mocking views of those assumptions. "To those whelps studying at the academies and quoting wisdom they've just read to each other, we're venerable gods with bad teeth and cobwebs in our hair. Just ignore all that nonsense, my boy," he'd told a young Gharek, who'd gawked at a crowd of the older librarians poring over a large, tattered-looking tome with frayed pages and a strange proclivity to twitch when the sun slanting through the windows in a certain way landed on it. "We're just gassy old men going blind from reading in bad light." One day, Gharek thought, he might relay that story to Siora. *If you manage to survive Zaredis and his promise to execute you,* his inner heckler mocked.

The narrow stairwell wound in a loose coil toward an upper

floor, opening onto a small landing made even smaller by baskets full of scrolls and books stacked there. They covered nearly all the floor space except a slender path leading to a corridor in much the same state. The smell of dust and ink permeated the stale air, and the midsummer heat pulsed in the cramped confines like a heart.

"It's miserable up here," Siora said and wiped her brow with her sleeve. "How does anyone work or live without roasting alive in this bread oven?"

"Most of the doors you see lead to storerooms," he said. "The ones at the end of this hallway branch off and line the back of the library. Those are the rooms the master librarians occupy. They have windows."

He didn't mind the heat as much as she did, mostly because the sights and smells of this place reminded him of better days long past, when he'd dreamed of becoming one of those esteemed scholars himself, surrounded by the accumulated knowledge of centuries. Instead he'd grown up to become a soldier and then an assassin. He'd spilled more blood than ink in his lifetime so far.

The hallway branched out to another, then ran perpendicular to it, and Gharek led Siora down one side to a door at the very end. He rapped three times on one of its carved panels and waited. Moments crawled by on shuffling steps, marked by the swirl of dust motes illuminated in the dim light of a single lamp hung from a chain attached to a ceiling joist. Siora shifted restlessly beside him.

"This is a funeral pyre waiting to happen," she said, pointing to one of the countless baskets of scrolls and then at the lamp. "Maybe we can coax your librarian to chat with us outside."

Her unease wasn't without merit. There was nothing here to disturb the lamp's flame or knock into it, but one small spark in the windowless corridor falling on what amounted to a wagonload of tinder would start a massive fire. His brief joy at returning to a place of fond memories evaporated, and he rapped harder on the door again, this time with the side of his fist instead of his knuckles.

"Stop that racket, you arsewipe! I'm coming," a reedy voice snarled from the door's other side. Siora covered her mouth with her hand to stifle her laughter. She jumped back when the door was suddenly flung open, leaving Gharek with his fist raised again to knock, facing whatever fury confronted them.

A man, as ancient and weathered as cured leather abandoned in the sun, stood on the threshold, glaring at them and holding a quill as if it were a dagger he was about to stab into his visitor's eye. His scowl turned the wrinkles in his face into trenches. "Go away," he snapped, the quill's feather quivering in his grip. "I don't know how you slipped past the guards downstairs, but you're not welcome here." His long beard, gray and as coarse-looking as a horse's tail, was a matted waterfall cascading down the front of his robes. He made to shut the door and was prevented by Gharek's hand pushing it open.

"Manaran," he said, hoping the librarian still had enough of his mental faculties to recognize him. "I need your help."

The old man released his hold on the door handle before edging farther into the hallway for a closer look at these intruders. He peered at Gharek, cloudy gaze passing over his face and body. A surprised gladness replaced the glare. "Gharek," he said, the scowl chased away by a broken-tooth smile. "You aren't dead."

Gharek shook his head. "Not yet, my friend." He glanced down the still-empty hallway. "May we come inside?"

Manaran started, then ushered them past him, nodding to Siora, who paused to give him a quick bow.

"He's not a nobleman," Gharek whispered to her once they found a place to stand in a chamber even more cluttered than the hallways and stairwell.

She shrugged. "He's better. He's a librarian."

He couldn't agree more and offered his own shallow bow to the man who'd once given time, patience, and access to the wonders of this place to a boy starved for all three.

Manaran closed the door and barred it before joining them. He pointed to a bench buried under stacks of parchment, frowned, then pointed to another one equally covered. He sighed. "I'd invite you to sit, but there's no place to do so."

Gharek chuckled. "It doesn't matter. We're here for a very short time." He was more interested in finding the room's coolest spot and motioned for Siora to join him next to the chamber's open window. She made a delighted sound at the whip of a breeze snapping into the room to flutter some of the parchment stacks and send a few leaves scuttling across a large and very messy desk.

Manaran's look was no less speculative for his squint as he eyed his visitors. "Domora is the last place you should be. If I had a *belsha* for every person looking to put your head on a pike, I'd be a wealthy man."

"You're already a wealthy man," Gharek replied. Librarians weren't paid handsome sums of money, but those who reached Manaran's level of scholarship typically came from wealthy families, ones who offered to act as patrons and made generous donations to the royal library as a way of elevating their name and social standing, not to mention the favor of the reigning monarch. Such currying of favor had been lost on Dalvila, but her predecessors had set great stores by the munificence their courtiers bestowed on the royal library.

The librarian pointed to Siora. "Who is this?"

Gharek could have spent an afternoon trying to explain to Manaran who Siora was or what he was learning she was. Instead he wrapped an arm around her waist to snuggle her against his side in a show of affection. She didn't resist. "My mistress, Siora."

Siora blushed under Manaran's regard, but she didn't drop her gaze from his. Gharek could almost hear the old man's thoughts. Where had he found this woman and did she know the reputation of the man she'd taken to her bed when she agreed to become his mistress?

"You could do to dress her better," Manaran said after several moments of awkward silence.

If only he'd seen her before she'd gotten new clothes. "A fall from grace has made me a beggar myself."

The other man raised a hoary eyebrow. "I'm not surprised. The fact you're still alive defies the odds, but you were always a survivor, Gharek." He picked his way around the obstacle course that was the floor and sat in a chair behind the parchment-strewn desk. "You aren't here for a social visit, son. What can I do for you?"

"I need help in understanding how a protection ward might be created and how it might be broken."

"And why would the cat's-paw need such knowledge?" Manaran's voice changed, became guarded, and the squinty, half-puzzled expression now held the sharpness of a newly polished blade.

This was the Manaran Gharek remembered best. The man his mother had taken as a lover because of his wit, his intelligence, and his ability to gauge a person's character in a single glance. It was one of two things Gharek held on to, and reminded himself that while broken and drowning in the muck of his own murderous history, the abyss hadn't yet swallowed him whole. His daughter still loved him and Manaran still spoke to him. He deserved honesty from Gharek, but an honesty he'd have to parse out from carefully chosen words.

"Wards keep things out and hold things in. I need something powerful. A spell that can do both if necessary. Something that doesn't require ritual or the participation of many. Something that can be wielded by a single mage and that can raise any ward or break one."

"One invoked on the sly that won't garner attention until too late," Manaran added with an enigmatic look.

"That would be a benefit, yes."

It was honesty in that Gharek had told Manaran exactly what he needed from him, just not why. He'd dance that dance if the librarian requested it of him.

More silence passed as the other man studied him, then Siora, who remained quiet beside him. "Have you been to the Maesor?" he asked suddenly, that same grizzled eyebrow quirking upward as Siora started. "I thought so," he said before Gharek could answer. "The market is a grave now. I lost two koops to whatever hunter is terrorizing its streets. A third one barely managed to make it back to tell the tale. I don't think he's slept a full night since without the help of a sleeping draft."

Like the vendors in the Maesor, the royal library hired koops to find and recover rare books and manuscripts while others, such as private collectors, employed them to find equally rare magical artifacts. They were valued for their skills and most of all for their discretion. Koopman had hired out an army of koops to his clients, thus the name by which he was known to them.

The Maesor was a risky place to do business, both for the nature of its market and the laws against sorcery that made dealing with it in any way, shape, or form an invitation to one's own execution. Even then, those who worked for the library faced fewer risks than others because Herself and her enforcers bent the rules when it came to the library and conveniently turned a blind eye. Sorcery was outlawed, but it thrived in the Empire, just behind closed doors, in the shadows, and in the whisper of transactions exchanged in secret.

"We were in the market," he told Manaran. "Whatever you do, don't send any more of your people in there. What hunts those empty streets and awaits prey is powerful and without mercy."

Manaran scowled. "You shouldn't have gone in there. You're lucky you got out at all. The Maesor squats on the boundary between worlds. It has always been as strange as Midrigar, though not so malevolent—until now. You were lucky."

While he couldn't risk telling the librarian of Zaredis and his plans for stealing the Windcry, he could reveal some details for why they needed a grimoire or some other spellbook to help them. Manaran might be even more motivated to help. "Ghosts aren't so lucky," he said. "Siora is a shade speaker. A true one. Something in Midrigar is literally devouring the spirits of the dead and is now reaching for the living. The creatures in the Maesor either do its bidding or are manifestations of the same entity."

Siora added her voice to his persuasion. "My father's spirit lingers in this realm. I want to protect him and others as well from whatever this abomination is. I fear if it's ignored, it will only grow stronger and more ravenous, and it won't stop with just the dead."

Manaran's gaze drifted to the open window where the view showed a landscape of rooftops and the shadow of the palace in the haze of a summer's day. Gharek was sure the old man saw none of the scenery but instead some inner place spooling across his mind's eye. His gaze abruptly snapped back to Gharek. "Why are you suddenly playing hero instead of villain, lad?"

Because my daughter's life is at risk. Because we're all at risk and no one should meet whatever end those unfortunates—ghosts and living people—had suffered. He could only base his certainty on instincts that screamed he run when caught in the throes of a malevolent bewitchment, knowing that end would surely redefine what horror meant.

He answered truthfully, avoiding the trap of believing just because Manaran was aged, he was easy to fool. "There's nothing heroic about my motivation. We've seen what the ghost-eater can do, felt its sorcery, watched its power grow and stretch beyond the wards of Midrigar and now into the Maesor. And it will find a way through the gates. Of that I have no doubt. Whatever tear in the fabric separating worlds that allows the Maesor to exist, it's also allowing something through that hungers and is never satiated, that doesn't belong to this world."

His answer must have satisfied Manaran because he reached inside his robes and produced a ring of keys. "Come with me," he said.

For all that he'd taken his time shuffling to open the door at Gharek's knock, he descended the stairs with surprising speed. Once on the ground floor again, they followed him into a maze of short corridors lined with towering shelves behind the main hall where the visitors and students mingled.

While the top floor might have been the venerable, if sweltering, sanctuary reserved for the master librarians to study and research in serenity, this part was a hive of activity, with scribes rushing to and fro like foraging bees. They halted long enough to salute Manaran as he passed before rushing off to complete their tasks. None questioned him or his two guests as they traveled through the maze to reach a set of three doors. Manaran unlocked the middle one, gesturing for Gharek to grab an oil lamp and follow him inside.

Once in, he closed the door and Gharek held up the lamp to reveal wall-to-wall shelves stuffed with scrolls. Unlike the hallways on the top floor and Manaran's chamber itself, this one was neat and orderly, boasting a table in its center and chairs on either side. Blank parchment sat neatly stacked next to two full ink pots and a row of quills laid out precisely next to each other.

Manaran gestured to the tableau. "Use what you need. The scrolls and books in here deal with sorcery, the shelf there"—he pointed to the tallest one spanning the room's back wall—"focuses on wards. Start there. They might be of some use, though you'll need a sorcerer to actually work any spell, and you may have a hard time finding an authentic one. After a century of persecution, most are reluctant to reveal their talents, even now with Herself good and dead."

"I may know someone," Gharek said. Or at least knew of him, remembering Zaredis's imported mage.

Manaran's lips twitched. "Of course you do. I'll give you an hour. There's ink and parchment there if you wish to copy anything.

Don't even try stealing the books. They're more heavily warded than a virgin's bedchamber. All of Domora will know the moment you cross the threshold that you've taken something from the library."

"Noted."

Manaran handed Gharek the door's key. "Again, you have one hour. It's all I can give you before someone gets curious, so make the best of it." He strode out of the room, all traces of enfeebled grandfatherly type gone. They overheard him order the scribes to leave his guests in peace until he returned. After witnessing their deference to him, Gharek doubted anyone would defy his command.

He turned to Siora, who was already crouched in front of the lowest row of scrolls to pull them from their slots. "You said you can read. How fast?"

She eyed him over her shoulder, face grim. "Not fast enough to go through these books for the information you need." She gestured to the ink pots. "I've a clear hand though and am quick enough with a quill."

He joined her and began pulling scrolls from the upper shelves, careful not to crush or bend them, gentle with the more fragile ones that felt like powder held together by prayer, ancient parchment whose contents might be completely faded thanks to time and age. With any luck, the knowledge they needed rested on pages not on the verge of disintegrating.

"That will work," he said. "I'll give you the pages I want copied. We'll be lucky to walk out of here with five at most, but it's better than nothing, and Zaredis should be satisfied with what we give him when we go back."

It was a daunting task, one he doubted with each unfurling of a scroll would yield the results they needed in so little time. Siora scribbled constantly as he either dictated some bit of spellwork or note he though Zaredis and Rurian might use in breaking the wards protecting the Windcry. The hour sped by on winged feet, and he wanted to punch his fist into the wall from sheer frustration when Manaran knocked to signal their time was up.

"Did you find something useful?" He followed Gharek into the room and closed the door behind him.

Gharek shrugged. "Maybe, maybe not. There's a great deal to sift through and ten lifetimes needed to do it. It doesn't help that I'm not a sorcerer to know specifically what to look for."

Manaran tipped his chin toward Siora, busy rolling scrolls and returning them to their proper place. "What about your shade speaker?"

Siora smiled. "My skills are limited, master. I talk with the dead, but no ghostly mages have paid us a visit to help while we were here." Her teasing lightened the mood in the room.

Manaran sighed. "Ah well, maybe your notes will offer what you need." He moved around the table to help gather scrolls. One of his robes' voluminous sleeves dragged across the table like a wave, sweeping ink, parchment, and books to the floor.

Siora scrambled to catch some as they fell and returned them to the table. Manaran cursed and bent to help. Gharek crouched down beside him, offering his forearm as support for the older man to stand.

"I grow clumsy with old age," Manaran muttered on a sour note. He gave Gharek an unexpected wink and suddenly the weight of something pressed to his side. He glanced down to discover

Manaran shoving a small book at him. He took it, using the sleight of hand that had always been one of his most useful skills, to tuck it into his tunic.

He gave Manaran a nod of thanks. Even if he and Siora found nothing useful in their notes, he was certain they'd find it in the small tome the librarian had sneaked to him. He waved to Siora. "Let's go. The scribes can put the rest of this away."

Before they left, Gharek clasped forearms with Manaran, noting the thinness of the other man's arm, remembering him as a younger, more robust figure who filled his ears with fantastic stories and loaned him precious books to read. "Any alarms I should worry about when we leave?"

Manaran shrugged. "Unless you stole something, not at all." A melancholy smile flitted across his mouth. "You still have your mother's eyes. It's how I recognized you under that beard. Good luck, Gharek."

Gharek thanked him again, and soon he and Siora were once more riding pillion on the free trader gelding through Domora.

"I don't think it's a good idea to stay any longer in the city," she told him.

"Nor I." He guided the horse toward one of Domora's gates. "We'll camp farther away from Domora and take the paths leading to Kraelag. Fewer travelers that way, and Zaredis will have moved his army toward there to delay clashing with any of Tovan's troops before he's ready."

He released the breath he'd been holding once they were through the gates and beyond the siege walls but stayed tense and ready to bolt until they were on the road leading to what remained of the old capital. Nothing of that city remained except soot marks and charred bone, which suited him fine. No crowds of people to contend with, and while it might be haunted, it wasn't cursed like Midrigar. God-fire, in all its ferocity, had destroyed Kraelag; a cleansing immolation unlike the poison of old spells laid upon Midrigar to trap her dead inside, as much prisoners of calculated evil as the trap shadows in their fabric cages. No curse would have dared settle on Kraelag, and if fortune favored them, neither would a ghost-eater.

They rode until nightfall, stopping on the edge of a farmer's field where a small lean-to with barely enough room for a pair of sheep stood empty under a sky speckled with stars and scudding clouds. It was as good a place as any, providing shelter in case it rained, and a floor cushioned with a layer of hay not too infested with insects and other vermin. "Pray whoever owns this land won't chase us off before we can get some sleep," he told Siora. "If we're out of here before dawn and don't build a fire, we might be gone before they even learn we were here."

Siora unsaddled and tethered the horse this time, crooning a few words so that its ears flickered back and forth. "Good idea. Besides, what we have left from the foodstuffs Halani packed for us doesn't need to be cooked. It's too warm anyway to huddle up to a fire."

Once they settled down for the night and shared a meal, Siora unpacked the other satchel one of the free traders had tied to their saddle. Two tunics, heavily embroidered but that had seen better days, were inside, along with a handful of drying cloths, a coin-size round of soap, and a corked pot of ointment for tending the scratches she and Gharek had sustained courtesy of the trap shadow.

Gharek paged through the book he'd taken from his tunic; a

small grimoire with some of the spells translated into languages he could read and some he couldn't. His burgeoning excitement over what he read was difficult to contain, and Siora paused in her task to give him a puzzled look. "Whatever you're reading, it's done what I doubt few besides Estred have managed: made you truly smile."

"Then I find amusement in dark things." He held up the book. "Manaran must be more terrified than I first thought, that what struck the Maesor will strike Domora. He thinks I've already found a sorcerer to work the right spells. He slipped this to me before we left. A spellbook with certain pages marked." He passed the book to her.

She turned it over in her hands, flipped through some of the pages, perused their contents, and returned it to him, her expression guarded. "Him knocking things off the table. That was a ruse and distraction to pass it to you. I thought it was just being clumsy."

"Clumsy with purpose." Gharek cracked the book open once more to one of the pages Manaran had marked with a folded corner. A spell for how to break a ward that required the spittle of a leper. His lip curled. Who, he wondered, thought up some of this tripe? Why couldn't potions involve the juice of fruits or a nicely aged wine? "Manaran isn't anything like the cloudy-minded mystic he enjoys playing for the entertainment of others."

She eyed the book as if its contents had been written with the spit of a leper. "I hope it will have what Zaredis needs and what we all need to stop the ghost-eater."

After experiencing the blood-freezing compulsion to race to his own death and devouring, Gharek couldn't agree more. The thoughts made him remember the empty Maesor. Not completely empty—if one counted faceless hunters pale as corpses and demented trap shadows freed. He shoved the memory aside. They had a place to sleep, something to offer Zaredis when they returned, and the chance to retrieve Estred. His own fate remained a question, but for now he'd set aside that grim thought as well and enjoy the squalid comforts of a lean-to for the night alongside a woman he once considered his enemy.

"How's your back?" he asked.

While she'd physicked the deep scratch on his cheek, it had been Halani who'd done the same for Siora. The free trader woman knew her herbals. The ointment she'd made possessed near miraculous healing qualities. It had already done wonders to the wound on his cheek as well as his bruises, and less than two days had passed since they left their camp.

"It still stings," Siora said. "I'm glad there was only one trap shadow to deal with in the Maesor. Between it and the hunter, we were in a bad spot." She rubbed her shoulder and winced. "Halani's salve stopped the sting most of the day, but I think it's worn off. She sent more to use if I needed it." She pointed to his face. "Your cheek looks already half healed."

"Do you want me to wash the scratches again? I can check to see if they're poisoning. I noticed the free traders kindly put a flask of spirits in the packs. It's good for cleaning wounds, though it'll make the sting worse for a moment." He fully expected her to refuse but asked anyway. Even a small part of him questioned why he'd made the offer. He wasn't a kind man or a charming one or one to display compassion, yet he was moved to do so now, to repay Siora's own generous well of kindness with something she might appreciate, something that didn't involve violence or ferocity.

She gazed at him without expression before giving a quick nod and turning her back to him. She unwound the sash snugging her tunic to her middle and set it aside. Her small hands gathered the garment at its hem and eased it up her legs and hips, past her waist, to bunch it under her arms. Her back, pale in the moonlight, was a mural of scabbed scratches marring a smooth landscape of skin stretched taut over the bridge of her spine and swoop of her shoulder blades.

Arrested by the sight, both elegant and harsh, Gharek could only stare for a moment before scooting closer so that he sat behind her, one leg splayed on either side of hers. His fingers traced the air just above the scratches, and though he didn't touch her skin, the goose flesh rose there in reaction to his nearness. "They're red," he said, hoping his voice didn't give away the rush of desire spilling through him. "But healing well. I won't need the spirits to cleanse them unless you wish it. I can just reapply the salve to relieve the stinging."

She turned her head to see him. "Yes, please. I'll sleep better."

Gharek suspected he could swim in a vat of the stuff and still not sleep at all this night, not with the beautiful shade speaker stretched out beside him. The thought made him freeze for a second as he reached for one of the satchels containing the salve. He glanced at her, but she remained with her back to him, quiet and contemplative. He was going as mad as the trap shadow in the Maesor if such thoughts were scurrying about in his mind.

He made small talk to distract himself and relieve the odd anticipatory tension that had settled between them when he'd foolishly offered to tend her back. "The free traders are generous to those who render aid to them. They gave you two tunics."

"Asil's doing, I think." A smile entered Siora's voice. "She is beloved by them all." She gestured to the bag where the salve and clothes shared space. "You can have the other tunic if you want to change."

No amount of small talk could dissipate the thrumming awareness growing between them or the slow heating of his blood as he gently applied the ointment to her back, painting the salve with light fingers over each mark. Several stretched from the top of her shoulders to the twin dimples indenting her lower back. Some of her hair had escaped its plait to fan along her backbone and the shadowy outline of her ribs on one side. Gharek gathered the stray locks in his palm, careful not to smear ointment on them, and twitched them over Siora's shoulder. She offered him a fine view of her profile with its strong jaw, straight nose, and resolute chin.

"Thank you, Gharek," she said softly, and his name on her lips was a more seductive caress than any touch he'd ever known from a woman.

She was small and beautifully made, inside and out. He bent to an unscratched part of her back. Flawless skin that tempted him to brush his lips there and learn her softness. Learn her taste. He'd known desire many times, but it had been long and long since he'd felt it coupled with affection.

Condemning and forgiving in equal parts, Siora had been a catalyst of change for him from the moment he'd met her, though he hadn't known it at the time or truly recognized it until now. His fear for Estred inspired him to survive at all costs. His growing feelings for Siora tangled him in knots.

The realization made him scramble to his feet. "I'm finished. I spotted a well on the other side of this barn. There's bound to be a bucket available. I'll wash and return soon with a bucket for you." If his blood ran any hotter in his veins, he'd have to do more than wash his hands. He'd need a full dunking.

His observations held true and he found the well with a bucket attached by rope and bar to a crank that lowered and raised it for water. He filled the first bucket and used it to wash the remnants of ointment off his hands, then washed his face and neck, as much to cool a passion as to rinse away the sweat and dust from the day's earlier heat.

He dumped the remainder of the water and refilled the bucket before lugging it back to the lean-to for Siora to have a quick wash if she chose. He'd stand guard nearby, though there was no one to be seen for leagues in either direction.

He discovered her asleep, curled on her side as she usually slept, one hand tucked under her cheek while the other stretched out in front of her, palm flat against the spot where he'd lay down for the night. The book Manaran gave him lay beside that hand, partially open. He set the bucket to one side and approached their sleeping spot. She didn't move, her breathing slow and deep. He took the book and checked the page she'd been reading before sleep claimed her.

His eyebrows rose. A list of necromantic spells, the start of a section that included fortune-telling, divination, and forms of spying using the skills and foreknowledge of an enslaved ghost. No wonder she wore a frown as she slept. Even before magic was outlawed, the dark art of raising the dead for a number of nefarious purposes was reviled by most, and necromancers operated in secret or risked being burned or torn apart by outraged villagers and townsmen.

Siora had insisted she was no necromancer, only a shade speaker, and believed there was a defining difference between the two. Gharek wasn't so sure. Her explanation for why her touch made Kalun visible to others made sense. A living twin could be an anchor to the world for a dead one, a beacon to follow until the spirit chose to pass on. The same explanation might work for her father as well, but there were still holes in her reasoning. Most shade speakers were frauds, but the few who were authentic, like Siora, were connected to the spirit world in a way only those gifted—or cursed—with necromantic magic since birth could be. In his opinion the only true difference between a necromancer and a real shade speaker was that one sought to enslave the dead and the other did not.

He gently slid her hand closer to her body and sat down beside her, angling the book so the moonlight illuminated the page. He wished he could build a fire but doing so risked drawing the attention of whoever owned the field, and he wanted to avoid one more confrontation.

"Can you actually see the words?" Siora asked in a drowsy voice. "I gave up."

He did the same, closing the book to set it beside him. Siora remained recumbent on her part of the horse blanket. Dappled in shadows, she reminded him of the night-blooming flowers in the garden he'd had planted in his courtyard for Estred. Her round eyes shone in the argent light and the frown was gone, replaced by a more pensive expression. "I didn't mean to wake you," he said.

"You didn't. I was just dozing." She continued to stare at him, an obvious question hovering on her lips.

"What?" He wondered what manner of question she planned

to flense him with this night. "I can tell you want to ask me something."

She gnawed on her bottom lip as if deciding how to say what she wanted, and Gharek braced for the expected moment when she'd knock his feet out from under him. She didn't disappoint.

"Do you hate your wife for abandoning Estred?"

He exhaled a long sigh and turned to stare out the door to the silver-plated fields beyond. Did this woman ever ask anything that was simple to answer? He could take the easy path, tell her it was none of her concern and put his back to her to sleep, but whatever urged him to peel back another layer of himself for her perusal in their earlier conversations wanted him to do the same thing now.

A memory of Tanarima, the charming, flirty daughter of a wool merchant, bloomed before him. She had enamored him from the moment he met her in the busy market of a village whose name he couldn't recall. He was a lowly census counter for the Empire, but his profession required he travel, and for a girl whose entire world consisted of the confines of her small village, he seemed to her an exotic world traveler.

Those initial infatuations hadn't survived, just as most didn't, and the reality of marriage between very disparate personalities insured a tumultuous relationship. They were both relieved when he chose to join the Kraelian army for better pay, especially with a baby on the way. He would leave with his regiment for a troubled spot in the Empire but return in time to welcome his child into the world. Things never went as planned, and months stretched to years, and the daughter he'd sired had been born with the burden and stigma of disfigurement to a woman alone and overwhelmed by that reality.

Siora's question resurrected more memories that were, to his surprise, no longer painful. They flitted across his mind's eyes as if Tanarima and his marriage to her were the shades of another life belonging to another man. He chose to answer the question.

"Once," he said. "Once, a lifetime ago, I hated her. Now I'm indifferent. And pitying. She was handed a hard fate by the gods. People would have blamed her for birthing a monster, shunned her, maybe even attacked her as they've attacked Estred. She was alone, and I was too far away to be of any use to her. I believe now she did what she thought was necessary."

"Do you know where she is now?"

He shrugged. "Dead from fever not long after she left Estred with her sister. I don't rejoice in her death, but I don't sorrow either. She gave me Estred. It's enough." He met that deep gaze, wondering if shade speakers saw more clearly than others. "Why do you ask such questions?"

She sat up and mimicked his shrug. "To understand better."

"There's nothing to understand. I'm a father, a murderer, a fugitive, and an exile. And once more a cat's-paw to a different master." Summing up his character aloud made him wither a little inside, and the chilly blackness that always threatened to subsume him encroached further into his soul with grasping fingers. If he avoided the eater of ghosts long enough, there would be nothing left of him for it to take when it finally netted him for good.

Siora leaned toward him until she was so close he could see the way her long lashes curved and the remnant of a tiny scar marring the skin under her left cheekbone. "There's more," she said, raising a hesitant hand to touch his head and then his cheek. He didn't pull away this time, caught in a trap of bewitchment more powerful than that of any Midrigar monstrosity. "More beyond the blackness and the terror. A candle flame almost guttered but still there."

He might have corrected her, mocked her for believing there was more to him than what he'd just told her. Instead, he gathered her into his arms, and she went, stupidly trusting, beautifully sensual.

Her arms slid over his shoulders. The weight of her clasped hands rested just below his nape. Her body fit neatly into the cove his made, her pelvis seated against his where she'd surely feel his desire for her nudge and seek. Her small breasts pressed against his chest as she embraced him.

She smelled of parchment dust and wildflowers and the apple they'd shared as part of their supper earlier. Her gaze mapped every detail of his face as if to commit it to memory, and he wondered what she saw there that he could not in any mirror's reflection. That flame she insisted still burned in the darkness? She leaned in and he met her halfway, capturing her lips, soft as a rose petal, before he teased her mouth open to accept the sweep of his tongue.

Siora moaned, a tiny sound of pleasure that drove the hot blood in his body straight into his cock. He grasped her hips and surged against her, rocking back and forth with her as they explored each other: mouths, cheeks, temples, and throats. Shoulders and backs, hips and legs.

She was a slight woman, built of bird bones and cobwebs. Fragile but strong. Incredibly so. She'd have to be to survive the life she'd lived. Friendless beggar, Flower of Spring, voice for the dead, prey of a cat's-paw. If he was honest with himself—and he indulged in such moments sometimes—she'd fascinated him as much as she'd unnerved him from the moment he'd met her. She was as different from Tanarima as the moon was to the sun, and yet the same, because she believed him to be something far more than he actually was, unswerving in her certainty despite evidence to the contrary.

He peeled her away from him, tipping her off his lap. She blinked at him, confused, a delectable temptation he would be wise to avoid yet nearly helpless to do so. "You see what isn't there, Siora" he told her in his harshest tones, flinching inwardly at the way her features froze. "I've no more answers for your questions."

CHAPTER EIGHT

S iora had never considered herself a reckless sort, even when she shielded Estred from a stoning with her own body or helped a draga rescue an old woman by betraying an assassin. Doing the right thing wasn't reckless, it was just that—the right thing. Kissing Gharek of Cabast, on the other hand, was reckless. There was no justification for it, no nobility attached to it unless one wanted to put desire on a pedestal. Neither right nor wrong but still incautious, and she regretted none of it, even when he set her aside and turned his back to her.

His words, designed to cut, had done their job at first, making her bleed inside with mortification but only for a breath or two. Her greatest talent might be conversing with the dead, but she was an excellent judge of people as well. It was why she'd never given up on the cat's-paw, seeing under all that cold brutality a man worth her faith and patience, even if only for the sake of his daughter.

She remained awake the rest of the night, counting the number of shooting stars passing overhead and the breaths of the sleeping man beside her as she replayed that lovely kiss in her mind, dwelling on the ephemeral moment and wishing it had lasted far longer, gone further than just the kiss. While she'd never admit it to anyone, he'd always intrigued her. Dangerous men usually made her wary and eager to avoid them. Even Malachus, whose character was more merciful than Gharek's despite being a draga, had made her glad to end their brief alliance and escape into the city's labyrinth once she'd shown him where Asil was hidden. Gharek was the exception. Sometimes the draw of another couldn't be explained, and he'd been a lodestone for her from the moment she met him in a Domoran alleyway, his daughter in her arms.

Her musings turned to the charm Asil gave her, one that was far more than the bits and scraps of thread and flowers woven into a disk. Siora wasn't gifted with magic, but she could sense it, and the charm had practically breathed with the sorcery of earth when Asil had adorned her with the gift. The old woman herself had the feel of earth magic about her, Halani even more so. Siora wondered who had created it—mother or daughter? Whoever had done so carried the power of rock and soil, plant and all manner of living things in their fingers. Gharek might not have felt the charm's power, but to Siora it was unmistakable. And valued. She and her companion could use every bit of protection given to them.

By the time sleep overtook her, Gharek was shaking her awake. "Time to go," he said, and his shuttered expression warned he wasn't in the mood for questions, explanations, or conversation in general. They were back on the road just before the sun crested the horizon, and Siora saw at the edge of the fields a thin seam of light in the window of a distant house. The farmer who worked these fields was awake. They'd chosen the right time to leave.

With hours and leagues ahead of them, and Gharek's demeanor as dour as a thunderstorm, she stayed quiet. Only once did he speak and that, a three-word command. "Take the reins." While she guided Suti on the road, he read the grimoire Manaran had given them, the crackle of pages turned loud in her ear.

Curious as to what he discovered, she braved a question. "Have you found anything useful in that book?" He might bite her head off, but she was undeterred. She didn't regret kissing him and refused to apologize, even if he stewed over it.

To her delight, he answered her without snarling, though a thin edge of ice lined his voice. "Several things, though not one that might break the Windcry's ward. Then again, I'm not a sorcerer. Zaredis's dog-mage might see something here I don't. Or a combination of things." He muttered something under his breath.

"What is it?"

His voice warmed a little more with each word. "This book is a codex of sorts. A guide to spells of different sorceries—the elements, potions, scrying, necromancy." A lengthy pause followed and his tone shifted. "You realize, as a true shade speaker you're a necromancer?"

Siora lurched in the saddle, hard enough to make the gelding stop, confused. Gharek signaled him with a tap of his heels and a click of his tongue to walk again and pick up the pace. "I'm not a necromancer," she snapped, every warm thought she'd indulged in about him this morning driven out by his remark. "I don't summon the dead, enslave the dead, or use them to foretell the future."

"If this book is accurate, there's more to necromancy than that. There's a spell in here you might find of particular interest."

He stretched his arm over her shoulder, nudging the book into her hand while he recaptured the reins with his other hand. He held the book open in one spot with his thumb. "Read this page."

She almost refused. Her interest in the grimoire had turned to wary revulsion when she'd thumbed through its pages while Gharek had gone to pull water from the nearby well the previous night. She didn't fear sorcery in general. There were clean and unclean magics, and not all were created equal. Her own shade-speaking might not be true sorcery, but she'd always had a sense of others who possessed the real thing. The fire witch in the cloister prison below Kraelag's notorious Pit, the Savatar commander with his desperate gaze when he questioned her about the witch—a hint of magic had hung on him. Even Halani, kind and solemn, who thrummed with a power that made Siora think of spring and wild-flowers and newly harvested fields. To her knowledge she hadn't crossed paths yet with anyone who possessed death magic—if one didn't count the thing swallowing up the dead as food.

Necromancy was an abomination of sorcery, not because it dealt in death but because it dealt in slavery. She'd seen the ruin-ation of a soul imprisoned too long as a trap shadow by some nec-romancer who likely counted such enslavement as the least of his evils.

People had sometimes asked why she didn't summon ghosts to tell the future. Her answer was always the same. "I'm a shade speaker, not a slaver. They come to me of their own accord." This book, with its many invocations and incantations, protections and blessings, also contained summoning magic and bind spells that forced the dead into serving the will of the living.

"Necromancy is filthy magic," she said. "You should tear that page from the book and burn it."

Gharek's "hmm" was noncommittal. "Don't be so quick to judge or discount. According to the book, the spell known as Holdfast traps a summoned ghost and binds it to the spellcaster to do their bidding until the caster chooses to set it free."

She twisted in the saddle to give him a dark look. "Whyever wouldn't I judge such a horrendous thing? Jumped-up slave mongers. Necromancy is the scourge of all sorcery."

Undaunted by her outrage, he poked the hornet's nest again. "But what if it could protect your father or the general's brother from whatever is snacking on hapless spirits?"

His question gave her pause. Such a scenario had never before presented itself to her, and until now, it had been easy to take a stand when there was no scenario. Harder now to hold that line when someone she loved was in danger, and she struggled with the grim reality of compromise when needs must conflicted with morality. "Is this one of those bitter choices an honorable person must make to protect the vulnerable?"

For one lovely moment, his arms came fully around her and tightened. His low sigh was depressingly resigned. "Fair innocent, oceans of blood have been spilled thanks to the honorable intentions of those who seek to do good."

"Our world is very dark in your eyes."

"And surprisingly bright in yours," he replied. The light brush of his cheek against her hair sent a shivery warmth through her.

She held on to the book and even read some of the spells in the section devoted to necromancy despite her reservations. The one called Holdfast was easy in terms of execution, impossible to invoke if one wasn't gifted with the power of death magic. Zaredis's magician had wielded a spell that stopped the ghost-eater for a short time, a ward that acted like a shield wall and took the entity by surprise so that it retreated. She doubted it would try the same approach or be taken unawares a second time. Rurian wasn't a necromancer; if he was, Zaredis would have employed him to protect his brother instead of bargaining for the help of a lowly shade speaker. The straightforward Holdfast spell was useless to him no matter how great his particular power. Death called to death, and nothing else would do.

The swelter of a late afternoon drugged her into a torpor as they closed the distance between them and what was left of the old capital, Kraelag. She dozed in Gharek's arms, waking when he nudged her shoulder and repeated her name. She blinked under the sun's harsh light and rubbed her eyes. At some point during her nap, Gharek had rescued the book from her hands and tucked it out of sight.

They cut across a fallow field adjacent to the giant burn scar on the landscape. The acrid smell of smoke assaulted her nostrils long before she saw the stretch of scorched ground—still blackened after several seasons—that had once been the largest city in the Kraelian Empire. "Kraelag," she said aloud.

"Even if I hadn't seen it, I'd know we were close," Gharek said. "The air smells burnt." He guided the gelding toward the ruins and the overgrown avenue that led to where a double set of formidable walls with a quartet of majestic gates once surrounded the city. Nothing of either remained.

His voice took on an almost reverential tone, as if they rode toward a sacred place to pay respects. "I remember the first time I saw it after it was destroyed. It still glowed hot in spots and lit the night sky above it."

He'd seen the aftermath; Siora had witnessed the actual destruction. "I saw the Savatar goddess burn Kraelag." There was no bard skilled enough to capture the awful majesty of the fire goddess rising as a colossal pillar of flame surrounding the shape of a woman just before she immolated an entire city and most of an army in a matter of moments. "I remember watching her rise from the center of the city. Gigantic, enrobed in flame, tall as a mountain it seemed at the time. You don't know how insignificant you truly are until you stand in the presence of a deity. The fire witch I mentioned? She was the goddess's avatar. One of the Savatar chieftains was her lover."

Gharek's low whistle tickled the top of her head. "Of the lovers I'd take to my bed, the avatar of a goddess would be one of my last choices."

"I don't think she survived the possession." Siora still thought of the fire witch on occasion. A woman possessing a stare that burned holes through a person. Old eyes in a young face and a mouth thinned with bitterness more often than not. Much like Siora's current companion, and like him, she'd revealed a fleeting vulnerability—guilt and despair, briefly assuaged when Siora passed on a message of forgiveness to her from the ghost of a woman named Pell.

The gelding Suti suddenly snorted and pranced sideways as they climbed a short slope that dropped once more on the other side and opened onto an enormous swath of blackened field littered with mounds of charred wood and stone that had once been structures and walls, gates and homes. Here the stench of soot and ash grew choking, and Suti fought his rider's control with increasing fervor.

Siora no longer paid attention to the remains of Kraelag, caught instead by the sight of a massive swarm of ghosts hovering over the burned fields, some shifting aimlessly in the wind like pale flags while others stood resolute and aware of their surroundings, their hollow-eyed gazes locked on the approaching riders.

Gharek cursed the gelding, muttering about the foolhardiness of buying unreliable nags from free traders.

"It isn't his fault," Siora said, holding tight to the saddle pommel as he steered the animal away from the burn field. Suti quieted, and Siora swept a hand toward the gathering wraiths she could see and Gharek could not. "For all that Domora is emptied of spirits, these lands surrounding Kraelag are not. If the wolf of the cursed city expands its reach this far, it will find a feast waiting for it. We stand on the shore of a sea of ghosts."

As if her words opened a gate and released a dammed river, phantoms rushed toward them in torrents, spilling over and around them in an icy miasma that sent Suti into a bucking, rearing panic. The horse whinnied and tried to bolt.

"Gods damn it," Gharek snarled, his breath floating in front of him in a chilled cloud. "Tell them to back off before I lose control of this fucking animal!"

She didn't get the chance. The wave of wraiths retreated like an ebbing tide, though not far, and Suti settled down. Voices swelled in a cacophony of furious wails in Siora's head. She clapped her hands to her ears in a futile attempt to block out the sound.

Cries for help, pleas to be set free, demands for revenge, questions about loved ones, and worst of all, the frightened sobs of childish voices confused by their altered existence and calling out for their mothers or fathers.

Tears blinded her and she sobbed aloud. Gharek held her tight to him with one arm, himself a barrier against the battering of the hopeless and despairing dead.

"What are they saying?" His voice was a lifeline tossed to her. She grasped it and held on tight.

"Many things." She gasped out her answer. "So many voices. Thousands of them. I can't make sense of them all."

Suti, shivering and snorting, half reared, and Siora nearly leapt from the saddle when Gharek bellowed, "Enough! Shut the fuck up, all of you!"

It must have looked truly bizarre to see a man on a skittish horse yelling at an empty field to be quiet in the saltiest terms, but the unorthodox response worked. The thunder of dead voices in Siora's head went instantly quiet, and she swayed in her seat from the sudden dizziness it caused.

Gharek's arm tightened around her. "Are you all right?"

She nodded and after a moment was steady enough to focus her attention on the large ethereal crowd watching her. One wraith separated from the mass of others, floating closer, only stopping when Suti's ears laid back flat and he pranced backward.

The phantasmic shape rippled ceaselessly, a waterfall of ethereal mist with the hint of a young face, though Siora couldn't tell if it was a man or a woman. *Have you come to free us, witch of the dead?*

The question made every hair on Siora's body stand straight up. She shook her head. *I'm no witch, and though I can see you and talk to you, I don't have the ability to free you from whatever chains you here. You must do it yourself.*

The towering wave of desolation at her reply broke against her and nearly broke her. Their voices didn't rise again to deafen her mind, but she drowned in their anguish. "I am so sorry," she said aloud. "What is your name?" she asked the ghost.

We are all one name now, the spirit said, and all replied in unison. *Forgotten.*

The melancholy word worked its own sorcery, and the turbulent sea of sorrowing dead faded until it was just the flat plain and the haunted ash of a city's remains.

Siora hugged Gharek's muscled arm to where it pressed hard against her middle. "Thank you, Gharek. They're gone."

He didn't let go of her. "Are you sure? No spirits still lingering for a bout of confession?"

"No. They don't mean any harm. They aren't like trap shadows. They're lost, confused, caught between an awareness of their death but also still tied to the memories of lives lived in a certain place. This can happen when death is violent or sudden. It doesn't help that the earth itself remembers and chains them here."

"Are you certain they're harmless?" Doubt riddled his question.

His experience with the dead so far always included the eater of ghosts. Siora understood his suspicions. "Yes. Memory brings them here. It would be impossible to forget the punishment of a fire goddess."

She missed the hard comfort of his embrace when he released her and leaned to the side to search through one of the satchels tied to the cantle. A flask appeared in front of her.

"Drink this." She did as he ordered, swallowing two mouthfuls of Karsa's plum wine. It cleared her head and set fire to her gut in an instant. "Better?"

She nodded and coughed. "There is no possible way that stuff is just wine," she said between gasps.

"True, but it's effective." He took the flask back and had a drink himself before closing and returning it back to its pack. "If we push on through the night, we can reach Zaredis's camp by late tomorrow, but the gelding needs to rest, and you look like you could use some as well. We can delay a few hours, eat and sleep and be on the road before dawn."

"I don't mind," she said, "but can we put distance between us and here before we stop for the night?" She didn't fear the dead. The living were much more frightening, but these lost souls, bound to an earth whose own violent memory of their deaths in the conflagration of god-fire wouldn't let them go . . . The knowledge crushed her own spirit just by their proximity.

This was why, when she watched Kraelag's immolation from the questionable safety of a Savatar army camp, she'd felt the very fabric of the earth ripple and warp around the living suddenly made phantoms in one cataclysmic moment.

"You'll get no argument from me," Gharek said. "I've grown more sick of the dead than the living lately and that's saying something."

They traveled until twilight edged the horizon, stopping twice to rest the gelding. A summer rain shower briefly darkened the sky with gravid gray clouds. They fractured open, pierced by bars of sunlight, to spill walls of rain across the land. It didn't last long, and the storm galloped south, leaving behind two thoroughly drenched people and one equally wet horse.

Siora didn't care. She was soaked to the skin but grateful for the unexpected bath that washed away the stickiness of sweat and heat clinging to her as well as the lingering despair that had spilled over her when she faced the ghosts at Kraelag. The words of the one spirit who acted as their speaker still brought tears to her eyes, as did the voices of phantom children crying for dead parents whose own ghosts had broken free and no longer traveled this plane. *We are all one name now. Forgotten.*

The destruction of Kraelag had been on everyone's lips for months after god-fire had consumed it. People who hadn't seen it immolated talked as if they'd run for their lives through the gates to escape the flames, embellishing the fictional experience with a few details to give it more validity. They spoke of the colossal goddess made of fire, of the Kraelian army and the Savatar cavalry alike fleeing from the battlefield in terror, the fighting between them forgotten as they tried to escape the burning wrath of an angry goddess.

It was epic, dramatic, perfect fodder for storytellers and traveling bards to earn their keep by enchanting tavern patrons and market day visitors with the tale. They didn't speak of the dead, of the absolute annihilation of bodies, burned in a fire so hot it turned the sands of the infamous Pit into glass and left no remains to bury or mourn.

The dead made terrible subjects for storytelling. People wanted tales of heroic deeds and adventure, not the confused loneliness of the perished whose spirits hung trapped in an earthly realm where they remained invisible, unheard, and, after a time, no longer remembered.

Relieved to put distance between them and Kraelag, she was even happier when they discovered a way station on the road offering room and board—until she learned of the exorbitant price for a night's stay. Gharek pointed to the patrons who entered or exited the building, then to a cluster of sedans and fine covered carts pulled by oxen or horses dressed in even finer harness.

"Even if we had the coin to afford a room, I'd be recognized in an instant. This is a tavern and inn devoted to the service of wealthy travelers. They wouldn't let us near the stables much less through the tavern's front entrance, and fighting off one assassin wanting my head for his master was one time too many."

"There are abandoned places scattered throughout this area," she said. "Especially this close to a large city, or what's left of one. We still have a little daylight left. Can we search until then?" While she'd appreciated the rain bath, the horse blanket they used for bedding was as waterlogged as they were, and she didn't fancy sleeping on wet ground.

Gharek reined Suti away from the tavern. "Tell me the way, and we'll ride there."

She was more familiar with this corner of the Empire than she was with Domora and its surrounding villages. She'd grown up not far from the old capital in a comfortable household of a mid-ranking Kraelian officer. That all changed in an instant when her father's commander, resentful and wary of a subordinate's climb through the ranks, named him traitor. Sold as a slave to the gladiatorial schools, Skavol had died in the bloodbaths there, never to see his wife or daughter again, at least not as a living man.

Siora and her mother had remained close to Kraelag, and Siora had buried her less than a league south from where she and Gharek were now. If she and the cat's-paw completed this task successfully, and he managed to survive Zaredis's promise to execute him, she'd invite him and Estred to see the breathtaking beauty of the land where her mother rested, under snow in winter and wildflowers in spring. It was a lovely thought that would never come to fruition, but she allowed it to remain in the back of her mind, a sweet delusion to distract her as they searched for dry shelter.

She directed Gharek to the remains of what had once been a free trader camp. All that was left were bits of refuse and an abandoned wagon, all four of its wheels gone, as was its entrance door and the carved decorations that were the signature styles of a free trader's home.

Gharek brought Suti to a halt in front of the wagon. He stared at it for several moments before declaring, "Well, it has a roof and possibly a floor, and if you're willing to fight the rats for a space inside, we can stay here for a few hours and have a fire."

They set up their temporary camp, Gharek to face down whatever vermin had taken up residence in the wagon and she to gather kindling and bits of discarded wood to build the fire. There was plenty of tinder among the garbage, and she didn't have to go far for sticks. When she returned, Gharek had Suti unsaddled, his lead rope staked to the ground with a loop at one end, the other end knotted to his halter. He grazed happily on the rain-drenched grass around him.

Siora set her bundle of scavenged fuel next to the spot Gharek indicated they'd have the fire. "Were there any residents in the wagon?" She imagined a floor covered in rodent droppings and dead spiders.

He set to work on building a small fire pit. "A few. They left without argument, and it's cleaner in there than some of the tavern rooms for rent in Domora, though I can't guarantee an absence of fleas."

As wet ground was their only other option, she was happy to put up with a few flea bites in exchange for a dry place to sleep.

They used the fire he built to start drying the heavy horse blanket as well their outer garments. Siora stripped down to her shift, the thin linen drying in no time while she stood close to the fire's heat but far enough from the flame to unbraid her hair and dry the wet locks.

Gharek stripped off his wet clothes as well. All of them. Unconcerned or unaware of how the firelight sculpted his nude body into a breathtaking example of male beauty, he reached for one of the blankets and wrapped it around his narrow waist, knotting the corners so it stayed in place. Siora watched him askance while she tended the fire and pretended the glorious sight of him had no effect on her.

"This wagon was a bit of good luck for a change," she said, proud of her voice's casual tone. "Maybe it will continue and we won't be visited by brigands." Truth be told, she had little concern over such a visitation. They were off a beaten path and in a spot where they'd see a party of riders coming from leagues away, especially under the bright quarter moon, but she needed to distract herself from gawking at her companion.

He lifted one shoulder, unconcerned, and dug through the nearly empty food satchel. "Most don't plague the roads in the small hours, as there aren't travelers to waylay this late. At least not ones with anything worth stealing." He held up a shriveled orange and the last hunk of stale bread to prove his point.

Obviously he'd forgotten the book. It would mean nothing to thieves wanting *belshas* and jewelry, but its value was great to her and Gharek, even if she disliked its contents. And of course they had Suti. "We have things worth stealing."

His knowing smile told her he hadn't forgotten either item. "True, and it will be a sorry morning for any who try to steal from me."

Not a boast or a threat, just a statement of fact. Siora was re-minded of why the cat's-paw had been feared throughout the Empire.

They shared the orange and bread, soaking the second in a cup of the plum wine to make it more palatable. Siora's stomach still rumbled when they were done, and Gharek's eyebrows rose at one particularly loud protest emanating from her belly. "I can trap something and bring it back to dress and cook if you're still hungry," he said.

She waved away the offer but thanked him nonetheless. A hunger pang or two wasn't the end of the world and nothing new to her. "Neither of us will fade away before morning. I'm more tired than hungry, despite what my belly is saying, and I'm eager to reach Zaredis's encampment."

Light from the fire brightened the anticipatory gleam in Gharek's eyes, as well as the fear. "I dream of Estred every night and wake up in a sweat of worry," he said, exposing a vulnerability someone else might use against him. She wasn't one of those, and if he admitted that small but revealing detail to her, he knew that without her even saying so.

"She's your daughter," she said. "Why wouldn't you wake afraid for her?"

His broad shoulders flexed and he tilted his head to one side, studying her. "You judge me yet never ridicule. Your sympathy is never pity, and you don't hesitate to wield the whip if you think there's an injustice done. You're an endless puzzle, Siora."

She could very well apply the last to him too, and somewhere in that observation she heard criticism, praise, admiration, even disapproval—all the things she felt for him. "I'm just me," she said.

"I follow where my spirit leads, even if that's off a cliff sometimes." She offered him a wry smile.

He chuckled. "I think your spiritual failures are more honorable than the successes of others."

She blushed but refused to look down or look away. "Thank you, Gharek," she said softly.

He inclined his head before gesturing to the wagon. "Go inside and set up the bedding as you prefer. I'll join you soon."

The way he said that sent another wave of heat through her that had nothing to do with the night air. A promise in that voice and in those eyes, usually so cold and now hotter than the sun at noon.

She gathered the things that had dried and could be layered into a makeshift mattress and laid them down on the elevated portion of the wagon that had once served as a bed. The space wasn't as confined as she'd assumed before she entered, with room for two people. It snugged up against a wall with a cut-out that could be removed and allow the circulation of air to flow through the interior from one end to the other. The musty scent and heat soon washed away on the breeze, leaving the space cooler and far more pleasant. Best of all, it was dry.

Without the horse blanket as a mattress, the layers of clothing she used in its place were a poor substitute for softening the wooden platform's unforgiving surface, but it was off the floor, and as Gharek had pointed out earlier, a lot cleaner than some of the rooms for rent in Domora, or elsewhere for that matter.

She crawled onto the platform and stretched out, hiking her shift to her knees so the breeze would cool her skin. Her position allowed her a view through the back wall's cut-out of a piece of sky full of stars.

The wagon creaked and shifted once more when Gharek entered, his features in shadow, his tall frame a black silhouette that seemed to fill the space from wall to wall, though he had room to stretch his arms straight out on either side.

A flutter of movement and the sound of fabric rustling, followed by the sudden weight of a warm blanket falling across her lap told her he'd shed the covering he'd worn either for comfort or modesty, though she had doubts about the last. "Wrap in it to keep warm if you get cold, or use it as a pillow," he said. A thread of amusement wove through his next words. "Or to cover your eyes if the sight of me offends you, but I'll sweat to death under that thing in here."

"I can't be offended," she said, scooting closer to the wall to make room for him as he climbed onto the platform and lay on his back beside her. "It's so dark in the wagon, I can barely see you." Not that she'd be offended if the moon illuminated him in a blaze of silver light. He was a pleasure to look upon, to lie beside, even here in a dilapidated free trader wagon.

He crooked his outside arm to cradle his head in his hand as a makeshift pillow. The position offered him the same view she had, and the moonlight caressed his face, casting shadows under the hollows of his wide cheekbones. He glanced at her, then at the cut-out with its view of the night sky. "What do you see?"

Her answer might seem macabre to others but was a comfort to her. "All of those who died before us. I'd like to think every star is the light of a person who looks down upon the world, waiting for their loved ones to join them up there. I don't believe we ever truly die. We just change into something else."

He didn't debate or mock her, remaining silent, his gaze fixed on the heavens as if he counted the stars. How many belonged to those he'd once loved and lost? Did he fear counting Estred's there before she could count his? Siora pointed to a spot in the sky where the pattern of stars everyone called the Lady Slipper decorated a space in the celestial fabric. "Did you know Estred can name every constellation and how they got their names?"

Gharek turned his head to regard her, his expression enigmatic, eyes dark and guarded. "No, I didn't know. Did you teach her?"

She nodded. "Sometimes after the household went to bed and you were gone for an evening, the two of us would climb to the roof with a blanket and lie down on our backs to stare up at the sky. My father taught me about the stars when I was a little younger than Estred now, and so I taught her."

Once more they slipped into silence, but while Siora returned to her observation of the night sky, Gharek's gaze never drifted from her. The weight of it finally made her look back at him. "What?"

The moon's light on him wasn't gentle any longer and carved his features into even harsher angles as he continued to study her. "She cried for days when you left, even in her sleep. I could do nothing to comfort her. It didn't help that we were fleeing Domora for a safe place to hide, away from the chaos after Herself was eaten by the draga."

Siora cringed inside, and she didn't stop the tears suddenly blurring her vision from trickling down her cheeks. "I never wanted to hurt her. Truly. Sometimes when I wield the whip you describe, I strike others by accident."

Leaving Estred without explanation had been one of the hardest things she'd ever done and had troubled her most. The little girl had suffered abandonment before and terrible mistreatment when she was still young enough to be on lead strings. Such a trauma remained throughout one's life even if one didn't remember the details. How much of that pain had Siora resurrected for Estred when she left and didn't return?

She tried to wrestle her emotions—a whirlwind of anguish and guilt—into submission, to shove them under a layer of reason that told her she couldn't change past actions, only try to rectify them in the present or future. She latched on to something Gharek had said that didn't make her bleed or cry. "Malachus said he didn't eat the empress."

He snorted, his legs shifting restlessly, sliding against hers. "I would have. Even if she'd tasted vile, I would have devoured her, then shat her out."

Siora didn't doubt him. Hate drove Gharek even harder than love and almost as hard as fear did, and he'd hated Dalvila. He would have consumed every bone, entrail, and last strand of hair that was the Spider of Empire.

The distraction of those ponderings centered her thoughts, and while the guilt still ate at her, and tears still streaked her cheeks, she could now speak around a very tight throat and not sob out the words in an incoherent jumble. "If Estred's at Zaredis's camp when we return, I'd like to talk to her. Apologize then for leaving without saying goodbye."

"She might not want to talk to you."

The knowledge stung, but she'd expected it. "That's all right. I wouldn't want to talk to me either if I were her."

Gharek rolled to his side to face her. She matched his actions until they lay pressed together, hip to hip, breast to chest. He raised a hand and smeared one of her tears with his thumb, bringing it to his mouth to taste her sorrow. Questions danced in his eyes, along with that puzzlement she was growing used to seeing when he looked at her. "Why do you so love a child who isn't yours?"

An easy answer, one Siora was happy to give. She touched her fingertips to his cheek as his hand came to rest on her hip before sliding along its contours to the dip in her waist, taking the hem of her shift with it. "Because she deserves it. As does her father." There, she'd said aloud what her heart had always believed. Gharek could make of it what he wished. His breath, a light caress against her fingers, stuttered for a moment. "Estred has persevered. She's good-natured and funny, with all the quirks and annoying traits of any child her age. She embraces who she is even when others won't. There's strength of character in her that most of us don't possess, even those of us much older than her. She's an admirable child. She will be an amazing woman, and some of that is thanks to her father's love."

"You have stars in your eyes," he said in a voice that stroked her as seductively as the hand continuing its exploration of her body's profile—hip, waist, shoulder, and neck, with a steady foray across her collarbone and down one breast. Her nipple drew tight in anticipation of his touch. Siora gasped when he cupped her there and arched her back.

"And you have shadows in yours," she replied when the sizzling sensations racing through her body allowed her to speak. She began her own exploration of him, mapping every line and ridge of his face, pausing at his mouth to feel his lips move under her fingertips when he spoke.

"You can't fix me or save me, not even with a good swiving. I know nothing of nobility."

"But everything of devotion," she replied. Her heart ached at the hopelessness in his voice. "I don't intend to fix you. That's a burden too heavy for another to bear. Your love for Estred should inspire you to be a better man, not a worse one. In the end, only you can save you."

This wasn't about rescue or redemption but something far simpler, truer, and honest. It was desire without justification, affection without explanation, maybe even love if she wanted to step onto that thin ledge and risk a terrible fall.

More confusion, this time mixed with doubt and the fire of a rising passion. His hand slipped from her breast to ride her lower back before cupping her buttock. "Then why?"

"Why not?" she asked in a voice that shook. Her own hand slid down his neck to the hollow of his throat, then over the slope of one shoulder. His skin was smooth and hot, stroked by the night breeze so that his nipples pebbled just as hers did.

"I don't think I will ever comprehend you, Siora of the dead."

She smiled, arching fully into him and sliding her arms around his neck to bring his head down for a kiss. "You don't have to, Gharek of Cabast, to find comfort in my arms."

She buried her hands in his hair and moaned into his mouth when he parted her lips and swept his tongue inside, learning the shape and taste of her as she learned him. He rolled until he rested partially on top of her, heavy and hard, his hips thrusting gently against hers in a silent coaxing for her to spread her thighs and invite him to settle in the valley there.

Siora abandoned carding his hair through her fingers to grasp her shift and yank it higher so that her legs were free, and her knees splayed wide to accommodate him. His cock nudged against her, erect and made slippery by her own desire as he sought entrance to her body. She kissed him even harder, her tongue battling his, a truce declared only long enough to breathe or allow her to suckle his lower lip while he nibbled at her upper one.

His hips rocked against her, a teasing half thrust that made her gasp and then made her squirm when he forsook her mouth to nuzzle her breast and torture her nipple with his tongue. By the time he finished there and moved to her other breast, she was reduced to mewling noises as she bucked in his embrace and dug her fingers into his buttocks to urge him closer and bring him inside her. She clawed at him when he suddenly pulled away only to lift her into a half-sitting position and tug her shift off her body. It landed on the floor atop the blanket Gharek had abandoned.

"Thank the gods," she said when he laid her down and settled his weight once more on her, bending one of her knees and positioning her other leg until it hung off the platform. The position opened her to him even more, and he grinned at her enthusiastic gratitude.

"Did you miss me?" he teased, rubbing the length of his cock against her so that each back and forth motion stroked her body's most sensitive pleasure point. The motion set fire to every nerve under her skin and curled her toes.

Siora's arms flexed hard on his back as she met each provocative movement with one of her own, angling so that every thrust forward forced the tip of his cock into her despite his half-hearted resistance and wish to prolong his teasing.

"I crave you," she said. He was heavy, his presence overwhelming and wondrous.

He smiled. "For once your honesty doesn't cut deep." He made love to her mouth in a leisurely fashion, exploring the shape of her lips, the taste of her tongue, the ridges of her teeth.

Siora clamped her knees against his hips, tensed her thighs and forced him down even as she surged upward. The motion drove him deep into her. Gharek broke the kiss to gasp, his eyes glittering in the shadows. Siora echoed the sound and dug her fingers into his arms, savoring the feel of him within her, her passage stretching to accommodate his girth, her inner muscles squeezing around him so that he groaned her name.

"Wait," he implored. His muscular arms quivered under her palms.

"Why?" Siora raised one hand to caress his cheek. "This is right. This is good. As I always knew it would be."

It was true. Unexplainable maybe but so very true, and she'd never been one to turn away from a truth, even when it frightened or confused her.

He surrendered on another groan, sliding his hands under her backside to lift her. His cock pulsed even deeper inside her, that pulse mimicked by the delicate skin at his temple where her fingertips rested.

It wasn't the swiving he'd referred to earlier, though Siora would have been happy with that as well. This was more—lovemaking fierce and passionate, of equal sharing. A breathless glimpse into the sleeping heart of a man who'd once known what it was to love a woman but had forgotten.

When Siora cried out at the force of her climax, it was an incoherent sound bordering on a dry sob. Gharek's name was a whisper on her lips and a cry in her mind.

A pair of thrusts and he found his own pleasure after her, his utterances a drawn-out moan ending on a prayer to unnamed gods.

Afterward they lay entwined, legs and arms entangled, feverish skin cooling in the night air. Gharek's breaths fanned over her hair, and Siora mapped the planes of his face with her fingers. He matched her affections by gliding his palm down the valley of her waist and over the swell of her hip, making a return journey several times over.

The quiet between them was peaceful, easy, comforting. Gharek finally ended it by saying, "I never imagined this when I retrieved my daughter and her protector from a street mob." His voice was soft, contemplative, with a hint of disbelief as if he couldn't quite fathom how the two of them had ended up in this place, in this moment, in this circumstance.

"Do you regret it?" Asking the question made her stomach clench. Waiting for the answer made it knot, but she refused to look away. No matter his answer, she'd never regret this, never regret holding the cat's-paw in her arms and in her body. In her heart as well. Acknowledging the last, even if he'd never know, nearly took her breath away.

There was no future for her with Gharek beyond the task set for them by General Zaredis, but these moments were hers, to be treasured, held close, and fondly recalled once they parted ways and his memory of her grew cloudy with time and distance.

His hand paused on her hip. "No. I regret many things but not this. Never this." He kissed her in a way that assured her he meant every word and stood by his statement. They made love a second time, an unhurried, more deliberate exploration of each other's bodies but no less passionate. Once more Siora beseeched Gharek by name in her mind even as she pressed her mouth to his neck and gasped her pleasure at his touch.

He held her for the remainder of the night, her body tucked into the curve of his despite the wagon's warmth and the bed's narrow confines that made it even warmer. He breathed softly, steadily, the cadence of a lullaby to tease her ear; it should have lulled her to sleep but didn't. Instead she lay awake, torturing herself with fanciful imaginings of an impossible life she'd never know—at least not with this man or in this Empire on the brink of collapse.

No regrets, she reminded herself.

She finally drifted off shortly before dawn, only to be awakened with what felt like moments later by ticklish kisses on her nape.

"Time to go, Siora," Gharek whispered in her ear. "The world beyond this one commands our hours."

She heard the disappointment in his voice, and it warmed her to know he felt as she did—reluctant to leave this ramshackle sanctuary where, for a few stolen moments, they could forget the grim and terrifying realities of ghost-eaters, hostage children, inevitable war, and the certain knowledge that Gharek's reward for succeeding in his endeavors was a death made mercifully swift instead of brutally slow.

Neither lingered in their morning ablutions, though Gharek

interspersed his preparations to leave with quick pauses to kiss her or stroke her back as he passed to saddle Suti while she packed their meager gear. This time when they rode pillion, she relaxed against him, taking the reins while he caressed her through her clothes. They didn't speak, and Siora savored the moments, the silence, and Gharek's touch as the sun fully crested the horizon and bathed the landscape in a wash of yellow and orange.

They still had a fair distance to cover, but with Suti bearing two riders, Gharek warned they'd have to go slow so as not to exhaust the gelding. "I worry for Estred, but I'll not get to her any faster if I kill this nag from running him into the ground and end up having to walk the rest of the way."

He took advantage of the leisurely pace and her handle on the reins to retrieve the book the master librarian had given him and read aloud some of the spells written there. Siora didn't worry he might invoke anything. He wasn't a sorcerer. She changed her mind when he once more recited the necromancer's spell to raise and trap the dead.

"Why are you reading that foul spell?" Gharek had a pleasant voice when he wasn't snarling at someone, but the words themselves sent splinters of cold into her skin. "And out loud?"

She felt him shrug against her.

"I commit things better to memory if I say them aloud several times."

"It wouldn't matter. You aren't a necromancer. It won't work for you."

Another shrug. "But if I lose the book, I can just write down the spell again and sell it to a newly minted necromancer wanting his own household staff of obedient spirits."

Siora twisted in the saddle, trying to see his expression. Humor had laced his voice, though she found nothing amusing about the idea. He gazed at her, lips curved in a hint of a smile. "You wouldn't," she said.

One of his dark eyebrows arched. "Wouldn't I?"

She frowned, unwilling to further challenge his question. He was the cat's-paw. He'd done many things others considered questionable, even heinous. Things he considered just as heinous but necessary. What was one more? She gestured to the book with a lift of her chin. "Maybe you should recite some of the other spells in there. Things like the ward breakers so you can steal the Windcry."

Gharek scoffed. "I'll leave that up to Zaredis's mage. He can contribute something other than swanning about in his robes, trying to look mysterious."

Be that as it may, she had no interest in listening to him repeat the vile incantation over and over. It was already etched in her mind, playing like the lyrics to a grim dirge. "At least recite the spell in a quieter voice. Half the Empire can hear you right now."

To her surprise, he acquiesced, closing the book before tucking it back into the satchel tied to the saddle. He contented himself with nuzzling her hair and kissing either side of her neck, a far more pleasant way to spend the time in her opinion.

Those too-brief moments of intimacy ended with the approach of a dozen riders appearing over the ridge of a gentle slope that hid from view what lay on the other side. Siora's stomach plummeted and didn't rise, even when she realized the approaching band were part of General Zaredis's army. A scout must have seen her and Gharek riding across the plain and sent word back to the general.

"An escort," Gharek said in the driest tones. "How nice."

"I thought we still had a few hours left before we reached the camp," she said, watching as the soldiers galloped toward them and praying they were truly just an escort sent by their commander and not some hotheaded bunch of idiots wanting to prove their mettle to each other.

Gharek sat rigid behind her now, no longer pressed to her back with relaxed affection. "I'll wager the camp has moved closer to Domora."

He was right. Once those sent to bring them back to the camp verified Gharek's identity, they said nothing more, even when he questioned them about Estred. Siora stroked his thigh where it rested against hers in reassurance. His daughter was more valuable to Zaredis alive than dead, the one thing that guaranteed the cat's-paw's complete cooperation. The general wouldn't jeopardize that while he relied on Gharek to help him gain the Windcry.

They topped the ridge on which their escort had first appeared, and she gasped at the sight before her. "So many! I didn't think his army was this large."

At the bottom of the gentle slope, a dark shadow made of tents, soldiers, and horses, numbering in the thousands, covered the plain. Siege engines in various states of construction perched on wagons, waiting to be rolled to their destination, and there were as many oxen as there were horses to toil in their traces as they pulled the great machines across fields and rutted roads.

This wasn't the camp they'd left. It had swelled in size many times over, a true measure of the might Zaredis commanded and why he felt confident that he'd still win Domora from its current emperor even without the aid of the Windcry.

She couldn't see Gharek's expression behind her, and his flat voice revealed nothing of his thoughts as they rode toward the encampment. "We only saw the first contingent of troops," he said. "The rest have since crossed the channel. What you're seeing here is what the people of Domora will face from behind its walls, and they have no idea what comes toward them."

"He doesn't need the Windcry," she said. "Not with a force such as this." It was vast, as far as the eye could see.

Behind her, Gharek snorted. "He needs it. Word has surely reached the capital that Zaredis is amassing here and plans to march soon. Kraelag may be an uninhabitable ruin, but its harbor still functions. By the time Zaredis makes it to Domora, General Tovan will have the forces of both army and navy behind him, a match for Zaredis's troops. If Zaredis wants a victory instead of a bloodbath, he'll need the artifact."

They spoke to each other in low voices. The soldiers surrounding them didn't ride close enough to hear them clearly.

Siora's gut twisted into a knot of dread. Gharek was returning to Zaredis willingly, to his own death with open arms because his daughter depended on his arrival, though she probably had no idea the kind of risks her father was taking. *What a grim reward for a task completed*, she thought, and blinked hard to suppress the tears welling in her eyes. Reunited with his child only to die for the sake of empty vengeance. Zaredis could kill Gharek a hundred times over, each time more brutal than the last, and it would still never bring his brother back. If only she could have done more, executed some grand feat of rescue that would unite father and daughter without the chains of extortion and threat of death.

"I wasn't much help to you on this trip," she said. "I'd hoped to offer you more."

His body shifted against her as he shrugged. "You warned me of that assassin and helped us escape from the creatures in the Maesor."

"My father did that."

"But only because you were there. And your bargaining with Zaredis to help Kalun bought me both time and leverage." His voice softened even more as he leaned in to nuzzle her ear. "Are you sure you don't want to try the Holdfast spell? There's a summoning one as well right before it."

She shuddered at the idea. "How many times must I say I'm not a necromancer? And even if I were, I certainly wouldn't enslave my own father."

A note of exasperation entered Gharek's voice. "You can always set him free. Holdfast is a spell with both a lock and a key."

This was a man who saw ethics more as a nuisance than a code. "That isn't the point."

"Your honor blinds you," he said, straightening away from her.

"And your lack of it twists you," she replied in an equally sharp tone.

They didn't say anything more after that until they reached the edge of the camp. Gharek's loose clasp around her waist tightened as they rode toward its center, every eye upon them as they passed. Siora did her best not to meet any one person's gaze, certain if she did, it would set off the pack aggression of wolves, and they were already in a dangerous situation as it was.

The captain who'd first captured her and Gharek as they fled the fighting at Wellspring Holt met them in the center of camp. Mild surprise animated his lined face, though his comment was no more polite than those he'd previously tossed their way. "I see you and your whore came back alive and well, cat's-paw." His gaze raked Siora, pausing on the sight of Gharek's arm wrapped snug around her middle. One eyebrow rose, and a gleam entered his eyes when he turned his attention to Gharek. "Obviously you found comfort on the trip. Or at least your prick did."

Coarse laughter from the soldiers surrounding them made Siora's face heat. She didn't reply to the man's vulgar remark, refusing to be baited. Gharek didn't either, though his arm tightened enough around her waist to squeeze a tiny squeak from her.

Disappointed by the lack of response from his target, the captain lost his derisive smile. His features once more settled into a dour expression. He gestured with one hand for them to follow. "Come. The general has been gnawing at the bit, wondering when or even if you'd return. Probably tired of playing nanny to your armless brat."

"I'll play nanny to that sweet young piece any day, even if she doesn't have arms," one soldier in the crowd called out.

One moment Gharek was holding Siora against him, the next he was pushing her away from him. She couldn't see what he was doing, only the result of his actions. A flash of steel shot through the air. A dull thunk followed, and the man whose vile comment made Siora's stomach curdle in revulsion fell to the ground on his back, Gharek's blade half embedded in his forehead.

The shock and silence that followed lasted no more than a heartbeat before the crowd rushed the gelding to drag Gharek from the saddle and Siora along with him. She cried out, holding the pommel in an iron grip as she hung off the side and the gelding whinnied its panic. The animal began to buck, back legs lashing out, and a few voices cursed in pain as powerful hooves connected with bodies standing too close. It was mayhem around them, and Siora lost sight of Gharek amid a flailing of bodies around her and under her thrashing horse.

"Cease before I have every one of you drawn and quartered," a voice bellowed above the din, and suddenly General Zaredis was there, hurtling into the fray.

It was the command of a man but might as well have been the edict of a god the way every soldier halted what they were doing and snapped to attention, leaving a bloodied, bedraggled, but thankfully still alive Gharek sprawled on the ground.

Siora dismounted, giving the gelding a reassuring pat. Its dark eyes still showed the white of fear as it watched her and the crowd surrounding them. Gharek had already sprung to his feet and shook himself off by the time she reached him. Blood streamed from his nose, and a mottled red stain with the promise of a bruise to come marred the entire length of his jaw and part of one cheek. They stood in the center of a makeshift arena created by Zaredis's men, many glaring at Gharek with murder in their eyes. The general himself wore a different expression, one of disapproval but also relief. She didn't imagine the second, having never been one for fanciful thoughts. Zaredis might hate the cat's-paw as much as his men, but he was glad for his return.

"What is the meaning of this?" he barked, leveling that sword-sharp gaze on his captain, who'd lost his snide demeanor and now looked a little pale under his leader's unwavering regard.

Ready to interrupt and contradict the lies she expected to hear regarding the reason for the soldier's death and Gharek's part in it, she was stunned when the captain gave the truth of what happened without embellishment. When he finished, the crowd parted so

Zaredis could have a better look at the man the cat's-paw had killed. The general shoved the body with the tip of his boot, his face a cool mask that gave nothing away. He was quiet for the longest time before turning to Gharek.

"You shouldn't have killed him," he said. "At least not so quickly. I would have given him to you to torture first if you wished."

A unified gasp went up, Siora's included. She had expected ruthlessness from Zaredis, had seen the calculating mind behind his eyes, fueled by an ambition that understood the unavoidable brutality of collateral damage, of extortion in negotiation, and the absolute certainty that he didn't bluff. She hadn't expected an understanding of Gharek's action or the expression in his gaze that told everyone he considered the killing just.

"I'll keep that in mind," Gharek said, keeping a wary eye on Zaredis's men still surrounding him.

"Do you have information for me?" Zaredis asked, no longer interested in the corpse at his feet.

"Yes." Gharek's features tightened. "My daughter . . ."

"Is safe and cared for. She's waiting for you in my tent. You can see her, and then I want your information." Zaredis's kindness ended there. "Try any trick to escape with her, and I'll kill you both." He turned his attention to Siora and the gelding. "Where did you get the horse?"

She answered before Gharek did, the words sour on her tongue as she mixed honesty with mendacity. "Free traders who helped us when we escaped Midrigar." That was the truth, and Zaredis's eyebrows rose with his interest. "I once helped the mother of one of them. They repaid my kindness by giving me this gelding." She had no intention of admitting Gharek had paid Malachus nearly all of the coin Zaredis had given them. If he knew, he'd consider the gelding his and take it. He could still take it anyway, even if he thought it rightfully Siora's, but she hoped he'd leave the horse with her.

"That must have been some kindness," the general said in a doubtful voice.

"Oh it was," Gharek replied for her, the acid in his tone making her wince. His feelings for her had changed, softened. Of that she had no doubt, but he still carried a resentment for what he considered as her betrayal of him and Estred, even if he had a better understanding for why she'd done so.

"Come," Zaredis said. "Your daughter awaits you, and I and my sorcerer await your news." He narrowed his eyes at his captain and gestured to the dead man. "Dispose of him and bring me the cat's-paw's knife. Put the shade speaker's mount in with one of the herds for now."

She and Gharek followed the general on foot back to his tent, an entourage of soldiers and ministers following at a respectful distance. Zaredis didn't bother keeping up conversation. The lack of hospitality didn't surprise her. They were neither friends nor honored guests but informants under duress. This wasn't a social visit.

Gharek glanced at her as they walked. "For once you don't judge me," he said softly.

His sentence made her heart contract with a hard squeeze. "Killing that soldier?" She shook her head. "No. I can't find compassion or mercy inside me for such a monster. In your place I might have reacted differently, chosen another path, but I understand why you did what you did. Estred is your daughter, a victim of the world and those like him who occupy it."

"What would you have done? If Estred was yours?"

He was asking her far more than the question he spoke aloud. Would you kill without remorse? Kill on command? Abduct the innocent and exploit the unwary? Sell yourself if it meant helping or saving a loved one?

All questions with answers that made justice a slippery slope, honor an empty word, and hope a myth. She reached for his hand, startling him. Her fingers twined with his, and she gave his hand a squeeze. "You ask me the questions you've already answered for yourself, but I'm not you, Gharek. My experiences aren't yours. I perceive the world differently from you. I don't know what I would have done. I begin to understand the fear that drives you as a parent, but maybe you should consider how it rules you so."

She wished they could stop, for just a moment, so she could enfold him in her arms and hold him close. This brittle, hard-edged man had made love not only to her body but to her heart, bewitching her not only with his touch but with the glimpses into his soul. She'd had peeks into it before, when she lived in his household as Estred's nurse and watched the way he interacted with his daughter. Then she wondered if two spirits occupied the same body, one loving if melancholy, the other dark, frigid, calculating. She'd learned in these last weeks a spirit had many facets of light and dark, and this man in particular was made up of countless hues and shades of both.

They reached Zaredis's spacious tent before Gharek could respond, and Siora watched, enchanted, as a noticeable change came over him. Dusty, bloodied, and bruised, he nearly glowed with anticipation of seeing Estred again, even if it was in the last place he wanted her to be.

Zaredis must have seen it as well, and in an odd gesture of kindness pulled the tent flap open and waved Gharek in. "Go ahead. She's waiting."

Gharek didn't hesitate. He bent to swoop into the interior. A child's high-pitched "Papa!" carried through half the camp, and Siora smiled at the general, who returned it with a half one of his own. He motioned for her to follow Gharek.

She entered the tent to discover Estred held tight in her father's embrace, his muscular forearms quivering with the effort not to crush her small body to him. She had no arms to return the hug, but she managed in her own way, her spindly legs wrapped tight around Gharek's middle as she nuzzled her face into his shoulder. Siora kept her silence, not wanting to intrude on the moment between the two. Zaredis came to stand silently behind her, and she caught an arrested expression on his features before he hid it. One of longing and regret.

Gharek pulled back enough to tip Estred's face up to the tent's lamplight for a closer look at her small features. Father and daughter stared at each other for several moments. "You're well, Estred?" he finally asked.

She nodded, grinning for a moment before an indignant frown chased it away. "I'm fine, though they came and got me before the sun was even up, and we had to ride horses all day and sit in a hot tent a lot of the time." The grin returned, tinged with pride as well as puzzlement. "They say you're one of the general's soldiers now."

The thin smile he returned lacked any humor. "Not quite, love, though I answer to him for the moment."

Zaredis's faint snort captured Estred's attention. Her eyes rounded, and her mouth fell open when she caught sight of Siora standing next to him.

Siora waggled her fingers in a small wave, her heartbeat thundering in her ears as dread dug a pit in her belly. Gharek had warned her Estred had grieved the sudden loss of her nurse, a vanishing without warning, without goodbyes. To a child, it was the worst sort of abandonment. "Hello, Estred," she said in a voice that warbled from the knot of tears stuck in her throat. "You've grown since we last saw each other, and you're still the prettiest girl I know. I've missed you."

Estred's stunned expression instantly changed to one of hurt, of resentment. She buried her face in Gharek's neck and refused to look at her erstwhile nurse. He turned his head, an I-told-you-so look on his face, along with a surprising touch of pity.

Siora nodded. "You warned me. I knew to expect it." That didn't mean it stung any less.

A respectful moment of quiet for the reunion and Zaredis returned to business. He left his place at the tent's entrance to stride to the table and chair set up for him at the back of the tent. The action must have been a signal for the two sentries posted on either side of the entrance, for they bent and motioned for a small stream of advisers and lieutenants to enter the space and await their commander's pleasure.

Zaredis leaned back in his chair and steepled his fingers just under his chin as he regarded them all. "I've kept my part of our bargain, cat's-paw. Your daughter is unharmed and well cared for. Even the maid who accompanied her is enjoying my hospitality in a tent she shares only with young Estred here, and they are guarded day and night."

Siora wondered if Zaredis expected a thank-you from Gharek. If so, he'd no doubt be disappointed. If the cat's-paw actually survived this entire ordeal, he wouldn't remember the general had been kind to Estred, only that he'd taken her hostage, for which Zaredis had made an enemy for life.

Gharek didn't gave away any of his thoughts as he held Estred close. "And I've kept mine," he said. "The Windcry is where it's always been, still warded against thieves. It's only a matter of time before the current puppet or Tovan himself finds the various secret passages and the Windcry itself, but for now it's undiscovered and undisturbed. I can draw you a map to every secret entrance into the palace as well as those at the city walls your spies may not yet have found." He gestured to his satchel that a soldier had delivered to the tent and which now lay at Zaredis's feet. "There's a grimoire in there that will be of use to your sorcerer for breaking the ward and possibly protecting your brother's spirit."

As he spoke, the air next to Siora wavered and turned chilly enough to raise goose flesh on her arms, even in the sweltering tent. A familiar form took shape.

Welcome back, shade speaker, Kalun's ethereal voice whispered in her mind.

She smiled and returned the thought-greeting. *It's good to see you, Kalun. Has the ghost-eater returned?*

Palpable fear wrapped around his misty form in black tendrils. *Not yet, but I think it waits and watches. Can you help?*

She might have refused to read aloud the foul necromantic spells in Gharek's book, but she hadn't discarded his words or the possibility he'd put forth to her—that she might be more than a shade speaker, might possess a dark power that made her shudder with its potential. *I don't know, and if I can, you might not want such help. It comes in the form of a necromancer's enslavement spell.*

Zaredis interrupted their silent conversation, his eyes glittering as his gaze moved from her to the seemingly empty space beside her, and back again. "Is my brother here, shade speaker?" She nodded. "Show me."

Siora held out her hand, the icy caress of the grave on her fingers and palm where Kalun held her. Her touch made him visible, eliciting a gasp from those in the tent who hadn't previously witnessed her ability. Estred squeaked in fright, shoving her body harder into Gharek's, who held her close and whispered assurances in her ear.

It was an arresting sight, one that brought tears to Siora's eyes and an ache to her heart. It was like watching two spirits battle for possession of one body—the cat's-paw who'd done Dalvila's dirty work and killed without remorse and this fiercely devoted father who soothed a child's fright.

She turned away, unable to look any longer, and settled on the equally distressing sight of Zaredis staring at his brother's revenant with a kind of despairing affection. His expression wiped clean when he noticed Siora watching him.

He swept a hand in a wide arc to include all who stood in the tent. "Someone find Rurian and send him to me. Clear off one of these tables. Bring parchment, ink, and food." He pulled the spellbook out of Gharek's satchel, turning it over in his hands before opening it to fan the pages with his fingers. He finally gifted Gharek with a distracted glance. "Put your daughter down so she can go back to her maid. You've work to do."

Gharek's eyes narrowed to slits, and his mouth thinned to a mutinous line. He made no move to let go of Estred.

Alarmed by what promised to be a battle of wills between cat's-paw and general, Siora spoke. "She is quiet, lord, and well-behaved. If you don't mind losing sight of your brother for a short time, I can keep her entertained while Gharek works. They've been separated a long time. He'll be less distracted if she's in his sight, and I'll make sure she doesn't interrupt."

The two adversaries stared at her before turning to eye each other. It was a standoff in which she held her breath and prayed her argument and assurance would sway Zaredis. She breathed a soundless exhalation when he nodded.

"Very well," he said. "But the first bit of noise and she goes back to her tent. Now tell me the details of your journey and what you discovered."

Well done, Kalun told her, fading before all but her as he let go of her hand. *You're a natural diplomat, combining reason with persuasion.*

The hard part hasn't started, she replied. *Keeping a small child occupied and quiet is no small task.*

They watched as Gharek whispered something to Estred, who first shook her head, refusing whatever offer he made to her, then finally nodded. He set her down, watching with a hawk's gaze as she made her way toward Siora. The condemnation in the child's eyes made Siora shrivel inside, but she offered Estred a smile.

Gharek mouthed "thank you" and turned his attention to the waiting Zaredis.

Like Gharek, Siora scrutinized Estred from head to toe, noting she looked healthy, clean, and uninjured. Zaredis didn't lie, at least not in this. He'd seen to it that his young hostage had not come to harm.

She pointed to where servants laid out numerous platters heaped with various foods, including meats and cheeses, fresh fruits, and pastries. "Have you eaten, love? There's plenty there to tempt the pickiest eater."

"Don't call me that," Estred snapped.

Siora hid her flinch, cursing herself for the inadvertent slip. Though she'd expected her former charge's anger, Estred's rejection of her verbal affection stung. "I'm sorry, Estred," she said, keeping her voice mild. "My mistake. Would you still like to eat? It's a good way to be quiet and not disturb your father and the general with a lot of chatter, and you can stay in the tent."

"I'm not hungry," Estred said in a whisper. Her resentment turned to curiosity. "Can I see the ghost again?"

Siora glanced at Kalun, who grinned and nodded. "You can, but let's go to the corner there." She pointed to the far side of the tent. "We can talk without bothering anyone. Just keep your voice low."

The spot they occupied held an array of Zaredis's weapons as well as his armor. Estred showed no interest in those, waiting instead with wide eyes and an eagerness free of fear at the chance to meet the phantom who'd appeared before them earlier.

"Ooh," she said on a slow exhale when Siora held Kalun's hand once more and he materialized in front of her. "It's magic!"

Fear sizzled through Siora's veins at the word, and Kalun's face assumed a contemplative expression tinged with a wariness that hadn't been there before. "No, Estred. Not magic. Shade-speaking isn't magic. It's like fortune-telling, that's all. Those people read the bones, the cards, or the leaves to gain information. I just talk to the dead."

Estred wasn't put off. "But how did you make him appear so we can see him?"

That is more than chatting with the dead, Siora, Kalun said. *Fortune-telling and second sight don't make us visible. Necromancy does.*

Was that accusation in his words? Siora scowled at him. *I'm not a necromancer.*

Are you sure? He nodded toward the book held in his brother's hand as he talked to Gharek. *Did you not say you might have help to offer against the ghost-eater? Help I might not want because it's necromantic?*

Estred interrupted their silent conversation. "Can I touch you?" she asked Kalun. She stretched out a bare foot, one hesitant toe a hairsbreadth from where he stood. He nodded.

"He won't be solid," Siora told her. "More like a cold mist to you."

Kalun held still as Estred ran her toe across and then through his leg. She snatched her foot back for a moment before approaching again, this time pointing all five toes. Once more her foot glided through his misty shape. "Does it hurt?"

Kalun grinned and Siora translated for him. "No, it doesn't hurt. Maybe a tickle here and there."

Estred grinned back, no longer as hesitant and far more fascinated. A tiny frown creased her forehead, and she eyed Siora with suspicion. "How come your hand doesn't go through his when you hold it? Is that what a shade speaker can do when they talk to ghosts?"

Siora had never seen another shade speaker touch a ghost and make them visible to others. If they possessed the same capabilities she did, they didn't make it known to all and sundry for fear of hanging or burning or suffering any number of gruesome executions for the crime of practicing magic and not just fortune-telling. "I don't know how it works like it does," she told Estred honestly. "Sometimes we can't explain why things happen the way they do."

"You said something like that to me when people were throwing rocks at us," Estred said. "You just said *people* instead of *things*."

Siora tightened her mouth and looked away, blinking hard to chase away the tears blurring her vision. Estred had brought up the first time Siora had met her, a frightened child on the verge of being stoned to death. Siora wished that memory was nothing more than a wispy cloud of fading recollection, but if Estred remembered what her savior had told her regarding why people would try to hurt her when she'd done nothing wrong, then she remembered the events of that day with the same crystal clarity that Siora recalled them.

She wished she might bend to hug the girl, but Estred, like her father, wasn't quick to forgive, and Siora didn't doubt she'd squirm away with a snarl and a warning not to touch her. "I did say that, didn't I?" She glanced at Kalun, who gave her a measuring look.

"Siora saved me from people who were throwing rocks at me in an alley one day," Estred told him.

A ghostly eyebrow rose. *Is that so?* he said. *Very brave of her. You must mean a lot to her to face down a mob to defend you.*

"Kalun says those people probably regret what they did," Siora translated instead.

Liar. The word boomed in her thoughts, and Kalun's scowl matched hers. *Why didn't you tell her what I said instead of that horseshit?*

Because she doesn't need to be burdened with a sense of obligation or the idea that I'm something more than what I am. I'm not brave or a hero. People just shouldn't be throwing rocks at children.

A brush on her free hand made her turn. Estred frowned. "Are you two arguing? Your faces are crinkled ugly."

Siora eyed the ghost with a half smile. "Kalun is a very stubborn ghost and likes to argue with people."

Kalun's indignant snort was even louder in her mind than his previous accusation. Instead of relying on her to translate for him, he used exaggerated hand motions and facial expressions that conveyed very clearly to the now grinning Estred that he wasn't the only one who was stubborn and enjoyed arguing.

The loud flutter of the tent flap as it was slapped aside heralded the arrival of Zaredis's enigmatic sorcerer. Rurian took in his surroundings with a sweeping glance, pausing briefly on Siora and Kalun. He joined Gharek and Zaredis at one of the tables where a large sheaf of parchment had been rolled out. The cat's-paw was sketching something there with a combination of broad strokes and more careful scratches with a shaving of coal. The map of the palace in Domora and the path to the Windcry.

Siora turned to Estred, pressing a finger to her lips. "Let's hear what the sorcerer has to say," she told her charge.

Zaredis had Gharek repeat what he'd told him about the palace and the Windcry's protection spells. Rurian listened in stoic silence until Zaredis held out the book the master librarian had given Gharek in Domora.

His strange eyes lit up, and his long fingers curved over the book with the touch of a lover. Unlike Zaredis, he didn't flip carelessly through the pages with only brief pauses to scan arcane words or note a sigil drawing. Instead, he turned each page slowly, fingertips gliding along the edges as if he listened to as well as read the words written there.

Gharek's eyes were narrowed as he watched the sorcerer. "Can you read?"

Rurian's answering smile held no amusement but plenty of dislike. "Better than you, I'd wager." He ignored Gharek after that, concentration firmly seated on the book's contents. The cat's-paw went back to drawing, and Zaredis back to watching him and occasionally asking questions.

Once, the sorcerer lowered his head to peer closer at one page, his mouth moving in silent speech. He finally straightened, only to pin Siora to the spot where she stood with a long stare that did its best to peel her skin back for a look inside her soul. He didn't have to say anything for her to know he'd just come across the section on necromancy.

In her mind she prepared a denial of being anything other than a lowly shade speaker. A true voice for the dead but not a wielder of death magic. Instead Rurian returned his attention to the book, speaking up only after reading a few more pages and stopping on a particular one for a long moment.

"Lord," he said, holding the book out to Zaredis, thumb holding up the pages to the spot he wanted the general to read. "This spell might work to break the ward that guards the Windcry, though the advantage of an ambush attack would be lost once the ward is broken. I can do it, but even then the cat's-paw will find it a challenge to steal the Windcry and not get caught."

"I'm very motivated to not get caught," Gharek said.

Kalun's chilly grip on Siora's hand tightened. *Tell my brother I wish to speak with him with just you to hear and translate.*

She nodded and relayed the message to Zaredis. Gharek's and the sorcerer's eyebrows rose, but the general didn't hesitate. He crossed the tent in a few strides, passing Estred, who took advantage of the interruption to be with her father again.

Zaredis's puzzled gaze moved between shade speaker and shade. "What do you wish to tell me?"

"Do you still intend to execute the cat's-paw?" Kalun tipped his chin toward Gharek, whose attention was fully on Estred as she pointed to the things on the map he was drawing.

Judging by his expression, the question caught Zaredis by surprise. Siora as well, though she did her best to keep any emotion out of her voice while she relayed Kalun's words to his brother. The general eyed her suspiciously for a moment. "I'm only repeating what he tells me," she assured him. "Nothing more. Nothing less."

She wanted so badly to implore Zaredis to reconsider his quest for vengeance against Gharek, to beg for mercy—if not for Gharek than for Estred, who needed him. Estred had Siora should she lose her father, but a homeless shade speaker couldn't offer much to an orphan.

Zaredis answered Kalun's question with one of his own. "Why do you ask?"

"*You always were a cagey one with your answers,*" Kalun replied with a smile. The smile melted away. "*Because his life has been of more benefit to you, and his death will serve no purpose. I'm dead and will remain dead, whether or not you kill him. The only real impact will be on his daughter. The innocent suffer enough in this world as it is, brother. Why add to the misery?*"

Siora avoided meeting Zaredis's eyes as she translated, afraid the emotion she managed to keep out of her voice would be blatantly painted on her face for him to see. His features took on a more severe cast at Kalun's remarks. "Do you not want vengeance? You were innocent of wrongdoing and died a savage death for trying to help. All thanks to the cat's-paw."

An ethereal sigh of regret drifted across Siora's soul, and Kalun stared at his brother with wistful melancholy. "*He fetched me with only the knowledge that I was summoned to heal his liege. He didn't know what she would do, though I doubt he was surprised when Dalvila turned on us.*" A flash of anger tightened his misty features for a moment. "*This is an empty vengeance. The person I'd want to extract it from is dead, the manner of her death a justice none of us could have imagined but more befitting than anything you or I or anyone else could have dealt her.*"

The struggle to keep her tone emotionless grew harder and harder with every sentence Siora translated for Kalun. This uneasy spirit, still lingering, had become Gharek's best chance of avoiding a death sentence and Estred's best hope of keeping her father, and it was her own strong belief that he, above all others, would be the one to sway his brother toward clemency.

Gharek wouldn't meekly submit to dying. He played puppet to Zaredis first to buy time and then to protect Estred. For him, all roads led back to her. Still, Siora didn't doubt he'd worked out in his mind some plan of escape for himself and his daughter. In her opinion, his chances of succeeding were slim at best, but if the general was inclined to change his mind . . . *Please*, she silently begged Zaredis. *Please reconsider.* His answer disappointed her, though it still allowed her to hope.

"I'll think on your argument," he told Kalun, his frown even darker now. "For now he's in no danger from me. I still need him to help me retrieve the Windcry."

"*I can help with that,*" Kalun said. Siora gave him a questioning look. So did Zaredis.

"How so?" He nodded to Siora. "Without her, none can see you or hear your words, not even Rurian. And it makes no sense to bring her. She'll only be a hindrance while we sneak inside."

As much as she disliked the notion of being a hindrance for anyone about anything, she had to agree and told Kalun, "Your brother's right. The more people trying to sneak past Domoran guards, the greater the challenge in doing so."

"*The dead have ways of alerting the living when they so desire,*" Kalun argued. "*A shade speaker is damn convenient but not necessary. My brother and I can figure out a way for me to warn him and the cat's-paw, if there's trouble afoot or they're about to be discovered.*"

Siora could almost hear the calculations, the strategies, and the risks weighed and measured as Zaredis stared at his brother's ghost. "So be it." He held out a forearm, which Kalun clasped in a phantom grip, his hand and arm vague shadows against Zaredis's living flesh. "I welcome your help, brother. Once I see the cat's-paw's completed map, we can plan in detail."

He gestured for Siora and Kalun to follow him back to the table where Gharek continued sketching an impressively detailed map of the summer palace's interior. Rurian stood beside him, silent except for an occasional question about true distance between one hallway and another or the position of a staircase and where it stood in relation to a guard's line of sight.

Estred, who'd soon grown bored with her father's dull task, approached Siora. She still wore the remnants of that condemning expression, a mask to conceal the hurt shining so clear in her eyes. Guilt sat heavy on Siora's chest, as did regret, making it hard to breathe. Still, the girl closed the distance to stand beside her, small toes pointed to pet the folds of Siora's dirty skirts.

Siora glanced at Gharek, who watched them both with his hawk's gaze. He nodded once as if to say, "Well done."

It wasn't forgiveness, but it was a start.

Rurian still held the book Gharek had brought with him, reluctantly passing it back to Zaredis when he gestured for its return. The general held the tome up to Siora. "How does this book help my brother?"

She wasn't sure if it could. Before she could explain why, a bone-shuddering chill blasted into the tent, colder than Kalun's touch, colder than the presence of any ghost she'd ever faced. Numerous gasps echoed throughout the tent. The rising terror inside her was reflected on both Gharek's face and Kalun's as well.

It's here, Kalun said. *The ghost-eater.*

To her horror, a second ghost joined Kalun in the tent. Skavol's revenant swirled in an endlessly changing mass that warped his features, as if he couldn't control his manifestation in the world of the living. *Help me, daughter!*

The cry boomed in her mind, greater than any full-throated

shout. A second frigid blast of air blew out the tent's sides like the wings of a bird in flight. Darkness edged this draft, serpentine and purposeful and smelling of decay.

Chaos erupted in the tent. Siora jerked her hand free of Kalun's to hoist a cowering Estred into her arms and shield her from the debris of parchment, candlesticks, plates, and cups hurling about the space in a whirlwind, striking people who dove for cover.

She caught a glimpse of Gharek lunging toward her, features pale with terror and fury. The otherworldly voice she'd heard in Midrigar rose above the howl and maelstrom, an echo of a command that still made her soul shrivel at the words.

"Come, meat. I hunger. I starve."

Despair and suffering, an endless gnawing on the bones of the soul by something whose ravenous appetite knew no end. More ghosts swarmed into the tent, dragged there helplessly by the ghost-eater.

Or drawn to her, for protection, for sanctuary. A shield against that which would devour them.

Her thoughts raced, and she barely felt the hard grip of Gharek's hand on her elbow as he finally reached her. All her life Siora had seen ghosts, talked with them. That dark gift was the hallmark of a shade speaker, but it wasn't sorcery. She knew nothing of necromancy nor wanted to, had never tried to learn or invoke any of the horrid spells such magic users employed to enslave the dead. Even had she been tempted, there was no reason to try. She didn't possess magic, couldn't wield it.

Or could she?

Her father's terrified face. Kalun's as well, and all the other phantoms surrounding her, begging for help. Gharek's hard words as they returned to Zaredis's camp. *Your honor blinds you.*

To be devoured or be enslaved. Shades of evil made gray or black by the motivation behind the act.

"Hold fast," she bellowed into the din, reciting the simple spell she'd memorized despite her revulsion for its purpose. "I am bound to earth and you to me. I name you, Skavol of Kraelag," she told her father. "And you, Kalun, brother of Zaredis, to serve my will and only my will. Hold fast!"

A greater darkness erupted this time, spilling from Siora's skin. She wanted to scream but found the sound locked in her throat. She made to wrench Estred off of her to give to Gharek for safe-keeping. She was no longer a safe haven for the living, only for the dead. Shadowy hands clawed at her as she tried to free herself from Estred, whose unthinking terror only made her cling harder, her slender legs wrapped so tightly around her erstwhile nurse's middle, Siora wheezed.

The memory of Kraelag with its vast crowd covering the summer fields in a chilly haze burst across her mind's eye. She didn't know the individual names of those apparitions fleeing the wolf that gave chase, but one at Kraelag, who'd called her "witch of the dead," had named them all.

She repeated the spell, changing part of it to capture all who hovered around her, begging for help in ethereal voices only she could hear. "I name you, the Forgotten, to serve my will. Hold fast!"

More darkness burst from her like blood and just as thick. Siora no longer saw Gharek beside her or Estred still in her arms.

She couldn't see the ghosts either, Kalun or her father. But they were still there, beside her, more solid than before.

A raging, shrieking howl drowned out all voices, and suddenly Siora was jerked backward so hard, she thought someone had grabbed her spine and tried to wrench it free of her body. Estred screamed into her neck, and far off, as if he shouted from the edge of a distant field, Gharek cried out his daughter's name and Siora's as well in an anguished voice.

Blackness swallowed her.

CHAPTER NINE

G ods damnit, move!" Gharek shouted, knocking people aside as he lunged toward the spiraling vortex that had wrenched Estred and Siora out of his arms, sucking them into a black maw that diminished at alarming speed. For a brief moment, he felt the awful compulsion to obey as the ghost-eater demanded its meat, only this time, instead of resisting, he thrust his hand toward its center, uncaring what might grab him on the other side. The spinning darkness collapsed abruptly, winking out of existence with a final blast of frigid air, taking Siora and Estred with it.

"No!" His bellow erupted from his throat, carried on a wave of helpless terror as he stared at the empty space where his purpose and his redemption had both vanished. He spun and rushed for the tent's entrance. He needed a horse and a blessing of speed from the gods to reach Midrigar, where the eater of ghosts lurked.

"Stop him!" Zaredis thundered behind him. "Don't kill him."

Gharek had a foot outside the tent when he went airborne before landing on his back with a breath-stealing thump. An explosion of color burst across his vision, splinters of agony lancing the inside of his skull. Several hands held him down in punishing grips. One overly enthusiastic soldier knelt on his chest with all his weight, compressing every bit of air out of Gharek's lungs until his sight grayed at the edges.

"Let him up," Zaredis ordered.

Gharek inhaled on a gasp when the soldier kneeling on him stood. He was hauled to his feet, still held prisoner in the grip of the general's minions.

Dark eyes flashing with the same fury consuming his captive, Zaredis grasped Gharek's chin to halt his struggles. "Listen to me." Rough fingers dug deeper into his cheeks. "Listen!" Gharek stilled. "That thing has my brother as well as your daughter and your woman. Do you want to save them?" At his stilted nod, Zaredis dropped his hand. "Then you finish drawing that map and make it right."

Blind rage nearly choked Gharek. "Fuck you and fuck your map," he said in a guttural voice.

One of the soldiers holding him growled and struck him on the back of his head for the impertinence.

Unmoved by his prisoner's profanity, Zaredis held up a hand to halt any more retribution. "The map," he told Gharek, his features resolute as horror wrenched his expression. "And when you're done, we ride to Domora and you take us to the Windcry. Rurian will break the ward. I'll release you to save your daughter and the shade speaker when we have the Windcry. If you try to escape, I'll kill the only hope either of them have of surviving."

Gharek's thoughts reeled at his nemesis's words. A choice wrapped in a bargain and enrobed in a threat. Zaredis might love his dead twin but taking the throne came first.

He'd never been one to trust or accept the word of another

without initial suspicion or follow-up investigation. The second wasn't an option for him here, and suspicion was an indulgence of time to spare. He didn't have that either. He was forced once more to accept Zaredis's bargain and trust the man meant to keep his word. His insides knotted at the thought.

"You said nothing of your brother," he pointed out to the general.

Anguish glittered in Zaredis's eyes even though his stoic facade didn't change. "He's dead already, and we all heard your shade speaker invoke the enchantment. He's bound to her until she frees him." The corners of his mouth quirked. "Seems there's more to her than just a voice for ghosts." His grim humor faded. "Give me your answer. We're wasting time."

There was only one answer to give. "Done," Gharek said.

Another person might have been too distracted by fear and worry for their captured loved ones to concentrate on such things as the complexity of an accurate map drawn strictly from memory, but Gharek had no issue. His value as a cat's-paw hadn't only been in his ruthlessness but in his ability to focus on the task at hand and see it to its completion. His mind remained quiet even if his spirit was howling in panic.

He employed that skill to finish the map, his memory sharp as he recalled the details of the corridors he'd walked, the hidden doors he'd passed through, the chambers he'd visited, and the path he'd taken to the coveted Windcry with its numerous wards in place to protect it from thieves.

He ignored Zaredis and Rurian, who stood on either side of him, watching as the map changed from a rough sketch to a detailed rendering with every swoop and scrawl of the charcoal he held.

"It's complete," he finally said, surprised to see that lamps had been lit in the reordered tent and a wedge of night instead of sunlight could be seen at its entrance.

"Are you certain?" Zaredis eyed the map with an admiring gaze.

Gharek nodded. "Absolutely. With this map in hand and your sorcerer beside you, you won't need me at all to take the Windcry." He resisted the temptation to snipe at Rurian for not stopping the ghost-eater from abducting his daughter and Siora. Surely the spell the sorcerer had cast before to drive the entity away would have worked a second time. Disgusted, his lip curled. Useless. The magician put more effort into looking mysterious than actually employing helpful magic when it truly counted.

"Nice try, cat's-paw." Zaredis's flinty regard hardened even more. "But you'll be accompanying us along with the map. I'll cut you loose when I have the Windcry in my hands. Not a moment sooner."

He'd expected Zaredis's refusal. He didn't lie when he said the map would direct the general to the Windcry without Gharek's help, but despite that, he'd remain a hostage until Zaredis had the prize in his hands.

Rurian bent closer to the map for a moment, stared at a section of it, then flipped through the spellbook Zaredis had returned to him.

"What is it?" Zaredis asked as the sorcerer's attention darted back and forth between the map and the page he'd marked in the tome.

Rurian didn't answer, instead firing a question of his own at Gharek. "How much of the book did you read?"

Made wary, Gharek shrugged. "Thoroughly? Not much. I skimmed all of it though. Why?"

The sorcerer pointed to a symbol Gharek had drawn on the map, a simple engraving with the look of a child's artwork decorating the lintel of the door that opened to the chamber holding the Windcry. "This is on your map, the marker for the chamber holding the Windcry."

"So?"

Rurian turned the open book outward so Gharek and Zaredis could see a replica of the symbol on the map sketched on the page. "The same mark is in the book. It's a sigil, which means there's more to the protection than a powerful warding spell." His somber visage turned darkly grim. "This chamber is protected by a demon."

The revelation twisted a knot in Gharek's gut. Thank the gods he hadn't sought to break the wards and steal the Windcry himself on that first reconnoitering mission into the palace. Even if he'd possessed the ability to break a ward, he was too cautious to try something so risky alone and without a well-crafted plan. He'd never accounted for a demon in this hastily constructed plan, and judging by his companions' scowls, neither had they.

"I can't do anything about a demon," he told Rurian. "I'm not a sorcerer to control such beings. This sort of thing is your expertise." Though he didn't have much faith in the sorcerer's abilities at the moment.

Rurian's gaze glittered with icy dislike, as if he'd heard Gharek's critical thoughts. "If the ward is broken, the sigil is broken and the demon set free," the sorcerer told Zaredis. "We'll be dead before we can blink if that happens."

Zaredis sighed, dragging a hand down his face. "What do you suggest?"

Impatient with this volleying of concerns and desperate to get free of Zaredis's demands so he could try to save those he actually cared about, Gharek snapped at Rurian. "Don't you have a binding spell you can mutter to hold it? Siora successfully enslaved two spirits while in the middle of a whirlwind and she didn't even know she was a necromancer."

For a sliver of time, Rurian's face went blank and tiny forks of pale blue lightning danced between his fingers before fading. His features lost their distant menace, softening the smallest bit with a touch of sympathy. "I understand your anger. Your desperation."

Gharek couldn't care less if he did. "That's nice. Now how do you get past the demon?"

Rurian's sympathy died a quick death. "I can create a ward within a ward. Carve a sanctuary out for us," he said. "Once we break the existing ward, the demon will attack us." He pointed again to the map, tracing the air just above it with a fingertip to stop over one spot. "This corridor. It's the only one leading to the room?" Gharek nodded. "Then it won't do us much good to lead it there. We'd have to run a gauntlet with it waiting for us. It needs to stay in the Windcry room. I can make use of the chamber's design and the position of the artifact to build a different ward that won't be affected by the ward breaker."

"And if that isn't enough?" Zaredis asked the most important question of all.

Rurian didn't hesitate. "I'll distract the demon while you steal the Windcry."

Gharek's eyebrows rose. Rurian's loyalty to Zaredis must be far fiercer than he first imagined if he was willing to use himself as bait to occupy a demon's attention while they stole the Windcry. He was torn as to whether the sorcerer was mad, stupid, courageous, or a combination of all three. There was no question regarding his devotion if he was willing to act the part of possible sacrificial victim so Zaredis could have his weapon. "Your bravery is epic," he finally conceded.

Rurian gave a soft snort. "Speed will serve us better than courage. Demons are fast."

"I've experienced many firsts since my unfortunate capture by your master," Gharek replied. "A ghost-eater and its ethereal wolves, and now a demon waiting to consume anyone foolish enough to attempt stealing the Windcry." Before he could face the horror in Midrigar, he'd have to face the horror in Domora, and for once it wasn't the now-deceased Empress Dalvila. One bright spot in this madness.

With the map complete, Zaredis chose not to wait until the following day to ride to Domora. His councilors tried to talk him out of going with Rurian and the cat's-paw, arguing that his army needed to see their general among them to keep up morale.

Zaredis had given them all a disgusted look. "My men aren't children, and I'm not a nursemaid. The majority of my forces made it here under command of my captains without seeing me for months. I'll be gone for a few days at most. I expect this camp to be ready to march on the capital as soon as I return."

Gharek understood what Zaredis didn't say. He wanted to be the one to personally steal the Windcry and didn't trust another to do so, not even Rurian, who was willing to act as demon bait if necessary so his master could obtain his prize.

The three men left for Domora in the deep of night, taking the main road instead of the drover paths with their rutted byways. Zaredis and Rurian were heavily armed. Gharek was not. His knife had been returned to him but hidden away in his satchel, which was tied to Zaredis's horse. He rode the gelding Suti once more, grateful for Siora's quick thinking and her mendacity for saying the animal was hers. Zaredis had allowed her to keep Suti, unaware it had been his funds that purchased the horse from the free traders.

The journey gave him time to think, to plan. Planning prevented him from worrying until his heart froze in his chest or did the opposite and burst past his breastbone from the frantic beat of terror that threatened to swallow him whole.

Estred, the light of his soul, was trapped somewhere in the grip of a thing that ate the dead, hunted the living, and had no place in this world. At least she had Siora with her, though his fear for her was nearly as great as that for his daughter.

The woman whose selfless compassion had saved his child, then motivated her to betray him, was all that stood between one small girl and a monstrous, ancient force he suspected made the brutal Dalvila seem like a sweet-natured infant by comparison.

A woman repulsed by the idea of necromancy, forced to wield such magic in one shattering moment. He had suspected her powers went far beyond that of a medium, especially after she made

Kalun appear before them all. Her name meant *raven*, those carrion-eaters that helped vultures clear battlefields of decaying corpses. Even her name was associated with the dead. Was it any wonder chance and circumstance had unveiled her true power? He didn't consider necromancy the abomination she did. Magic was magic. It was men who twisted it for nefarious purposes. Still, he wished she might have embraced her newly discovered power without the threat of a ghost-eater.

He'd caught only a glimpse of her fright and the resolve that had hardened her delicate features as she invoked a necromancer's spell in a bid to save her father and Kalun before she was snatched from Gharek's arms, Estred along with her.

To Midrigar. Of that, he had no doubt. And while Zaredis was assured of the cat's-paw's extorted alliance, Gharek schemed to slip away at the first opportunity. Domora offered the best chance and a means for him to reach Midrigar via the Maesor. The general was welcome to the artifact and Domora itself. Gharek just wanted his daughter—and his lover—back. He wanted Siora in his arms, in his bed, in his life. She, who gave him no quarter and allowed none of his excuses, had been generous in her mercy with him, her understanding. From the time she'd entered his house as Estred's nurse, her presence had begun to alter him, remind him of the gentler man he'd once been so long ago. She'd turned his rage away, cooled the fire of his vengeance and made him question his purpose for it. She'd had no reason to help him with Zaredis's task or defend him to the general, yet she had, and put herself in danger for the doing. Siora made him whole when he was with her, made him believe there was something inside himself not yet rotten or splintered beyond repair. Something ultimately redeemable.

Schemes and memories occupied his thoughts and kept at bay the grimmer reality of her and Estred's current circumstances. He barely noticed the way the sun crested the horizon to bring forth the dawn until Zaredis signaled a stop.

"These roads will soon have a fair number of travelers as we get closer to Domora," he said. "I've been a long time away from this part of the Empire. I doubt I'll be recognized. You, however," he eyed Gharek, "are notorious and hunted. Even your beard won't fool the sharp-eyed for long."

He was right. Gharek had already pushed his luck more than once by visiting Domora. He recalled the assassin who'd appeared at the abandoned brothel that was one of the gateways to the Maesor, a killer dispatched by one of many who sought revenge against the cat's-paw. Someone had recognized him then, and there was only so far a beard or a head wrap would go. "What do you suggest then? I don't think I'll make a very convincing woman if you have such a disguise in mind."

"I have something better than a shoddy disguise as an exceptionally ugly milkmaid," Zaredis said. "I have a sorcerer."

Instantly alarmed by the implication of his remark, Gharek halted Suti and leapt from the saddle to run. Too late.

His feet had barely hit the ground before a wash of sensation like thousands of tiny thorns dug into his skin, covering his entire body. The feeling lasted no more than a couple of moments. He stood next to the patient Suti, who stayed beside him and took advantage of their short rest to nibble grass at the roadside. "What did you do to me?" Gharek snarled at Rurian, ready to charge the mage in his fury and pull the uppity bastard from his mount so he could strangle him.

"Peace, cat's-paw," Rurian said, one hand raised in truce. "You wear a disguise, an illusion, though not that of a milkmaid. It's a temporary spell but works better than any dress, hat, or beard ever could."

Zaredis handed Gharek the small shield he carried. "Take a look for yourself."

Gharek held the shield up, its low polished surface not much of a mirror but reflective enough that he could make out the face staring back at him. It was one he didn't recognize. One no one looking for the cat's-paw would ever suspect hid their quarry in plain sight. The anger drained away, and he glanced at Rurian, impressed. "You're more useful than I thought. I could have used such help on my first trip back to Domora."

"You'll do," Rurian said. "But you can't wander far. The spell's strength is limited by distance from the spellcaster. Get too far from me and it will fade."

They set off once more, arriving at the double walls that girdled Domora and were manned by guards in towers and on the battlements.

Zaredis stared at the formidable fortifications with an eye for strategy. "It's changed since I last saw it. I think it might have been half its current size when I lived here. And Herself added another three stretches of walls."

Rurian pointed to a section built of recently quarried stone. It shone brighter than the more weathered squares on either side of it. "That's a repair. Bigger or not, someone managed to breach that section."

Gharek gave a bitter chuckle. "Work of a draga," he said. "The one who ate the empress." He recalled Malachus's long-suffering expression as he denied eating Dalvila.

"A draga would be very useful to us," Zaredis said on a wistful note.

"And beyond any control you might fancy you had over it," Gharek replied.

"If that repair work is any indicator and the Kraelian stories are true, it will be nothing for the artifact to conquer," Rurian said in a low voice.

Gharek noted the mage avoided calling the Windcry by name. They were on the perimeter of the heaviest traffic flowing into and out of the city. Rurian would have had to shout his remark for any beyond the three of them to hear, but one could never be too cautious when discussing the siege of a city, especially when one stood just outside its gates.

The inaugural test of Rurian's spell on Gharek came when they were stopped by a trio of gate guards. One demanded to know who they were and what business brought them to Domora.

This was the first time Gharek had seen the lazy gate guards actually do their jobs and question visitors. It was also the first time he'd seen so many soldiers in the city at a given moment, even more than when he and Siora were here days earlier. Regiments marched through the gates, all wearing General Tovan's heraldry on their shields or their horses' barding. Word had obviously reached Domora that an army amassed and prepared to march on the capital.

Zaredis answered the guard's questions with an easy smile. "Whores for the army," he said. "I'm Baleetis of South Dale. I've brought over a nice crop of cunts from Wester Way. I hear Tovan likes to keep his men happy, and these mares are a fine lot to tempt the choosiest prick. I'm here to barter."

The guard's eyes lit up as if he might have a chance to purchase the services of these nonexistent prostitutes. He gave both Gharek and Rurian no more than a passing glance before waving them through the gate. The pungent crush of people and horses surrounding them reminded Gharek why he didn't miss most things about living here, even if he was effectively a homeless exile.

He glanced at Zaredis. "A whoremonger? How the great have fallen in the world."

The general shrugged, unfazed by the mockery. "If there's one thing that will gain you access to most places, it's the possibility of a good fuck. Free or paid for, it doesn't matter."

Were they not adversaries, Gharek would have enjoyed Zaredis's company. He was pragmatic, straightforward, and ruthlessly resolved when necessary. His observations were insightful and no less accurate for their occasional vulgarity. Too bad the man had threatened to execute him, held Estred hostage, and refused to set him free so he could rescue her and Siora. Gharek wouldn't think twice about sinking a knife into the general if it aided in his escape, but he'd regret doing it. The Empire, crumbling away every day, might actually survive and thrive under Zaredis's rule.

They made the trek to the palace, Gharek uneasy despite Rurian's spell as they passed numerous members of Domoran nobility on the royal avenue, many who'd happily disembowel him on the spot with their bare hands if they recognized him.

They left their mounts in a public stable within walking distance of the palace, strolling toward the grand building as if they were provincial sightseers on a walking tour. At the palace itself, Gharek directed them to one of the hidden entrances noted on the map he'd drawn. Zaredis kept a knife to his back as they sneaked into the royal residence while Rurian read the map, checking every verbal instruction or hand gesture the cat's-paw made against the map to verify they matched.

When they reached the palace's inner most sanctum, the center of a labyrinth of corridors and warren of rooms, the mage swiftly dispatched the two guards standing sentry at a door made of wood darkened with age and engraved with arcane symbols whose power made the air around the frame pulse. The sigil Rurian noted earlier was carved deepest into the lintel above, glowing the crimson shade of fresh blood.

Zaredis poked Gharek in the back. "Take the keys off the guard there," he ordered. "And unlock the door."

The dead guard was the size of an ox, and Gharek grunted with the effort to turn him over and retrieve the keys trapped under his corpse. He held them up and waited, noting that the general had traded his knife for a sword, prepared for battle. He knew what the man would tell him and didn't argue when Zaredis said, "Now open the door."

The key screeched in a lock not turned for centuries, but the mechanism submitted and a series of clicks and snaps told them the door was unlocked.

Gharek nudged it open with his foot. It swung inward on squealing hinges. *So much for any element of surprise*, he thought.

No monstrosity perched on the threshold waiting for them to cross so it could pounce and enjoy a quick meal of general, sorcerer, and cat's-paw. Zaredis gestured for Gharek to go inside first. He and Rurian followed behind him.

He'd scouted the path to this room earlier. It was a spartan chamber except for mysterious glowing runes painted on the walls. They mimicked those etched on the floors. Gharek didn't need to translate them to know these were protection symbols used to build a sorcerous cage that housed a powerful artifact.

The legendary Windcry sat on a plain table in the center of the room, looking exactly as he remembered it when he'd first seen it while serving as Dalvila's henchman. Every survival instinct Gharek possessed snapped to attention. There was more in this room than a magical artifact and three would-be thieves. Demon. The guardian trapped in the cage with the Windcry. Gharek's skin crawled with the sense of otherness that practically breathed in this room.

Different from the ghost-eater of Midrigar but pulsing with the same kind of waiting malice as it bided its time and watched what its prey would do.

He glanced askance at Zaredis, catching the man sketch a protection symbol in the air with his fingers. From some hidden distance something gave a low, mocking, inhuman laugh

It was Rurian who strode first to the table. The Windcry looked like a piece of decorative glass, one of those expensive and utterly useless things aristo women wasted their wealth on and put on a shelf so they could boast about their acquisition to their equally rich and envious friends.

Gharek hung back as Zaredis joined his sorcerer. "This is truly the Windcry?" Doubt colored his voice, as if he couldn't quite believe something so fragile-looking had and could level an entire city and win a siege for an army.

"The one and only," Gharek said. He joined the two men, who stood on the perimeter of another, smaller glowing circle that was carved into the floor and surrounded the table.

"It looks fragile." Rurian bent to peer more closely at the artifact.

"I'd suggest not throwing it about once you have your hands on it," Gharek said.

The mage frowned at his mockery. "Obviously."

Zaredis gazed at his sorcerer, then his prisoner. "Are you ready? I've a city to conquer and you, cat's-paw, have a woman and child to rescue."

Rurian unhooked a flask from his belt, unstoppering the cork to carefully shake out a green powder that began to smoke as soon as it hit the flagstone floor. The runes glowed even brighter as he used the powder to create a wedge-shaped pattern, with the narrow end touching a part of the smaller circle around the table and the wider end connecting to the larger one at the door's threshold. A path, a safe avenue leading from one warded space to another. They could safely travel from the table to the door once the original wards were broken as long as they didn't cross the new lines Rurian's powder was etching into the floor.

"Clever," Gharek said, watching as tendrils of smoke wafted off blistered stone.

"Cautious," Rurian replied. "I've no wish to be torn apart by demon kind." He cursed all of a sudden as he shook out the last of the powder. A thin cascade managed to close the ward but just barely.

Zaredis bent to survey the spot. "Can't you just spread some of the powder from other spots that have more?"

Rurian shook his head. "It isn't the powder itself that's magic. It's simply the means to disperse it, and that magic has already played into the stone where the powder fell. What you see now is nothing more sorcerous than a baker's bowl of flour or sand on a beach." He blew away a portion of the green stuff to reveal the wedge shape carved deep into the stone and glowing as bright as the runes—except for one spot no longer than a small dirk and no wider than the blade itself.

"That," Rurian said, scowling at the place where the etching was more shallow and the sorcerous glow dimmer, "is the weak point. I think it will still prevent the demon from reaching us but keep your distance just in case."

"You think?" In that moment Gharek was tempted to revisit his earlier murderous urges and snatch Zaredis's sword from his hand and skewer the sorcerer with it. "We all might end up bloody stains on the walls because you didn't measure correctly?"

"Silence," the general snapped. He didn't look any happier about Rurian's announcement than Gharek felt, but he gave the sorcerer a nod. "I need the Windcry. It's worth the risk. Break the ward."

Rurian wasted no time. He pulled the grimoire with its ward-breaker spells from the bag at his belt and motioned for his companions to stand with him in the wedge's safety. His voice took on a sonorous cadence as he recited one of the spells, the invocation echoing with a hollowness one might hear in a vast, vaulted cave instead of a windowless chamber in the palace.

Every hair on Gharek's nape and arms stood at attention when a snap, more felt than heard, bludgeoned not only his ears but his entire body. The runes decorating the chamber flashed blindingly bright once, then returned to their milder glow. Except for those on the floor. Those had gone dark, including the two circles. Only Rurian's wedge continued to shimmer, along with portions of the old wards where they made up parts of the wedge.

Rurian didn't pause in his invocation, and his eyes had turned an otherworldly ice blue from which the pinpoints of his pupils glittered like shards of obsidian. His voice was soon drowned out by the most gods-awful howling shriek Gharek had ever heard. A roiling miasma of pus, blood, fangs, and darkness suddenly burst into existence from thin air.

"Gods have mercy on us all," he said on a thin breath, his gaze rising up and up as the awakened demon grew in size until it brushed the ceiling, a colossus made up of every foul and sharp thing that had plagued humanity from the dawn of time. It left an oily smear where it scraped the ceiling, a smear that soon drooled toward the floor in dull black droplets of some foul ichor.

Gharek instinctively ducked and covered his head, shuddering at the anticipation of being splashed on. Zaredis did the same. The oozing black rain fell but never struck them, stopped by the wedge's invisible barrier. Rurian's ward had a roof.

"I've seen horrors of the battlefield," Zaredis said, his voice stricken as he straightened and gazed at the demon with wide eyes. "But not this. Never this."

Gharek too had seen the brutality and hard death of a battle-field but this demon surpassed any nightmare memory of the worst atrocities committed on the field. This thing defined atrocity.

As if insulted by the general's remark, the demon hurled itself at them, only to bounce back with a frustrated scream. It did it over and over again, rabid in its efforts to reach prey.

Rurian had finished his invocation. "Now, my lord!" He had to shout above the cacophony. "Take the Windcry so we may escape this place!"

Zaredis jogged to the table and snatched up the fragile artifact. He held it like an infant in his arms and raced back to where Rurian and Gharek waited. Intent on not dropping his prize and triumphant over claiming it, he made a careless misstep and jogged too close to the weak part of Rurian's ward.

"Too close!" Gharek bellowed a warning.

Too late.

The demon, seeing an opportunity, slammed into that side of the wedge with all its formidable might. The ward held, barely, but the force of the impact made Zaredis fall. He had the presence of mind to pitch the Windcry to the man closest to him, and Gharek caught it just as the general went down, the tip of his left foot sliding outside of the wedge's protection.

The general's terrified howl matched the demon's victorious shriek as skeletal fingers made of shadow and stronger than steel grasped Zaredis's boot, prepared to yank him fully across the ward line. Gharek was certain he was about to witness the thing paint the walls red with Zaredis's blood and entrails.

Rurian leapt toward his liege, using all his strength to hold him inside the wedge.

In that moment time slowed to a crawl, and the cat's-paw's thoughts raced far ahead of it. The demon's gnarled fingers wrapping around the general's foot. Zaredis bellowing for help as he tried to squirm back across the ward's protective line. Rurian's desperate expression as he wrapped his arms around his lord's shoulders and held on, the cords in his neck rigid with the effort. All

Gharek had to do was toss the Windcry aside and sprint for the door and freedom while the demon did away with his biggest problem. Rurian wouldn't stop him, too busy trying to save Zaredis, and he couldn't drop the ward that protected them all and provided clear passage to the door. By the time the mage lost any hope of saving the general and chased after him, Gharek would be long gone. He'd be free of Zaredis's threat, and with Estred no longer a hostage, he'd find her and Siora, rescue them, and disappear into the hinterlands beyond the Empire's reach.

Those considerations were lightning flashes in his mind, swift and bright, as he watched the barbarian mage struggle to keep his lord from becoming demon food. *I know nothing of nobility*, he'd told Siora.

Her gaze, once so condemning, had rested on him, soft with compassion and a spark of something that had robbed him of breath: admiration. *But everything of devotion*, she'd said. *Your love for Estred should inspire you to be a better man, not a worse one.*

Beggar maid of untapped power and an ear for the dead. He'd sought and found comfort in her arms and wisdom in her words. She was right. Love, especially that of a parent for a child, should fuel courage instead of ruthlessness.

"Fuck," he growled and set the Windcry down. "I'm going to regret this."

Rurian called out spells that kept Zaredis still inside the ward but had no impact on the demon itself. Gharek was a cat's-paw, not a mage. He couldn't cast a spell, but he was good with a blade. He grabbed the sword Zaredis had dropped when he fell, prayed to any useless god listening for mercy, and stepped outside the wedge enough to bring the sword down on the demon's hand gripping the general's foot. The blade sliced through both with ease. Zaredis screamed as did the demon, one in agony, the other in fury.

Rurian snapped Zaredis back across the ward's barrier, leaving a red smear where the man's foot bled into the stones. Gharek darted back across the ward, narrowly avoiding a clawed swipe from the enraged demon that would have disemboweled him on the spot.

Heart thundering in his chest and his ears, he abandoned the sword to scoop up the Windcry and assist Rurian in helping Zaredis stand. "We have to get out of here," he said. "Half of Domora has heard the demon's shrieking. A pack of guards will be down here in no time."

Rurian nodded. "Hold him up." He abandoned the two for a moment to retrieve the sword Gharek had dropped. The general was pale, shivering. Gharek didn't think he'd bleed to death, but he was in danger of passing out.

"You cut off my toes, cat's-paw," he accused in a faintly slurred voice.

"Be glad it wasn't your head, general," Gharek stumbled a little as Zaredis swayed hard against him.

Rurian returned to share the burden. He held Zaredis's sword in his free hand.

"I hope you know how to use that," Gharek said. "Because your master can't at the moment." He had to shout to be heard, the demon's fury so loud, he was nearly deafened by the noise.

"The door," Rurian shouted back. "Just get through the door. We'll worry about the rest later."

To Gharek's amazement they managed to escape the chamber

with their skins still attached, and the Windcry unbroken and in their possession, though Zaredis had left his toes behind with the demon.

A touch of color had returned to the injured man's skin, though sweat poured down his face, and he clenched his jaw with every limp into the corridor. Despite the pain and the bloody wound that was once his toes, he was focused solely on the artifact. "The Windcry," he said between gritted teeth. "Where is it?"

Gharek held it up. "Never let it be said you're easily distracted from your goals."

Zaredis offered him a weak smile. "But they aren't your priorities." The smile fell away. "I release you from your obligation." Gharek inhaled sharply. "Consider my clemency a debt repaid for you saving my life. Now save your woman and daughter."

The thunder of running feet sounded above them, and the demon screeched behind the warded door.

"Go now before you're trapped in this hallway," Rurian said. "Leave the Windcry with us."

Gharek gladly handed the artifact to the sorcerer. "Even with the map, you'll never outrun palace soldiers, especially now." He nodded toward Zaredis.

The sorcerer's eyes, no longer the eerie ice blue from earlier, gleamed in the corridor's dim torchlight. "Your doubt in my abilities is humbling, cat's-paw. Have no fear that you'll see the general at the head of his army as the walls of Domora fall." He gestured with a lift of his chin. "Now go. My magic is stronger spent on two instead of three."

Dozens of footsteps thundered toward them. Gharek didn't need to be told twice. He sprinted for one of the corridors that led deeper into the bowels of the palace, to a tunnel that ascended once more. At its end an exit into the royal gardens lay behind a vicious barricade of thorny roses.

He ran, euphoria and fear giving his feet wings. He raced toward another battle, another monster, to save the two people who reminded him what it was to love and to hope.

CHAPTER TEN

Siora held her hands up to the sullen sky in supplication, allowing her cupped palms to fill with rainwater until it threatened to spill over her knuckles. She bent then and tipped her makeshift cup to Estred's lips. The child drank greedily until Siora's palms were empty.

"More?" At Estred's enthusiastic nod, Siora stretched her hands out a second time, just enough beyond their meager shelter and the ward she'd drawn in the dirt around them. Except for the gray sheets of a spring shower falling from a jaundiced sky, the dead city of Midrigar was silent. She let Estred drink her fill before soothing her own parched lips and throat with rain.

The sky above had transformed since her last foray here, now an eerie tapestry of oddly changing light in which the sun moved at unnatural speed across the horizon, slinging shadows against decrepit structures like paint splashes. A sliver of twilight already graced the far edges of the heavens. It was as if time outside the walls rushed by in increments of moments instead of hours, leaving dead Midrigar an island to stagnate in an abyss.

Thirst, hunger, and the demands of a bladder were the only ways she could guess how much time had passed since the eater of ghosts had abducted her and Estred, dropping them among the ruins along with a crowd of the dead. Were she alone, Siora might have succumbed to terror and screamed herself senseless. Instead she'd raced for shelter, useless though it was in such circumstances, and sketched a shallow protection ward in the dirt. The rain couldn't reach it to wash parts of the circle away, but a strong wind would, and she prayed neither she, Estred, nor nature itself sneezed. If she guessed right, they'd hidden under the shadow of a partially toppled building for more than a day, two at most, surrounded by a tattered fog of ghosts bound to her by the vile Holdfast spell.

The irony of a necromantic spell of enslavement managing to protect many from the ghost-eater's predation wasn't lost on her. Revulsion still gripped her at the possibility of possessing such magic but for now it had its uses. Even the protection ward in which she and Estred stood sprang from this poisoned well. It kept away the dozen pale, faceless wolves lurking nearby, creatures like the pair that had stalked her and Gharek in the Maesor. They raised their heads to sniff the air, scarlet tongues in equally scarlet mouths flickering out like a serpent's before sliding back behind needle-like teeth.

Siora held Estred even tighter. The little girl clung like an ivy vine, her tears wet on Siora's neck. "Where's my papa?"

Siora patted her back. "Shh. Safe, love. Don't talk." She didn't want any more attention drawn to them than what was already there, and Estred's young, living voice was surely a confection the ghost-eater and his minions couldn't resist.

Their voices, at normal volume, seemed strangely loud in the destroyed city, and the ever-changing light made it difficult for Siora to focus her gaze. She blinked several times, watching as the faceless hunters crept ever closer. A pair slunk like great cats, moving on all fours with a sinuous gait. Others scuttled like insects, and more crawled down the walls of broken buildings, their forms shifting back and forth between amorphous shapes that rippled like water and solid bodies the shade of a corpse with their white skin and bloody mouths.

An icy touch on her arm made Siora jump with a gasp. She turned to discover her father next to her and Kalun adjacent to him. "Papa!" she exclaimed. "Kalun! Thank the gods!" The ghost-eater hadn't taken them. Her hastily invoked Holdfast spell had worked. Not only on them but on the many other phantoms huddling close to her.

Skavol's apparition gazed at her with both pride and apprehension. *Your mother and I always suspected your magic to be far greater than hers, far greater than that of a lowly fortune-teller.*

She said aloud what he didn't, her voice mournful. "Necromancer." She held the shaking Estred closer for warmth, shivering herself with terror. *I have to get out of here, Papa. Get Estred to safety.* He turned to stare at all the ghostly shapes, bound by magic that kept them from becoming a ghost-eater's dinner but enslaved them just the same to a desperate, newly minted spellcaster. *I'm afraid,* she told Skavol.

Kalun joined the conversation. *But you're not alone, Siora.* Skavol nodded. *We're yours to command. In the world outside Midrigar, we are as nothing, but here, where the city straddles two existences, we can help.*

Siora pointed to one of the creeping hunters. *Can you help with that?*

Kalun nodded. *But you have to command us. You are our mistress now. We serve you.*

His words brought only despair and a generous helping of guilt. All around her were the remnants of a city punished, annihilated; its populace slaughtered, then cursed. And at its shriveled heart, a thing had taken up residence in a nearby temple and fed first on those trapped for a millennium, then on the denizens of the Maesor. It had come for more. It had also come for her. She'd known in her gut the ghost-eater hadn't scooped her up by chance. It had sensed a rival's power even before she herself became aware of it.

As if the ghost-eater knew her thoughts, its command rang throughout the city in an abyssal voice. *"Give to me what is mine, witch of the dead."*

The ghosts around her wailed, and even her father and Kalun cowered before the entity who demanded she surrender the spirits she held in thrall.

That arrogant, entitled command snapped her out of the fear threatening to choke her, replacing it with righteous anger. "No," she yelled back. "These people are not yours, nor are they meat as you call them."

A wrathful snarl filled what remained of the plaza in which she stood with her phantom audience. *"To me, meat!"* the ghost-eater thundered, and the ghosts rippled as one misty shade, pulled toward the grand temple whose dark interior faced the plaza and housed a thing that watched from behind a facade of crumbling pillars.

"Stay," Siora cried out, only half believing that her command would counteract the ghost-eater's power. She stared at her father, at Kalun, a slow grin turning up her mouth when neither of them moved from their place beside her.

You're doing it, daughter, Skavol said, his misty face beaming like sunlight through glass.

"*KILL!*"

This time the entity's screech almost cracked her skull in half. Estred screamed in her arms and called out for her father. Siora wanted to call out for him too.

Neither she nor Estred would make it out of Midrigar alive. The ghost-eater's wolves leapt at the implacable command, rushing toward them, their excited chattering making Siora's blood run cold. The ghost-eater might not be any more corporeal than those it considered food, but the pale hounds were solid, feral, and eager to rend her and Estred asunder with their clawed hands.

Command us, daughter, if you want to live, Skavol urged her.

To protect her father, Zaredis's brother, and a whole host of spirits fleeing the ghost-eater, she'd had to enslave them. To command them now was to use them.

Gharek had tossed ethics out the window and done the dirty work of a twisted empress to protect his daughter and provide for her. It seemed Siora would see some small part from his perspective of what that was like, and for the same reason.

One of the wolves was nearly upon her when she called out in a loud voice. "To me! Defend! Protect!"

It was as if lightning suddenly struck, igniting the ethereal host so that they were no longer misty apparitions but fiery columns of light. Several shot toward the first attacking hunter, swallowing it whole in a shower of flame that showed hints of phantom hands, arms, and legs. Siora gasped in shock as the ghosts tore the creature apart until it was nothing more than tattered flags of bloodless flesh scattered across the plaza.

Its fate didn't stop the others from attacking. Some met the same end as the first. Others slammed headlong into an unbreachable wall of spirits, with Siora and Estred behind it, safe for the moment from the ghost-eater's hounds.

The ghost-eater shrieked in glee. *"You aren't above me, witch! You destroy your own."*

Its words made no sense at first until she watched an invisible hand pluck one of the hunters off the ground, dangling it in midair. It was a bizarre, terrifying sight to behold. The creature's mouth opened and closed with that same mad chittering noise. For a moment, a flicker of a different shape; a different, fully developed face superimposed itself over the hunter, and Siora's stomach somersaulted in horror at the realization of what the ghost-eater's taunt meant.

Its hounds had once been human.

"Is that a man or a woman?"

Siora turned from the ghastly sight to discover Estred's gaze transfixed on the terrible chimera squirming in midair. "Close your eyes, love." She covered the girl's eyes with one hand. "You don't want to dream about this." She forced the words past a knot in her throat. *Papa,* she called and instantly Skavol was by her side. *The ghost-eater can't take you?*

He shook his head. *Not while we serve you.*

And those wolves. Can you kill them? Destroy them utterly so the ghost-eater can no longer use them? Again he nodded. *Do it,* she said, allowing angry tears to slide down her cheeks. *Show no mercy and obliterate every last one of them in this entire wretched place.*

Had that been the fate of the missing folk in the Maesor? Not food for the ghost-eater, but hounds to serve its will? Would this have been Gharek's fate had she not knocked him unconscious and broken the ghost-eater's bewitchment?

Two score or more of ghosts stayed with her, including Kalun. The others shot away in all directions, hunters themselves, and no longer so afraid as they tracked the ghost-eater's minions.

Estred's weight was an anvil in her arms, and the draining feel of sudden fatigue made Siora sway.

Kalun spoke next to her. *You have to get out of Midrigar, Siora. All magic has costs. We serve you, but it's your life force that shackles us to you, and we are many with an enemy doing its best to take us from you. Your first loyalty is to the living, not the dead. To Estred. Even to yourself.*

He was right, though she dared not think beyond the idea of escaping Midrigar. How, in good conscience, could she release those ghosts bound to her when a terrifying fate awaited them? How could she, in good conscience, keep them in thrall to her, even to protect them?

She took his advice and began a jog to the gate, reluctant to turn her back on the temple now behind her, knowing the ghost-eater observed her every move. Her diminished entourage swelled in numbers again as they returned from their tasks of destroying the pale wolves. Her father had yet to reappear.

She wasn't far from the gate when a familiar voice called her name. Estred jumped in Siora's arms, squirming like an eel. "Papa!"

Siora could hardly believe her eyes. Gharek sprinted toward them, long legs effortlessly closing the distance. She lost her hold on Estred, who met Gharek halfway to jump into his embrace.

Siora gawked at him when he finally came to stand in front of her. The cat's-paw, her lover, alive and well and reunited with his daughter in the worst possible place for the living and the dead to be at the moment. "How?" she asked, stunned.

"I'll explain later," he said. "Once we're past the gate."

She didn't argue or ask if he saw the ghosts all around them. Instead she kept pace with him as they fled toward Midrigar's shattered gates and the uncertain safety of the living world beyond them. Siora's heart beat hard as they ran, a rhythm born of equal fear and joy even as the weight of responsibility dragged at her heels and the weight of a choice kindled the first sparks of a crazed idea surely bound to fail.

They reached the gates without a single hound snapping at their heels or the ghost-eater stopping them. Siora skidded to a halt right before the gates and exhaled a relieved sigh when Gharek crossed the city's border, one foot in the woodland. It was late afternoon, but if she guessed rightly, of a different day than the one she'd left when the ghost-eater had taken her.

It only took a moment for Gharek to realize she was no longer beside him. He spun around to gawk at her. "Hurry, Siora."

An odd ripple of air seemed to warp the broken gates even more. She offered him and Estred a melancholy smile. "Forgive me," she said. "I must abandon you once more. My work here isn't done." She couldn't leave, not while there was a sliver of hope that she might somehow save her father, Kalun, and all the dead she subjugated. Save the living as well from the parasite in Midrigar.

Gharek's dark eyebrows crashed down in a ferocious scowl. He took a step toward the gate, glanced at Estred staring at Siora, and stopped, conflicted. "Don't do this," he implored. "Come through the gate. What binds you to Midrigar but not to us?"

His words seemed rushed, bleeding together. Tears blurred her vision. "My father. Hundreds of souls who don't deserve the fate of those unfortunate ones who came before them, those who will be at risk of that same fate when they too die."

He frowned, confused, and she wondered if her own words sounded slow and laborious to his ears. "Life is sacrifice, Siora," he said. "Hard choices. Stay with me and Estred. Share your hours and days with us." The plea in his question wrenched her to her soul.

She couldn't think of anything finer, and his words—his expression—sent her heart soaring, then plummeting. "The ghost-eater can't remain here. I have to exile it somehow, cast it out of Midrigar, out of this world entirely. For you, for Estred, for all of us—so that when we die, we won't dread what comes afterward."

"You have no idea how to battle such a monster," he snapped, eyes flashing with frustration and fear. Fear for her.

"No, I don't, but I'll figure it out." She exhaled a sigh of relief when her father's spirit appeared beside her, bolstering her conviction she was doing the right thing, making the right choice, though it felt as if someone were slashing at her insides. She yearned with her entire being to step beyond Midrigar's gates and join the father and daughter she'd fallen in love with in different times and different ways. It was not to be.

Siora raised a hand to wave. "You both sleep in my soul," she said. "Farewell." She put her back to the gate and walked away, not turning around once, not even when Gharek shouted her name and begged her to come back.

CHAPTER ELEVEN

S he'd abandoned them yet again for some noble cause that would likely get her killed, and even worse, get her soul devoured like those she sought to save.

Gharek cried out Siora's name several times, imploring her to join him and Estred, to flee Midrigar. Estred herself had called out as well, the child's siren song powerful enough to make Siora pause in walking away but not powerful enough to make her turn around. Her slim shoulders shook for a moment before her back stiffened and she strode deeper into Midrigar to disappear behind a derelict building, the strange mist trailing alongside her.

"Will she come back?" Estred asked with a sniffle.

"Yes, love," he replied, and hugged her. If he had any say in the matter. He just had to figure out how without endangering Estred. He kept a tight hold on his daughter and took her farther into the woodland but always with the gate in sight in case Siora decided to abandon her maddening nobility and return to them.

It would be best if he took Estred and left altogether, put leagues between him and the cursed city with its fatal bewitchments and an ethereal shackle with his name on it.

"We can't leave Siora, Papa," Estred protested, thumping his shoulder with her chin.

"We aren't, love. Just putting some distance between us and trouble while I think of a plan." He leaned back to peer into her worried features. "Are you all right? No injuries?"

His heart had trebled its already rapid beat when he caught sight of her in Siora's arms, surrounded by an eerie luminescence in the middle of a plaza under a weirdly convulsing sky. His blood had curdled in his veins as he drew closer to a grandiose temple whose entrance spilled a blackness over the steps, reeking of malice, of hunger. The awful, familiar tug on his spine froze the blood in his veins.

The terrifying compulsion of the geas had made running away a hard struggle. He hadn't paused for niceties or assurances before taking Estred and urging Siora to flee with him to the gates, feet flying across uneven ground in a bid to outrun the inevitable net cast by the ghost-eater.

"I'm fine," Estred said. "But I'm thirsty."

Gharek paused in replying when the sound of voices reached his ears. He pressed a finger to his lips to signal silence. Estred nodded. He carried her toward a concealing clump of underbrush and let her slip from his arms. At his wordless gesture, she crouched behind the barrier of scrubby vegetation.

He paced several steps away from her and pulled the newly acquired knife he'd taken from a Maesor stall as he passed through the market to reach Midrigar. He was prepared to defend against whatever adversary was headed in their direction. The tree he stood behind didn't offer much in the way of concealment, but it didn't matter. He only needed to stay hidden long enough to gain the upper hand in an ambush.

Judging by volume, one person was close. "Maybe they've already cleared out."

"They'd have to be faster than a deer to cover that much ground in so little time," another said.

They hadn't yet made it into his field of view, but Gharek thought he recognized the second voice.

"It could have been a deer."

"Shouting curses and calling someone's name? What kind of deer have you come across when you're out hunting?"

Gharek's hopes soared, though he remained wary and reminded Estred with a series of hand motions to stay where she was. He tucked the knife away but still within easy reach in case he was wrong and had to face another new threat.

At the snap of a twig underfoot, he stepped out from behind the tree and almost took a crossbow bolt to the gut for his trouble. "Don't shoot," he said, arms spread in a gesture of surrender.

Kursak, the wagon master for the free trader caravan that had a draga living among them, held a crossbow aimed on him and a bolt nocked and ready to fire. His eyes rounded. "Cat's-paw?"

Gharek nodded. "I need your help," he said. "So does Siora."

The wagon master lowered his bow a fraction, his expression wary and not at all welcoming. "What are you doing back here at Midrigar, and where is Siora?"

His eyebrows arched and the crossbow lowered a little more when Gharek told him, "I have my daughter with me." At her father's signal, Estred slowly emerged from her hiding place before darting to shelter behind him.

Confusion replaced the suspicion on Kursak's face. His companion's expression mirrored the wagon master's. "What are you doing lurking about Midrigar at all, much less with your child in tow?" He didn't wait for Gharek's reply before firing off another question. "And was that you shouting nonsense to the heavens earlier?"

"It was, and I'll ask you a similar question. What are you doing back here?"

Kursak didn't hesitate, and his answer sent stark horror roaring through Gharek's body, along with panic. "Asil tried to return here twice more, so Malachus is going to burn this cesspit down with draga fire."

"No!" Gharek took a hasty step forward only to halt when the other free trader whose name he didn't know raised his own crossbow in warning. "He can't! Not yet. Siora is in there."

Kursak gaped at him. "You left her in Midrigar?"

"No time to explain," Gharek said, "but you have to stop Malachus."

"Why is nothing we do without some problem?" the wagon master groused. He turned to the other free trader. "Run like someone set your arse on fire and tell Malachus to wait and tell him why. We'll be right behind you."

The free trader nodded and raced in the direction he and Kursak had come—the opposite end of the city from where the main gates stood.

"We've gathered there," Kursak said. "Farthest from the road. Not all of us. Most are back at the camp, an hour's brisk walk as the crow flies." He eyed Estred, still hiding behind Gharek. "What's wrong with your daughter?"

Gharek hadn't missed the way the two free traders had stared at Estred's shoulders. "Not a damn thing," he snapped, instantly defensive.

Untroubled by the sharp response, Kursak shrugged. He addressed Estred directly. "Girl, is there anything wrong with your legs?" Estred shook her head. "Good. Then you'll need to stretch them long and keep up because your da and I are going to run to where my people are waiting. Are you ready?"

Gharek glanced down to see a wide smile grace her features. She gave the wagon master an enthusiastic nod.

"Good," Kursak said. "Let's go."

They followed the path the other free trader had taken, through the wood and adjacent to the broken walls surrounding Midrigar until they reached the far side of the city. Estred kept up effortlessly, for which Gharek was both pleased and grateful. Nor was she panting nearly as hard as he and Kursak were by the time they met more free traders halfway to their destination.

Malachus, that imposing nemesis who'd altered the course of Gharek's life when he confronted him in Domora, didn't bother with a greeting and got straight to the point. "Why is Siora in Midrigar, Gharek?"

Gharek took a few more deep breaths before spilling out a summary of what had happened since his last encounter with the free traders. During the telling, both Halani and Asil had approached Estred. It was to Asil the little girl went first, drawn by whatever natural enchantment the childlike woman possessed.

"What is Siora planning to do to save the dead?" Malachus demanded, his scowl dark, worried.

Gharek shrugged. "I don't know. I don't think she knows

either, but you can't set fire to the city yet. I wanted to go in there and bring her out, over my shoulder if necessary, but I had Estred."

Halani spoke up. "If you trust us enough, Estred can stay with us while you get Siora out of that horrible place." The healer's voice still held a thread of dislike for him, but she'd just tossed aside his greatest obstacle with her simple offer. The trust part fell to him.

They were a small group, numbering no more than eight and made up of an equal number of men and women. Gharek was surprised to see Asil and Halani there considering what Kursak had told him about Asil succumbing to the ghost-eater's summons. Why Malachus would agree to the heavily pregnant Halani accompanying him anywhere near Midrigar puzzled him even more. Her gravid belly looked even larger since he'd last seen her.

He wondered if Malachus was a mind reader as well as a draga dressed in the trappings of a man when he said, "We brought Asil to tell us if the compulsion that keeps luring her here dies when I destroy the rest of the city."

"And I won't leave my mother," Halani chimed in.

Gharek understood that level of mulish devotion, though he had to put it aside for Estred now if he wanted to enter Midrigar and find Siora. These people had been generous with him so far despite the grim history between them. They were not folk to take revenge on a man through his children.

Estred's enthusiasm at the idea of spending time with the odd but fascinating Asil put him at ease, and he thanked Halani for the offer of watching over her while he was gone.

"I'll give you two hours," Malachus told him as he prepared to leave. "And then I start the burn."

It was more than enough time. "If we're not on this side of the wall by then," Gharek replied, "it won't matter to either of us if you set it alight." They'd already be dead by then. Or worse.

He turned back to Halani. "You now have a greater power over me than any other because I place in your care that which has given my life meaning."

"I'm not interested in power over another," Halani retorted. "But I'm pleased to help a father, his daughter, and the woman that father so clearly cherishes." Her solemn face brightened a little. "Estred can entertain Asil while we wait. It will keep them both occupied."

Estred leaned into him as he held her and stroked her bedraggled braid. "Come back, Papa," she implored in a soft voice. "These people are nice, but I want to be with you and Siora."

Gharek kissed her forehead. "I want that too," he said. "I'll be back before you realize I'm even gone. Listen to Halani. She'll take good care of you."

Asil stopped him before he walked away. She lifted a cord over her head to reveal a charm strung on its length. She'd done the same for Estred at their first departure from the free traders. This bauble was more than the rustic craftwork of foraged herbs and whispered spells. It was a strange combination of expensive silver medallion entwined with scraps and bits of dried weeds and flowers bound with twine. "Take this," she said. "Halani made me wear it to protect me from Midrigar's evil."

"No, Mama." Halani's alarm was unmistakable.

Asil shushed her. "He needs it more than I do if he's going in there alone." She grinned at Gharek. "It will look pretty on you." She motioned for him to bend so she could adorn him, and he complied.

He lifted the bauble for a closer look, noting the craftsmanship of the silver medallion with its trio of interlocking pieces that resembled a draga, a horse, and a woman. He didn't imagine the vibration it sent through his palm or the way it lay almost too hot against his chest when he let it fall.

"Halani made it for me to keep me tethered here," Asil said. "I wander off too much." Her unapologetic smile made him smile as well and pity her daughter. That unfortunate predilection was how he'd gotten his hands on Asil in Domora.

"Thank you, Asil," he told her.

Halani, on the other hand, was not amused. "My mother is generous to a fault," she said. "Forgiving as well." She nodded toward the charm where it rested just below his collarbones. "You wear the gift of a fire witch who once held the power of a goddess in her hands. Those symbols are the foundation of this world, the herbs the children of its bounty."

"An anchor," he said.

"Just so. May it serve you and Siora well and bring you both back to Estred."

"Two hours," Malachus reminded him before Gharek sprinted toward the opening of broken wall that allowed entrance into Midrigar for any fool brave or stupid enough to visit. Or driven and desperate as he was.

There were no faceless abominations to give chase as he raced through the city toward the plaza with its vile temple. The silence was like nothing he'd experienced before; a twisted, living thing that throbbed around him and drifted over his skin with a crawling touch that left invisible but viscous traceries. Asil's charm grew even hotter, and he was grateful for his shirt that acted as a barrier against its blistering heat. But the compulsion he felt every time he ended up in this awful place was gone, suppressed by the clean, vital magic of the earth this city no longer truly occupied.

He shouted Siora's name the moment he saw her standing alone at the base of the steps leading to the temple's portico and the black mouth of a door.

He gasped when she turned in response to his shout. The Siora who'd given him her back at the gates and returned to the city's poisoned heart had been a woman with life blood pinking her cheeks and youth in her face and body. That woman was gone, replaced by a shade of grayish skin, sunken eyes, and lips bleached of color. The hollows under her cheeks lent a skull-like cast to her face, and the contorting play of light and shadow from a warping sky passed through her as if she were a windowpane.

Horrified by her transformation, he sprinted toward her, snatching one of her hands in his grip when he was close enough. They both gasped, he from the iciness of her touch, and she from some force in his that brought color to her face and solidity to her form. A wave of fatigue overwhelmed him for a moment before dissipating, as if she'd drawn a small portion of his own life into her fading form.

"Why did you come back?" she said. Her eyes widened with alarm. "Where's Estred?"

"Safe," he said. "With your free trader friends." He tugged gently on her still chilly hand. "We can't stay, Siora, not even to help your ghosts. This entire city will soon burn with draga fire."

"Malachus," she said. Gharek nodded, and she frowned. "It won't help." She pointed to the temple. "This is a door that needs to be shut before it's destroyed. Even draga fire can't do it." Her pallid smile ratcheted his fear for her up another notch. "But I think I know how to do it." She paused. "If I'm strong enough."

They couldn't stay; Siora refused to leave, and Gharek wouldn't leave without her. Resigned, he stroked the back of her hand with his thumb. "What can I do to help you?"

"Why did you come back?" she asked him a second time.

He ran a light finger along her jaw. "Surely it's obvious, shade speaker."

Siora tilted her head in puzzlement, though the light in her eyes was one of joy mixed with a tiny bit of disbelief. "You wanted vengeance not so long ago," she pointed out with a half smile.

Honesty wasn't one of his strong traits, but it came easily when he dealt with her. "I did, but Estred made me put vengeance aside, and you made me forget it altogether." He brought her cold hand to his lips and kissed her knuckles. "We're yours, Estred and I. And you're ours, whether you know it or not. You belong with us."

Tears sheened her eyes for a moment. She lifted his hand to press it to her cold cheek. "I should insist you leave, be brave and show my love by sending you away where you'll be safe. But I'm weak and afraid, and so very glad you're here with me."

"That's a good thing because I'm not going anywhere, so you can tell your annoying nobility to piss off."

Her answering laugh was cut short when a pulse of black light burst from the temple to wash down the steps toward them in a tumbling tide.

"Don't let go of me," Siora said, lacing her fingers with his.

Gharek did more than that, wrapping her in his arms and turning her away from the spectral wave of venomous emotion that threatened to drown them—fury, despair, horror, and, worst of all, a ravenous, unending hunger that knew nothing beyond the urge to devour and destroy.

"Give me my meat, witch!"

The command was a scream, razoring across Gharek's senses until his ears popped and blood trickled from his nostrils. Siora shuddered in his arms. All around them, a chorus of shrieks filled the air. He bent under their burden.

She abruptly pulled away from him, though her hand remained firm in his. A triumphant glint lit her gaze. "Our dead are the creature's foothold," she told him. "The ghost-eater can only find purchase in this world if it eats continuously. It can't take the dead I have in thrall. They protected me and Estred from the wolves without faces." Her features saddened. "Those creatures were people once, Gharek. Living people stolen from the Maesor and warped by the ghost-eater."

That explained the uncanny absence of their kind when he traveled through the Maesor a second time to reach Midrigar fully prepared to battle one, if not several of the abominations to reach Midrigar. He shivered, wondering if the vicious Koopman was counted among their number.

Another wave of black light poured over them, this time saturated with the tortured wails of spirits the ghost-eater had consumed.

"You can't stand in Midrigar casting Holdfast spells on every ghost this thing pulls through the gate." He had to shout the words.

"I don't have to!" Siora yelled back. "The spell relies on naming a spirit to enslave it to the caster." The wails died away, and she lowered her voice to its customary softness. "I knew my father's name and Kalun's. The dead outside Kraelag called themselves Forgotten. I was able to tether them to me by using that name."

Gharek's eyes widened as he followed her line of reasoning. "Meat," he said. "The thing calls them meat and drags them to it with that term. It's a name."

She nodded. "I can't save all it's taken, but surely enough can be drawn back. Enough to weaken its presence here."

"And lose the foothold."

It was a hope, a fragile one with consequences that made him recoil inside if Siora failed. His heart wrenched at the knowledge of what it would cost if she succeeded. "All sorcery has a price to be paid, Siora," he said softly.

She caressed his cheek. "And I may pay with my life, but it's a sacrifice worth making." Her palm remained chilly on his skin. "If the gods haven't abandoned us or this world, it won't come to that, and you and I can watch as Malachus cleanses this horrible place once and for all in fire."

She ran a hand over the spot where Asil's charm lay obscured by the folds of his shirt. Gharek started as Siora's features once more regained a vitality lost. She seemed unaware of the change and only lifted her head for him to kiss her.

He pressed her hand to the charm even as he pressed his mouth to hers. Her lips warmed under his, plumped with life. She tasted of berries and summer, those pleasures this warped city had long forgotten and which the ghost-eater would never know or understand.

When they parted, Gharek wasn't surprised to see Siora almost glowing with health. And all around him hundreds of spectral shapes, unseen before, shifted and roiled around them. Spirits in thrall to her. Prey for the ghost-eater who slavered for the power they gave it.

Asil's charm, gifted by Halani, was more than just a protection ward, more than a shield or an anchor. It was earth magic in its purest form. Life unrefined and unfiltered. A way to save the woman he loved as she strove to save the dead and the world of the living.

"I had hoped to kiss you one last time," Siora told him.

"And I hope to kiss you many more times," he retorted. "And swive you all night." He made her laugh again, the sound a welcomed one after the din made by the damned. "Are you ready to end this game and go back with me?" She nodded, no longer laughing. Fear pinched her face, but there was resolve there too, and the courage that had gained her his respect from the moment he met her. He held her clasped hand against his chest, against the charm. "Remember, you're not alone in this. I stand with you."

Siora invoked the Holdfast spell once more, her voice no longer soft but thunderous, as vast as the ghost-eater's and more commanding. "Hold fast!" The spell amplified her command, making the ground shudder beneath their feet. "I am bound to earth and you to me. I name you, ye whom the abomination has called *meat*, to serve my will and only my will. Hold fast!"

A shockwave of dark power exploded out of the temple in a bludgeoning tide. Gharek was nearly thrown off his feet. Siora stumbled with him but didn't fall. He bent his knees and braced for another wave, holding her to him. This time a blast of cold burst from the temple and with it a miasma gravid with souls newly freed from one prison to become slaves of a well-meaning necromancer.

Triumph and fear lit Siora's face, even as the vitality of life drained out of her like water through a sieve, leaving her once more on the knife's edge of becoming a shade herself.

Gharek almost broke her fingers in the grip held on her hand, and the charm beneath it. The smell of charred cloth filled his nostrils, and a hot pain burned a circle in his skin where the charm rested. Its power too was being leached away by the Holdfast spell, and the sheer number of spirits responding to its summons.

The compulsion that the charm had fended off returned with punishing force, pounding through every fiber of his being like a drum before the call to battle. Gharek's muscles seized, and he clenched his teeth against the nearly uncontrollable urge to shove Siora from him and race up the temple steps to fling himself into the abyssal maw. His face felt frozen or clad in stone, smoothed over, and his vision began to fade at the edges. Siora's horrified expression filled his diminishing view.

"No!" she wailed. "Please, gods, not you!"

Whatever she saw as she stared at him raised a deeper fury inside her. Once more her voice took on the vast echo of a being far greater in size than her own delicate frame. "Return what isn't yours, defiler! You are outcast and unwelcome. All here ARE MINE!"

A shrieking maelstrom blasted across the plaza, blowing out the weakened walls of several ruins, shattering columns as if they were glass. Gharek was thrown backward, Siora still in his unyielding hold. He landed on his back, she atop him, her weight that of a feather. The compulsion's vise grip shattered, and he gasped from the shock and pain of its release. Color blossomed across his vision, and his face felt almost liquid compared to moments earlier.

A last whistling scream of air followed by a distant wail above him made him look up. The stairs to the temple were mostly unchanged except for the shrapnel of stone and brick littered across the treads. The temple itself was gone, completely wiped away as if builders had finished the steps and walked away, never to return to construct the place of worship. Above them, the sky arced in a peaceful, slow-moving vault.

Gharek tucked his chin down to look at Siora. A new fear surged through him at her stillness. He rolled them both to their sides and gently tilted her face up to his. Nearly a wraith herself, she opened her eyes to stare at him.

Her pale tongue flicked out to lick her equally pale lips. "Is it gone?" Her voice was a thready whisper.

He caressed her cheek, ice-cold under his palm. "It's gone. And you closed the door."

"That's good." Exhaustion weighted her words. "I can set them free now."

Gharek stiffened when two misty shapes suddenly took form and came to hover on either side of them. Siora only smiled. "You're free, Papa," she told one of the shapes. "And you, Kalun," she told the other. "You are all free. I release you from my service."

The pair of specters lingered a moment longer, one to curl around Siora in a diaphanous embrace before drifting back to join what looked to Gharek like a massive fog bank that roiled across the plaza. There was no dramatic exit of ghosts, no moans or wails, just a gradual, silent fading until the square was clear and still.

Siora's eyes rolled back and her head lolled. Gharek lifted her easily. She felt no more substantial than a cobweb, and he prayed nonstop as he raced through Midrigar with his precious burden that she wouldn't soon join her father and those thousands of souls she had so valiantly saved.

Estred joyfully shouted his name when he emerged from the opening in the broken wall to where the free traders still waited. She rushed toward him, her enthusiasm blunted as she demanded to know what was wrong with Siora. Gharek strode past her without answering, his eyes trained solely on Halani, who met him halfway.

"Help her," he begged the healer.

Halani motioned for him to lay Siora on the ground in front of her. With his hands free, he reached inside his shirt to grasp the charm. Maybe it would help. Both he and Halani gasped when he brought forth a blackened disk of distorted silver and a handful of charred stems, which was all that remained of the dried herbs. The life magic of the charm had been drained dry.

Gharek cursed and shrugged off the charm, setting it aside. He lifted one of Siora's hands to kiss her palm. "Stay," he told her, praying she listened, praying she heeded his beseeching. "Stay and allow me the privilege of becoming worthy of your faith in me."

He looked to Halani when she laid a hand on his arm. "All will be well, Gharek," she said, a terrible sympathy in her solemn gaze.

The most inane, foolish, and outright false statement ever uttered by anyone, in his opinion, and he'd love to punch whoever it was that first coined it. Instead he nodded and held on to Siora's limp hand while Halani did her work as a healer and her draga husband turned Midrigar into an inferno to rival Kraelag's destruction.

EPILOGUE

Siora stood with Gharek and Estred among a crowd of free traders and watched from a distance as the walls of fair Domora collapsed under the sorcerous power of the Windcry. A strange keening sound drifted toward her, along with the low rumble of stone as it disintegrated into rubble. Siora couldn't tell if the first noise was that of the artifact as it sang destruction or the wail of the people who'd assumed themselves safe within the city's confines.

"It seems Zaredis's plan worked after all," Gharek said beside her. "Tovan can't hold Domora against him, not even with help from his navy. Zaredis's forces are larger, stronger."

His words carried neither triumph nor joy, only a grim acceptance that made Siora wish for a different fate for the city once thought of as the jewel in the Empire's crown. She sighed. "How much blood will be spilled today so that one man might wrest the throne of a dying empire from another?"

"Far more than either one deserves," Malachus said from nearby. He stood behind Halani, his arm draped loosely across her shoulders. "I have no good memory of Domora, but it was never my home. Those who fight there will do so to save what they consider theirs from others who'll try to take it. Only the few faithful actually fight for the generals they serve under." His gaze slid to Gharek. "Or am I wrong about that, cat's-paw?"

Gharek shook his head. "Not wrong. As a soldier, I fought so I'd get paid and send those monies back to my family. As the cat's-paw, I did Dalvila's dirty work to provide a better life for Estred." He glanced to where Estred played with a group of free trader children, laughing and running as they all chased a ball thrown between them. "Misguided though it might have been."

Siora recalled the barbarian mage, both pale and colorful. "What about Rurian?"

He gave a huff of disdain. "One of the faithful few. I'm certain he's the one who figured out how to make the Windcry work. No doubt he's beside Zaredis now even as we speak. Loyal minion to the end."

Another high singing sound, fading in places as it carried on the breeze, reached them. Another part of the girdle wall fell amidst a colossal plume of dust.

"I've seen enough." Halani stepped out of Malachus's embrace. She tucked a spiral of curly hair behind her ear and turned away from the sight of the besieged city. "The chaos and the fighting will spread beyond Domora. We've been here too long."

A chorus of low-voiced agreement followed her remarks. Malachus watched her leave to descend the ridge on which they stood, accompanied by Kursak, Asil, and several of the free traders. A few, less troubled by the sight of Domora's fall, lingered to observe a little longer. The children continued their game farther down the hillside, Estred still among them. Siora noted how Gharek kept one eye on her and one on the draga.

Malachus nodded briefly to Siora before settling an implacable gaze on Gharek. Her stomach fluttered, instinct warning her she wouldn't like what he was about to say and neither would the cat's-paw.

"You've lived among us for nearly a fortnight now. Taken shelter with us, shared food. This free trader band did the same for me when I first came to these lands." He shrugged. "They're generous. I think to a fault sometimes." His face hardened, and Siora swallowed a gasp as a shadow of something not entirely human moved behind his eyes. *Not a man*, she reminded herself. *Only a being dressed as one.* "That generosity only goes so far." He glanced at Siora, regret replacing the strange shadow in his eyes. "I once denied you sanctuary with us because of the danger you represented."

No one with their wits still about them wanted the notorious cat's-paw stalking them. Despite Siora helping Malachus rescue Asil, the free trader band had too much to lose by offering her a place among them. Sometimes doing what was right and doing what was necessary conflicted too much with each other, and hard choices were made. She didn't resent Malachus for the one he made. "I understand," she said. "Then and now."

She fully expected him to say the free trader band would continue east to find relative safety among the Gobani peoples and their allies, the nomadic Savatar. Their guests would not be invited to travel with them. Instead Malachus caught her off guard.

He bowed to her briefly before returning his attention to Gharek. "While Asil has been quick to forgive what you did, Halani hasn't. Nor have the others. You abide with us for Siora's sake and that of Estred's."

Gharek's expression remained impassive. "Of course. I'd expect as much. Give us the rest of the day to gather our things, and we'll be gone by tonight." He shot a quick look to Siora as if to ask for her agreement. She didn't hesitate, nodding a yes in answer to his silent question.

Malachus observed their interaction, and for a moment his features softened before turning stern once more. "I'm not finished. Siora and Estred are welcome to stay with us for as long as they wish, become part of our family and live as free traders themselves. You," he said, pointing at Gharek, "are not." At Siora's gasp, a gleam of sympathy lit his gaze. "You have until sundown to decide what you wish to do." He left them to join Halani, gesturing to those still on the ridge to follow him down the slope to the waiting wagons where the rest of the camp were busy packing up to travel during the night.

"I never expected such a kindness. But maybe I should. They've helped us without hesitation several times before this." Gharek stared at Malachus's retreating back, puzzlement lining his forehead in shallow grooves.

Siora moved closer to him and rested her hand on his arm. At her touch, his regard shifted from Malachus to her. "I think it will take time before your view of others isn't quite so dark, even when you have proof of good intentions and well-meaning motives." Gharek was still broken, but there was a different light in his eyes now, a spark of renewed hope, a willingness to try to repair inside him what had been shattered years ago. She too watched Malachus for a moment, smiling when he pulled Halani into his arms and held her as close as her pregnant belly would allow. "Maybe with time Halani will soften and find it in herself to forgive."

"If she had done to me and mine what I did to hers, there

would be no forgiveness. Ever." He said the words without anger, without resentment. Just a simple statement of fact and beneath it an unspoken warning: woe betide any who harmed his loved ones, for there would be a harsh reckoning. Gharek of Cabast was not Halani the free trader.

A sick feeling settled in Siora's stomach when Gharek's gaze settled on Estred and turned bleak. "Malachus is right. Just as you were once, I'm a threat to his family now. I'm still a hunted man, and even if these free traders have a draga who can turn a city into an ash heap and break a thousand-year-old curse traveling with them, the danger isn't lessened by that fact. It would be wrong of me to stay, even if he'd made the offer. But Estred . . ." He turned, lifted Siora's hand and pressed a kiss to her knuckles. "And you would be safe among them. Part of their family, with other children for Estred to grow up with and be accepted by. For you to find home and hearth and speak to ghosts among people who'll view your gift with admiration instead of suspicion."

Her nausea grew worse with every word. Siora licked her lips before speaking, the inside of her mouth dry with fear. "You'd leave Estred for others to raise? After all you've been through for her?" She didn't dare ask if he'd leave her. She didn't want to hear that answer.

Gharek closed his eyes, the anguish in his expression so surprising, so awful, that a despairing sound escaped past Siora's lips. When he opened his eyes again, the bleakness there was even deeper, darker. "You once said being her father should inspire me to be a better man, not a worse one. Giving her up to protect her was never an option until now. She'd be safer with them than with me, Siora. You know this."

334

She shook her head. "Maybe, but not happier. Of the many things she needs and of those that can be given by these free traders, none of them will equal the presence of her father in her life. None of them." Tears made her eyes throb and she blinked them away. "Trust me. I say this from experience." A day hadn't yet gone by in which she didn't miss her father, even now when she knew his spirit had moved beyond this world and found peace.

Gharek tugged on her hand, drawing her closer until she pressed against him. He released her hand to splay his across her lower back. "And you?" he said. The terrible anguish had faded, replaced by cautious hope tinged with a touch of dread. "What will you do?"

The easy answer would be to counter his question with one of her own: what do you want me to do? But Siora had never known easy in her life, and in her opinion, the difficult roads had the most satisfying endings. It just took courage to travel them. Terrified, she walked this road too.

She slid her palms up to cup his face. "I will beg you to keep me and Estred with you. To make the three of us a family, one where we protect each other, befriend each other, love each other. Where we feel the safest and most cherished. Estred and I don't need an entire free trader band to have these things. We just need you, Gharek."

Her heart thundered so hard and fast in her chest, she was afraid she might faint. She'd spoken without pause or hesitation, no stutters or hints of uncertainty. Inside though, she was like the walls of Domora, breaking and tumbling before the hammering of his silence. For one terrible moment, his features shuttered closed, and Siora feared she might retch. She was a breath away from jerking out of his arms when he crushed her to him, nearly breaking her ribs. The hand not pressed to her lower back buried itself in her hair as he pressed the side of his face to hers. He loosened his hold long enough to allow her an inhalation, one cut short by the hard kiss he planted on her lips. A kiss no longer flavored with bitterness or rage but joy. When they finally separated, Siora's lips throbbed and both she and Gharek panted as if they'd raced up and down the hill on which they stood.

His eyes were soft as he stared at her, a stunning expression she thought never to see on his features. "I can never go back, Siora. Only forward and strive to be worthy of you and Estred."

She stroked his cheek. "Is that not a kind of redemption?"

He shrugged. "I don't know. All I know is you make me better, make me whole."

"And you make me brave."

She laughed when he lifted her in his arms and twirled her around before setting her down. They kissed again, ending the moment at the sound of Estred calling their names as she raced up the slope toward them. Gharek gave her a quick wave before turning back to Siora. "Will you stay with me beyond the rising of the sun and the fall of the Empire, shade speaker?"

This time she felt no fear in answering his question. "Beyond the life of stars and the end of days, cat's-paw. When we're all ghosts and the only voice I'll want to hear is yours."

ACKNOWLEDGMENTS

Some say that writing is a solitary process. Building a book, however, is a team effort. Completing this one and finalizing it took not only my efforts but those of my amazing editor, Anne Sowards, as well as the patience and support of my husband and children. My eternal gratitude to them for helping me cross this finish line.

ABOUT THE AUTHOR

Grace Draven is a Louisiana native living in Texas with her husband, kids, and two doofus dogs. She is the winner of the RT Reviewers' Choice Award for Best Fantasy Romance of 2016 and a *USA Today* bestselling author.

CONNECT ONLINE

GraceDraven.com
🅕 GraceDravenAuthor
🐦 GraceDraven

Ready to find
your next great read?

Let us help.

Visit prh.com/nextread